Poseidonis and Other Lost Realms

THE GARDEN OF HECATE

POSEIDONIS

and Other Lost Realms

Clark Ashton Smith

Edited by Ronald S. Hilger

Introduction by Robert M. Price

Hippocampus Press

New York

Published by Hippocampus Press
P.O. Box 641, New York, NY 10156.
www.hippocampuspress.com

Cover illustration, design, and map on p. 26 by Dan Sauer.
Frontispiece "The Garden of Hecate" by Clark Ashton Smith.
Hippocampus Press logo designed by Anastasia Damianakos.

First Paperback Edition
1 3 5 7 9 8 6 4 2

ISBN 978-1-61498-475-7 trade paperback

Contents

Dedicated to the memory of
Scott Connors (1957–2024)
A friend and scholar without equal

The Myth of the Lost Continent

Why are we so intrigued by the possibility of there having been whole continents that have now gone missing? It appears to be a fact that once-sizable land masses have sunk beneath the oceans, and that is fascinating in its own right. At the very least, such world-transforming events must make us pause to realize that the physical world we like to think of as "Terra Firma" is not quite as "firma" as we thought. Of course, earthquake survivors have that realization forced upon them more swiftly and catastrophically. But even as we commiserate with the victims of volcanism, who have lost dear ones, homes, and possessions, we cannot help asking, "What if it should happen to *us?*" But such worry will pass, as it must.

But the question of lost continents remains a magnet attracting our thoughts. Otherwise many shelves filled with stories of Atlantis, Lemuria, Mu, and Hyperborea would stand empty and vacant. Colonel Churchward, Lewis Spence, Madame Blavatsky, Clark Ashton Smith, Henry Kuttner, Lin Carter, and others would have been forced to find other worlds to conquer (with a pen, not a sword)—which of course they did anyway! You and I are avid partisans of these creative and scholarly (or sometimes *pseudo*-scholarly) writers. But let us not forget that our "knowledge" of that preeminent lost continent, Atlantis (though, personally, my favorite is Lemuria, usually esteemed as silver next to Atlantis's gold), comes from what was already a mythic fiction about that vanished empire and its watery doom. Plato tells the tale in his *Timaios,* crediting it (fictively) to an old Egyptian priest. (Tell me *that* doesn't sound like something from *Weird Tales*!)

But then we get to the *Critias*. There we read that one of the crea-
tions of the Demiurge ("Craftsman"), a deity just subordinate to the ultimate Creator, produced an elite litter of divine offspring: the Olympian
gods familiar from inherited myths, poems, plays, and epics. Though
they were not all-powerful (they required nourishment, among other
things), these beings possessed an assured immortality extrinsically decreed by their Creator. These anthropomorphic deities lived upon the
earth, each dwelling in a palace or temple, though eventually relocating
to high mountains or somewhere in the sky. Each was assigned a fief-
dom to rule. Each created humans/mortals to populate each god's
realm, then formulated laws and rites for their nascent societies. These
gods would take mortal females to wife and beget demigods to rule the
societies, enforcing the god-derived law codes. As long as they reigned,
peace and coexistence reigned.

The trouble began when each new royal wedding between demigods
and mortals produced kings with progressively smaller shares of divine
nature. This meant that the once semi-divine rulers were more and more
subject to the unbridled lusts and animal instincts of their "humanimal"
natures. War, arrogance, and envy became the rule. The several king-
doms began to covet the resources of their neighbors and to resort to
war to seize them. When the kingdom of Atlantis began a program of
imperialism and conquest, Athens gathered allies and went to war with
Atlantis. They finally won, but by that time Zeus, king of the Immortals,
had seen enough and decided to make a wash of the whole thing, drowning the world and sinking Atlantis to clear the chessboard and start over.

As Russell E. Gmirkin (*Plato's* Timaeus *and the Biblical Creation Ac-
counts*) has recently demonstrated, this Platonic narrative formed the ba-
sis of the early chapters of the biblical Book of Genesis. In chapter 1,
we read of Elohim ("God") creating the earth, the sky, the stars, and the
planets. Chapter 2 (cf. Deuteronomy 32:8–9) relates (or implies) how

Yahweh (a.k.a. Jehovah), the subordinate Demiurge, created some seventy lesser gods, placing each in charge of a single nation. Each of these deities created his or her country's population. Then it jumps along to the intermarriage of these national gods with mortal women, spawning demigods, who likewise wedded mortal females, after which the human race becomes corrupt. Remember, Plato's version explains this, though the Genesis writer skipped it: the amount of divine genetic inheritance became increasingly diluted with every subsequent generation until the animalistic nature of mere humans took over and produced wars and violence. Plato said Poseidon was sick of it, especially when his own Atlantis went to war with Athens, so he flooded out the lot of them and started over. In the Greek original it was Deucalion and Pyrrha who survived the Deluge inside an Ark, just like Noah and his family in Genesis. Thus the Atlantis myth, albeit anonymously, even made it into the Bible!

When we ask why these tales of sunken continents are so potent—much more so, for instance, than myths of unicorns and dragons—we start to realize that these continents have sunk deeper than we thought, all the way down into the ocean floor of the Jungian Unconscious. They mean something. So what say we get that winch around them and raise them up to the surface?

In teaching the Bible, I often find myself trying to dispel what C. S. Lewis dubbed "chronological snobbery," the smug assumption that the ancients were stupid, as attested by the fairy-tale atmosphere of their myths. I never tire of explaining that the ancients only lacked our modern research tools and technology. If they had actually been simply a bunch of stupid dullards, they would not have come up with the mythic "explanations" of natural phenomena that they did. For instance: "What? They thought the rainbow was God's war bow, hung up in the sky as a pledge he would never flood the world again? What a bunch of morons!" No, my friend, I'm afraid *you're* the moron! Fred Flintstone and Alley Oop couldn't possibly have known about light refraction, but their knowledge-hungry brains were determined to figure the thing out.

They had to come up with *something!* Gotta give 'em an A for effort!

Well, the Atlantis myth is just the opposite of chronological snobbery. It is like several "Golden Age" myths popular today in various quarters. Marxists plan a "return" to a postulated dawn age of "primitive communism." How many churchgoers are flogged from the pulpit with the rhetorical appeal to the supposedly perfect "Early Church," so superior to backslidden slobs like us? Feminists insist that things would be better without "toxic" masculinity if we could "get back to the Garden" when a righteous matriarchy held sway. But of course, all these "Golden Ages" are really modern blueprints of Utopian "New Orders" retrojected into the past. The advantage of placing it in the past is to say, "You see? It *can* happen because back then it *did* happen."

By the same token, Atlantis myths serve as cautionary tales. After all, someone is going to ask why such an ideal condition no longer exists. The propagandist must have an explanation up his or her sleeve, or hearers will suspect such perfection did not last because it *cannot* last. It would have to be abandoned as a fool's paradise. So the skeptic will be offered a story of Perfection's downfall, assuring us that, since we know what they did to screw things up, we are forewarned and can steer clear of their fatal mistakes.

A prime example would be that of the city of Sodom, obliterated by God for her many sins (Genesis 18–19). There actually *was* a great city of Sodom. It is mentioned in trade records surviving from the Ebla Empire in present-day Syria. Presumably it was destroyed by earthquakes. The destruction was so terrible that the ancients asked Jesus' question: "And those eighteen crushed in the collapse of the tower in Siloam—do you think they were worse sinners than all other Jerusalemites?" (Luke 13:4). Sodom's neighboring towns answered with a big and unequivocal "Yes!" So what was their damning sin that they "must" have committed? Ezekiel 16:49 says it was Sodom's overweening pride and her neglect of her poor. The later rabbis made the Sodom story a parallel to the myth of Theseus putting the fiendish innkeeper Procrustes out of his business of murdering and robbing his guests. Finally, the Sodomite sin was interpreted in Jude 7 as "unnatural lust" between humans and angels, as in Genesis 6:1–4. In any case, it "must have" been something intolerably bad.

But it is just here that modern fictions of sunken continents attach themselves to the legends. In these stories we frequently find doomed protagonists somehow or other rediscovering vestiges of the advanced knowledge of Atlantis, et al., whether scientific or sorcerous. What an opportunity for civilization to make up for lost time! Mastering the secrets of Atlantis, Hyperborea, or Göbekli Tepi might enable us to take a shortcut toward the levels they achieved! But the discoverer has forgotten that the ancients were not ready for what they discovered—and we aren't either! We repeat their mistakes and in our remaining seconds we realize our mistake. Maybe the *Weird Tales* writers were issuing a warning we ought to take seriously. Who knows? Our own cherished continents may find themselves on the demolition schedule.

What was Clark Ashton Smith's special angle on the Atlantis myth? There is an intriguing suggestion implicit in Lin Carter's observation that occultists Helena Petrovna Blavatsky and William Scott-Elliot* invented Poseidonis as the last island fragment of Atlantis to sink after a respectably long life of its own. What is interesting about this is that it portrays Atlantean (Poseidonian) characters as looking back on Atlantis as a sunken continent even while they are living on it still above the surface! The tales, both comic books and movies, of Aquaman and the Sub-Mariner achieve the same effect by portraying Atlantis as anciently sunken— yet still inhabited!

---

*HPL, followed by Lin Carter, used to cite, as a single volume, "W. Scott-Elliot's *Atlantis and the Lost Lemuria*," but there were originally two separate books, *The Story of Atlantis* (1896) and *The Lost Lemuria* (1904). They were eventually reissued in a single volume called *Atlantis and the Lost Lemuria* (1925). Carter also erred in giving 1896 as the publication date for the combined edition.

Okay, I admit I'm going out on a limb here, but I believe I sense in Smith's Poseidonis the exotic tang of Buddhism. Nor is Poseidonis the only case of this. I have long suspected Smith derived the name "Ubbo-Sathla" from a Buddhist meditation ritual, the *uposattha*. But who knows? Nonetheless, the Poseidonis stories enshrine the futility of heaping up material treasures (jewels, rare tomes, even secular power). Don't tell me Malygris was some innocent spiritual seeker like Prince Siddhartha! His mighty powers are equivalent to the parlor-trick thaumaturgy of corrupt yogis, distracting off-ramps on the path to Enlightenment. Zooey Glass said it best:

> As a matter of simple logic, there's no difference at all, that *I* can see, be-tween the man who's greedy for material treasure—or even intellectual treasure – and the man who's greedy for spiritual treasure. As you say, treas-ure's treasure, God damn it, and it seems to me that ninety per cent of all the world-hating saints in history were just as aquisitive and unattractive, basically, as the rest of us are. (J. D. Salinger, *Franny and Zooey*)

Or, if you prefer hearing it from an official Buddhist take a look at Chögyam Trungpa's great book *Cutting Through Spiritual Materialism.*

But aren't Smith's occultist masters seeking spiritual knowledge? It seems they will do anything to attain it, take any soul-imperiling risk, right? Wrong. They have not learned an elementary lesson from the Buddha: that there are many metaphysical "questions that tend not unto edification."

> It's just as if a man were wounded with an arrow thickly smeared with poison. His friends and companions, kinsmen and relatives would provide him with a surgeon, and the man would say, 'I won't have this arrow re-moved until I know whether the man who wounded me was a noble war-rior, a priest, a merchant, or a worker.' He would say, 'I won't have this arrow removed until I know the given name and clan name of the man who wounded me . . . until I know whether he was tall, medium, or short . . . until I know whether he was dark, ruddy-brown, or golden-colored . . . until I know his home village, town, or city . . . until I know whether the bow with which I was wounded was a long bow or a crossbow . . . until I know whether the bowstring with which I was wounded was fiber, bamboo threads, sinew, hemp, or bark . . . until I know whether the shaft with which

I was wounded was wild or cultivated . . . until I know whether the feathers of the shaft with which I was wounded were those of a vulture, a stork, a hawk, a peacock, or another bird . . . until I know whether the shaft with which I was wounded was bound with the sinew of an ox, a water buffalo, a langur, or a monkey.' He would say, 'I won't have this arrow removed until I know whether the shaft with which I was wounded was that of a common arrow, a curved arrow, a barbed, a calf-toothed, or an oleander arrow.' The man would die and those things would still remain unknown to him.

But in the Poseidonis tales it's even worse than that. Malygris and his colleagues spend a great deal of time seeking (and finding and using) archaic sources of necromantic knowledge, ancient tomes containing even more ancient lore, all derived from the ancient dead who first learned it and recorded it—and from mummies, liches, phantoms, revenants, and fallen angels! No wonder this coveted information yields nothing but *death* to those who go to such trouble to rediscover it!

So, then, are Smith's stories true cautionary tales? Is he trying to warn impressionable youths to stay the hell away from the Dark Arts? You know better! He didn't take such things seriously and would have been happy to sign the committal papers if you did! It's just perpetual Halloween!

Finally, let no one deny that Clark Ashton Smith was one of the great *literary* wizards, conjuring illusory wonders with dazzling words of power!

ROBERT M. PRICE
HIEROPHANT OF THE HORDE

30 November 2024

A Note on the Text

Clark Ashton Smith began writing weird fiction for the pulp magazines shortly before the onset of the Great Depression, completing some 100 short stories between 1929 and 1936. This decision was not one of choice but rather of necessity, as his first and strongest love was always poetry. Like many self-respecting poets, he considered fiction writing to be a rather demeaning prospect, as indicated in a letter to his mentor George Sterling in October 1926: "Too bad you have to write prose. It's a beastly occupation." And again a few weeks later: "I don't blame you for writing prose, if you can make money by it. But it's a hateful task, for a poet, and shouldn't be necessary in any true civilization." Smith was also successful as a poet, having published *The Star-Treader and Other Poems* in 1912, *Ebony and Crystal* in 1922, and *Sandalwood* in 1925. But while these volumes earned him a reputation as a youthful prodigy and gifted poet, he was nevertheless the epitome of the starving artist, earning nowhere near enough from his poetry to support himself. So it was that during a camping trip to the Sierras in the summer of 1927, his lady friend Genevieve Sully suggested that he could better support himself and his aging parents by writing fiction rather than poetry. This advice, along with the encouragement and inspiration from his close friend and correspondent H. P. Lovecraft, who was already gaining a reputation as a writer of horror fiction for the pulps, led Smith to embark upon the writing career for which he is best known today.

One of Smith's earliest efforts in his new career as fiction writer was "The Last Incantation," written on 23 September 1929 and published in *Weird Tales* in June 1930. His first story set in Poseidonis, this melancholy tale features Malygris, an aging sorcerer who seeks to bring back Nylissa, the lost love of his youth who had died on the eve of their wedding day from a sudden and mysterious illness. Being omnipotent, he naturally succeeds, but the result is not what he had hoped for. "A Voyage to Sfanomoë" was Smith's next Atlantis-related tale and was completed on 17 May 1930. This tale deals with two brother scientists who build a space vessel in order to escape the imminent foundering of Poseidonis, and travel to Sfanomoë, which is the Atlantean name for the planet Venus. "A Vintage from Atlantis" takes place after the sinking of Atlantis and tells of a pirate ship and crew that lands on a deserted island to stash their ill-gotten treasure. There they discover a large urn full of an ancient wine from lost Poseidonis and foolishly decide to sample this rare vintage.

Widely recognized as one of Smith's most popular tales, "The Double Shadow" was nevertheless twice rejected by *Weird Tales* editor Farnsworth Wright; and although accepted by *Strange Tales,* it was left unpublished when the magazine folded in 1932. Being well aware of its merits and encouraged by Lovecraft, who wrote that the story was "full of vivid colour & creeping menace, & with an atmosphere tension worthy of E.A.P.," (Edgar Allan Poe). Smith self-published the tale as the title story of *The Double Shadow and Other Fantasies,* issued by the Auburn Journal Press in 1933. "The Death of Malygris" was written in March 1933 and was the last Atlantis tale written by Smith. This tale describes the incredible tyranny Malygris actively exerted over Susran, the capital city of Poseidonis, for over a year from the actual time of his demise.

With the completion of this story Smith seems to have closed the book on his relatively sparse Poseidonis cycle, focusing instead upon the more popular Zothique and Hyperborean tales. The Atlantis stories are certainly consistent with his best work insofar as literary quality and atmospheric detail are concerned, so why would Smith abandon this promising story cycle altogether? Part of the answer may be found in the following lines from the prose poem "To the Daemon":

> . . . for I am a little weary of all recorded years and chartered lands; and the isles that are westward of Cathay, and the sunset realms of Ind, are not

remote enough to be made the abiding-place of my conceptions; and Atlantis is over-new for my thoughts to sojourn there, and Mu itself has gazed upon the sun in aeons that are too recent.

Smith often spoke of his desire to create *everything* in his imaginative fiction, as mentioned in this letter to George Sterling in November 1926: "Indeed, my fondest dream is to find a Hyperborea beyond Hyperborea, in the realm of imaginative poetry. I have the feeling that my best and most original work is still to be done." Assuming that this desire pertained to fiction as well as to poetry, it seems likely that the already well-worked vein of lost Atlantis was a bit too commonplace for him and he hoped to conceive a more original setting for his best work.

The Poseidonis grouping of tales is followed by "Orientales," a title Smith often used to describe stories with Oriental or Arabian settings. "The Willow Landscape" is a poignant story of an art lover from a noble family who has fallen on hard times and is forced to sell his beloved family heirlooms in order to survive—a situation Smith himself understood all too well. While he created many paintings, drawings, and sculptures for the sole purpose of selling them, it is easy to imagine that he might have preferred to keep many of his favorite pieces. This tale also appeared in *The Double Shadow and Other Fantasies* and thus stands free from the over-editing and needless revisions that plagued so many of Smith's pulp appearances.

"The Third Episode of Vathek" is a rare example of "posthumous collaboration," in which Smith completes a tale left unfinished by William Beckford. Beckford, after writing the Arabian novel *Vathek* (1787), wrote three "episodes" that were designed to be inserted into the novel; but the third remained unfinished. The episodes themselves remained unpublished until they appeared as *The Episodes of Vathek* (1912). Lovecraft suggested the completion of the third episode to Smith in 1933, stating that Smith could "capture the general atmosphere better than anyone else in the gang." Although he was doubtful of its salability, Smith completed the 4000-word ending with such skill in duplicating

Beckford's style and probable conclusion that the tale reads seamlessly throughout. The transition takes place a little more than three-quarters into the tale where Beckford ends with "All around were ranged black chests, whose steel padlocks seemed crusted with blood . . ." At this point Smith takes over and brings the story to its conclusion. "The Third Episode of Vathek" appeared in R. H. Barlow's mimeographed magazine *Leaves* (Summer 1937) and was reprinted in Smith's fourth Arkham House collection, *The Abominations of Yondo* (1960). "The Ghoul" is another tale that takes place during the reign of the Caliph Vathek and details the plight of Noureddin Hassan, who runs afoul of some ghastly demon and finds himself hopelessly trapped in a proverbial "deal with the devil."

"Told in the Desert" is a beautifully poignant story that reads much like an extended prose poem in light of its structure and sustained poetic descriptions. The tale begins much as it ends: "Out of the fiery furnace of the desert sunset, he came to meet our caravan. He and his camel were a single silhouette of shadow-like thinness that emerged above the golden-crested dunes and disappeared by turns in their twilight-gathering hollows." Compare these opening lines to the conclusion: ". . . we saw that the man and his dromedary had disappeared. And far-off in the ghostly light a doubtful shadow passed from dune to dune like a fever-driven phantom. And it seemed to us that the shadow was the single silhouette of a camel and its rider." This story is similar in theme and construction to the prose poem "The Passing of Aphrodite," which tells of a poet who finds and then loses the perfect beauty and love of all his romantic desires.

The final grouping here is "Lemuria" and collects Smith's stories and poems relating to Lemuria as well as other tales with a similar "Lost Realm" setting. "An Offering to the Moon" and "The Uncharted Isle" are stories that deal with lost Lemuria and utilize elements of time travel, but in very different ways. In "Offering," the protagonist Morley seems to relive a past life on Lemuria, while in "The Uncharted Isle" a sailor is blown off course to a mysterious island whose inhabitants are completely unaware of his presence, and it isn't clear whether he has gone back in time or the island itself has been somehow removed from its proper time period.

"The Abominations of Yondo," written in 1925, constitutes Smith's first real attempt at writing weird fiction. An obvious expansion of the techniques used in his prose poetry, "Yondo" extends this poetic style to the length of a short story with admirable success. Indeed, Donald Sidney-Fryer has described such tales as "Sadastor," "The Abominations of Yondo," "The Last Incantation," and "Told in the Desert" as extended poems in prose because of their sustained poetic style, structure, and atmosphere throughout. When George Sterling first read "Yondo" he praised it as "a magnificent exercise in imagination" but strongly discouraged Smith from pursuing this particular genre, referring to it as "outworn and childish"; he further cautioned him that he would probably find no magazine willing to pay for such material. Smith rejected this advice and in 1926 "Yondo" appeared in the *Overland Monthly*, presumably earning him some much-needed cash.

There will always be some stories that defy classification; "The Letter from Mohaun Los" is a case in point. This tale begins with the disappearance of a wealthy young eccentric who, apparently unmoved by his recent breakup with a fiancée of several years, devotes all his time and resources toward the development of a time machine. He rationalizes his decision thus:

> I have always been irked by the present age, have always been devoured by a sort of nostalgia for other times and places. It has seemed so oddly and capriciously arbitrary that I should be *here* and not *otherwhere*, in the infinite, eternal ranges of being; and I have long wondered if it would not be possible to gain control of the laws that determine our temporal or cosmic situation, and pass at will from world to world or from cycle to cycle.

He succeeds in building the time machine but soon discovers that traveling in time also has the effect of changing his relative location in space as the Earth and stars simply move away from him. This is a concept Smith had previously explored in "The Eternal World." While this would seem to place the story firmly in the science fiction genre, what follows is a wild ride through infinite cosmic dimensions that can only be described as an adventure in exploration during which the protagonist and his Chinese manservant are joined by fascinating alien companions as they jump from world to world.

In his introduction to the Ballantine Adult Fantasy Series edition of *Zothique* (1970), Lin Carter makes this interesting observation:

> [Smith] began to hit his stride in about 1929; between then and August 1936, he produced more than one hundred short stories and novelettes. At that point, although still only in his early forties, he for some unknown reason virtually stopped writing. The remaining twenty-five years of his life—Smith died on August 14th, 1961—produced only a negligible output. No one has yet come forth with a convincing explanation of this curious and very unfortunate decline.

In the fifty-five years since Carter wrote this, much research has revealed that the death of his parents (Frances Smith passed away in 1935 and Timeus Smith in 1937) removed much of the financial pressure he was under at the time. Moreover, the passing of his great friend H. P. Lovecraft, also in 1937, would deprive him of what was probably his main source of encouragement and inspiration for fiction writing. This, along with the capricious rejection of much of his best work by various pulp editors, is now recognized as the main reason for Smith's withdrawal from the pulp markets. While he would resume writing fiction to some small degree in the late 1940s and 1950s, he would never revisit the promising story-cycles of Posedonis, Lemuria, or Xiccarph again.

Poseidonis and Other Lost Realms marks the fifth volume in the Hippocampus Press series of thematically related tales of Clark Ashton Smith's fiction, leaving only the Hyperborean tales and perhaps enough miscellaneous stories to make up one final volume. While the majority of Smith's most popular fiction may be found within his various story-cycles of Averoigne, Zothique, and Hyperborea, his remaining stories, whether classified as science fiction, fantasy, horror, satire, or just plain weird, are still prime examples of the best from the *Weird Tales* era. The brevity of Smith's fiction-writing career has been the focus of much lamentation and discussion among his still-growing devotees. In response I can only echo these words of Lin Carter: "But there is little point in bemoaning the [stories] he left unwritten. Let us be very grateful for the glorious tales he *did* write." To this I heartily agree and wish readers happy sojourning as they explore the fascinating lost realms of Poseidonis and Lemuria as well as the many other marvelous worlds of Clark Ashton Smith.

Poseidonis

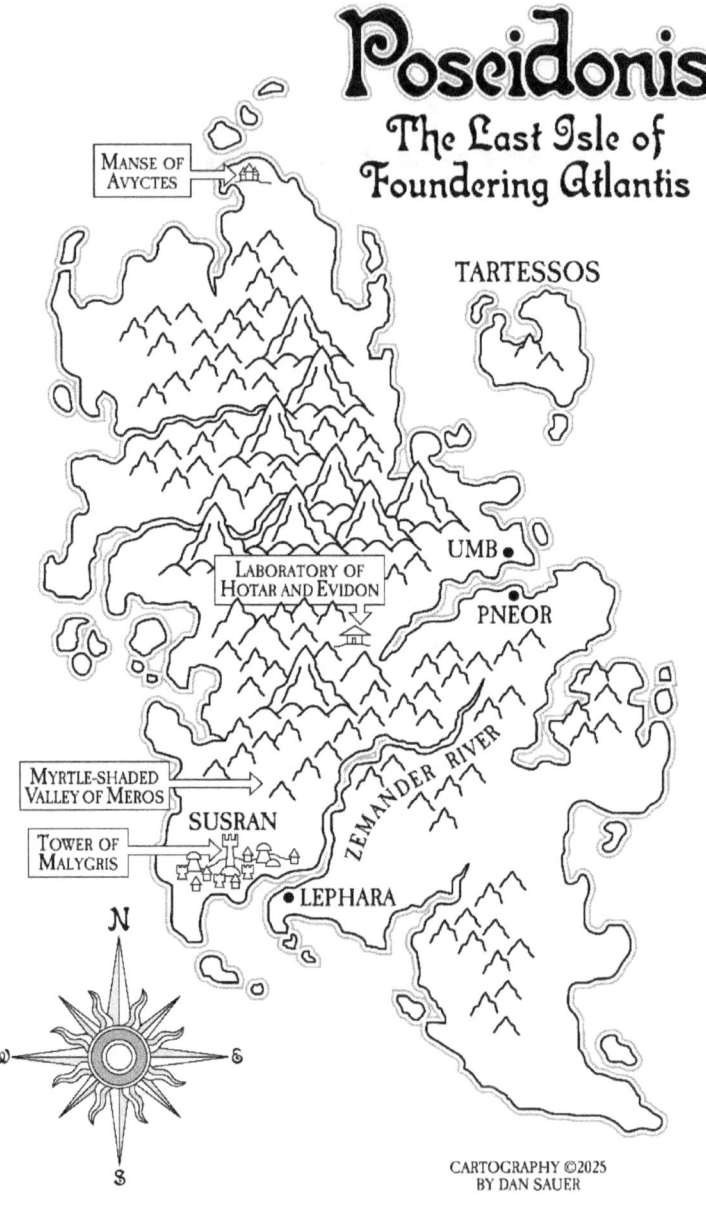

Poseidonis
The Last Isle of Foundering Atlantis

MANSE OF AVYCTES

TARTESSOS

LABORATORY OF HOTAR AND EVIDON

UMB •

• PNEOR

MYRTLE-SHADED VALLEY OF MEROS

SUSRAN

TOWER OF MALYGRIS

ZEMANDER RIVER

• LEPHARA

N

W

E

S

CARTOGRAPHY ©2025
BY DAN SAUER

FROM A LETTER

**** Will you not join me in Atlantis, where we will go down through streets of blue and yellow marble to the wharves of orichalch, and choose us a galley with a golden Eros for figurehead, and sails of Tyrian sendal? With mariners that knew Odysseus, and beautiful amber-breasted slaves from the mountain-vales of Lemuria, we will lift anchor for the unknown fortunate isles of the outer sea; and, sailing in the wake of an opal sunset, will lose that ancient land in the glaucous twilight, and see from our couch of ivory and satin the rising of unknown stars and perished planets. *** Perhaps we will not return, but will follow the tropic summer from isle to halcyon isle, across the amaranthine seas of myths and fable: We will eat the lotos, and the fruit of lands whereof Odysseus never dreamt; and drink the pallid wines of faery, grown in a vale of perpetual moonlight. I will find for you a necklace of rosy-tinted pearls, and a necklace of yellow rubies, and crown you with precious corals that have the semblance of sanguine-coloured blossoms. We will roam in the marts of forgotten cities of jasper, and carnelian-builded ports beyond Cathay; and I will buy you a gown of peacock azure damascened with copper and gold and vermilion; and a gown of black samite with runes of orange, woven by fantastic sorcery without the touch of hands, in a dim land of spells and philtres.

THE LAST INCANTATION

Malygris the magician sat in the topmost room of his tower that was builded on a conical hill above the heart of Susran, capital of Poseidonis. Wrought of a dark stone mined from deep in the earth, perdurable and hard as the fabled adamant, this tower loomed above all others, and flung its shadow far on the roofs and domes of the city, even as the sinister power of Malygris had thrown its darkness on the minds of men.

Now Malygris was old, and all the baleful might of his enchantments, all the dreadful or curious demons under his control, all the fear that he had wrought in the hearts of kings and prelates, were no longer enough to assuage the black ennui of his days. In his chair that was fashioned from the ivory of mastodons, inset with terrible cryptic runes of red tourmalines and azure crystals, he stared moodily through the one lozenge-shaped window of fulvous glass. His white eyebrows were contracted to a single line on the umber parchment of his face, and beneath them his eyes were cold and green as the ice of ancient floes; his beard, half white, half of a black with glaucous gleams, fell nearly to his knees and hid many of the writhing serpentine characters inscribed in woven silver athwart the bosom of his violet robe. About him were scattered all the appurtenances of his art; the skulls of men and monsters; phials filled with black or amber liquids, whose sacrilegious use was known to none but himself; little drums of vulture-skin, and crotali made from the bones and teeth of the cockodrill, used as an accompaniment to certain incantations. The mosaic floor was partly covered with the skins of enormous black and silver apes; and above the door there hung the head of a unicorn in which dwelt the familiar demon of Malygris, in the form of a coral viper with pale green belly and ashen mottlings. Books were piled everywhere: ancient volumes bound in serpent-skin, with verdigris-eaten clasps, that held the frightful lore of Atlantis, the pentacles that have power upon the demons of the earth and the moon, the spells that transmute or disintegrate the elements; and runes from a lost language of Hyperborea, which, when uttered aloud, were more deadly than poison or more potent than any philtre.

But, though these things and the power they held or symbolized were the terror of the peoples and the envy of all rival magicians, the thoughts of Malygris were dark with immitigable melancholy, and weariness filled his heart as ashes fill the hearth where a great fire has died. Immovable he sat, implacable he mused, while the sun of afternoon, declining on the city and on the sea that was beyond the city, smote with autumnal rays through the window of greenish-yellow glass, and touched his shrunken hands with its phantom gold, and fired the balas-rubies of his rings till they burned like demonian eyes. But in his musings there was neither light nor fire; and turning from the greyness of the present, from the darkness that seemed to close in so imminently upon the future, he groped backward among the shadows of memory, even as a blind man who has lost the sun and seeks it everywhere in vain. And all the vistas of time that had been so full of gold and splendor, the days of triumph that were colored like a searing flame, the crimson and purple of the rich imperial years of his prime, all these were chill and dim and strangely faded now, and the remembrance thereof was no more than the stirring of dead embers. Then Malygris groped backward to the years of his youth, to the misty, remote, incredible years, where, like an alien star, one memory still burned with unfailing luster—the memory of the girl Nylissa whom he had loved in days ere the lust of unpermitted knowledge and necromantic dominion had ever entered his soul. He had well-nigh forgotten her for decades, in the myriad preoccupations of a life so bizarrely diversified, so replete with occult happenings and powers, with supernatural victories and perils; but now, at the mere thought of this slender and innocent child, who had loved him so dearly when he too was young and slim and guileless, and who had died of a sudden mysterious fever on the very eve of their marriage-day, the mummy-like umber of his cheek took on a phantom flush, and deep down in the his orbs was a sparkle like the gleam of mortuary tapers. In his dreams arose the irretrievable suns of youth, and he saw the myrtle-shaded valley of Meros, and the stream Zemander, by whose ever-verdant marge he had walked at eventide with Nylissa, seeing the birth of summer stars in the heavens, the stream, and the eyes of his beloved.

Now, addressing the demonian viper that dwelt in the head of the unicorn, Malygris spoke, with the low monotonous intonation of one who thinks aloud:

"Viper, in the years before you came to dwell with me and to make your abode in the head of the unicorn, I knew a girl who was lovely and frail as the orchids of the jungle, and who died as the orchids die… Viper, am I not Malygris, in whom is centered the mastery of all occult lore, all forbidden dominations, with dominion over the spirits of earth and sea and air, over the solar and lunar demons, over the living and the dead? If so I desire, can I not call the girl Nylissa, in the very semblance of all her youth and beauty, and bring her forth from the never-changing shadows of the cryptic tomb, to stand before me in this chamber, in the evening rays of this autumnal sun?"

"Yes, master," replied the viper, in a low but singularly penetrating hiss, "you are Malygris, and all sorcerous or necromantic power is yours, all incantations and spells and pentacles are known to you. It is possible, if you so desire, to summon the girl Nylissa from her abode among the dead, and to behold her again as she was ere her loveliness had known the ravening kiss of the worm."

"Viper, is it well, is it meet, that I should summon her thus? . . . Will there be nothing to lose, and nothing to regret?"

The viper seemed to hesitate. Then, in a more slow and measured hiss: "It is meet for Malygris to do as he would. Who, save Malygris, can decide if a thing be well or ill?"

"In other words, you will not advise me?" the query was as much a statement as a question, and the viper vouchsafed no further utterance.

Malygris brooded for awhile, with his chin on his knotted hands. Then he arose, with a long-unwonted celerity and sureness of movement that belied his wrinkles, and gathered together, from different coigns of the chamber, from ebony shelves, from caskets with locks of gold or brass or electrum, the sundry appurtenances that were needful for his magic. He drew on the floor the requisite circles, and standing within the centermost he lit the thuribles that contained the prescribed incense, and read aloud from a long narrow scroll of grey vellum the purple and vermilion runes of the ritual that summons the departed. The fumes of the censers, blue and white and violet, arose in thick clouds and speedily filled the room with ever-writhing interchanging columns, among which the sunlight disappeared and was succeeded by a wan unearthly glow, pale as the light of moons that ascend from Lethe. With preternatural slowness, with unhuman solemnity, the voice of the necromancer went on in a priest-like chant till the scroll was ended and the last echoes lessened and died out in hollow sepulchral vibrations. Then the colored vapors cleared away, as if the folds of a curtain had been drawn back. But the pale unearthly glow still filled the chamber, and between Malygris and the door where hung the unicorn's head there stood the apparition of Nylissa, even as she had stood in the perished years, bending a little like a wind-blown flower, and smiling with the unmindful poignancy of youth. Fragile, pallid, and simply gowned, with anemone blossoms in her black hair, with eyes that held the new-born azure of vernal heavens, she was all that Malygris had remembered, and his sluggish heart was quickened with an old delightful fever as he looked upon her.

"Are you Nylissa?" he asked—"the Nylissa whom I loved in the myrtle-shaded valley of Meros, in the golden-hearted days that have gone with all dead aeons to the timeless gulf?"

"Yes, I am Nylissa," Her voice was the simple and rippling silver of the voice that had echoed so long in his memory... But somehow, as he gazed and listened, there grew a tiny doubt—a doubt no less absurd than intolerable, but nevertheless insistent: was this altogether the same Nylissa he had known? Was there not some elusive change, too subtle to be named or defined, had time and the grave not taken something away—an innominable something that his magic had not wholly restored? Were the eyes as tender, was the black hair as lustrous, the form as slim and supple, as those of the girl he recalled? He could not be sure, and the growing doubt was succeeded by a leaden dismay, by a grim despondency that choked his heart as with ashes. His scrutiny became searching and exigent and cruel, and momently the phantom was less and less the perfect semblance of Nylissa, momently the lips and brow were less lovely, less subtle in their curves; the slender figure became thin, the tresses took on a common black and the neck an ordinary pallor. The soul of Malygris grew sick again with age and despair and the death of his evanescent hope. He could believe no longer in love or youth or beauty; and even the memory of these things was a dubitable mirage, a thing that might or might not have been. There was nothing left but shadow and greyness and dust, nothing but the empty dark and the cold, and a clutching weight of insufferable weariness, of immedicable anguish.

In accents that were thin and quavering, like the ghost of his former voice, he pronounced the incantation that serves to dismiss a summoned phantom. The form of Nylissa melted upon the air like smoke and the lunar gleam that had surrounded her was replaced by the last rays of the sun. Malygris turned to the viper and spoke in a tone of melancholy reproof:

"Why did you not warn me?"

"Would the warning have availed?" was the counter-question. "All knowledge was yours, Malygris, excepting this one thing; and in no other way could you have learned it."

"What thing?" queried the magician. "I have learned nothing except the vanity of wisdom, the impotence of magic, the nullity of love, and the delusiveness of memory. . . . Tell me, why could I not recall to life the same Nylissa whom I knew, or thought I knew?"

"It was indeed Nylissa whom you summoned and saw," replied the viper. "Your necromancy was potent up to this point; but no necromantic spell could recall for you your own lost youth or the fervent and guileless heart that loved Nylissa, or the ardent eyes that beheld her then. This, my master, was the thing that you had to learn."

THE DEATH OF MALYGRIS

A t the hour of interlunar midnight, when lamps burned rarely and
far apart in Susran, and slow-moving autumn clouds had muffled
the stars, King Gadeiron sent forth into the sleeping city twelve of his
trustiest mutes. Like shadows gliding through oblivion, they vanished
upon their various ways; and each of them, returning presently to the
darkened palace, led with him a shrouded figure no less silent and discreet than himself.

In this manner, groping along tortuous alleys, through blind cypress-
caverns in the royal gardens, and down subterranean halls and steps,
twelve of the most powerful sorcerers of Susran were brought together
in a vault of oozing, death-grey granite, far beneath the foundations of
the palace.

The entrance of the vault was guarded by earth-demons that obeyed
the arch-sorcerer, Maranapion, who had long been the king's councillor.
These demons would have torn limb from limb any who came unpre-
pared to offer them a libation of fresh blood. The vault was lit dubiously
by a single lamp, hollowed from a monstrous garnet, and fed with vipers'
oil. Here Gadeiron, crownless, and wearing sackcloth dyed in sober purple, awaited the wizards on a seat of limestone wrought in the form of
a sarcophagus. Maranapion stood at his right hand, immobile, and
swathed to the mouth in the garments of the tomb. Before him was a
tripod of orichalchum, rearing shoulder-high; and on the tripod, in a
silver socket, there reposed the enormous blue eye of a slain Cyclops,
wherein the archimage was said to behold weird visions. On this eye,
gleaming balefully under the garnet lamp, the gaze of Maranapion was
fixed with death-like rigidity.

From these circumstances, the twelve sorcerers knew that the king had convened them only because of a matter supremely grave and secret. The hour and fashion of their summoning, the place of meeting, the terrible elemental guards, the mufti worn by Gadeiron—all were proof of a need for preternatural stealth and privity.

For awhile there was silence in the vault, and the twelve, bowing deferentially, waited the will of Gadeiron. Then, in a voice that was little more than a harsh whisper, the king spoke:

"What know ye of Malygris?"

Hearing that awful name, the sorcerers paled and trembled visibly; but, one by one, as if speaking by rote, several of the foremost made answer to Gadeiron's question.

"Malygris dwells in his black tower above Susran," said the first. "The night of his power is still heavy upon Poseidonis; and we others, moving in that night, are as shadows of a withered moon. He is overlord of all kings and sorcerers. Yea, even the triremes that fare to Tartessos, and the far-flown eagles of the sea, pass not beyond the black falling of his shadow."

"The demons of the five elements are his familiars," said the second. "The gross eyes of common men have beheld them often, flying like birds about his tower, or crawling lizard-wise on the walls and pavements."

"Malygris sits in his high hall," avowed the third. "Unto him, tribute is borne at the full moon from all the cities of Poseidonis. He takes a tithe of the lading of every galley. He claims a share of the silver and incense, of the gold and ivory sacred to the temples. His wealth is beyond the opulence of the sunken kings of Atlantis . . . even those kings who were thy forefathers, O Gadeiron."

"Malygris is old as the moon," mumbled a fourth. "He will live forever, armed against death with the dark magic of the moon. Death has become a slave in his citadel, toiling among other slaves, and striking only at the foes of Malygris."

"Much of this was true formerly," quoth the king, with a sinister hissing of his breath. "But now a certain doubt has arisen . . . for it may be that Malygris is dead."

A communicated shiver seemed to run about the assembly.

"Nay," said the sorcerer who had affirmed the immortality of Malygris. "For how can this thing have come to pass? The doors of his tower stood open today at sunset; and the priests of the ocean-god, bearing a gift of pearls and purple dyes, went in before Malygris, and found him sitting in his tall chair of the ivory of mastodons. He received them haughtily, without speaking, as is his wont; and his servants, who are half ape and half man, came in unbidden to carry away the tribute."

"This very night," said another, "I saw the steadfast lamps of the sable tower, burning above the city like the eyes of Taaran, god of Evil. The familiars have departed not from the tower as such beings depart at the dying of a wizard: for in that case, men would have heard their howling and lamentation in the dark."

"Aye," declared Gadeiron, "men have been befooled ere this. And Malygris was ever the master of illuding shows, of feints, and beguilements. But there is one among us who discerns the truth. Maranapion, through the eye of the Cyclops, has looked on remote things and hidden places. Even now, he peers upon his ancient enemy, Malygris."

Maranapion, shuddering a little beneath his shroud-like garments, seemed to return from his clairvoyant absorption. He raised from the tripod his eyes of luminous amber, whose pupils were black and impenetrable as jet.

"I have seen Malygris," he said, turning to the conclave. "Many times I have watched him thus, thinking to learn some secret of his close-hidden magic. I have spied upon him at noon, at evenfall, and through the drear, lampless vigils of midnight. And I have beheld him in the ashen dawn and the dawn of quickening fire. But always he sits in the great ivory chair, in the high hall of his tower, frowning as if with meditation. And his hands clutch always the basilisk-carven arms of the chair, and his eyes turn evermore, unshutting, unblinking, toward the orient window and the heavens beyond, where only high-risen stars and clouds go by.

"Thus have I beheld him for the space of a whole year and a month. And each day I have seen his monsters bring before him vessels filled with rare meat and drink; and later they have taken away the vessels untouched. And never have I discerned the least movement of his lips, nor any turning or tremor of his body.

"For these reasons, I deem that Malygris is dead; but by virtue of his supremacy in evil and in art magical, he sits defying the worm, still undecayed and incorrupt. And his monsters and his familiars attend him still, deceived by the lying appearance of life; and his power, though now an empty fraud, is still dark and awful upon Poseidonis."

Again, following the slow-measured words of Maranapion, there was silence in the vault. A dark, furtive triumph smouldered in the face of Gadeiron, on whom the yoke of Malygris had lain heavily, irking his pride. Among the twelve sorcerers, there was none who wished well to Malygris, nor any who did not fear him; and they received the annunciation of his demise with dreadful, half-incredulous joy. Some there were who doubted, holding that Maranapion was mistaken; and in the faces of all, as in somber mirrors, their awe of the master was still reflected.

Maranapion, who had hated Malygris above all others, as the one warlock whose art and power excelled his own, stood aloof and inscrutable like a poising vulture.

It was King Gadeiron who broke the gravid silence.

"Not idly have I called ye to this crypt, O sorcerers of Susran: for a work remains to be done. Verily, shall the corpse of a dead necromancer tyrannize over us all? There is mystery here, and a need to move cautiously, for the duration of his necromancy is yet unverified and untested. But I have called ye together in order that the hardiest among ye may take council with Maranapion, and aid him in devising such wizardry as will now expose the fraud of Malygris, and evince his mortality

to all men, as well as to the fiends that follow him still, and the minis-
tering monsters."

A babble of disputation rose, and they who were most doubtful of
this matter, and feared to work against Malygris in any fashion, begged
Gadeiron's leave to withdraw. In the end, there remained seven of the
twelve....

Swiftly, by dim and covert channels, on the day that followed, the
death of Malygris was bruited throughout the isle Poseidonis. Many dis-
believed the story, for the might of the wizard was a thing seared as with
hot iron on the souls of them that had witnessed his thaumaturgies.
However, it was recalled that during the past year few had beheld him
face to face; and always he had seemed to ignore them, speaking not,
and staring fixedly through the tower window, as if intent on far things
that were veiled to others. During that time, he had called no man to his
presence, and had sent forth no message, no oracle or decree; and they
who had gone before him were mainly bearers of tribute and had followed a long-established custom.

When these matters became generally known, there were some who
maintained that he sat thus in a long swoon of ecstasy or catalepsy, and
would awaken therefrom in time. Others, however, held that he had
died, and was able to preserve the deceitful aspect of life through a spell
that endured after him. No man dared to enter the tall, sable tower; and
still the shadow of the tower fell athwart Susran like the shadow of an
evil gnomon moving on some disastrous dial; and still the umbrage of
the power of Malygris lay stagnant as the tomb's night on the minds of
men.

Now, among the five sorcerers who had begged Gadeiron's leave to
depart, fearing to join their fellows in the making of wizardry against
Malygris, there were two that plucked heart a little afterward, when they
heard from other sources a confirmation of the vision beheld by Maranapion through the Cyclops' eye.

These two were brothers, named Nygon and Fustules. Feeling a certain shame for their timidity, and desiring to rehabilitate themselves in the regard of the others, they conceived an audacious plan.

When night had again fallen upon the city, bringing no moon, but only obscure stars and the scud of sea-born clouds, Nygon and Fustules went forth through the darkened ways and came to the steep hill at the heart of Susran, whereon, in half-immemorial years, Malygris had established his grim citadel.

The hill was wooded with close-grown cypresses, whose foliage, even to the full sun, was black and somber as if tarnished by wizard fumes. Crouching on either hand, they leaned like misshapen spirits of the night above the stairs of adamant that gave access to the tower. Nygon and Fustules, mounting the stairs, cowered and trembled when the boughs swung menacingly toward them in violent gusts of wind. They felt the dripping of heavy sea-dews, blown in their faces like a spittle of demons. The wood, it seemed, was full of execrably sighing voices, and weird whimpers and little moanings as of imp-children astray from Satanic dams.

The lights of the tower burned through the waving boughs, and seemed to recede unapproachably as they climbed. More than once, the two regretted their temerity. But at length, without suffering palpable harm or hindrance, they neared the portals, which stood eternally open, pouring the effulgence of still, unflaring lamps on the windy darkness.

Though the plan they had conceived was nefarious, they deemed it best to enter boldly. The purpose of their visit, if any should challenge or interrogate them, was the asking of an oracle from Malygris, who was famed throughout the isle as the most infallible of soothsayers.

Freshening momently from the sea beyond Susran, the wind clamored about the tower like an army of devils in flight from deep to deep, and the long mantles of the sorcerers were blown in their faces. But, entering the wide portals, they heard no longer the crying of the gale, and felt no more its pursuing rudeness. At a single step they passed into

mausolean silence. Around them the lamplight fell unshaken on caryat-
ides of black marble, on mosaics of precious gems, on fabulous metals
and many-storied tapestries; and a tideless perfume weighed upon the
air like a balsam of death.

They felt an involuntary awe, deeming the mortal stillness a thing
that was hardly natural. But, seeing that the tower vestibule was un-
guarded by any of the creatures of Malygris, they were emboldened to
go on and climb the marmorean stairs to the apartments above.

Everywhere, by the light of opulent lamps, they beheld inestimable
and miraculous treasures. There were tables of ebony wrought with sorcerous runes of pearl and white coral; webs of silver and samite, cunningly pictured; caskets of electrum overflowing with talismanic jewels;
tiny gods of jade and agate; and tall chryselephantine demons. Here was
the loot of ages, lying heaped and mingled in utter negligence, without
lock or ward, as if free for the taking of any casual thief.

Eyeing the riches about them with covetous wonder, the two sorcerers mounted slowly from room to room, unchallenged and unmo-
lested, and came ultimately to that upper hall in which Malygris was
wont to receive his visitors.

Here, as elsewhere, the portals stood open before them, and lamps
burned as if in a trance of light. The lust of plunder was hot in their
hearts. Made bolder still by the seeming desolation, and thinking now
that the tower was uninhabited by any but the dead magician, they went
in with little hesitancy.

Like the rooms below, the chamber was full of precious artifacts;
and iron-bound volumes and brazen books of occult, tremendous necromancy, together with golden and earthen censers, and vials of unshat-
terable crystal, were strewn in weird confusion about the mosaic floor.
At the very center, there sat the old archimage in his chair of primeval
ivory, peering with stark, immovable eyes at the night-black window.

Nygon and Fustules felt their awe return upon them, remembering
too clearly now the thrice-baleful mastery that this man had wielded, and

the demon lore he had known, and the spells he had wrought that were irrefragable by other wizards. The specters of these things rose up before them as if by a final necromancy. With down-dropped eyes and humble mien, they went forward, bowing reverentially. Then, speaking aloud, in accordance with their predetermined plan, Fustules requested an oracle of their fortunes from Malygris.

There was no answer, and lifting their eyes, the brothers were greatly reassured by the aspect of the seated ancient. Death alone could have set the greyish pallor on the brow, could have locked the lips in a rigor as of fast-frozen clay. The eyes were like cavern-shadowed ice, holding no other light than a vague reflection of the lamps. Under the beard that was half silver, half sable, the cheeks had already fallen in as with beginning decay, showing the harsh outlines of the skull. The grey and hideously shrunken hands, whereon the eyes of enchanted beryls and rubies burned, were clenched inflexibly on the chair-arms, which had the form of arching basilisks.

"Verily," murmured Nygon, "there is naught here to frighten or dismay us. Behold, it is only the lich of an old man after all, and one that has cheated the worm of his due provender overlong."

"Aye," said Fustules. "But this man, in his time, was the greatest of all necromancers. Even the ring on his little finger is a sovereign talisman. The balas-ruby of the thumb-ring of his right hand will conjure demons from out the deep. In the volumes that lie about the chamber, there are secrets of perished gods and the mysteries of planets immemorial. In the vials, there are syrups that give strange visions, and philtres that can revive the dead. Among these things, it is ours to choose freely."

Nygon, eyeing the gems greedily, selected a ring that encircled the right forefinger with the sixfold coils of a serpent of orichalchum, bearing in its mouth a beryl shaped like a griffin's egg. Vainly, however, he tried to loosen the finger from its rigid clutch on the chair-arm, to permit the removal of the ring. Muttering impatiently, he drew a knife from his girdle and prepared to hew away the finger. In the meanwhile, Fustules had drawn his own knife as a preliminary before approaching the other hand.

"Is thy heart firm within thee, brother?" he inquired in a sort of sibilant whisper. "If so, there is even more to be gained than these talismanic rings. It is well known that a wizard who attains to such supremacy as Malygris, undergoes by virtue thereof a complete bodily transformation, turning his flesh into elements more subtle than those of common flesh. And whoso eats of his flesh even so much as a tiny morsel, will share thereafter in the powers owned by the wizard."

Nygon nodded as he bent above the chosen finger. "This, too, was in my thought," he answered.

Before he or Fustules could begin their ghoulish attack, they were startled by a venomous hissing that appeared to emanate from the bosom of Malygris. They drew back in amazement and consternation, while a small coral viper slid from behind the necromancer's beard, and glided swiftly over his knees to the floor like a sinuous rill of scarlet. There, coiling as if to strike, it regarded the thieves with eyes that were cold and malignant as two drops of frozen poison.

"By the black horns of Taaran!" cried Fustules. "It is one of Malygris' familiars. I have heard of this viper—"

Turning, the two would have fled from the room. But, even as they turned, the walls and portals seemed to recede before them, fleeing giddily and interminably, as if unknown gulfs had been admitted to the chamber. A vertigo seized them; reeling, they saw the little segments of mosaic under their feet assume the proportions of mighty flags. Around them the strewn books and censers and vials loomed enormous, rearing above their heads and barring their way as they ran.

Nygon, looking over his shoulder, saw that the viper had turned to a vast python, whose crimson coils were undulating swiftly along the floor. In a colossal chair, beneath lamps that were large as suns, there sat the colossal form of the dead archimage, in whose presence Nygon and Fustules were no more than pigmies. The lips of Malygris were still immobile beneath his beard; and his eyes still glared implacably upon the blackness of the far window. But at that instant a voice filled the awful spaces of the room, reverberating like thunder in the heavens, hollow and tremendous:

"Fools! ye have dared to ask me for an oracle. And the oracle is—death!"

Nygon and Fustules, knowing their doom, fled on in a madness of terror and desperation. Beyond the towering thuribles, the tomes that were piled like pyramids, they saw the threshold in intermittent glimpses, like a remote horizon. It withdrew before them, dim and unattainable. They panted as runners pant in a dream. Behind them, the vermilion python crawled; and overtaking them as they tried to round the brazen back of a wizard volume, it struck them down like fleeing dormice....

In the end, there was only a small coral viper, that crept back to its hiding-place in the bosom of Malygris. . . .

Toiling by day and night, in the vaults under the palace of Gadeiron, with impious charms and unholy conjurations, and fouler chemistries, Maranapion and his seven coadjutors had nearly completed the making of their sorcery.

They designed an invultuation against Malygris, that would break the power of the dead necromancer by rendering evident to all the mere fact of his death. Employing an unlawful Atlantean science, Maranapion had created living plasm with all the attributes of human flesh, and had caused it to grow and flourish, fed with blood. Then he and his assistants, uniting their wills and convoking the forces that were blasphemy to summon, had compelled the shapeless, palpitating mass to put forth the limbs and members of a new-born child; and had formed it ultimately, after all the changes that man would undergo between birth and senescence, into an image of Malygris.

Now, carrying the process even further, they caused the simulacrum to die of extreme age, as Malygris had apparently died. It sat before them in a high chair, facing toward the east, and duplicating the very posture of the magician on his seat of ivory.

Nothing remained to be done. Forspent and weary, but hopeful, the sorcerers waited for the first signs of mortal decay in the image. If the spells they had woven were successful, a simultaneous decay would occur in the body of Malygris, incorruptible heretofore. Inch by inch, member by member, he would rot in the adamantine tower. His familiars would desert him, no longer deceived; and all who came to the tower would know his mortality; and the tyranny of Malygris would lift from Susran, and his necromancy be null and void as a broken pentacle in sea-girt Poseidonis.

For the first time since the beginning of their invultuation, the eight magicians were free to intermit their vigilance without peril of invalidating the charm. They slept soundly, feeling that their repose was well earned. On the morrow they returned, accompanied by King Gadeiron, to the vault in which they had left the plasmic image.

Opening the sealed door, they were met by a charnel odor, and were gratified to perceive in the figure the unmistakable signs of decomposition. A little later, by consulting the Cyclops' eye, Maranapion verified the paralleling of these marks in the features of Malygris.

A great jubilation, not unmingled with relief, was felt by the sorcerers and by King Gadeiron. Heretofore, not knowing the extent and duration of the powers wielded by the dead master, they had been doubtful of the efficacy of their own magic. But now, it seemed, there was no longer any reason for doubt.

On that very day it happened that certain sea-faring merchants went before Malygris to pay him, according to custom, a share of the profits of their latest voyage. Even as they bowed in the presence of the master, they became aware, by sundry disagreeable tokens, that they had borne tribute to a corpse. Not daring even then to refuse the long-exacted toll, they flung it down and fled from the place in terror.

Soon, in all Susran, there was none who doubted any longer the death of Malygris. And yet, such was the awe he had wrought through many lustrums, that few were venturous enough to invade the tower; and thieves were wary, and would not try to despoil its fabled treasures.

Day by day, in the blue, monstrous eye of the Cyclops, Maranapion saw the rotting of his dreaded rival. And upon him presently there came a strong desire to visit the tower and behold face to face that which he had witnessed only in vision. Thus alone would his triumph be complete.

So it was that he and the sorcerers who had aided him, together with King Gadeiron, went up to the sable tower by the steps of adamant, and climbed by the marble stairs, even as Nygon and Fustules before them, to the high room in which Malygris was seated. . . . But the doom of Nygon and Fustules, being without other witness than the dead, was wholly unknown to them.

Boldly and with no hesitation they entered the chamber. Slanting through the western window, the sun of late afternoon fell goldenly on the dust that had gathered everywhere. Spiders had woven their webs on the bright-jewelled censers, on the graven lamps, and the metal-covered volumes of sorcery. The air was stagnant with a stifling foulness of death.

The intruders went forward, feeling that impulse which leads the victors to exult over a vanquished enemy. Malygris sat unbowed and upright, his black and tattered fingers clutching the ivory chair-arms as of yore, and his empty orbits glowering still at the eastern window. His face was little more than a bearded skull; and his blackening brow was like worm-pierced ebony.

"O Malygris, I give thee greeting," said Maranapion in a loud voice of mockery. "Grant, I beseech thee, a sign, if thy wizardry still prevails, and hath not become the appanage of oblivion."

"Greeting, O Maranapion," replied a grave and terrible voice that issued from the maggot-eaten lips. "Indeed, I will grant thee a sign. Even as I, in death, have rotted upon my seat from that foul sorcery which was wrought in the vaults of King Gadeiron, so thou and thy fellows and Gadeiron, *living,* shall decay and putrefy wholly in an hour, by virtue of the curse that I put upon ye now."

Then the shrunken corpse of Malygris, fulminating the runes of an old Atlantean formula, cursed the eight sorcerers and King Gadeiron. The formula, at frequent intervals, was cadenced with fatal names of lethal gods; and in it were told the secret appellations of the black god of time, and the Nothingness that abides beyond time; and use was made of the titles of many tomb-lairing demons. Heavy and hollow-sounding were the runes, and in them one seemed to hear a noise of great blows on sepulchral doors, and a clangor of downfallen slabs. The air darkened as if with the hovering of seasonless night, and thereupon, like a breathing of the night, a chillness entered the chamber; and it seemed that the black wings of ages passed over the tower, beating prodigiously from void to void, ere the curse was done.

Hearing that maranatha, the sorcerers were dumb with the extremity of their dread; and even Maranapion could recall no counter-spell effectual in any degree against it.

All would have fled from the room ere the curse ended, but a mortal weakness was upon them, and they felt a sickness as of quick-coming death. Shadows were woven athwart their eyes; but through the shadows, each beheld dimly the instant blackening of the faces of his fellows, and saw the cheeks fall ruinously, and the lips curl back on the teeth like those of long-dead cadavers.

Trying to run, each was aware of his own limbs that rotted beneath him, pace by pace, and felt the quick sloughing of his flesh in corruption from the bone. Crying out with black tongues that shrivelled ere the cry was done, they fell down on the floor of the chamber. Life lingered in them, together with the dire knowledge of their doom, and they preserved something of hearing and sight. In the dark agony of their live corruption, they tossed feebly to and fro, and crawled inchmeal on the chill mosaic. And they still moved in this fashion, slowly and more imperceptibly, till their brains were turned to grey mould, and the sinews were parted from their bones, and the marrow was dried up.

Thus, in an hour, the curse was accomplished. The enemies of the necromancer lay before him, supine and shrunken, in the tomb's final posture, as if doing obeisance to a seated Death. Except for the garments, none could have told King Gadeiron from Maranapion, nor Maranapion from the lesser wizards.

The day went by, declining seaward; and, burning like a royal pyre beyond Susran, the sunset flung an aureate glare through the window, and then dropped away in red brands and funereal ashes. And in the twilight a coral viper glided from the bosom of Malygris, and weaving among the remnants of them that lay on the floor, and slipping silently down the stairs of marble, it passed forever from the tower.

TOLOMETH

In billow-lost Poseidonis
I was the black god of the abyss:
My three horns were of similor
Above my double diadem;
My one eye was a moon-bright gem
Found in a monstrous meteor.

Incredible far peoples came,
Called by the thunders of my fame,
And passed below my terraced throne
Where titan pards and lions stood,
As pours a never-lapsing flood

Before the wind of winter blown.
Below my glooming architraves
One brown eternal file of slaves
Came in from mines of chalcedon,
And camels from the long plateaus
Laid down their sard and peridoz,
Their incense and their cinnamon.

The star-born evil that I brought
Through all that ancient land was wrought;
All women took my yoke of shame;
I reared, through sumless centuries,
The thrones of hell-black wizardries,
The hecatombs of blood and flame.

*   *   *

But now, within my sunken walls,
The slow blind ocean-serpent crawls,
And sea-worms are my ministers,
And wandering fishes pass me now
Or press before mine eyeless brow
As once the thronging worshipers . . .

And yet, in ways outpassing thought,
Men worship me that know me not.
They work my will. I shall arise
In that last dawn of atom-fire,
To stand upon the planet's pyre
And cast my shadow on the skies.

THE DOUBLE SHADOW

My name is Pharpetron, among those who have known me in Poseidonis; but even I, the last and most forward pupil of the wise Avyctes, know not the name of that which I am fated to become ere tomorrow. Therefore, by the ebbing silver lamps, in my master's marble house above the loud, ever-ravening sea, I write this tale with a hasty hand, scrawling an ink of wizard virtue on the grey, priceless, antique parchment of dragons. And having written, I shall enclose the pages in a sealed cylinder of orichalchum, and shall cast the cylinder from a high window into the sea, lest that which I am doomed to become should haply destroy the writing. And it may be that mariners from Lephara, passing to Umb and Pneor in their tall triremes, will find the cylinder; or fishers will draw it from the wave in their seines of byssus; and having read my story, men will learn the truth and take warning; and no man's feet, henceforward, will approach the pale and demon-haunted house of Avyctes.

For six years, I have dwelt apart with the aged master, forgetting youth and its wonted desires in the study of arcanic things. Together, we have delved more deeply than all others before us in an interdicted lore; we have solved the keyless hieroglyphs that guard ante-human formulae; we have talked with the prehistoric dead; we have called up the dwellers in sealed crypts, in fearful abysses beyond space. Few are the sons of mankind who have cared to seek us out among the desolate, wind-worn crags; and many, but nameless, are the visitants who have come to us from further bourns of place and time.

Stern and white as a tomb, older than the memory of the dead, and built by men or devils beyond the recording of myth, is the mansion in which we dwell. Far below, on black, naked reefs, the northern sea climbs and roars indomitably, or ebbs with a ceaseless murmur as of armies of baffled demons; and the house is filled evermore, like a hollow-sounding sepulcher, with the drear echo of its tumultuous voices; and the winds wail in dismal wrath around the high towers, but shake them not. On the seaward side, the mansion rises sheerly from the straight-falling cliff; but on the other sides there are narrow terraces, grown with dwarfish, crooked cedars that bow always beneath the gale. Giant marble monsters guard the landward portals; and huge marble women ward the strait porticoes above the sea; and mighty statues and mummies stand everywhere in the chambers and along the halls. But, saving these, and the spirits we have summoned, there is none to companion us; and liches and shadows have been the servitors of our daily needs.

All men have heard the fame of Avyctes, the sole surviving pupil of that Malygris who tyrannized in his necromancy over Susran from a tower of sable stone; Malygris, who lay dead for years while men believed him living; who, lying thus, still uttered potent spells and dire oracles with decaying lips. But Avyctes lusted not for temporal power in the manner of Malygris; and having learned all that the elder sorcerer could teach him, withdrew from the cities of Poseidonis to seek another and vaster dominion; and I, the youth Pharpetron, in the latter years of Avyctes, was permitted to join him in this solitude; and since then, I have shared his austerities and vigils and evocations . . . and now, likewise, I must share the weird doom that has come in answer to his summoning.

Not without terror (since man is but mortal) did I, the neophyte, behold at first the abhorrent and tremendous faces of them that obeyed Avyctes: the genii of the sea and earth, of the stars and the heavens, who passed to and fro in his marmorean halls. I shuddered at the black writhing of submundane things from the many-volumed smoke of the braziers; I cried in horror at the grey foulnesses, colossal, without form, that crowded malignly about the drawn circle of seven colors, threatening unspeakable trespass on us that stood at the center. Not without revulsion did I drink wine that was poured by cadavers, and eat bread that was purveyed by phantoms. But use and custom dulled the strangeness, destroyed the fear; and in time I believed implicitly that Avyctes was the lord of all incantations and exorcisms, with infallible power to dismiss the beings he evoked.

Well had it had been for Avyctes—and for me—if the master had contented himself with the lore preserved from Atlantis and Thule, or brought over from Mu and Mayapan. Surely this should have been enough: for in the ivory-sheeted books of Thule there were blood-writ runes that would call the demons of the fifth and seventh planets, if spoken aloud at the hour of their ascent; and the sorcerers of Mu had left record of a process whereby the doors of far-future time could be unlocked; and our fathers, the Atlanteans, had known the road between the atoms and the path into far stars, and had held speech with the spirits of the sun. But Avyctes thirsted for a darker knowledge, a deeper empery; and into his hands, in the third year of my novitiate, there came the mirror-bright tablet of the lost serpent-people.

Strange, and apparently fortuitous, was our finding of the tablet. At certain hours, when the tide had fallen from the steep rocks, we were wont to descend by cavern-hidden stairs to a cliff-walled crescent beach behind the promontory on which stood the house of Avyctes. There, on the dun, wet sands, beyond the foamy tongues of the surf, would lie the worn and curious driftage of alien shores, and trove that hurricanes had cast up from unsounded deeps. And there we had found the purple and sanguine volutes of great shells, and rude lumps of ambergris, and white flowers of perpetually blooming coral; and once, the barbaric idol of green brass that had been the figurehead of a galley from far hyperborean isles.

There had been a great storm, such as must have riven the sea to its nethermost profound; but the tempest had gone by with morning, and the heavens were cloudless on that fatal day when we found the tablet, and the demon winds were hushed among the high crags and chasms; and the sea lisped with a low whisper, like the rustle of gowns of samite trailed by fleeing maidens on the sand. And just beyond the ebbing wave, in a tangle of russet sea-weed, we beheld a thing that glittered with blinding sun-like brilliance. And running forward, I plucked it from the wrack before the wave's return, and bore it to Avyctes.

The tablet was wrought of some nameless metal, like never-rusting iron, but heavier. It had the form of a triangle and was broader at the widest than a man's heart. On one side it was wholly blank; and Avyctes and I, in turn, beheld our features mirrored strangely, like the drawn, pallid features of the dead, in its burnished surface. On the other side many rows of small crooked ciphers were incised deeply in the metal, as if by the action of some mordant acid; and these ciphers were not the pictorial symbols or alphabetic characters of any language known to the master or to me.

Of the tablet's age and origin, likewise, we could form no conjecture; and our erudition was altogether baffled. For many days thereafter we studied the writing and held argument that came to no issue. And night by night, in a high chamber closed against the perennial winds, we pondered over the dazzling triangle by the tall straight flames of silver lamps. For Avyctes deemed that knowledge of rare value (or haply some secret of an alien or elder magic) was holden by the clueless crooked ciphers. Then, since all our scholarship was in vain, the master sought another divination, and had recourse to wizardry and necromancy. But at first, among the devils and phantoms that answered our interrogation, none could tell us aught concerning the tablet. And any other than Avyctes would have despaired in the end . . . and well would it have been if he had despaired, and had sought no longer to decipher the writing. . . .

The months and years went by with a slow thundering of seas on the dark rocks, and a headlong clamor of winds around the white towers.

Still we continued our delvings and evocations; and further, always further we went into lampless realms of space and spirit; learning, perchance, to unlock the hithermost of the manifold infinities. And at
whiles, Avyctes would resume his pondering of the sea-found tablet; or
would question some visitant from other spheres of time and place regarding its interpretation.

At last, by the use of a chance formula, in idle experiment, he summoned up the dim, tenuous ghost of a sorcerer from prehistoric years;
and the ghost, in a thin whisper of uncouth, forgotten speech, informed
us that the letters on the tablet were those of a language of the serpent-
men, whose primordial continent had sunk aeons before the lifting of
Hyperborea from the ooze. But the ghost could tell us naught of their
significance; for, even in his time, the serpent-people had become a dubious legend; and their deep, ante-human lore and sorcery were things
irretrievable by man.

Now, in all the books of conjuration owned by Avyctes, there was
no spell whereby we could call the lost serpent-men from their fabulous
epoch. But there was an old Lemurian formula, recondite and uncertain,
by which the shadow of a dead man could be sent into years posterior
to those of his own life-time, and could be recalled after an interim by
the wizard. And the shade, being wholly insubstantial, would suffer no
harm from the temporal transition, and would remember, for the information of the wizard, that which he had been instructed to learn during
the journey.

So, having called again the ghost of the prehistoric sorcerer, whose
name was Ybith, Avyctes made a singular use of several very ancient
gums and combustible fragments of fossil wood; and he and I, reciting
the responses to the formula, sent the thin spirit of Ybith into the far
ages of the serpent-men. And after a time which the master deemed
sufficient, we performed the curious rites of incantation that would recall Ybith from his alienage. And the rites were successful; and Ybith
stood before us again, like a blown vapor that is nigh to vanishing. And

in words that were faint as the last echo of perishing memories, the specter told us the key to the meaning of the letters, which he had learned in the primeval past; and after this, we questioned Ybith no more, but suffered him to return unto slumber and oblivion.

Then, knowing the import of the tiny, twisted ciphers, we read the writing on the tablet and made thereof a transliteration, though not without labor and difficulty, since the very phonetics of the serpent tongue, and the symbols and ideas expressed in the writing, were somewhat alien to those of mankind. And when we had mastered the inscription, we found that it contained the formula for a certain evocation which, no doubt, had been used by the serpent sorcerers. But the object of the evocation was not named; nor was there any clue to the nature or identity of that which would come in answer to the rites. And moreover there was no corresponding rite of exorcism nor spell of dismissal.

Great was the jubilation of Avyctes, deeming that we had learned a lore beyond the memory or prevision of man. And though I sought to dissuade him, he resolved to employ the evocation, arguing that our discovery was no chance thing but was fatefully predestined from the beginning. And he seemed to think lightly of the menace that might be brought upon us by the conjuration of things whose nativity and attributes were wholly obscure. "For," said Avyctes, "I have called up, in all the years of my sorcery, no god or devil, no demon or lich or shadow, which I could not control and dismiss at will. And I am loath to believe that any power or spirit beyond the subversion of my spells could have been summoned by a race of serpents, whatever their skill in demonism and necromancy."

So, seeing that he was obstinate, and acknowledging him for my master in all ways, I consented to aid Avyctes in the experiment, though not without dire misgivings. And then we gathered together, in the chamber of conjuration, at the specified hour and configuration of the stars, the equivalents of sundry rare materials that the tablet had instructed us to use in the ritual.

Of much that we did, and of certain agents that we employed, it were better not to tell; nor shall I record the shrill, sibilant words, difficult for beings not born of serpents to articulate, whose intonation formed a signal part of the ceremony. Toward the last, we drew a triangle on the marble floor with the fresh blood of birds; and Avyctes stood at one angle, and I at another; and the gaunt umber mummy of an Atlantean warrior, whose name had been Oigos, was stationed at the third angle. And standing thus, Avyctes and I held tapers of corpse-tallow in our hands, till the tapers had burned down between our fingers as into a socket. And in the outstretched palms of the mummy of Oigos, as if in shallow thuribles, talc and asbestos burned, ignited by a strange fire whereof we knew the secret. At one side we had traced on the floor an infrangible ellipse, made by an endless linked repetition of the twelve unspeakable Signs of Oumor, to which we could retire if the visitant should prove inimical or rebellious. We waited while the pole-circling stars went over, as had been prescribed. Then, when the tapers had gone out between our seared fingers, and the talc and asbestos were wholly consumed in the mummy's eaten palms, Avyctes uttered a single word whose sense was obscure to us; and Oigos, being animated by sorcery and subject to our will, repeated the word after a given interval, in tones that were hollow as a tomb-born echo; and I, in my turn, also repeated it.

Now, in the chamber of evocation, before beginning the ritual, we had opened a small window giving upon the sea, and had likewise left open a high door on the hall to landward, lest that which came in answer to us should require a spatial mode of entrance. And during the ceremony, the sea became still and there was no wind, and it seemed that all things were hushed in awful expectation of the nameless visitor. But after all was done, and the last word had been repeated by Oigos and me, we stood and waited vainly for a visible sign or other manifestation. The lamps burned stilly in the midnight room; and no shadows fell, other than were cast by ourselves and Oigos and by the great marble women along the walls. And in the magic mirrors we had placed cunningly, to reflect those that were otherwise unseen, we beheld no breath or trace of any image.

At this, after a reasonable interim, Avyctes was sorely disappointed, deeming that the evocation had failed of its purpose; and I, having the same thought, was secretly relieved. And we questioned the mummy of Oigos, to learn if he had perceived in the room, with such senses as are peculiar to the dead, the sure token or doubtful proof of a presence undescried by us the living. And the mummy gave a necromantic answer, saying that there was nothing.

"Verily," said Avyctes, "it were useless to wait longer. For surely in some way we have misunderstood the purport of the writing, or have failed to duplicate the matters used in the evocation, or the correct intonement of the words. Or it may be that in the lapse of so many aeons, the thing that was formerly wont to respond has long ceased to exist, or has altered in its attributes so that the spell is now void and valueless."

To this I assented readily, hoping that the matter was at an end. So, after erasing the blood-marked triangle and the sacred ellipse of the linked Signs of Oumor, and after dismissing Oigos to his wonted place among the other mummies, we retired to sleep. And in the days that followed, we resumed our habitual studies, but made no mention to each other of the strange triangular tablet or the vain formula.

Even as before, our days went on; and the sea climbed and roared in white fury on the cliffs, and the winds wailed by in their unseen, sullen wrath, bowing the dark cedars as witches are bowed by the breath of Taaran, god of evil. Almost, in the marvel of new tests and cantraips, I forgot the ineffectual conjuration, and I deemed that Avyctes had also forgotten it.

All things were as of yore, to our sorcerous perception; and there was naught to trouble us in our wisdom and power and serenity, which we deemed secure above the sovereignty of kings. Reading the horoscopic stars, we found no future ill in their aspect; nor was any shadow

of bale foreshown to us through geomancy, or other modes of divination such as we employed. And our familiars, though grisly and dreadful
to mortal gaze, were wholly obedient to us the masters.

Then, on a clear summer afternoon, we walked, as was often our
custom, on the marble terrace behind the house. In robes of ocean-pur-
ple, we paced among the windy trees with their blown, crooked shadows; and there, following us as we went to and fro, I saw the blue
shadow of Avyctes and my own shadow on the marble; and between
them, an adumbration that was not wrought by any of the cedars. And
I was greatly startled, but spoke not of the matter to Avyctes, and observed the unknown shadow with covert care.

I saw that it followed closely the shadow of Avyctes, keeping ever
the same distance. And it fluttered not in the wind, but moved with a
flowing as of some heavy, thick, putrescent liquid; and its color was not
blue nor purple nor black, nor any other hue to which man's eyes are
habituated, but a hue as of some unearthly purulence; and its form was
altogether monstrous, having a squat head and a long, undulant body,
without similitude to beast or devil.

Avyctes heeded not the shadow; and still I feared to speak, though
I thought it an ill thing for the master to be companioned thus. And I
moved closer to him, in order to detect by touch or other perception
the invisible presence that had cast the adumbration. But the air was
void to sunward of the shadow; and I found nothing opposite the sun
nor in any oblique direction, though I searched closely, knowing that
certain beings cast their shadows thus.

After a while, at the customary hour, we returned by the coiling
stairs and monster-flanked portals into the high house. And I saw that
the strange adumbration moved ever behind the shadow of Avyctes,
falling horrible and unbroken on the steps and passing clearly separate
and distinct amid the long umbrages of the towering monsters. And in
the dim halls beyond the sun, where shadows should not have been, I

beheld with terror the distorted loathly blot, having a pestilent, unnamable hue, that followed Avyctes as if in lieu of his own extinguished shadow. And all that day, everywhere that we went, at the table served by specters, or in the mummy-warded room of volumes and books, the thing pursued Avyctes, clinging to him even as leprosy to the leper. And still the master had perceived it not; and still I forbore to warn him, hoping that the visitant would withdraw in its own time, going obscurely as it had come.

But at midnight, when we sat together by the silver lamps, pondering the blood-writ runes of Hyperborea, I saw that the shadow had drawn closer to the shadow of Avyctes, towering behind his chair on the wall between the huge sculptured women and the mummies. And the thing was a streaming ooze of charnel pollution, a foulness beyond the black leprosies of hell; and I could bear it no more; and I cried out in my fear and loathing, and informed the master of its presence.

Beholding now the shadow, Avyctes considered it closely and in silence; and there was neither fear nor awe nor abhorrence in the deep, graven wrinkles of his visage. And he said to me at last:

"This thing is a mystery beyond my lore; but never, in all the practice of my art, has any shadow come to me unbidden. And since all others of our evocations have found answer ere this, I must deem that the shadow is a veritable entity, or the sign of an entity, that has come in belated response to the formula of the serpent-sorcerers, which we thought powerless and void. And I think it well that we should now repair to the chamber of conjuration, and interrogate the shadow in such manner as we may, to inquire its nativity and purpose."

We went forthwith into the chamber of conjuration, and made such preparations as were both necessary and possible. And when we were prepared to question it, the unknown shadow had drawn closer still to the shadow of Avyctes, so that the clear space between the two was no wider than the thickness of a necromancer's rod.

Now, in all ways that were feasible, we interrogated the shadow, speaking through our own lips and the lips of mummies and statues. But there was no determinable answer; and calling certain of the devils and phantoms that were our familiars, we made question through the mouths of these, but without result. And all the while, our magic mirrors were void of any reflection of a presence that might have cast the shadow; and they that had been our spokesmen could detect nothing in the room. And there was no spell, it seemed, that had power upon the visitant. So Avyctes became troubled; and drawing on the floor with blood and ashes the ellipse of Oumor, wherein no demon nor spirit may intrude, he retired to its center. But still within the ellipse, like a flowing taint of liquid corruption, the shadow followed his shadow; and the space between the two was no wider than the thickness of a wizard's pen.

Now, on the face of Avyctes, horror had graven new wrinkles; and his brow was beaded with a deathly sweat. For he knew, even as I, that this was a thing beyond all laws, and foreboding naught but disaster and evil. And he cried to me in a shaken voice, and said:

"I have no knowledge of this thing nor its intention toward me, and no power to stay its progress. Go forth and leave me now; for I would not that any man should witness the defeat of my sorcery and the doom that may follow thereupon. Also, it were well to depart while there is time, lest you too should become the quarry of the shadow and be compelled to share its menace."

Though terror had fastened upon my inmost soul, I was loath to leave Avyctes. But I had sworn to obey his will at all times and in every respect; and moreover I knew myself doubly powerless against the adumbration, since Avyctes himself was impotent.

So, bidding him farewell, I went forth with trembling limbs from the haunted chamber; and peering back from the threshold, I saw that the alien umbrage, creeping like a noisome blotch on the floor, had touched the shadow of Avyctes. And at that moment the master shrieked aloud like one in nightmare; and his face was no longer the face of Avyctes but was contorted and convulsed like that of some helpless madman who wrestles with an unseen incubus. And I looked no more, but fled along the dim outer hall and through the high portals giving upon the terrace.

A red moon, ominous and gibbous, had declined above the terrace and the crags; and the shadows of the cedars were elongated in the moon; and they wavered in the gale like the blown cloaks of enchanters. And stooping against the gale, I fled across the terrace toward the outer stairs that led to a steep path in the riven waste of rocks and chasms behind Avyctes' house. I neared the terrace edge, running with the speed of fear; but I could not reach the topmost outer stair; for at every step the marble flowed beneath me, fleeing like a pale horizon before the seeker. And though I raced and panted without pause, I could draw no nearer to the terrace edge.

At length I desisted, seeing that an unknown spell had altered the very space about the house of Avyctes, so that none could escape therefrom to landward. So, resigning myself in despair to whatever might befall, I returned toward the house. And climbing the white stairs in the low, level beams of the crag-caught moon, I saw a figure that awaited me in the portals. And I knew by the trailing robe of sea-purple, but by no other token, that the figure was Avyctes. For the face was no longer in its entirety the face of man, but was become a loathly fluid amalgam of human features with a thing not to be identified on earth. The transfiguration was ghastlier than death or the changes of decay; and the face was already hued with the nameless, corrupt and purulent color of the strange shadow, and had taken on, in respect to its outlines, a partial likeness to the squat profile of the shadow. The hands of the figure were not those of any terrene being; and the shape beneath the robe had lengthened with a nauseous undulant pliancy; and the face and fingers seemed to drip in the moonlight with a deliquescent corruption. And the pursuing umbrage, like a thickly flowing blight, had corroded and distorted the very shadow of Avyctes, which was now double in a manner not to be narrated here.

Fain would I have cried or spoken aloud; but horror had dried up the fount of speech. And the thing that had been Avyctes beckoned me in silence, uttering no word from its living and putrescent lips. And with eyes that were no longer eyes, but had become an oozing abomination, it peered steadily upon me. And it clutched my shoulder closely with the soft leprosy of its fingers, and led me half-swooning with revulsion along the hall, and into that room where the mummy of Oigos, who had assisted us in the threefold incantation of the serpent-men, was stationed with several of his fellows.

By the lamps which illumed the chamber, burning with pale, still, perpetual flames, I saw that the mummies stood erect along the wall in their exanimate repose, each in his wonted place with his tall shadow beside him. But the great, gaunt shadow of Oigos on the marble wall was companioned by an adumbration similar in all respects to the evil thing that had followed the master and was now incorporate with him. I remembered that Oigos had performed his share of the ritual, and had repeated an unknown stated word in turn after Avyctes; and so I knew that the horror had come to Oigos in turn, and would wreak itself upon the dead even as on the living. For the foul, anonymous thing that we had called in our presumption could manifest itself to mortal ken in no other way than this. We had drawn it from unfathomable depths of time and space, using ignorantly a dire formula; and the thing had come at its own chosen hour, to stamp itself in abomination uttermost on the evocators.

Since then, the night has ebbed away, and a second day has gone by like a sluggish ooze of horror. . . . I have seen the complete identification of the shadow with the flesh and the shadow of Avyctes . . . and also I have seen the slow encroachment of that other umbrage, mingling itself with the lank shadow and the sere, bituminous body of Oigos, and turning them to a similitude of the thing which Avyctes has become. And I have heard the mummy cry out like a living man in great pain and fear, as with the throes of a second dissolution, at the impingement of the shadow. And long since it has grown silent, like the other horror, and I know not its thoughts or its intent. . . . And verily I know not if the thing that has come to us be one or several; nor if its avatar will rest complete with the three that summoned it forth into time, or be extended to others.

But these things, and much else, I shall soon know; for now, in turn, there is a shadow that follows mine, drawing ever closer. The air congeals and curdles with an unseen fear; and they that were our familiars have fled from the mansion; and the great marble women seem to tremble where they stand along the walls. But the horror that was Avyctes, and the second horror that was Oigos, have left me not, and neither do they tremble. And with eyes that are not eyes, they seem to brood and watch, waiting till I too shall become as they. And their stillness is more terrible than if they had rended me limb from limb. And there are strange voices in the wind, and alien roarings upon the sea; and the walls quiver like a thin veil in the black breath of remote abysses.

So, knowing that the time is brief, I have shut myself in the room of volumes and books and have written this account. And I have taken the bright triangular tablet, whose solution was our undoing, and have cast it from the window into the sea, hoping that none will find it after us. And now I must make an end, and enclose this writing in the sealed cylinder of orichalchum, and fling it forth to drift upon the wave. For the space between my shadow and the shadow of the horror is straitened momently . . . and the space is no wider than the thickness of a wizard's pen.

A Voyage to Sfanomoë

There are many marvellous tales, untold, unwritten, never to be recorded or remembered, lost beyond all divining and all imagining, that sleep in the double silence of far-recessive time and space. The chronicles of Saturn, the archives of the moon in its prime, the legends of Antillia and Moaria—these are full of an unsurmised or forgotten wonder. And strange are the multitudinous tales withheld by the light-years of Polaris and the Galaxy. But none is stranger, none more marvellous, than the tale of Hotar and Evidon and their voyage to the planet Sfanomoë, from the last isle of foundering Atlantis. Harken, for I alone shall tell the story, who came in a dream to the changeless center where the past and future are always contemporary with the present; and saw the veritable happening thereof; and, waking, gave it words:

Hotar and Evidon were brothers in science as well as by consanguinity. They were the last representatives of a long line of illustrious inventors and investigators, all of whom had contributed more or less to the knowledge, wisdom, and scientific resources of a lofty civilization matured through cycles. One by one they and their fellow-savants had learned the arcanic secrets of geology, of chemistry, of biology, of astronomy; they had subverted the elements, had constrained the sea, the sun, the air, and the force of gravitation, compelling them to serve the uses of man; and lastly they had found a way to release the typhonic power of the atom, to destroy, transmute, and reconstruct the molecules of matter at will.

However, by that irony which attends all the triumphs and achievements of man, the progress of this mastering of natural law was coincidental with the profound geologic changes and upheavals which caused the gradual sinking of Atlantis. Age by age, aeon by aeon, the process had gone on: huge peninsulas, whole sea-boards, high mountain ranges, citied plains and plateaus, all went down in turn beneath the diluvial waves. With the advance of science, the time and location of future cataclysms was more accurately predictable; but nothing could be done to avert them.

In the days of Hotar and Evidon, all that remained of the former continent was a large isle, called Poseidonis. It was well known that this isle, with its opulent sea-ports, its aeon-surviving monuments of art and architecture, its fertile inland valleys, and mountains lifting their spires of snow above semi-tropic jungles, was destined to go down ere the sons and daughters of the present generation had grown to maturity.

Like many others of their family, Hotar and Evidon had devoted long years of research to the obscure telluric laws governing the imminent catastrophe; and had sought to devise a means of prevention, or, at least, of retardation. But the seismic forces involved were too deeply seated and too widespread in their operation to be controllable in any manner or degree. No magnetic mechanism, no zone of repressive force, was powerful enough to affect them. When the two brothers were nearing middle age, they realized the ultimate futility of their endeavors; and though the peoples of Poseidonis continued to regard them as possible saviors, whose knowledge and resource were well-nigh superhuman, they had secretly abandoned all effort to salvage the doomed isle, and had retired from sea-gazing Lephara, the immemorial home of their family, to a private observatory and laboratory far up in the mountains of the interior.

Here, with the hereditary wealth at their command, the brothers surrounded themselves not only with all the known instruments and materials of scientific endeavor, but also with a certain degree of personal luxury. They were secluded from the world by a hundred scarps and precipices and by many leagues of little-trodden jungle; and they deemed this seclusion advisable for the labors which they now proposed to themselves, and whose real nature they had not divulged to anyone.

Hotar and Evidon had gone beyond all others of their time in the study of astronomy. The true character and relationship of the world, the sun, the moon, the planetary system, and the stellar universe, had long been known in Atlantis. But the brothers had speculated more boldly, had calculated more profoundly and more closely than anyone else. In the powerful magnifying mirrors of their observatory, they had given special attention to the neighboring planets; had formed an accurate idea of their distance from the earth; had estimated their relative size; and had conceived the notion that several, or perhaps all, might well be inhabited by creatures similar to man; or, if not inhabited, were potentially capable of supporting human life.

Venus, which the Atlanteans knew by the name of Sfanomoë, was the planet which drew their curiosity and their conjecture more than any other. Because of its position, they surmised that it might readily resemble the earth in climatic conditions and in all the prerequisites of biological development.

And the hidden labor to which they were now devoting their energies was nothing less than the invention of a vehicle by which it would be possible to leave the ocean-threatened isle and voyage to Sfanomoë.

Day by day the brothers toiled to perfect their invention; and night by night, through the ranging seasons, they peered at the lustrous orb of their speculations as it hung in the emerald evening of Poseidonis, or above the violet-shrouded heights that would soon take the saffron footprints of the dawn. And ever they gave themselves to bolder imaginings, to stranger and more perilous projects.

The vehicle they were building was designed with complete foreknowledge of all the problems to be faced, of all the difficulties to be overcome. Various types of air-vessels had been used in Atlantis for epochs; but they knew that none of these would be suitable for their purpose even in a modified form. The vehicle they finally devised, after much planning and long discussion, was a perfect sphere, like a miniature moon; since, as they argued, all bodies traveling through etheric space were of this shape. It was made with double walls of a metallic alloy whose secret they themselves had discovered—an alloy that was both light and tough beyond any substance classified by chemistry or mineralogy. There were a dozen small round windows lined with an unbreakable glass, and a door of the same alloy as the walls that could be shut with hermetic tightness. The explosion of atoms in sealed cylinders was to furnish the propulsive and levitative power and would also serve to heat the sphere's interior against the absolute cold of space. Solidified air was to be carried in electrum containers and vaporized at the rate which would maintain a respirable atmosphere. And foreseeing that the gravitational influence of the earth would lessen and cease as they went further and further away from it, they had established in the floor of the sphere a magnetic zone that would simulate the effect of gravity and thus obviate any bodily danger or discomfort to which they might otherwise be liable.

These labors were carried on with no other assistance than that of a few slaves, members of an aboriginal race of Atlantis, who had no conception of the purpose for which the vessel was being built; and who, to ensure their complete discretion, were deaf-mutes. There were no interruptions from visitors, for it was tacitly assumed throughout the isle that Hotar and Evidon were engaged in seismologic researches that required a concentration both profound and prolonged.

At length, after years of toil, of vacillation, doubt, anxiety, the sphere was completed. Shining like an immense bubble of silver, it stood on a westward-facing terrace of the laboratory, from which the planet Sfanomoë was now visible at eventide beyond the purpling sea of the jungle. All was in readiness: the vessel was amply provisioned for a journey of many lustrums and decades, and was furnished with an abundant supply of books, with implements of art and science, with all things necessary for the comfort and convenience of the voyagers.

Hotar and Evidon were now men of middle years, in the hale maturity of all their powers and faculties. They were the highest type of the

Atlantean race, with fair complexions and lofty stature, with the features of a lineage both aristocratic and intellectual. Knowing the nearness of the final cataclysm, they had never married, they had not even formed any close ties; but had given themselves to science with a monastic devotion. They mourned the inevitable passing of their civilization, with all its epoch-garnered lore, its material and artistic wealth, its consummate refinement. But they had learned the universality of the laws whose operation was plunging Atlantis beneath the wave—the laws of change, of increase and decay; and they had schooled themselves to a philosophic resignation—a resignation which, mayhap, was not untempered by a foresight of the singular glory and novel, unique experiences that would be entailed by their flight upon hitherto-untraveled space.

Their emotions, therefore, were a mingling of altruistic regret and personal expectancy, when, on the evening chosen for their departure, they dismissed their wondering slaves with a writ of manumission, and entered the orb-shaped vessel. And Sfanomoë brightened before them with a pulsing luster, and Poseidonis darkened below, as they began their voyage into the sea-green heavens of the west.

The great vessel rose with a buoyant ease beneath their guidance; till soon they saw the lights of Susran the capital and its galley-crowded port Lephara, where nightly revels were held and the very fountains ran with wine that people might forget awhile the predicted doom. But so high in the air had the vessel climbed, that Hotar and Evidon could hear no faintest murmur of the loud lyres and strident merry-making in the cities beneath. And they went onward and upward, till the world was a dark blur and the skies were aflame with stars that their optic mirrors had never revealed. And anon the black planet below was rimmed with a growing crescent of fire, and they soared from its shadow to unsetting daylight. But the heavens were no longer a familiar blue, but had taken on the lucid ebon of ether; and no star nor world, not even the littlest, was dimmed by the rivalship of the sun. And brighter than all was Sfanomoë, where it hung with unvacillating lambence in the void.

Mile by stellar mile the earth was left behind; and Hotar and Evidon, peering ahead to the goal of their dreams, had almost forgotten it. Then, gazing back, they saw it was no longer below but above them, like a vaster moon. And studying its oceans and isles and continents, they named them over one by one from their maps as the globe revolved; but vainly they sought for Poseidonis, amid an unbroken glittering waste of sea. And the brothers were conscious of that regret and sorrow which is the just due of all evanished beauty, of all sunken splendor. And they mused awhile on the glory that had been Atlantis, and recalled to memory her obelisks and domes and mountains, her palms with high and haughty crests, and the fire-tall plumes of her warriors, that would lift no longer to the sun.

Their life in the orb-like vessel was one of ease and tranquillity, and differed little from that to which they were accustomed. They pursued their wonted studies, they went on with experiments they had planned or begun in past days, they read to each other the classic literature of Atlantis, they argued and discussed a million problems of philosophy or science. And time itself was scarcely heeded by Hotar and Evidon; and the weeks and months of their journey became years, and the years were added into lustrums, and the lustrums into decades. Nor were they sensible of the change in themselves and in each other, as the years began to weave a web of wrinkles in their faces, to tint their brows with the yellow ivory of age and to thread their sable beards with ermine. There were too many things to be solved or debated, too many speculations and surmises to be ventured, for such trivial details as these to usurp their attention.

Sfanomoë grew larger and larger as the half-oblivious years went by; till anon it rolled beneath them with strange markings of untraveled continents and seas unsailed by man. And now the discourse of Hotar and Evidon was wholly concerning the world in which they would so soon arrive, and the peoples, animals, and plants which they might expect to find. They felt in their ageless hearts the thrill of an anticipation without parallel, as they steered their vessel toward the ever-widening orb that swam below them. Soon they hung above its surface, in a cloud-laden atmosphere of tropic warmth; but though they were childishly eager to set foot on the new planet, they sagely decided to prolong their journey on a horizontal level till they could study its topography with some measure of care and completeness.

To their surprise, they found nothing in the bright expanse below that in any manner suggested the work of men or living beings. They had looked for towering cities of exotic aerial architecture, for broad thoroughfares and canals and geometrically measured areas of agricul-tural fields. Instead, there was only a primordial landscape of mountains, marshes, forests, oceans, rivers, and lakes.

At length they made up their minds to descend. Though they were old, old men, with five-foot ermine beards, they brought the moon-shaped vessel down with all the skill of which they would have been capable in their prime; and opening the door that had been sealed for decades, they emerged in turn—Hotar preceding Evidon, since he was a little the elder.

Their first impressions were of a torrid heat, of dazzling color and overwhelming perfume. There seemed to be a million odors in the heavy, strange, unstirring air—odors that were almost visible in the form of wreathing vapors—perfumes that were like elixirs and opiates, that conferred at the same time a blissful drowsiness and a divine exhilara-tion. Then they saw that there were flowers everywhere—that they had descended in a wilderness of blossoms. They were all of unearthly forms, of supermundane size and beauty and variety, with scrolls and volutes of petals many-hued, that seemed to curl and twist with a more than vegetable animation or sentiency. They grew from a ground that their overlapping stems and calyxes had utterly concealed; they hung from the boles and fronds of palm-like trees they had mantled beyond recognition; they thronged the water of still pools; they poised on the jungle-tops like living creatures winged for flight to the perfume-drunken heavens. And even as the brothers watched, the flowers grew and faded with a thaumaturgic swiftness, they fell and replaced each other as if by some legerdemain of natural law.

Hotar and Evidon were delighted, they called out to each other like children, they pointed at each new floral marvel that was more exquisite and curious than the rest; and they wondered at the speed of their miraculous growth and decay. And they laughed at the unexampled bizarrerie of the sight, when they perceived certain animals new to zoology, who were trotting about on more than the usual number of legs, with orchidaceous blossoms springing from their rumps.

They forgot their long voyage through space, they forgot there had ever been a planet called the earth and an isle named Poseidonis, they forgot their lore and their wisdom, as they roamed through the flowers of Sfanomoë. The exotic air and its odors mounted to their heads like a mighty wine; and the clouds of golden and snowy pollen which fell upon them from the arching arbors were potent as some fantastic drug. It pleased them that their white beards and violet tunics should be powdered with this pollen and with the floating spores of plants that were alien to all terrene botany.

Suddenly Hotar cried out with a new wonder, and laughed with a more boisterous mirth than before. He had seen that an oddly folded leaf was starting from the back of his shrunken right hand. The leaf unfurled as it grew, it disclosed a flower-bud; and lo! the bud opened and became a triple-chaliced blossom of unearthly hues, adding a rich perfume to the swooning air. Then, on his left hand, another blossom appeared in like manner; and then leaves and petals were burgeoning from his wrinkled face and brow, were growing in successive tiers from his limbs and body, were mingling their hair-like tendrils and tongue-shaped pistils with his beard. He felt no pain, only an infantile surprise and bewilderment as he watched them.

Now from the hands and limbs of Evidon, the blossoms also began to spring. And soon the two old men had ceased to wear a human semblance, and were hardly to be distinguished from the garland-laden trees about them. And they died with no agony, as if they were already part of the teeming floral life of Sfanomoë, with such perceptions and sensations as were appropriate to their new mode of existence. And before long their metamorphosis was complete, and every fiber of their bodies had undergone a dissolution into flowers. And the vessel in which they had made their voyage was embowered from sight in an ever-climbing mass of plants and blossoms.

Such was the fate of Hotar and Evidon, the last of the Atlanteans, and the first (if not also the last) of human visitors to Sfanomoë.

ATLANTIS

A bove its domes the gulfs accumulate.
Far up, the sea-gales blare their bitter screed:
But here the buried waters take no heed—
Deaf, and with welded lips pressed down by weight
Of the upper ocean. Dim, interminate,
In cities over-webbed with sombre weed,
Where galleons crumble and the krakens breed,
The slow tide coils through sunken court and gate.

From out the ocean's phosphor-starry dome,
A ghostly light is dubitably shed
On altars of a goddess garlanded
With blossoms of some weird and hueless vine;
And, wingéd, fleet, through skies beneath the foam,
Like silent birds the sea-things dart and shine.

A Vintage from Atlantis

I thank you, friend, but I am no drinker of wine, not even if it be the rarest Canary or the oldest Amontillado. Wine is a mocker, strong drink is raging . . . and more than others, I have reason to know the truth that was writ by Solomon the Jewish king. Give ear, if ye will, and I shall tell you a story such as would halt the half-drained cup on the lips of the hardiest bibber.

We were seven-and-thirty buccaneers, who raked the Spanish Main under Barnaby Dwale, he that was called Red Barnaby for the spilling of blood that attended him everywhere. Our ship, the *Black Falcon*, could outfly and outstrike all other craft that flew the Jolly Roger. Full often, Captain Dwale was wont to seek a remote isle on the eastward verge of the West Indies, and lighten the vessel of its weight of ingots and doubloons.

The isle was far from the common course of maritime traffic, and was not known to maps or other mariners; so it suited our purpose well. It was a place of palms and sand and cliffs, with a small harbor sheltered by the curving outstretched arms of rugged reefs, on which the dark ocean climbed and gnashed its fangs of white foam without troubling the tranquil waters beyond. I know not how many times we had visited the isle; but the soil beneath many a coco tree was heavy with our hidden trove. There we had stored the loot of bullion-laden ships, the massy plate and jewels of cathedral towns.

Even as to all mortal things, an ending came at last to our visits. We had gathered a goodly cargo of loot, but might have stayed longer on the open main where the Spaniards passed, if a tempest had not impended. We were near the secret isle, as it chanced, when the skies began

74

to blacken; and wallowing heavily in the rising seas, we fled to our placid harbor, reaching it by night-fall. Before dawn the hurricane had blown by; and the sun came up in cloudless amber and blue. We proceeded with the landing and burying of our chests of coin and gems and ingots, which was a task of some length; and afterwards we refilled our water-casks at a cool sweet spring that ran from beneath the palmy hill not far inland.

It was now mid-afternoon. Captain Dwale was planning to weigh anchor shortly and follow the westering sun toward the Caribbees. There were nine of us, loading the last barrels into the boats, with Red Barnaby looking on and cursing us for being slower than mud-turtles; and we were bending knee-deep in the tepid, lazy water, when suddenly the Captain ceased to swear, and we saw that he was no longer watching us. On the contrary, he had turned his back and was stooping over a strange object that must have drifted in with the tide, after the storm: a huge and barnacle-laden thing that lay on the sand, half in and half out of the shoaling water. Somehow, none of us had perceived it heretofore.

Red Barnaby was not silent long.

"Come here, ye chancre-eaten coistrels," he called to us. We obeyed willingly enough, and gathered around the beached object, which our Captain was examining with much perplexity. We too were greatly be-wondered when we saw the thing more closely; and none of us could name it off-hand or with certainty.

The object had the form of a great jar, with a tapering neck and a deep, round, abdominous body. It was wholly encrusted with shells and corals that had gathered upon it as if through many ages in the ocean deeps, and was festooned with weeds and sea-flowers such as we had never before beheld; so that we could not determine the substance of which it was made.

At the order of Captain Dwale, we rolled it out of the water and beyond reach of the tide, into the shade of nearby palms; though it re-quired the efforts of four men to move the unwieldy thing, which was strangely ponderous. We found that it would stand easily on end, with its top reaching almost to the shoulders of a tall man. While we were handling the great jar, we heard a swishing noise from within, as if it were filled with some sort of liquor.

Our Captain, as it chanced, was a learned man.

"By the communion-cup of Satan!" he swore. "If this thing is not an antique wine-jar, then I am a Bedlamite. Such vessels—though mayhap they were not so huge—were employed by the Romans to store the goodly vintages of Falernus and Cecuba. Indeed, there is today a Spanish wine—that of Valdepenas—which is kept in earthen jars. But this, if I mistake not, is neither from Spain nor olden Rome. It is ancient enough, by its look, to have come from that long-sunken isle, the Atlantis whereof Plato speaks. Truly, there should be a rare vintage within, a wine that was mellowed in the youth of the world, before the founding of Rome and Athens; and which, perchance, has gathered fire and strength with the centuries. Ho! my rascal sea-bullies! We sail not from this harbor till the jar is broached. And if the liquor within be sound and potable, we shall make holiday this evening on the sands."

"Belike, 'tis a funeral urn, full of plaguey cinders and ashes," said the mate, Roger Aglone, who had a gloomy turn of thought.

Red Barnaby had drawn his cutlass and was busily prying away the crust of barnacles and quaint fantastic coral-growths from the top of the jar. Layer on layer of them he removed, and swore mightily at this increment of forgotten years. At last a great stopper of earthen-ware, sealed with a clear wax that had grown harder than amber, was revealed by his prying. The stopper was graven with queer letters of an unknown language, plainly to be seen; but the wax refused the cutlass-point. So, losing all patience, the Captain seized a mighty fragment of stone, which a lesser man could scarce have lifted, and broke therewith the neck of the jar.

Now even in those days, I, Stephen Magbane, the one Puritan amid that Christless crew, was no bibber of wine or spirituous liquors, but a staunch Rechabite on all occasions. Therefore I held back, feeling little concern other than that of reprobation, while the others pressed about the jar and sniffed greedily at the contents. But, almost immediately with its opening, my nostrils were assailed by an odor of heathen spices, heavy and strange, together with a powerful vinulence; and the very in-halation thereof caused me to feel a sort of giddiness, so that I thought it well to retreat still further. But the others were eager as midges around a fermenting-vat in autumn.

"'Sblood! 'Tis a royal vintage!" roared the Captain, after he had dipped a forefinger in the jar and sucked the purple drops that dripped from it. "Avast, ye slumdegullions! Stow the water-casks on board, and summon all hands ashore, leaving only a watch there to ward the vessel. We'll have a gala night before we sack any more Spaniards."

We obeyed his order; and there was much rejoicing amid the crew of the *Black Falcon* at the news of our find and the postponement of the voyage. Three men, grumbling sorely at their absence from the revels, were left on board; though, in that tranquil harbor, such vigilance was virtually needless. We others returned to the shore, bringing a supply of pannikins in which to serve the wine, and provisions for a feast. Then we gathered pieces of drift with which to build a great fire, and caught several huge tortoises along the sands, and unearthed their hidden eggs, so that we might have an abundance and variety of victuals.

In these preparations, I took part with no special ardor. Knowing my habit of abstention, and being of a somewhat malicious and torment-ing humor, Captain Dwale had expressly commanded my presence at the feast. However, I anticipated nothing more than a little ribaldry at my expense, as was customary at such times; and being partial to fresh tortoise-meat, I was not wholly unresigned to my lot as a witness of the Babylonian inebrieties of the others.

At nightfall, the feasting and drinking began; and the fire of drift-wood, with eerie witch-colors of blue and green and white amid the flame, leapt high in the dusk while the sunset died to a handful of red embers far on purpling seas.

It was a strange wine that the crew and Captain swilled from their pannikins. I saw that the stuff was thick and dark, as if it had been mingled with blood; and the air was filled with the reek of those pagan spices, hot and rich and unholy, that might have poured from a broken tomb of antique emperors. And stranger still was the intoxication of that wine; for those who drank it became still and thoughtful and sullen; and there was no singing of lewd songs, no playing of apish antics.

Red Barnaby had been drinking longer than the others, having begun to sample the vintage while the crew were making ready for their revel. To our wonderment, he ceased to swear at us after the first cupful, and no longer ordered us about or paid us any heed, but sat peering into the sunset with eyes that held the dazzlement of unknown dreams. And one by one, as they began to drink, the others were likewise affected, so that I marvelled much at the unwonted power of the wine. I had never before beheld an intoxication of such nature; for they spoke not nor ate, and moved only to re-fill their cups from the mighty jar.

The night had grown dark as indigo beyond the flickering fire; and there was no moon; and the firelight blinded the stars. But one by one, after an interval, the drinkers rose from their places and stood staring into the darkness toward the sea. Unquietly they stood, and strained forward, peering intently as men who behold some marvellous thing; and queerly they muttered to one another, with unintelligible words. I knew not why they stared and muttered thus, unless it were because of some madness that had come upon them from the wine; for naught was visible in the dark, and I heard nothing, save the low murmur of wavelets lapping on the sand.

Louder grew the muttering; and some raised their hands and pointed seaward, babbling wildly as if in delirium. Noting their demeanor, and doubtful as to what further turn their madness might take, I bethought me to withdraw along the shore. But when I began to move away, those who were nearest me appeared to waken from their dream, and restrained me with rough hands. Then, with drunken, gibbering words, of which I could make no sense, they held me helpless while one of their number forced me to drink from a pannikin filled with the purple wine.

I fought against them, doubly unwilling to quaff that nameless vintage, and much of it was spilled. The stuff was sweet as liquid honey to the taste, but burned like hell-fire in my throat. I turned giddy; and a sort of dark confusion possessed my senses by degrees; and I seemed to hear and see and feel as in the mounting fever of calenture.

The air about me seemed to brighten, with a redness of ghostly blood that was everywhere; a light that came not from the fire nor from the nocturnal heavens. I beheld the faces and forms of the drinkers, standing without shadow, as if mantled with a rosy phosphorescence. And beyond them, where they stared in troubled and restless wonder, the darkness was illumed with the strange light.

Mad and unholy was the vision that I saw: for the harbor waves no longer lapped on the sand, and the sea had wholly vanished. The *Black Falcon* was gone, and where the reefs had been, great marble walls ascended, flushed as if with the ruby of lost sunsets. Above them were haughty domes of heathen temples, and spires of pagan palaces; and beneath were mighty streets and causeys where people passed in a never-ending throng. I thought that I gazed upon some immemorial city, such as had flourished in Earth's prime; and I saw the trees of its terraced gardens, fairer than the palms of Eden. Listening, I heard the sound of dulcimers that were sweet as the moaning of women; and the cry of horns that told forgotten glorious things; and the wild sweet singing of people who passed to some hidden, sacred festival within the walls.

I saw that the light poured upward from the city, and was born of its streets and buildings. It blinded the heavens above; and the horizon beyond was lost in a shining mist. One building there was, a high fane above the rest, from which the light streamed in a ruddier flood; and from its open portals music came, sorcerous and beguiling as the far voices of bygone years. And the revellers passed gayly into its portals forever; but none came forth. The weird music seemed to call me and entice me; and I longed to tread the streets of the alien city; and a deep desire was upon me to mingle with its people and pass into the glowing fane.

Verily I knew why the drinkers had stared at the darkness and had muttered among themselves in wonder. I knew that they also longed to descend into the city. And I saw that a great causey, built of marble and gleaming with the red luster, ran downward from their very feet over meadows of unknown blossoms to the foremost buildings.

Then, as I watched and listened, the singing grew sweeter, the music stranger; and the rosy luster brightened, fair as the gleaming of lost suns recalled by necromancy from eternal night. Then, with no backward glance, no word or gesture of injunction to his men, Captain Dwale went slowly forward, treading the marble causey like a dreamer who walks in his dream. And after him, one by one, Roger Aglone and the crew followed in the same manner, going toward the city.

Haply I too should have followed, drawn by the witching music. For truly it seemed that I had trod the ways of that city in former time, and had known the things whereof the music told and the voices sang. Well did I remember why the people passed eternally into the fane, and why they came not forth; and there, it seemed, I should meet familiar and beloved faces, and take part in mysteries recalled from the foundered years.

All this, which the wine had remembered through its sleep in the ocean depths, was mine to behold and conceive for a moment. And well it was that I had drunk less of that evil and pagan vintage than the others, and was less besotted than they with its luring vision. For, even as Captain Dwale and his crew went toward the city, it appeared to me that the rosy glow began to fade a little. The walls took on a wavering thinness, and the domes grew insubstantial. The rose departed, the light was pale as a phosphor of the tomb; and the people went to and fro like phantoms, with a thin crying of ghostly horns and a ghostly singing. Dimly above the sunken causey the harbor waves returned; and Red Barnaby and his men walked down beneath them. Slowly the waters darkened above the fading spires and walls; and the midnight blackened upon the sea; and the city was lost even as the vanished bubbles of wine.

A terror came upon me, knowing the fate of those others. I fled swiftly, stumbling in darkness toward the palmy hill that crowned the isle. No vestige remained of the rosy light; and the sky was filled with returning stars. And looking oceanward as I climbed the hill, I saw a lantern that burned on the *Black Falcon* in the harbor, and discerned the embers of our fire that smouldered on the sands. Then, praying with a fearful fervor, I waited for dawn.

Orientales

CHINOISERIE

Ling Yang, the poet, sits all day in his willow-hidden hut by the riverside, and dreams of the Lady Moy. Spring and the swallows have returned from the timeless isles of myrrh and amaranth, further than the flight of sails in the unknown south; the silver buds of the willow are breaking into gold; and delicate jade-green reeds have begun to push their way among the brown and yellow rushes of yesteryear. But Ling Yang is heedless of the brightening azure, the light that lengthens; and he has no eye for the northward flight of the waterfowl, and the passing of the last clouds, that melt and vanish in the flames of an amber sunset. For him, there is no season save the moon of waning summer in which he first met the Lady Moy. But a sorrow deeper than the sorrow of autumn abides in his heart: for the heart of Moy is colder to him than the high mountain snows above a tropic valley; and all the songs he has made for her, the songs of the flute and the songs of the lute, have found no favour in her hearing.

Leagues away, in her pavilion of scarlet lacquer and ebony, the Lady Moy reclines on a couch piled with sapphire-coloured silks. All day, through the gathering gold of the willow-foliage, she watches the placid lake, on whose surface the pale green lily-pads have begun to widen. Beside her, in a turquoise-studded binding, there lie the verses of the poet Ling Yung, who lived six centuries ago, and who sang in all his songs the praise of the Lady Loy, who disdained him. Moy has no need to peruse them any longer, for they live in her memory even as upon the written page. And, sighing, she dreams ever of the great poet, Ling Yung, and of the melancholy romance that inspired his songs, and wonders enviously at the disdain that was shown toward him by the Lady Loy.

THE WILLOW LANDSCAPE

The picture was more than five hundred years old; and time had not changed its colors, unless to touch them with the mellow softness of ancient hours, with the gathering morbidezza of bygone things. It had been painted by a great artist of the Sung dynasty, on silk of the finest weave, and mounted on rollers of ebony tipped with silver. For twelve generations it had been one of the most cherished possessions of the forefathers of Shih Liang. And it was equally cherished by Shih Liang himself, who, like all his ancestors, was a scholar, a poet, and a lover of both art and nature. Often, in his dreamiest or most meditative moods, he would unroll the painting and gaze upon its idyllic loveliness with the feeling of one who retires to the seclusion and remoteness of a mountain-warded valley. It consoled him in a measure for the bustle and blare and intrigue of the imperial court, where he held an official post of no small honor; since he was not altogether native to such things and would have preferred, like the olden sages, the philosophic peace of a leaf-embowered hermitage.

The picture represented a pastoral scene of the most ideal and visionary beauty. In the background arose lofty mountains rendered vague by the slow withdrawal of morning mists; in the foreground there ran a little stream, descending in mimic turbulence to a tranquil lake, and crossed on its way by a rustic bridge of bamboo, more charming than if it were made of royal lacquer. Beyond the stream and around the lake were willows of vernal green more lovely and delicious than anything that was ever beheld except in vision or memory. Incomparable was their grace, ineffable their waving: they were like the willows of Shou Shan, the Taoist Paradise; and they trailed their foliage as leaning women trail their unbound hair. And partly hidden among them was a tiny hut; and a maiden dressed in peony pink and white was crossing the little bamboo bridge. But somehow the picture was more than a painting, was more than a veritable scene: it possessed the enchantment of far-off things for which the heart has longed in vain, of years and of places that are lost beyond recall. Surely the artist had mingled with its hues the diviner iris of dream or of retrospect, and the wine-sweet tears of a nostalgia long denied.

Shih Liang felt that he knew the landscape more intimately than any actual scene. Each time that he gazed upon it, his sensations were those of a returning wanderer. It became to him the cool and sequestered retreat in which he found a never-failing refuge from the weariness of his days. And though he was of an ascetic turn and had never married nor sought the company of women, the presence of the peony maiden on the bridge was by no means exceptionable: in fact, her tiny figure, with its more than mortal charm, was somehow an essential part of the composition and was no less important to its perfection than the stream, the willows, the lake, and the far-off mountains with their riven veils of mist. And she seemed to companion him in the visits and sojournings of reverie, when he would imagine himself repairing to the little hut or roaming beneath the delicate foliage.

In truth, Shih Liang had need of such refuge and of such companionship, illusory though they were. For, aside from his younger brother, Po Lung, a boy of sixteen, he was alone and without living relatives or comrades; and the fortunes of the family, declining through several generations, had left him the heritor of many debts and little cash or property, except a number of priceless art-treasures. His life was increasingly sad, and oppressed by ill-health and poverty; for much of the stipend from his secretarial post at the court was necessarily devoted to the canceling of inherited obligations; and the remainder was barely enough for his own sustenance and the education of his brother.

Shih Liang was approaching middle-age; and his honorable heart was rejoicing over the payment of the last family debt, when there came a fresh stroke of misfortune. Through no fault or remissness of his own, but the machinations of an envious fellow-scholar, Shih Liang was suddenly deprived of his position and found himself without means of support. No other position offered itself; for a certain amount of unmerited disgrace was attached to the imperial dismissal. In order to procure the necessities of life, and continue his brother's education, Shih Liang was now forced to sell one by one many of the irreplaceable heirlooms, the antique carvings of jade and ivory, the rare porcelains and paintings of the ancestral collection. This he did with extreme reluctance, with a sense of utter shame and profanation, such as could be felt only by a true lover of such things, and by one whose very soul was consecrated to the past and to the memory of his fathers.

The days and years went by, the collection dwindled piece by piece; and the time drew near when the studies of Po Lung would be completed, when he would be a scholar versed in all the classics and eligible for a position of both honor and profit. But, alas! the porcelains and lacquers, the jades and ivories had all been sold; and the paintings were likewise gone, all except the willow landscape so dearly cherished by Shih Liang.

A mortal and inassuageable sorrow, a dismay that was colder than the chill of death itself, entered the heart of Shih Liang when he realized the truth. It seemed to him that he could no longer live if he should sell the picture. But if he did not sell it, how could he complete the fraternal duty which he owed to Po Lung? There was but one possible course; and he sent word at once to the Mandarin Mung Li, a connoisseur who had purchased other pieces of the old collection, telling him that the willow picture was now for sale.

Mung Li had long coveted this picture. He came in person, his eyes gleaming in his fat face with the avidity of a collector who scents a bargain; and the transaction was soon concluded. The money was paid immediately; but Shih Liang begged leave to retain the picture for another day before delivering it to the mandarin. And knowing that Shih Liang was a man of honor, Mung Li assented readily to this request.

When the mandarin had gone, Shih Liang unrolled the landscape and hung it on the wall. His stipulation to Mung Li had been prompted by the irresistible feeling that he must have one more hour of communion with the beloved scene, must repair once more in reverie to its inviolate retreat. After that, he would be as one without a home or a sanctuary; for he knew that in all the world there was nothing that could take the place of the willow picture or afford a like asylum for his dreams.

The mellowing rays of earliest eventide were sifted upon the silk volumen where it hung on the bare wall; but for Shih Liang, the painting was steeped in a light of supernal enchantment, was touched by more than the muted splendor of the falling sun. And it seemed to him that never before had the foliage been so tender with immortal spring, or the mist about the mountain so glamorous with eternally dissolving opal, or the maiden upon the rustic bridge so lovely with unfading youth. And somehow, by an unaccountable sorcery of perspective, the painting itself was larger and deeper than of yore, and had mysteriously assumed even more of reality, or the illusion of an actual place.

With unshed tears in his heart, like an exile who bids farewell to his natal valley, Shih Liang enjoyed the sorrowful luxury of looking upon the willow picture for the last time. Even as on a thousand former occasions, his fancy strayed beneath the branches and beside the mere, it inhabited the tiny hut whose roof was so tantalizingly revealed and concealed, it peered at the mountain-tops from behind the trailing foliage, or paused upon the bridge to converse with the peony maiden.

And now there happened a strange and inexplicable thing. Though the sun had gone down while Shih Liang continued to gaze and dream, and a twilight had gathered in the room, the picture itself was no less plain and luminous than before, as if it were lit by another sun than that of contemporary time and space. And the landscape had grown even larger, till it seemed to Shih Liang that he was looking through an open door on the veritable scene itself.

Then, as bewilderment assailed him, he heard a whisper that was not an actual voice, but which seemed to emanate from the landscape and become audible as a thought in his inmost mind. And the whisper said:

"Because you have loved me so long and so dearly, and because your heart is native here but alien to all the world beside, it is now permitted that I should become for you the inviolable refuge of which you have dreamed, and a place wherein you can wander and abide forever."

So, with the surpassing joy of one whose fondest vision has been verified, the rapture of one who inherits the heaven of his reverie, Shih Liang passed from the twilight room into the morning picture. And the ground was soft with a flower-embroidered grass beneath his heel; and the leaves of the willows murmured in an April wind that blew from long ago; and he saw the door of the half-hidden hut as he had never seen it before except in fancy; and the peony maiden smiled and answered his greeting when he approached her; and her voice was like the speech of the willows and the blossoms.

The disappearance of Shih Liang was a matter of brief and passing concern to those who had known him. It was readily believed that his financial sorrows had driven him to suicide, probably by drowning in the great river that ran athwart the capital.

Po Lung, having received the money left by his brother from the sale of the last painting, was enabled to finish his education; and the willow landscape, which had been found hanging on the wall of Shih Liang's abode, was duly claimed by the Mandarin Mung Li, its purchaser.

Mung Li was delighted with his acquisition; but there was one detail which puzzled him considerably when he unrolled the volumen and examined it. He could remember only one figure, a maiden in pink and white, on the little bamboo bridge; and now there were two figures! Mung Li inspected the second figure with much curiosity, and was more than surprised when he noted that it had a singular resemblance to Shih

Liang. But it was very tiny, like that of the maiden; and his eyes were dim from peering at so many porcelains and lacquers and paintings; so he could not be entirely sure. At any rate, the picture was very old; and he must have been mistaken about the number of the figures. However, it was undeniably peculiar.

Mung Li might have thought the matter still stranger, if he had looked more often at the painting. He might have found that the peony maiden and the person who resembled Shih Liang were sometimes engaged in other diversions than that of merely passing the time of day on the bamboo bridge!

THE JUSTICE OF THE ELEPHANT

Nikhal Singh, Rajah of Anapur, was acquiring the obese complacency of middle-age; and his memories were blurred and befogged by a liberal use of Rajput opium. It was seldom that he recalled Ameera; though, as a general rule, an unfaithful woman is not the easiest thing in the world to forget. But Nikhal Singh had possessed so many wives and concubines; and one more or less was of no great importance, even though she had been eyed like the sloe and footed like the gazelle and had preferred an elephant-driver to a Rajah. And as Nikhal Singh grew older, and became wearier of women and fonder of opium, such matters were even less memorable or worthy of consideration.

However, the incident had angered him greatly at the time; and the doom he had devised for Ameera was the most atrocious one conceivable. Her story was long remembered and whispered in the royal zenana; though whether or not the example had served to deter others from similar derelictions is a moot problem.

Ameera was a dancing-girl, and therefore of low birth; and her rise in the Rajah's favor had not been regarded with unqualified approval by his legitimate wives. Under the circumstances, it was highly unwise for Ameera to carry on a love affair with the comely young elephant-driver, Rama Das; for there were many jealous eyes to note the amour, and jealous tongues to bear tattle thereof to Nikhal Singh. Ameera had been watched; and a man was seen leaving her apartments in the early morning hours. The man was not positively identified as Rama Das; but the presence of anyone save the Rajah in those sacrosanct purlieus was enough to damn the unfortunate girl.

The punishment inflicted by Nikhal Singh was no less swift than dreadful. The girl was condemned to a death usually reserved for the lowest criminals; and her suspected lover, Rama Das, by a refinement of Rajput cruelty, was chosen as her executioner. She was made to kneel and place her head on a block of stone in the palace courtyard; and thereupon the great elephant ridden by Rama Das, at a signal from the driver, lifted one of his enormous hoofs and brought it down on the head of the dancing-girl, crushing her to an instant pulp. During the awful ordeal, no sign of recognition or emotion was betrayed either by Rama Das or Ameera; and the gloating Rajah was perhaps disappointed in this respect. A day or two afterward the young elephant-driver disappeared from Anapur; and no one knew whether he had been secretly made away with by Nikhal Singh or had vanished of his own accord.

Ten years had now passed; and the affair was overlaid, even in the minds of the Rajah's eldest wives, by a score of later scandals and by the petty happenings of the palace. And when the position of mahout to Ragna, the huge elephant that bore the Rajah himself on all formal occasions, became vacant through death, no one would have connected the half-forgotten Rama Das with the new applicant, Ram Chandar, who vowed his fitness to take charge of Ragna and offered credentials testifying to years of faithful and efficient service under the Maharajah of a state in Bundelcund. And least of all would it have occurred to Nikhal Singh himself that the grave, taciturn, heavy-bearded Ram Chandar and the blithe, beardless Rama Das were the same person.

Somehow, though there were many other applicants, Ram Chandar insinuated himself into the desired position. And since he was a competent driver, who had obviously mastered the language of elephants down to its last and most subtle inflection, no one, not even his fellow mahouts, found reason to disapprove or criticize his appointment. Ragna, also, appeared to like his new driver; and that ideal confidence and understanding which often exists between the mahout and the animal soon sprang up between these two. Ragna, after the fashion of a well-tutored elephant, was wise and erudite in regard to all that it was proper for him to know;

but he learned some new manners and graces beneath the instruction of Ram Chandar; and was even taught in private one or two tricks that are not usually part of the curriculum of a state elephant. Of these latter, no one dreamt; and Ram Chandar preserved an inscrutable silence. And Nikhal Singh was wholly unaware of the strange, sardonic, sinister regard with which he was watched by the new mahout from Bundelcund.

Nikhal Singh had grown fonder than ever of his opium, and cared less and less for other pleasures or distractions. But now, in his fortieth year, for political reasons, it was agreed upon by his ministers that he must take another wife. The Ranee had recently died without leaving him a male heir; and the young daughter of the neighboring Rajah of Ayalmere was selected as her successor. All the necessary arrangements and elaborate protocols were made; and the day was set for the marriage. Nikhal Singh was secretly bored by the prospect but was publicly resigned to his royal duty. The feelings of the bride, perhaps, were even more problematical.

The day of the marriage dawned in torrid saffron. A great procession coming from Ayalmere was to bring the bride into Anapur; and Nikhal Singh, with another stately procession, was to meet her outside the gates of his capital.

It was a gorgeous ceremony. Nikhal Singh, seated in a golden and jewel-crusted howdah on the superb elephant Ragna, passed slowly through the streets of Anapur followed by the court dignitaries on other elephants and a small army of horsemen, all splendidly caparisoned. There was much firing of jezails and cannon by the soldiers and banging of musical instruments among the populace. The mahout, Ram Chandar, grave and impassive as usual, sat on Ragna's neck. Nikhal Singh, who had fortified himself with a large lump of his favorite drug, was equally impassive on his broidered cushions in the howdah.

The procession emerged through the open gate of Anapur, and beheld at some distance, in a cloud of summer dust, the approach of the bride and her attendants, forming an array no less magnificent and sumptuous than that which was headed by Nikhal Singh.

As the two processions neared each other, an event occurred which was not a pre-arranged part of the ceremonial. At a secret signal from Ram Chandar, perceived and understood only by the elephant himself, Ragna suddenly halted, reached into the great howdah with his trunk, seized Nikhal Singh in a tenacious embrace, and haling the Rajah forth in a most undignified and ignominious manner, deposited him on his knees in the road and forced him to bow his head in the dust before the bride's approaching litter. Then, almost before his action was comprehended by the stupefied throng, Ragna raised one of his front hoofs and calmly proceeded to crush the Rajah's head into a flat, formless jelly. Then, trumpeting wildly, menacing all who stood in his way, and apparently defying the frantic signals and commands of his driver, Ragna plunged through the crowd and quickly vanished in the nearby jungle, still carrying Ram Chandar and the empty howdah.

Amid the confusion and consternation that prevailed, it was assumed that Ragna had been seized by the vicious madness to which elephants are sometimes liable. When a semblance of order had been restored, he was followed by a troop of the Rajah's horsemen, armed with jezails. They found him an hour later, browsing peacefully in a jungle-glade without his driver, and dispatched him with a volley, not trusting his appearance of renewed mildness.

The assumption that Ragna had gone *musth* was universal; and no one thought of Rama Das and the death of Ameera, ten years before. However, the disappearance of the new mahout, Ram Chandar, was no less a mystery than the earlier vanishment of Rama Das, if anyone had remembered to draw the parallel. The body of Ram Chandar was never found, and no one knew to a certainty whether he had been killed by Ragna in the thick jungle or had run away from Anapur through fear of being held responsible for Ragna's behavior. But mad elephants are prone to wreak their malignity on all accessible victims, even their own mahouts; so it was considered very unlikely that Ram Chandar could have escaped.

THE GHOUL

During the reign of the Caliph Vathek, a young man of good repute and family, named Noureddin Hassan, was haled before the Cadi Ahmed ben Becar at Bussorah. Now Noureddin was a comely youth, of open mind and gentle mien; and great was the astonishment of the Cadi and of all others present when they heard the charges that were preferred against him. He was accused of having slain seven people, one by one, on seven successive nights, and of having left the corpses in a cemetery near Bussorah, where they were found lying afterwards with their bodies and members devoured in a fearsome manner, as if by jackals. Of the people he was said to have slain, three were women, two were traveling merchants, one was a mendicant, and one a grave-digger.

Ahmed ben Becar was filled with the learning and wisdom of honorable years, and withal was possessed of much perspicacity. But he was deeply perplexed by the strangeness and atrocity of these crimes and by the mild demeanor and well-bred aspect of Noureddin Hassan, which he could in no wise reconcile with them. He heard in silence the testimony of witnesses who had seen Noureddin bearing on his shoulders the body of a woman at yester-eve in the cemetery; and others who on several occasions had observed him coming from the neighborhood at unseemly hours when only thieves and murderers would be abroad. Then, have considered all these, he questioned the youth closely.

"Noureddin Hassan," he said, "thou has been charged with crimes of exceeding foulness, which thy bearing and thy lineaments belie. Is there haply an explanation of these things, by which thou canst wholly clear thyself, or in some measure mitigate the heinousness of thy deeds, if so it be that thou art guilty? I adjure thee to tell me the truth in this matter."

Now Noureddin Hassan arose before the Cadi; and the heaviness of extreme shame and sorrow was visible on his countenance.

"Alas, O Cadi," he replied, "for the charges that have been brought against me are indeed true. It was I and none other, who slew these people; nor can I offer an extenuation of my act."

The Cadi was sorely grieved and astonished when he heard this answer.

"I must perforce believe thee," he said sternly. "But thou hast confessed a thing which will make thy name henceforward an abomination in the ears and mouths of men. I command thee to tell me why these crimes were committed, and what offense these persons had given thee, or what injury they had done thee; or if perchance thou slewest them for gain, like a common robber."

"There was neither offense given nor injury wrought by any of them against me," replied Noureddin. "And I did not kill them for their money or belongings or apparel, since I had no need of such things, and, aside from that, have always been an honest man."

"Then," cried Ahmed ben Becar, greatly puzzled, "what was thy reason, if it was none of these?"

Now the face of Noureddin Hassan grew heavier still with sorrow; and he bowed his head in a shamefaced manner that bespoke the utterness of profound remorse. And standing thus before the Cadi, he told this story:

The reversals of fortune, O Cadi, are swift and grievous, and beyond the foreknowing or advertence of man. Alas! for less than a fortnight agone I was the happiest and most guiltless of mortals, with no thought of wrong-doing toward anyone. I was wedded to Amina, the daughter of the jewel-merchant Aboul Cogia; and I loved her deeply and was much beloved by her in turn; and moreover we were at this time anticipating the birth of our first child. I had inherited from my father a rich estate and many slaves; the cares of life were light upon my shoulders; and I had, it would seem, every reason to count myself among those whom Allah has blest with an earthly foretaste of Heaven.

Judge, then, the excessive nature of my grief when Amina died in the same hour when she was to have been delivered. From that time, in the dire extremity of my lamentation, I was as one bereft of light and knowledge; I was deaf to all those who sought to condole with me, and blind to their friendly offices.

After the burial of Amina my sorrow became a veritable madness, and I wandered by night to her grave in the cemetery near Bussorah and flung myself prostrate before the newly lettered tombstone, on the earth that had been digged that very day. My senses deserted me, and I knew not how long I remained on the damp clay beneath the cypresses, while the horn of a decrescent moon arose in the heavens.

Then, in my stupor of abandonment, I heard a terrible voice that bade me rise from the ground on which I was lying. And lifting my head a little, I saw a hideous demon of gigantic frame and stature, with eyes of scarlet fire beneath brows that were coarse as tangled rootlets, and fangs that overhung a cavernous mouth, and earth-black nails that were longer and sharper than those of the hyena. And the demon said to me:

"I am a ghoul, and it is my office to devour the bodies of the dead. I have now come to claim the corpse that was interred today beneath the soil on which thou art lying in a fashion so unmannerly. Begone, for I have fasted since yester-night, and I am much anhungered."

Now, at the sight of this demon, and the sound of his dreadful voice, and the still more dreadful meaning of his words, I was like to have swooned with terror on the cold clay. But I recovered myself in a manner, and besought him, saying:

"Spare this grave, I implore thee; for she who lies buried therein is dearer to me than any living mortal; and I would not that her fair body should be the provender of an unclean demon such as thou."

At this the ghoul was angered, and I thought that he would have done me some bodily violence. But again I besought him, swearing by Allah and Mohammed with many solemn oaths that I would grant him anything procurable and would do for him any favor that lay in the power of man if he would leave undespoiled the new-made grave of Amina. And the ghoul was somewhat mollified, and he said:

"If thou wilt indeed perform for me a certain service, I shall do as thou askest." And I replied:

"There is no service, whatsoever its nature, that I will not do for thee in this connection, and I pray thee to name thy desire."

Then the ghoul said: "It is this, that thou shalt bring me each night, for eight successive nights, the body of one whom thou hast slain with thine own hand. Do this, and I shall neither devour nor dig the body that lies interred hereunder."

Now was I seized by utter horror and despair, since I had bound myself in all honor to grant the ghoul his hideous requirement. And I begged him to change the terms of the stipulation, saying to him:

"Is it needful to thee, O eater of corpses, that the bodies should be those of people whom I myself have slain?"

And the ghoul said: "Yea, for all others would be the natural provender of myself or of my kin in any event. I adjure thee by the promise thou hast given to meet me here tomorrow night, when darkness has wholly fallen or as soon thereafter as thou are able, bringing the first of the eight bodies."

So saying, he strode off among the cypresses, and began to dig in another newly made grave at a little distance from that of Amina.

I left the graveyard in even direr anguish than when I had come, thinking of that which I must do in fulfillment of my sworn promise, to preserve the body of Amina from the demon. I know not how I survived the ensuing day, torn as I was between sorrow for the dead and my horror of the coming night with its repugnant duty.

When darkness had descended, I went forth by stealth to a lonely road near the cemetery; and waiting there amid the low-grown branches of the trees, I slew the first passer with a sword and carried his body to the spot appointed by the ghoul. And each night thereafter, for six more

nights, I returned to the same vicinity and repeated this deed, slaying
always the very first who came, whether man or woman, or merchant or
beggar or grave-digger. And the ghoul awaited me on each occasion, and
would begin to devour his provender in my presence, with small thanks
and scant ceremony. Seven persons did I slay in all, till only one was
wanting to complete the agreed number; and the person I slew
yesternight was a woman, even as the witnesses have testified. All this I
did with utmost repugnance and regret, and sustained only by the remembrance of my plighted word and the fate which would befall the
corpse of Amina if I should break the bond.

This, O Cadi, is all my story. Alas! for these lamentable crimes have
availed me not, and I have failed in wholly keeping my bargain with the
demon, who will doubtless this very night consume the body of Amina
in lieu of the one corpse that is still lacking. I resign myself to thy judgment, O Ahmed ben Becar, and I beseech thee for no other mercy than
that of death, wherewith to terminate my double grief and my twofold
remorse.

When Noureddin Hassan had ended his narrative, the amazement
of all who had heard him was verily multiplied, since no man could remember hearing a stranger tale. And the Cadi pondered for a long time
and then gave judgment, saying:

"I must needs marvel at thy story, but the crimes thou has committed are none the less heinous, and Iblis himself would stand aghast before them. However, some allowance must be made for the fact that
thou hadst given thy word to the ghoul and wast bound as it were in
honor to fulfill his demand, no matter how horrible its nature. And allowance must likewise be made for thy connubial grief and the piety
which caused thee to forfend thy wife's body from the demon. Yet I
cannot adjudge thee guiltless, though I know not the punishment which
is merited in a case so utterly without example or parallel. Therefore, I
set thee free, with this injunction, that thou shalt make atonement for

thy crimes in the fashion that seemeth best to thee, and shalt render justice to thyself and to others in such degree as thou art able."

"I thank thee for this mercy," replied Noureddin Hassan; and he then withdrew from the court amid the wonderment of all who were present. There was much debate when he had gone, and many were prone to question the wisdom of the Cadi's decision. Some there were who maintained that Noureddin should have been sentenced to death without delay for his abominable actions, though others argued for the sanctity of his oath to the ghoul, and would have exculpated him altogether or in part. And tales were told and instances were cited regarding the habits of ghouls and the strange plight of men who had surprised such demons in their nocturnal delvings. And again the discussion returned to Noureddin, and the judgment of the Cadi was once more upheld or assailed with divers arguments. But amid all this, Ahmed ben Becar was silent, saying only:

"Wait, for this man will render justice to himself and to all others concerned, as far as the rendering thereof is possible."

So indeed it happened, for on the morning of the next day another body was found in the cemetery near Bussorah, lying half-devoured on the grave of Noureddin Hassan's wife, Amina. And the body was that of Noureddin, self-slain, who in this manner had not only fulfilled the injunction of the Cadi but had also kept his bargain with the ghoul by providing the required number of corpses.

THE THIRD EPISODE OF VATHEK

THE STORY OF THE PRINCESS ZULKAÏS AND THE PRINCE KALILAH

By *William Beckford and Clark Ashton Smith*

My father, lord, can scarcely be unknown to you, inasmuch as the Caliph Motassem had entrusted to his care the fertile province of Masre. Nor would he have been unworthy of his exalted position if, in view of man's ignorance and weakness, an inordinate desire to control the future were not to be accounted an unpardonable error.

The Emir Abou Taher Achmed, however—for such was my father's name—was very far from recognizing this truth. Only too often did he seek to forestall Providence, and to direct the course of events in spite of the decrees of Heaven. Ah! terrible indeed are those decrees! Sooner or later their accomplishment is sure! Vainly do we seek to oppose them!

During a long course of years, everything flourished under my father's rule, and among the Emirs who have successfully administered that beautiful province, Abou Taher Achmed will not be forgotten. Following his speculative bent, he enlisted the services of certain experienced Nubians, born near the sources of the Nile, who had studied the stream throughout its course, and knew all its characteristics, and the properties of its waters; and, with their aid, he carried out his impious design of regulating the overflow of the river. Thus he covered the country with a too luxuriant vegetation, which left it afterwards exhausted. The people, always slaves to outward appearances, applauded his enterprises, worked indefatigably at the unnumbered canals with which he intersected the land, and, blinded by his successes, passed lightly over any unfortunate circumstances accompanying them. If, out of every ten ships that he sent forth to traffic, according to his fancy, a single ship came back richly freighted after a successful voyage, the wreck of the other nine was counted for nothing. Moreover, as, owing to his care and vigilance, commerce prospered under his rule, he was himself deceived as to his losses, and took to himself all the glory of his gains.

Soon Abou Taher Achmed came to be convinced that if he could recover the arts and sciences of the ancient Egyptians, his power would be unbounded. He believed that, in the remote ages of antiquity, men had appropriated to their own use some rays of the divine wisdom, and thus been enabled to work marvels, and he did not despair of bringing back once again that glorious time. For this purpose he caused search to be made, among the ruins abounding in the country, for the mysterious tablets which, according to the report of the Sages who swarmed in his court, would show how the arts and sciences in question were to be acquired, and also indicate the means of discovering hidden treasures, and subduing the Intelligences by which those treasures are guarded. Never before his time had any Mussulman puzzled his brains over hieroglyphics. Now, however, search was made, on his behalf, for hieroglyphics of every kind, in all quarters, in the remotest provinces, the strange symbols being faithfully copied on linen cloths. I have seen these cloths a thousand times, stretched out on the roofs of our palace. Nor could bees be more busy and assiduous about a bed of flowers than were the Sages about these painted sheets. But, as each Sage entertained a different opinion as to the meaning of what was there depicted, arguments were frequent, and quarrels ensued. Not only did the Sages spend the hours of daylight in prosecuting their researches, but the moon often shed its beams upon them while so occupied. They did not dare to light torches upon the terraced roofs, for fear of alarming the faithful Mussulmans, who were beginning to blame my father's veneration for an idolatrous antiquity, and regarded all these painted symbols, these figures, with a pious horror.

Meanwhile, the Emir, who would never have thought of neglecting any real matter of business, however unimportant, for the pursuit of his strange studies, was by no means so particular with regard to his religious observances, and often forgot to perform the ablutions ordained by the law. The women of his harem did not fail to perceive this, but were afraid to speak, as, for one reason and another, their influence had considerably waned. But, on a certain day, Shaban, the chief of the eunuchs, who was very old and very pious, presented himself before his master, holding a ewer and golden basin, and said: "The waters of the Nile have been given for the cleansing of all our impurities; their source is in the clouds of heaven, not in the temples of idols; take and use those waters, for you stand in need of them."

The Emir, duly impressed by the action and speech of Shaban, yielded to his just remonstrances, and, instead of unpacking a large bale of painted cloths, which had just arrived from a far distance, ordered the eunuch to serve the day's collation in the Hall of the Golden Trellises, and to assemble there all his slaves, and all his birds—of which he kept a large number in aviaries of sandalwood.

Immediately the palace rang to the sound of instruments of music, and groups of slaves appeared, all dressed in their most attractive garments, and each leading in leash a peacock whiter than snow. One only of these slaves—whose slender and graceful form was a delight to the eye—had no bird in leash, and kept her veil down.

"Why this eclipse?" said the Emir to Shaban.

"Lord," answered he with joyful mien, "I am better than all your astrologers, for it is I who have discovered this lovely star. But do not imagine that she is yet within your reach; her father, the holy and venerable Iman Abzenderoud, will never consent to make you happy in the possession of her charms unless you perform your ablutions with greater regularity, and give the go-by to Sages and their hieroglyphics."

My father, without replying to Shaban, ran to snatch away the veil that hid the countenance of Ghulendi Begum—for such was the name of Abzenderoud's daughter—and he did so with such violence that he nearly crushed two peacocks, and overturned several baskets of flowers. To this sudden heat succeeded a kind of ecstatic stupor. At last he cried: "How beautiful she is, how divine! Go, fetch at once the Iman of Soussouf—let the nuptial chamber be got ready, and all necessary preparations for our marriage be complete within one hour!"

"But, Lord," said Shaban, in consternation, "you forget that Ghulendi Begum cannot marry you without the consent of her father, who makes it a condition that you should abandon..."

"What nonsense are you talking?" interrupted the Emir. "Do you think I am fool enough not to prefer this young virgin, fresh as the dew of the morning, to cartloads of hieroglyphics, mouldy and of the color of dead ashes? As to Abzenderoud, go and fetch him if you like—but quickly, for I shall certainly not wait a moment longer than I please."

"Hasten, Shaban," said Ghulendi Begum modestly, "hasten; you see that I am not here in case to make any very effectual resistance."

"It's my fault," mumbled the eunuch as he departed, "but I shall do what I can to rectify my error."

Accordingly he flew to find Abzenderoud. But that faithful servant of Allah had gone from home very early in the morning, and sought the open fields in order to pursue his pious investigations into the growth of plants and the life of insects. A death-like pallor overspread his countenance when he saw Shaban swooping down upon him like a raven of ill omen, and heard him tell, in broken accents, how the Emir had promised nothing, and how he himself might well arrive too late to exact the pious conditions he had so deeply pondered. Nevertheless, the Iman did not lose courage, and reached my father's palace in a very few moments; but unfortunately he was by this time so out of breath that he sank down on a sofa, and remained for over an hour panting and breathless.

While all the eunuchs were doing their best to revive the holy man, Shaban had quickly gone up to the apartment assigned to Abou Taher Achmed's pleasures; but his zeal suffered some diminution when he saw the door guarded by two black eunuchs, who, brandishing their sabres, informed him that if he ventured to take one more step forward, his head would roll at his own feet. Therefore he had nothing better to do than to return to Abzenderoud, whose gaspings he regarded with wild and troubled eyes, lamenting the while over his own imprudence in bringing Ghulendi Begum within the Emir's power.

Notwithstanding the care my father was taking for the entertainment of the new sultana, he had heard something of the dispute between the black eunuchs and Shaban, and had a fair notion of what was going on. As soon, therefore, as he judged it convenient, he came to find Abzenderoud in the Hall of the Golden Trellises, and presenting Ghulendi Begum to the holy man assured him that, while awaiting his arrival, he, the Emir, had made her his wife.

At these words, the Iman uttered a lamentable and piercing cry, which relieved the pressure on his chest; and, rolling his eyes in a fearful manner, he said to the new sultana: "Wretched woman, dost thou not know that rash and ill-considered acts lead ever to a miserable end? Thy father would have made thy lot secure; but thou hast not awaited the result of his efforts, or rather it is Heaven itself that mocks all human previsions. I ask nothing more of the Emir; let him deal with thee, and with his hieroglyphics, as he deems best! I foresee untold evils in the future; but I shall not be there to witness them. Rejoice for a while, intoxicated with thy pleasures. As for me, I call to my aid the Angel of Death, and hope, within three days, to rest in peace in the bosom of our great Prophet!"

After saying these words, he rose to his feet, tottering. His daughter strove in vain to hold him back. He tore his robe from her trembling hands. She fell fainting to the ground, and while the distracted Emir was striving to bring her back again to her senses, the obstinate Abzenderoud went muttering from the room.

At first it was thought that the holy man would not keep his vow quite literally, and would suffer himself to be comforted; but such was not the case. On reaching his own house, he began by stopping his ears by cotton wool, so as not to hear the clamor and adjuration of his friends; and then, having seated himself on the mats in his cell, with his legs crossed, and his head in his hands, he remained in that posture speechless, and taking no food; and finally, at the end of three days, expired according to his prayer. He was buried magnificently, and during the obsequies Shaban did not fail to manifest his grief by slashing his flesh without mercy, and soaking the earth with little rivulets of his blood; after which, having caused balm to be applied to his wounds, he returned to the duties of his office.

Meanwhile, the Emir had no small difficulty in assuaging the despair of Ghulendi Begum, and often cursed the hieroglyphics which had been its first efficient cause. At last his attentions touched the heart of the sultana. She regained her ordinary equability of spirits, and became pregnant; and everything returned to its accustomed order.

The Emir, his mind always dwelling on the magnificence of the ancient Pharaohs, built, after their manner, a palace with twelve pavilions—proposing, at an early date, to install in each pavilion a son. Unfortunately, his wives brought forth nothing but daughters. At each new birth he grumbled, gnashed his teeth, accused Mahomet of being the cause of his mishaps, and would have been altogether unbearable, if Ghulendi Begum had not found means to moderate his evil temper. She induced him to come every night into her apartment, where, by a thousand ingenious devices, she succeeded in introducing fresh air, while, in other parts of the palace, the atmosphere was stifling.

During her pregnancy my father never left the dais on which she reclined. This dais was set on a large and long gallery overlooking the Nile, and so disposed as to seem about on a level with the stream,—so close, too, that anyone reclining upon it could throw into the water the seeds of any pomegranate he might be eating. The best dancers, the most excellent magicians, were always about the palace. Every night pantomimes were performed to the light of a thousand golden lamps—

lamps placed upon the floor so as to bring out the fineness and grace of the performers' feet. The dancers themselves cost my father immense sums in golden-fringed slippers and sandals a-glitter with jewelry; and, indeed, when they were all in motion together the effect was dazzling.

But notwithstanding this accumulation of splendors, the sultana passed very unhappy days on her dais. With the same indifference that a poor wretch tormented by sleeplessness watches the scintillations of the stars, so did she see pass before her eyes all this whirl of performers in their brilliancy and charm. Anon she would think of the wrath, that seemed almost prophetic, of her venerable father; anon she would deplore his strange and untimely end. A thousand times she would interrupt the choir of singers, crying: "Fate has decreed my ruin! Heaven will not vouchsafe me a son, and my husband will banish me from his sight!" The torment of her mind intensified the pain and discomfort attendant on her condition. My father, thereupon, was so greatly perturbed that, for the first time in his life, he made appeal to Heaven, and ordered prayers to be offered up in every mosque. Nor did he omit the giving of alms, for he caused it to be publicly announced that all beggars were to assemble in the largest court of the palace, and would there be served with rice, each according to his individual appetite. There followed such a crush every morning at the palace gates that the incomers were nearly suffocated. Mendicants swarmed in from all parts, by land, and by river. Whole villages would come down the stream on rafts. And the appetites of all were enormous; for the buildings which my father had erected, his costly pursuit of hieroglyphics, and his maintenance of the Sages, had caused some scarcity throughout the land.

Among those who came from a very far distance was a man of an extreme age, and great singularity, by name Abou Gabdolle Guehaman, the hermit of the Great Sandy Desert. He was eight feet high, so ill-proportioned, and of a leanness so extreme, that he looked like a skeleton, and was hideous to behold. Nevertheless, this lugubrious and forbidden piece of human mechanism enshrined the most benevolent and religious spirit in the universe. With a voice of thunder he proclaimed the will of the Prophet, and said openly it was a pity that a prince who distributed rice to the poor, and in such great profusion, should be a lover of hieroglyphics. People crowded around him—the Imans, the Mullahs, the Muezins, did nothing but sing his praises. His feet, though ingrained with the sand of his native desert, were freely kissed. Nay, the very grains of the sand from his feet were gathered up, and treasured in caskets of amber.

One day he proclaimed the truth and the horror of the sciences of evil, in a voice so loud and resonant that the great standards set before the palace trembled. The terrible sound penetrated into the interior of the harem. The women and the eunuchs fainted away in the Hall of the Golden Trellises; the dancers stood with one foot arrested in the air; the mummers had not the courage to pursue their antics; the musicians suffered their instruments to fall to the ground; and Ghulendi Begum thought to die of fright as she lay on her dais.

Abou Taher Achmed stood astounded. His conscience smote him for his idolatrous proclivities, and during a few remorseful moments he thought that the Avenging Angel had come to turn him into stone— and not himself only but the people committed to his charge.

After standing for some time, upright, with arms uplifted, in the Gallery of the Daises, he called Shaban to him, and said: "The sun has not lost its brightness, the Nile flows peacefully in its bed, what means then this supernatural cry that has just resounded through my palace?"

"Lord," answered the pious eunuch, "this voice is the voice of Truth, and is spoken to you through the mouth of the venerable Abou Gabdolle Guehaman, the Hermit of the Sandy Desert, the most faithful, the most zealous, of the servants of the Prophet, who has, in nine days, journeyed three hundred leagues to make proof of your hospitality, and to impart to you the knowledge with which he is inspired. Do not neglect the teachings of a man who in wisdom, in piety, and in stature, surpasses the most enlightened, the most devout, and the most gigantic of the inhabitants of earth. All your people are in an ecstasy. Trade is at a standstill. The inhabitants of the city hasten to hear him, neglecting their wonted assemblies in the public gardens. The story-tellers are without hearers at the margins of the public fountains. Jussouf himself was not wiser than he, and had no greater knowledge of the future."

At these last words, the Emir was suddenly smitten with the desire of consulting Abou Gabdolle with regard to his family affairs, and particularly with regard to the great projects he entertained for the future advantage of his sons, who were not yet born. He deemed himself happy in being thus able to consult a living prophet; for, so far, it was only in the form of mummies that he had been brought into relation with these inspired personages. He resolved, therefore, to summon into his presence, nay, into his very harem, the extraordinary being now in question. Would not the Pharaohs have so dealt with the necromancers of their time, and was not he determined, in all circumstances, to follow the Pharaohs' example? He therefore graciously directed Shaban to go and fetch the holy man.

Shaban, transported with joy, hastened to communicate this invitation to the hermit, who, however, did not appear to be as much charmed by the summons as were the people at large. These latter filled the air with their acclamations, while Abou Gabdolle stood still, with his hands clasped, and his eyes uplifted to heaven, in a prophetic trance. From time to time he uttered the deepest sighs, and, after, remaining long rapt in holy contemplation, shouted out, in his voice of thunder: "Allah's will be done! I am but his creature. Eunuch, I am ready to follow thee. But let the doors of the palace be broken down. It is not meet for the servants of the Most High to bend their heads."

The people needed no second command. They all set hands to the work with a will, and in an instant the gateway, a piece of the most admirable workmanship, was utterly ruined.

At the sound of the breaking in of the doors, piercing cries arose within the harem, Abou Taher Achmed began to repent of his curiosity.

Nevertheless, he ordered, though somewhat reluctantly, that the passages into the harem should be laid open to the holy giant, for he feared lest the enthusiastic adherents of the prophet should penetrate into the apartments occupied by the women, and containing the princely treasures. These fears were, however, vain, for the holy man had sent back his devout admirers. I have been assured that on their all kneeling to receive his blessing he said to them, in tones of the deepest solemnity: "Retire, remain peacefully in your dwellings, and be assured that, whatever happens, Abou Gabdolle Guehaman is prepared for every emergency." Then, turning towards the palace, he cried: "O domes of dazzling brilliancy, receive me, and may nothing ensue to tarnish your splendor."

Meanwhile, everything had been made ready within the harem. Screens had been duly ordered, the door-curtains had been drawn, and ample draperies hung before the daises in the long gallery that ran round the interior of the building—thus concealing from view the sultanas, and the princesses, their daughters.

Such elaborate preparations had caused a general ferment; and curiosity was at its height, when the hermit, trampling under foot the ruined fragments of the doorways, entered majestically into the Hall of the Golden Trellises. The magnificence of the palace did not even win from him a passing glance, his eyes remained fixed, mournfully, on the pavement at his feet. At last he penetrated into the great gallery of the women. These latter, who were not at all accustomed to the sight of creatures so lean, gaunt, and gigantic, uttered piercing cries, and loudly asked for essences and cordials to enable them to bear up against the apparition of such a phantasm.

The hermit paid not the smallest heed to the surrounding tumult. He was gravely pursuing his way, when the Emir came forward, and, taking him by the skirt of his garment, led him, with much ceremony, to the dais of the gallery which looked out upon the Nile. Basins of comfits and orthodox liquors were at once served; but though Abou Gabdolle

Guehaman seemed to be dying of hunger, he refused to partake of these refreshments, saying that for ninety years he had drunk nothing but the dew of heaven, and eaten only the locusts of the desert. The Emir, who regarded this diet as conformable to what might properly be expected of a prophet, did not press him further, but at once entered into the question he had at heart, saying how much it grieved him to be without a male heir, notwithstanding all the prayers offered up to that effect, and the flattering hopes which the Imans had given him. "But now," he continued, "I am assured that this happiness will at last be mine. The Sages, the mediciners, predict it, and my own observations confirm their prognostications. It is not, therefore, with the purpose of consulting you with regard to the future that I have caused you to be summoned. It is for the purpose of obtaining your advice upon the education I should give to the son whose birth I am expecting—or rather, to the two sons, for, without doubt, in recognition of my alms, Heaven will accord to the Sultana Ghulendi Begum a double measure of fertility, seeing that she is twice as large as women usually are on such occasions."

Without answering a word, the hermit mournfully shook his head three times.

My father, greatly astonished, asked if his anticipated good fortune was in any wise displeasing to the holy man.

"Ah! too blind prince," replied the hermit, uttering a cavernous sigh that seemed to issue from the grave itself, "why importune Heaven with rash prayers? Respect its decrees! It knows what is best for all men better than they do themselves. Woe be to you, and woe be to the son whom you will doubtless compel to follow in the perverse ways of your own beliefs, instead of submitting himself humbly to the guidance of Providence. If the great of this world could only foresee all the misfortunes they bring upon themselves, they would tremble in the midst of their splendor. Pharaoh recognized this truth, but too late. He pursued the children of Moussa in despite of the divine decrees, and died the death of the wicked. What can alms avail when the heart is in rebellion? Instead of asking the Prophet for an heir, to be led by you into the paths of destruction, those who have your welfare at heart should implore him to cause Ghulendi Begum to die—yes, to die before she brings into the world presumptuous creatures, whom your conduct will precipitate into the abyss! Once again I call upon you to submit. If Allah's angel threatens to cut short the days of the sultana, do not make appeal to your magicians to ward off the fatal blow: let it fall, let her die! Tremble not with wrath, Emir; harden not your heart! Once again call to mind the fate of Pharaoh and the waters that swallowed him up!"

"Call them to mind yourself!" cried my father, foaming with rage, and springing from the dais to run to the aid of the sultana, who, having heard all, had fainted away behind the curtains. "Remember that the Nile flows beneath these windows, and that thou hast well deserved that thy odious carcass should be hurled into its waters!"

"I fear not," cried the gigantic hermit in turn; "the prophet of Allah fears naught but himself," and he rose on the tips of his toes and touched with his hands the supports of the dome of the apartment.

"Ha! ha! thou fearest nothing," cried all the women and eunuchs, issuing like tigers out of their den. "Accursed assassin, thou hast just brought our beloved mistress to death's door, and yet fearest nothing! Go, and become food for the monsters of the river!" Screaming out these words, they threw themselves, all at once, on Abou Gabdolle Guehaman, bore him down, strangled him without pity, and cast his body through a dark grating into the Nile, which there lost itself obscurely among the piers of iron.

The Emir, astonished by an act at once so sudden and so atrocious, remained with his eyes fixed on the waters; but the body did not again come to the surface; and Shaban, who now appeared upon the scene, bewildered him with his cries. At last he turned to look upon the perpetrators of the crime; but they had scattered in every direction, and hidden behind the curtains of the gallery, each avoiding the other, they were all overwhelmed by the thought of what they had done.

Ghulendi, who had only come to herself in time to witness this scene of horror, was now in mortal anguish. Her convulsions, her agonizing cries, drew the Emir to her side. He bedewed her hand with tears. She opened her eyes wildly, and cried: "O Allah! Allah! put an end to a wretched creature who has already lived only too long, since she has been the cause of so terrible an outrage, and suffer not that she should bring into the world—"

"Stop, stop," interrupted the Emir, holding her hands which she was about to turn against herself, "thou shalt not die, and my children shall yet live to give the lie to that demented skeleton, worthy only of contempt. Let my Sages be summoned instantly. Let them use all their art to keep thy soul from flitting hence and to save from harm the fruit of thy body."

The Sages were convened accordingly. They demanded that one of the courts in the palace should be placed entirely at their disposal, and there began their operations, kindling a fire whose light penetrated into the gallery. The sultana rose from her couch, notwithstanding all the efforts made to restrain her, and ran to the balcony overlooking the Nile. The view from thence was lonely and drear. Not a single boat showed upon the surface of the stream. In the distance were discernible reaches of sand which the wind, from time to time, sent whirling into the air. The rays of the setting sun dyed the waters blood-red. Scarcely had the deepening twilight stretched over the horizon, when a sudden and furious wind broke the open lattice-work of the gallery. The sultana, beside herself, her heart beating, tried to plunge back into the interior of the apartment, but an irresistible power held her where she was, and forced her, against her will, to contemplate the mournful scene before her eyes. A great silence now reigned. Darkness had insensibly covered the earth. Then suddenly a streak of blue light furrowed the clouds in the direction of the pyramids. The princess could distinguish their enormous mass against the horizon as clearly as if it had been noonday. The spectacle thus suddenly revealed, chilled her with fear. Several times did she try to call her slaves, but her voice refused its office. She endeavored to clap her hands, but in vain.

While she remained thus—as if in the grip of some horrible dream—a lamentable voice broke the stillness, and uttered these words: "My latest breath has just been exhaled into the waters of the river; vainly have thy servants striven to stifle the voice of truth; it rises now from the abysses of death. O wretched mother! see whence issues that fatal light, and tremble!"

Ghulendi Begum endured to hear no more. She fell back senseless. Her women, who had been anxious about her, hurried up at this moment, and uttered the most piercing cries. The Sages approached, and placed into the hands of my father, who was in terrible perturbation, the powerful elixir they had prepared. Scarcely had a few drops fallen on the sultana's breast, when her soul, which had seemed about to follow the orders of Asrael, the Angel of Death, came back, as if in nature's despite, to reanimate her body. Her eyes reopened to see, still illumining the pyramids, the fatal furrow of blue light which had not yet faded from the sky. She raised her arms, and, pointing out to the Emir with her finger that dread portent, was seized with the pains of childbirth, and, in the paroxysm of an unspeakable anguish, brought into the world a son and a daughter: the two wretched beings you see before you here.

The Emir's joy in the possession of a male child was greatly dashed when he saw my mother die before his eyes. Notwithstanding his excessive grief, however, he did not lose his head, and at once handed us over to the care of his Sages. The nurses, who had been engaged in great number, wished to oppose this arrangement; but the ancient men, all uttering incantations simultaneously, compelled them to silence. The cabalistic lavers in which we were to be immersed stood all ready prepared; the mixture of herbs exhaled a vapor that filled the whole palace. Shaban, whose very stomach was turned by the odor of these unspeakable drugs, had all the trouble in the world to restrain himself from summoning the Imans, and doctors of the law, in order to oppose the impious rites now in contemplation. Would to Heaven he had had the courage to do so! Ah, how terrible has been the influence upon us of the pernicious immersions to which we were then subjected! In short, Lord, we were plunged, both successively and together, into a hell-broth which was intended to impart to us a strength and intelligence more than human, but has only instilled into our veins the ardent elixir of a too exquisite sensibility, and the poison of an insatiable desire.

It was to the sound of brazen wands beating against the metal sides of the lavers, it was in the midst of thick fumes issuing from heaps of burning herbs, that invocations were addressed to the Jinns, and specially to those who preside over the pyramids, in order that we might be endowed with miraculous gifts. After this we were delivered over to the nurses, who scarcely could hold us in their arms, such was our liveliness and vivacity. The good women shed tears when they saw how our young blood boiled within us, and strove in vain to cool its effervescence, and to calm us by cleansing our bodies from the reeking mess with which they were still covered; but, alas! the harm was already done! Nay, if even, as sometimes happened in after days, we wished to fall into the ordinary ways of childhood, my father, who was determined at all hazards to possess children of an extraordinary nature, would brisk us up with heating drugs and the milk of negresses.

We thus became unendurably headstrong and mettlesome. At the age of seven, we could not bear contradiction. At the slightest restraint, we uttered cries of rage, and bit those who had us in charge till the blood flowed. Shaban came in for a large share of our attentions in this kind; sighing over us, however, in silence, for the Emir only regarded our spitefulness as giving evidence of a genius equal to that of Saurid and Charobé. Ah! how little did anyone suspect the real cause of our forwardness! Those who look long into the light are soonest afflicted with blindness. My father had not yet remarked that we were never arrogant and overbearing towards one another; that each was ready to yield to the other's wishes; that Kalilah, my brother, was never at peace save in my arms; and that, as for me, my only happiness lay in overwhelming him with caresses.

Up to this time, we had in all things been educated together: the same book was always placed before the eyes of both, each turned over the leaves alternately. Though my brother was subjected to a course of study rigorous, and above his years, I insisted on sharing it with him. Abou Taher Achmed, who cared for nothing save the aggrandisement of his son, gave directions that in this I should be humored, because he saw that his son would only fully exert himself when at my side.

We were taught not only the history of the most remote ages of antiquity, but also the geography of distant lands. The Sages never ceased to indoctrinate us with the abstruse and ideal moral code, which, as they pretended, lurked hidden in the hieroglyphics. They filled our ears with a magnificent verbiage about wisdom and foreknowledge, and the treasure houses of the Pharaohs, whom sometimes they compared to ants, and sometimes to elephants. They inspired us with a most ardent curiosity as to those mountains of hewn stone beneath which the Egyptian kings lie sepulchred. They compelled us to learn by heart the long catalogue of architects and masons who had labored at the building of them. They made us calculate the quality of provisions that would be required by the workmen employed, and how many threads went to every ell of silk with which Sultan Saurid had covered his pyramid. Together with all this rubbish, these most wearisome old dotards bewildered our brains with a pitiless grammar of the language spoken of old by the priests in their subterranean labyrinths.

The childish games in which we were allowed to indulge, during our playtime, had no charms for us unless we played them together. The princesses, our sisters, wearied us to death. Vainly did they embroider for my brother the most splendid vests. Kalilah disdained their gifts, and would only consent to bind his lovely hair with the muslin that had floated over the breast of his beloved Zulkaïs. Sometimes they invited us to visit them in the twelve pavilions which my father, no longer hoping to have that number of sons, had abandoned to their use—erecting another, and of greater magnificence, for my brother, and for myself. This latter building, crowned by five domes, and situated in a thick grove, was, every night, the scene of the most splendid revels in the harem. My father would come thither, escorted by his most beautiful slaves—each holding in her hand a candlestick with a white taper. How many times has the light of these tapers, appearing through the trees, caused our hearts to beat in sad anticipation? Everything that broke in upon our solitude was in the highest degree distasteful. To hide among the leafage, and listen to its murmur, seemed to us sweeter far than attending to the sound of the lute and the song of the musicians. But these soft luxurious reveries of ours were highly offensive to my father, he would force us back into the cupolaed saloons, and force us to take part in the common amusements.

Every year the Emir treated us with greater sternness. He did not dare to separate us altogether for fear of the effect upon his son, but tried rather to win him from our languorous dalliance by throwing him more and more into the company of young men of his own age. The game of reeds, so famous among the Arabs, was introduced into the courts of the palace. Kalilah gave himself up to the sport with immense energy; but this was only so as to bring the games to a speedier end, and then fly back to my side. Once reunited we would read together, read of the loves of Jussouf and Zelica, or some other poem that spoke of love—or else, taking advantage of our moments of liberty, we would roam through the labyrinth of corridors looking out upon the Nile, always with our arms intertwined, always with eyes looking into each other's eyes. It was almost impossible to track us in the mazy passages of the palace; and the anxiety we inspired did but add to our happiness.

One evening when we were thus tenderly alone together, and running side by side in childish glee, my father appeared before us and shuddered. "Why," said he to Kalilah, "why are you here and not in the great courtyard, shooting with the bow, or else with the horse-trainers training the horses which are to bear you into battle? Must the sun, as it rises and sets, see you only bloom and fade like a weak narcissus flower? Vainly do the Sages try to move you by the most eloquent discourses, and unveil before your eyes the learned mysteries of an older time; vainly do they tell you of warlike and magnanimous deeds. You are now nearly thirteen, and never have you evinced the smallest ambition to distinguish yourself among your fellow-men. It is not in the lurking haunts of effeminacy that great characters are formed; it is not by reading love poems that men are made fit to govern nations! Princes must act; they must show themselves to the world. Awake! Cease to abuse my patience which has too long allowed you to waste your hours by the side of Zulkaïs. Let her, tender creature that she is, continue to play among her flowers, but do you cease to haunt her company from dawn till eve. I see well enough that it is she who is perverting you."

Having spoken these words, which he emphasized by angry and threatening gestures, Abou Taher Achmed took my brother by the arm, and left me in a very abyss of bitterness. An icy numbness overcame me. Though the sun still shed its fullest rays upon the water, I felt as if it had disappeared below the horizon. Stretched at length upon the ground, I did nothing but kiss the sprays of orange flower that Kalilah had gathered. My sight fell upon the drawings he had traced, and my tears fell in greater abundance. "Alas!" said I, "All is over. Our blissful moments will return no more. Why accuse me of perverting Kalilah? What harm can I do him? How can our happiness offend my father? If it was a crime to be happy, the Sages would surely have given us warning."

My nurse Shamelah found me in this condition of languor and dejection. To dissipate my grief she immediately led me to the grove where the young girls of the harem were playing at hide-and-seek amid the golden aviaries of which the place was full. I derived some little solace from the song of the birds, and the murmur of the rillets of clear water that trickled round the roots of the trees, but when the hour came at which Kalilah was wont to appear these sounds did but add to my sufferings.

Shamelah noticed the heavings of my breast; she drew me aside, placed her hand upon my heart, and observed me attentively. I blushed, I turned pale, and that very visibly. "I see very well," said she, "that it is your brother's absence that so upsets you. This is the fruit of the strange education to which you have been subjected. The holy reading of the Koran, the due observance of the Prophet's laws, confidence in the known mercies of Allah, these are as milk to cool the fever heat of human passion. You know not the soft delight of lifting up your soul to Heaven, and submitting without a murmur to its decrees. The Emir, alas! would forestall the future; while, on the contrary, the future should be passively awaited. Dry your tears; perchance Kalilah is not unhappy though distant from your side."

"Ah!" I cried, interrupting her with a sinister look, "if I were not fully convinced that he is unhappy, I should myself be far more miserable."

Shamelah trembled at hearing me speak thus. She cried: "Would to Heaven that they had listened to my advice, and the advice of Shaban, and instead of handing you over to the capricious teaching of the Sages, had left you, like true believers, at peace in the arms of a blissful and quiet ignorance. The ardor of your feelings alarms me in the very highest degree. Nay, it excites my indignation. Be more calm; abandon your soul to the innocent pleasures that surround you, and do so without troubling yourself whether Kalilah shares in those pleasures or not. His sex is made for toil and manly hardship. How should you be able to follow him in the chase, to handle a bow, and to dart reeds in the Arab game? He must look for companions manly and worthy of himself, and cease to fritter away his best days here at your side amid bowers and aviaries."

This sermon, far from producing its desired effect, made me altogether beside myself. I trembled with rage, and, rising to my feet like one bereft of reason, I rent my veil into ten thousand pieces, and, tearing my breast, cried with a loud voice that my nurse had mishandled me.

The games ceased. Everyone crowded about me; and though the princesses did not love me overmuch, because I was Kalilah's favorite sister, yet my tears, and the blood that flowed from my self-inflicted wounds, excited their indignation against Shamelah. Unfortunately for the poor woman, she had just awarded a severe punishment to two young slaves who had been guilty of stealing pomegranates; and these two little vipers, in order to be revenged, bore testimony against her, and confirmed all I said. They ran, and retailed their lies to my father, who, not having Shaban at his side, and being, moreover, in a good temper because my brother had just thrown a javelin into a crocodile's eye, ordered Shamelah to be tied to a tree, and whipped without mercy.

Her cries pierced my heart. She cried without ceasing: "O you, whom I have carried in my arms, whom I have fed from my breast, how can you cause me to suffer thus? Justify me! Declare the truth! It is only because I tried to save you from the black abyss, into which your wild and unruly desires cannot fail to precipitate you in the end, that you are thus causing this body of mine to be torn to shreds."

I was about to ask that she should be released and spared further punishment, when some demon put into my mind the thought that it was she who, conjointly with Shaban, had inspired my father with the desire of making a hero of Kalilah. Whereupon I armed myself against every feeling of humanity, and cried out that they should go on whipping her till she confessed her crime. Darkness at last put an end to this horrible scene. The victim was unloosed. Her friends, and she had many, endeavored to close her wounds. They asked me, on their knees, to give them a sovereign balm which I possessed, a balm which the Sages had prepared. I refused. Shamelah was placed before my eyes on a litter, and, of set purpose, kept for a moment in front of the place where I stood. That breast, on which I had so often slept, streamed with blood. At this spectacle, at the memory of the tender care she had taken of my infancy, my heart at last was moved—I burst into tears; I kissed the hand she feebly extended to the monster she had nourished in her bosom; I ran to fetch the balm; I applied it myself, begging her, at the same time, to forgive me, and declaring openly that she was innocent, and I alone guilty.

This confession caused a shudder to pass among all who surrounded us. They recoiled from me with horror. Shamelah, though half dead, perceived this, and stifled her groans with the skirt of her garment so as not to add to my despair and the baleful consequences of what I had done. But her efforts were vain. All fled, casting upon me looks that were evil indeed.

The litter was removed, and I found myself alone. The night was very dark. Plaintive sounds seemed to issue from the cypresses that cast their shadows over the place. Seized with terror, I lost myself amid the black foliage, a prey to the most harrowing remorse. Delirium laid its hand upon me. The earth seemed to yawn before my feet, and I to fall headlong into an abyss which had no bottom. My spirit was in this distraught condition when, through the thick underwood, I saw shine the torches of my father's attendants. I noticed that the cortége stopped suddenly. Someone issued from the crowd. A lively presentiment made my heart beat. The footsteps came nearer; and, by the light of a faint and doleful glimmer, such as prevails in the place where we now are, I saw Kalilah appear before me.

"Dear Zulkaïs," cried he, intermingling words and kisses, "I have passed an age without seeing you, but I have spent it in carrying out my father's wishes. I have fought with one of the most formidable monsters of the river. But what would I not do when, for recompense, I am offered the bliss of spending a whole evening with you alone? Come! Let us enjoy the time to the full. Let us bury ourselves among these trees. Let us, from our retreat, listen, disdainful, to the tumultuous sound of music and dances. I will cause sherbet and cakes to be served on the moss that borders the little porphyry fountain. There I shall enjoy your sweet looks, and charming converse, till the first dawn of the new day.

Then, alas! I must plunge once more into the world's vortex, dart accursed reeds, and undergo the interrogatories of Sages."

Kalilah said all this with such volubility that I was unable to put in a word. He drew me after him, scarce resisting. We made our way through the leafage to the fountain. The memory of what Shamelah had said concerning my excessive tenderness for my brother, had, in my own despite, produced a strong impression upon me. I was about to withdraw my hand from his, when, by the light of the little lamps that had been lit on the margin of the fountain, I saw his charming face reflected in the waters, I saw his large eyes dewy with love, I felt his looks pierce to the very bottom of my heart. All my projects of reform, all my agony of remorse, made way for a ferment of very different feelings. I dropped on the ground by Kalilah's side, and, leaning his head upon my breast, gave a free course to my tears. Kalilah, when he saw me thus crying passionately, eagerly asked me why I wept. I told him all that had passed between myself and Shamelah, without omitting a single particular. His heart was at first much moved by the picture I drew of her sufferings; but, a moment after, he cried: "Let the officious slave perish! Must the heart's soft yearnings ever meet with opposition! How should we not love one another, Zulkaïs? Nature caused us to be born together. Has not nature, too, implanted in us the same tastes, and a kindred ardor? Have not my father and his Sages made us partakers in the same magic baths? Who could blame a sympathy all has conspired to create? No, Zulkaïs, Shaban and our superstitious nurse may say what they please. There is no crime in our loving one another. The crime would rather be if we allowed ourselves, like cowards, to be separated. Let us swear—not by the Prophet, of whom we have little knowledge, but by the elements that sustain man's existence—let us swear that, rather than consent to live the one without the other, we will take into our veins the soft distillation of the flowers of the stream, which the Sages have so often vaunted in our hearing. That essence will lull us painlessly to sleep in each other's arms, and so bear our souls imperceptibly into the peace of another existence."

These words quieted me. I resumed my ordinary gaiety, and we played and sported together. "I shall be very valiant tomorrow," Kalilah would say, "so as to purchase such moments as these, for it is only by the promise of such a prize that my father can induce me to submit to his fantastic injunctions."

"Ha, ha!" cried Abou Taher Achmed, issuing from behind some bushes, where he had been listening. "Is that your resolve! We will see if you keep to it! You are already fully paid this evening for the little you have done during the day. Hence! And as to you, Zulkaïs, go and weep over the terrible outrage you have committed against Shamelah."

In the greatest consternation we threw ourselves at his feet; but, turning his back upon us, he ordered the eunuchs to conduct us to our separate apartments.

It was no scruple with regard to the kind and quality of our love that exercised the Emir. His sole end was to see his son become a great warrior, and a potent prince, and with regard to the character of the means by which that end was to be obtained, he cared not one tittle. As for me, he regarded me only as an instrument that might have its uses; nor would he have felt any scruples concerning the danger of inflaming our passion by the alternation of obstacles and concessions. On the other hand, he foresaw that indolence and pleasure, too constantly indulged in, must necessarily interfere with his designs. He deemed it necessary, therefore, to adopt with us a harsher and more decided line of conduct than he had hitherto done; and in an unhappy moment he carried that resolution into effect. Alas! without his precautions, his projects, his accursed foresight, we should have remained in innocence, and never been brought to the horror of this place of torment!

The Emir, having retired to his apartments, caused Shaban to be summoned, and imparted to him his fixed resolve to separate us during a certain time. The prudent eunuch prostrated himself immediately, with his face to the ground, and then, rising to his feet, said: "Let my lord forgive his slave if he ventures to be of a different opinion. Do not loose upon this nascent flame the winds of opposition and absence, lest the final conflagration should be such as you are unable to master. You know the Prince's impetuous disposition; his sister has today given proofs, only too signal, of hers. Suffer them to remain together without contradiction; leave them to their childish propensities. They will soon grow tired of one another; and Kalilah, disgusted with the monotony of the harem, will beg you on his knees to remove him from its precincts."

"Have you done talking your nonsense?" interrupted the Emir impatiently. "Ah, how little do you know the genius of Kalilah! I have carefully studied him, I have seen that the operations of my Sages have not been void of their effect. He is incapable of pursuing any object with indifference. If I leave him with Zulkaïs, he will be utterly drowned in effeminacy. If I remove her from him, and make their reunion the price of the great things I require at his hands, there is nothing of which he will not prove himself capable. Let the doctors of our law dote as they please! What can their idle drivel matter so long as he becomes what I desire him to be? Know besides, O eunuch, that when he has once tasted the delights of ambition, the idea of Zulkaïs will evaporate in his mind as a light morning mist absorbed into the rays of the noonday sun—the sun of glory. Therefore enter tomorrow morning into the chamber of Zulkaïs, forestall her awakening, wrap her up in these robes, and convey her, with her slaves and all that may be necessary to make her life pleasant, to the borders of the Nile, where a boat will be ready to receive you. Follow the course of the stream for twenty-nine days. On the thirtieth you will disembark at the Isle of Ostriches. Lodge the princess in the palace which I have had built for the use of the Sages who roam those deserts—deserts replete with ruins and with wisdom. One of these Sages you will find there, called the Palm-tree-climber, because he pursues his course of contemplation upon the tops of the palm-trees. This ancient man knows an infinite number of stories, and it will be his care to divert Zulkaïs, for I know very well that, next to Kalilah, stories are the chief object of her delight."

Shaban knew his master too well to venture upon any further opposition. He went, therefore, to give the necessary orders, but sighed heavily as he went. He had not the slightest desire to undertake a journey to
the Isle of Ostriches, and had formed a very unfavorable opinion of the
Palm-tree-climber. He was himself a faithful Mussulman, and held the
Sages and all their works in abomination.

Everything was made ready all too soon. The agitation of the previous day had greatly fatigued me, so that I slept very heavily. I was taken
from my bed so quietly, and carried with such skill, that I never woke
till I was at a distance of four leagues from Cairo. Then the noise of the
water gurgling round the boat began to alarm me. It filled my ears
strangely, and I half fancied I had drunk of the beverage spoken of by
Kalilah, and been borne beyond the confines of our planet. I lay thus,
bewildered with strange imaginings, and did not dare to open my eyes,
but stretched out my arms to feel for Kalilah. I thought he was by my
side. Judge of the feelings of hateful surprise to which I was doomed,
when, instead of touching his delicate limbs, I seized hold of the horny
hand of the eunuch who was steering the boat, and was even older, and
more grotesquely ugly, than Shaban himself.

I sat up and uttered piercing cries. I opened my eyes, and saw before
me a waste stretch of sky, and of water bounded by bluish banks. The
sun was shining in its fullness. The azure heavens caused all nature to
rejoice. A thousand river birds played around amid the water-lilies,
which the boat shore through at every moment, their large yellow flowers shining like gold, and exhaling a sweet perfume. But all these objects
of delight were lost upon me, and, instead of rejoicing my heart, filled
me with a somber melancholy.

Looking about me, I saw my slaves in a state of desolation, and Shaban who, with an air at once of discontent and authority, was making
them keep silence. The name of Kalilah came at every moment to the
tip of my tongue. At last I spoke it aloud, with tears in my eyes, and
asked where he was, and what they intended to do with me. Shaban,

instead of replying, ordered his eunuchs to redouble their exertions, and to strike up an Egyptian song, and sing in time to the cadence of their oars. Their accursed chorus rang out so potently that it brought an even worse bewilderment in my brain. We shot through the water like an arrow. It was in vain that I begged the rowers to stop, or at least to tell me where I was going. The barbarous wretches were deaf to my entreaties. The more insistent I was, the louder did they roar out their detestable song so as to drown my cries. Shaban, with his cracked voice, made more noise than the rest.

Nothing can express the torments I endured, and the horror I felt at finding myself so far from Kalilah, and on the waters of the fearful Nile. My terrors increased with nightfall. I saw, with an inexpressible anguish, the sun go losing itself in the waters—its light, in a thousand rays, trembling upon their surface. I brought to mind the quiet moments which, at that same hour, I had passed with Kalilah, and, hiding my head in my veil, I gave myself up to despair.

Soon a soft rustling became audible. Our boat was shearing its way through banks of reeds. A great silence succeeded to the song of the rowers, for Shaban had landed. He came back in a few moments, and carried me to a tent, erected a few paces from the river's bank. I found there lights, mattresses stretched on the ground, a table covered with various kinds of food, and an immense copy of the Koran, unfolded. I hated the holy book. The Sages, our instructors, had often turned it into ridicule, and I had never read it with Kalilah. So I threw it contemptuously to the ground. Shaban took upon himself to scold me; but I flew at him, and endeavored to reduce him to silence. In this I proved successful, and the same treatment retained its efficacy during the whole course of the long expedition.

Our subsequent experiences were similar to those of the first day. Endlessly did we pass banks of water-lilies, and flocks of birds, and an infinite number of small boats that came and went with merchandise.

At last we began to leave behind us the plain country. Like all who are unhappy and thus led to look forward, I kept my eyes continually fixed on the horizon ahead of us, and one evening I saw, rising there, great masses of much greater height, and of a form infinitely more varied, than the pyramids. These masses proved to be mountains. Their aspect inspired me with fear. The terrible thought occurred to me that my father was sending me to the woeful land of the Negro king, so that I might be offered up as a sacrifice to the idols, who, as the Sages pretended, were greedy of princesses. Shaban perceived my increasing distress, and at last took pity upon me. He revealed our ultimate destination, adding that though my father wished to separate me from Kalilah, it was not forever, and that, in the meanwhile, I should make the acquaintance of a marvellous personage, called the Palm-tree-climber, who was the best story-teller in the universe.

This information quieted me to some extent. The hope, however distant, of seeing Kalilah again, poured balm into my soul, and I was not sorry to hear that I should have stories to my liking. Moreover, the idea of a realm of solitude, such as the Ostrich Isle, flattered my romantic spirit. If I must be separated from him whom I cherished more than life itself, I preferred to undergo my fate rather in some savage spot than amid the glitter and chatter of a harem. Far from all such impertinent frivolities, I purposed to abandon my whole soul to the sweet memories of the past, and give a free course to the languorous reveries in which I could see again the loved image of my Kalilah.

Fully occupied with these projects, it was with heedless eyes that I saw our boat approaching nearer and nearer to the land of mountains. The rocks encroached more and more upon the border of the stream, and seemed soon about to deprive us of all sight of the sky. I saw trees of immeasurable height whose intertwisted roots hung down in the water. I heard the noise of cataracts, and saw the boiling eddies flash in foam and fill the air with a mist thin as silver gauze. Through this veil I perceived, at last, a green island of no great size, on which the ostriches were gravely promenading. Still further forward I discerned a domed edifice standing against a hill all covered with nests. This palace was utterly strange of aspect, and had, in truth, been built by a noted cabalist. The walls were of yellow marble, and shone like polished metal, and every object reflected in them assumed gigantic proportions. I trembled when I saw what fantastic figures the ostriches presented as seen in that strange mirror; their necks seemed to go losing themselves in the clouds, and their eyes shone like enormous balls of iron heated red in a furnace.

My terrors were observed by Shaban, who made me understand the magnifying qualities of the palace walls, and assured me that even if the birds were really as monstrous as they appeared, I might trust, in all security, to their good manners, since the Palm-tree-climber had been laboring for over a hundred years to reduce their disposition to an exemplary mildness. Scarcely had he furnished me with this information, when I landed at a spot where the grass was green and fresh. A thousand unknown flowers, a thousand shells of fantastic shape, a thousand oddly fashioned snails, adorned the shore. The ardor of the sun was tempered by the perpetual dew distilled from the falling waters, whose monotonous sound inclined to slumber.

Feeling drowsy, I ordered a penthouse to be affixed to one of the palm-trees of which the place was full; for the Palm-tree-climber, who always bore at his girdle the keys of the palace, was at that hour pursuing his meditations at the other end of the island.

While a soft drowsiness took possession of my senses, Shaban ran to present my father's letters to the man of wisdom. In order to do this, he was compelled to attach the missives to the end of a long pole, as the Climber was at the top of a palm-tree fifty cubits high, and refused to come down without knowing why he was summoned. So soon as he had perused the leaves of the roll, he carried them respectfully to his forehead, and slipped down like a meteor; and indeed he had somewhat the appearance of a meteor, for his eyes were of flame, and his nose was a beautiful blood-red.

Shaban, amazed by the rapidity of the old man's descent, uninjured, from the tree, was somewhat outraged when asked to take him on his back; but the Climber declared that he never so far condescended as to walk. The eunuch, who loved neither Sages nor their caprices, and regarded both as the plagues of the Emir's family, hesitated for a moment; but, bearing in mind the positive order he had received, he conquered his aversion, and took the Palm-tree-climber on his shoulders, saying: "Alas, the good hermit Abou Gabdolle Guehaman would not have behaved after this manner, and would, moreover, have been much more worthy of my assistance."

The Climber heard these words in high dudgeon, for he had aforetime had pious squabbles with the hermit of the Sandy Desert; so he administered a mighty kick on to the small of Shaban's back, and thrust a fiery nose into the middle of his countenance. Shaban, on this, stumbled, but pursued his way without uttering a syllable.

I was still asleep. Shaban came up to my couch, and, throwing his burden at my feet, said, and his voice had a certain ring in it that woke me without difficulty: "Here is the Climber! Much good may he do you!"

At the sight of such an object, I was quite unable, notwithstanding all my sorrows, to help bursting out into a fit of uncontrollable laughter. The old man did not change countenance, notwithstanding; he jingled his keys with an air of importance, and said to Shaban, in grave tones: "Take me again upon your back; let us go to the palace, and I will open its doors, which have never, hitherto, admitted any member of the female sex save my great egg-layer, the queen of the ostriches."

I followed. It was late. The great birds were coming down from the hills, and surrounded us in flocks, pecking at the grass and at the trees. The noise they made with their beaks was such that I seemed to be listening to the feet of an army on the march. At last I found myself before the shining walls of the palace. Though I knew the trick of them, my own distorted figure terrified me, as did also the figure of the Climber on the shoulders of Shaban.

We entered into a vaulted apartment, lined with black marble starred with golden stars, which inspired a certain feeling of awe—a feeling to which, however, the old man's grotesque and amusing grimaces afforded some relief. The air was stifling and nearly made me sick. The Climber, perceiving this, caused a great fire to be lit, and threw into it a small aromatic ball which he drew from his bosom. Immediately a vapor, rather pleasant to the smell, but very penetrating, diffused itself throughout the room. The eunuch fled, sneezing. As for me, I drew near to the fire, and sadly stirring the ashes, began to form in them the cipher of Kalilah.

The Climber did not interfere. He praised the education I had received, and approved greatly of our immersions, just after birth, by the Sages, adding maliciously that nothing so sharpened the wits as a passion somewhat out of the common. "I see clearly," he continued, "that you are absorbed in reflections of an interesting nature; and I am well pleased that it should be so. I myself had five sisters; we made very light of Mahomet's teachings, and loved each other with some fervor. I still, after the lapse of a hundred years, bear this in my memory with pleasure, for we scarcely ever forget early impressions. Thus my constancy has greatly commended me to the Jinns whose favorite I am. If you are able, like myself, to persevere in your present sentiments, they will probably do something for you. In the meanwhile, place your confidence in me. I shall not prove surly or unsympathetic as a guardian and keeper. Don't get it into your head that I am dependent on the caprice of your father, who has a limited outlook, and prefers ambition to pleasure. I am happier amid my palms, and my ostriches, and in the enjoyments of the delights of meditation, than he in his divan, and in all his grandeur. I don't mean to say that you yourself cannot add to the pleasures of my life. The more gracious you are to me, the more shall I show civility to you, and make you the partaker in things of beauty. If you seem to be happy in this place of solitude, you will acquire a great reputation for wisdom, and I know, by my own experience, that under the cloak of a great reputation it is possible to hide whole treasures of folly. Your father in his letters has told me all your story. While people think that you are giving heed to my instructions, you can talk to me about your Kalilah as much as you like, and without offending me in anyway. On the contrary, nothing affords me greater pleasure than to observe the movements of a heart abandoning itself to its youthful inclinations, and I shall be glad to see the bright colors of a first love mantling on young cheeks."

While listening to this strange discourse, I kept my eyes on the ground; but the bird of hope fluttered in my bosom. At last I looked at the Sage, and his great red nose, that shone like a luminous point in that room of black marble, seemed to me less disagreeable. The smile accompanying my glance was of such significance that the Climber easily perceived I had swallowed his bait. This pleased him so mightily that he forgot his learned indolence, and ran to prepare a repast of which I stood greatly in need.

Scarcely had he departed, when Shaban came in, holding in his hand a letter, sealed with my father's seal, which he had just opened. "Here," said he, "are the instructions I was only to read when I reached this place; and I have read them only too clearly. Alas! how wretched it is to be the slave of a prince whose head has been turned by much learning! Unhappy princess! I am compelled, much against my will, to abandon you here. I must re-embark with all who have followed me hither, and only leave in your service the lame Mouzaka, who is deaf and dumb. The wretched Climber will be your only helper. Heaven alone knows what you will gain from his companionship. The Emir regards him as a prodigy of learning and wisdom; but as to this he must suffer a faithful Mussulman to have his doubts." As he spoke these words, Shaban touched the letter three times with his forehead, and then, leaping backwards, disappeared from my sight.

The hideous manner in which the poor eunuch wept on leaving me, amused me much. I was far indeed from making any attempt to keep him back. His presence was odious to me, for he always avoided all conversation about the only subject that filled my heart. On the other hand, I was enchanted at the choice of Mouzaka as my attendant. With a deaf and dumb slave, I should enjoy full liberty in imparting my confidences to the obliging old man, and in following his advice, if so be that he gave me advice of which I approved.

All my thoughts were thus assuming a somewhat rosy hue, when the Climber returned, smothered up in carpets and cushions of silk, which he stretched out on the ground; and he then proceeded, with a pleasant and contented air, to light torches, and to burn pastilles in braziers of gold. He had taken these sumptuous articles from the palace treasury, which, as he assured me, was well worthy of exciting my curiosity. I told him I was quite ready to take his word for it at that particular time, the smell of the excellent viands which had preceded him having very agreeably whetted my appetite. These viands consisted chiefly of slices of deer spiced with fragrant herbs, of eggs prepared after divers recipes, and of cakes more dainty and delicate than the petals of a white rose. There was besides a ruddy liquor, made of date juice, and served in strange translucent shells, and sparkling like the eyes of the Climber himself.

We lay down to our meal together in very friendly fashion. My amazing keeper greatly praised the quality of his wine, and made very good use of it, to the intense surprise of Mouzaka, who, huddled up in a corner, indulged in undescribable gestures which the marble reflected on all sides. The fire burnt gaily, throwing out sparks, which, as they darkened, exhaled an exquisite perfume. The torches gave a brilliant light, the braziers shone brightly, and the soft warmth that reigned in the apartment inclined to a voluptuous indolence.

The situation in which I found myself was so singular, the kind of prison in which I was confined was so different from anything I could have imagined, and the ways of my keeper were so grotesque, that from time to time I rubbed my eyes to make sure that the whole thing was not a dream. I should even have derived amusement from my surround-ings, if the thought that I was so far from Kalilah had left me for a single moment. The Climber, to distract my thoughts, began the marvellous story of the Giant Gebri, and the artful Charodé, but I interrupted him, and asked him to listen to the recital of my own real sorrows, promising that, afterwards, I should give ear to his tales. Alas! I never kept that promise. Vainly, at repeated intervals, did he try to excite my curiosity: I had none save with regard to Kalilah, and did not cease to repeat: "Where is he? What is he doing? When shall I see him again?"

The old man, seeing me so headstrong in my passion, and so well resolved to brave all remorse, became convinced that I was a fit object for his nefarious purposes, for, as my hearers will doubtless have already understood, he was a servant of the monarch who reigns in this place of torment. In the perversity of his soul, and that fatal blindness which makes men desire to find an entrance here, he had vowed to induce twenty wretches to serve Eblis, and he exactly wanted my brother and myself to complete that number. Far indeed was he, therefore, from re-ally trying to stifle the yearnings of my heart; and though, in order to fan the flame that consumed me, he seemed, from time to time, to be desir-ous of telling me stories, yet, in reality, his head was filled with quite other thoughts.

I spent a great part of the night in making my criminal avowals. To-wards morning I fell asleep. The Climber did the same, at a few paces' distance, having first, without ceremony, applied to my forehead a kiss that burned me like a red-hot iron. My dreams were of the saddest. They left but a confused impression on my mind; but, so far as I can recollect, they conveyed the warnings of Heaven, which still desired to open be-fore me a door of escape and of safety.

So soon as the sun had risen, the Climber led me into his woods, introduced me to his ostriches, and gave me an exhibition of his super-natural agility. Not only did he climb to the tremulous tops of the tallest and most slender palms, bending them beneath his feet like ears of corn, but he would dart like an arrow from one tree to another. After the display of several of these gymnastic feats, he settled on a branch, told me he was about to indulge in his daily meditations, and advised me to go with Mouzaka and bathe by the border of the stream, on the other side of the hill.

The heat was excessive. I found the clear waters cool and delicious. Bathing-pools, lined with precious marbles, had been hollowed out in the middle of a little level mead over which high rocks cast their shadow. Pale narcissi and gladioli grew on the margin, and, leaning towards the water, waved over my head. I loved these languid flowers, they seemed an emblem of my fortunes, and for several hours I allowed their perfumes to intoxicate my soul.

On returning to the palace, I found that the Climber had made great preparations for my entertainment. The evening passed like the evening before; and from day to day, pretty nearly after the same manner, I spent four months. Nor can I say that the time passed unhappily. The romantic solitude, the old man's patient attention, and the complacency with which he listened to love's foolish repetitions, all seemed to unite in soothing my pain. I should perhaps have spent whole years in merely nursing those sweet illusions that are so rarely realized, have seen the ardor of my passion dwindle and die, have become no more than the tender sister and friend of Kalilah, if my father had not, in pursuit of his wild schemes, delivered me over to the impious scoundrel who sat daily watching at my side to make me his prey. Ah! Shaban! ah, Shamelah! you, my real friends, why was I torn from your arms? Why did you not, from the very first, perceive the germs of a too passionate tenderness existing in our hearts, germs which ought then and there to have been extirpated, since the day would come when not fire and steel would be of any avail!

One morning when I was steeped in sad thoughts, and expressing in even more violent language than usual my despair at being separated from Kalilah, the old man fixed upon me his piercing eyes, and addressed me in these words: "Princess, you, who have been taught by the most enlightened of Sages, cannot doubtless be ignorant of the fact that there are Intelligences, superior to the race of man, who take part in human affairs, and are able to extricate us from the greatest difficulties. I, who am telling you this, have had experience, more than once, of their power; for I had a right to their assistance, having been placed, as you yourself have been, under their protection from birth. I quite see that you cannot live without your Kalilah. It is time, therefore, that you should apply for aid to such helpful spirits. But will you have the strength of mind, the courage to endure the approach of Beings so different from mankind? I know that their coming produces certain inevitable effects, as internal tremors, the revulsion of the blood from its ordinary course; but I know also that these terrors, these revulsions, painful as they undoubtedly are, must appear as nothing compared with the mortal pain of separation from an object loved greatly and exclusively. If you resolve to invoke the Jinn of the Great Pyramid, who, as I know, presided at your birth, if you are willing to abandon yourself to his care, I can, this very evening, give you speech of your brother, who is nearer than you imagine. The Being in question, so renowned among the Sages, is called Omoultakos: he is, at present, in charge of the treasure which the ancient cabalist kings have placed in this desert. By means of the other spirits under his command, he is in close touch with his sister, whom, by the by, he loved in his time just as you now love Kalilah. He will, therefore, enter into your sorrows just as much as I do myself, and will, I make no doubt, do all he can to further your desires."

At these last words, my heart beat with unspeakable violence. The possibility of seeing Kalilah once again excited a transport in my breast. I rose hastily, and ran about the room like a mad creature. Then, coming back to the old man's side, I embraced him, called him my father, and throwing myself at his knees, I implored him, with clasped hands, not to defer my happiness, but to conduct me, at whatever hazard, to the sanctuary of Omoultakos.

The crafty old scoundrel was well pleased, and saw with a malicious eye into what a state of delirium he had thrown me. His only thought was how to fan the flame thus kindled. For this purpose, he resumed a cold and reserved aspect, and said, in tones of great solemnity: "Be it known to you, Zulkaïs, that I have my doubts, and cannot help hesitating, in a matter of such importance, great as is my desire to serve you. You evidently do not know how dangerous is the step you propose to take; or, at least, you do not fully appreciate its extreme rashness. I cannot tell how far you will be able to endure the fearful solitude of the immeasurable vaults you must traverse, and the strange magnificence of the place to which I must conduct you. Neither can I tell in what shape the Jinn will appear. I have often seen him in a form so fearful that my senses have long remained numbed; at other times he has shown himself under an aspect so grotesque that I have scarcely been able to refrain from choking laughter, for nothing can be more capricious than beings of that nature. Omoultakos, mayhap, will spare your weakness; but it is right to warn you that the adventure on which you are bound is perilous, that the moment of the Jinn's apparition is uncertain, that while you are waiting in expectation you must show neither fear nor horror, nor impatience, and that, at the sight of him, you must be very sure not to laugh, and not to cry. Observe, moreover, that you must wait in silence, and the stillness of death, and with your hands crossed over your breast, until he speaks to you, for a gesture, a smile, a groan, would involve not only your destruction, but also that of Kalilah, and my own."

"All that you tell me," I replied, "carries terror into my bosom; but, impelled by such a fatal love as mine, what would one not venture!"

"I congratulate you on your sublime perseverance," rejoined the Climber, with a smile of which I did not then appreciate the full significance and wickedness. "Prepare yourself. As soon as darkness covers the earth, I will go and suspend Mouzaka from the top of one of my highest palm-trees, so that she may not be in our way. I will then lead you to the door of the gallery that leads to the retreat of Omoultakos. There I shall leave you, and myself, according to my custom, go and meditate at the top of one of the trees, and make vows for the success of your enterprise."

I spent the interval in anxiety and trepidation. I wandered aimlessly amid the valleys and hillocks on the island. I gazed fixedly into the depths of the waters. I watched the rays of the sun declining over their surface, and looked forward, half in fear and half in hope, to the moment when the light should abandon our hemisphere. The holy calm of a serene night at last overspread the world.

I saw the Climber detach himself from a flock of ostriches that were gravely marching to drink at the river. He came to me with measured steps. Putting his finger to his lips, he said: "Follow me in silence."

I obeyed. He opened a door, and made me enter, with him, into a narrow passage, not more than four feet high, so that I was compelled to walk half doubled up. The air I breathed was damp and stifling. At every step I caught my feet in viscous plants that issued from certain cracks and crevices in the gallery. Through these cracks the feeble light of the moon's rays found an entrance, shedding light, every here and there, upon little wells that had been dug to right and left of our path. Through the black waters in these wells I seemed to see reptiles with human faces.

I turned away my eyes in horror. I burned with desire to ask the Climber what all this might mean, but the gloom and solemnity of his looks made me keep silence. He appeared to progress painfully, and to be brushing aside with his hands something to me invisible. Soon I was no longer able to see him at all. We were going, as it seemed, round and round in complete darkness; and, so as not to lose him altogether in that frightful labyrinth, I was compelled to lay hold upon his robe.

At last we reached a place where I began to breathe a freer and fresher air. A solitary taper of enormous size, fixed upright in a block of marble, lighted up a vast hall, and discovered to my eyes five staircases, whose banisters, made of different metals, faded upwards into the darkness. There we stopped, and the old man broke the silence, saying:

"Chose between these staircases. One only leads to the treasury of Omoultakos. From the others, which go losing themselves to cavernous depths, you would never return. Where they lead you would find nothing but hunger, and the bones of those whom famine has aforetime destroyed."

Having said these words, he disappeared, and I heard a door closing behind him.

Judge of my terror, you who have heard the ebony portals, which confine us forever in this place of torment, grind upon their ebony hinges! Indeed, I dare to say that my position was, if possible, even more terrible than yours, for I was alone. I fell to the earth at the base of the block of marble. A sleep, such as that which ends our mortal existence, overcame my senses. Suddenly a voice, clear, sweet, insinuating like the voice of Kalilah, flattered my ears. I seemed, as in a dream, to see him on the staircase, the banisters of which were of brass. A majestic warrior, whose pale front bore a diadem, held him by the hand. "Zulkaïs," said Kalilah, with an afflicted air, "Allah forbids our union. But Eblis, whom you see here, extends to us his protection. Implore his aid, and follow the path to which he points you."

I awoke in a transport of courage and resolution, seized the taper, and began, without hesitation, to ascend the stairway with the brazen banisters. The steps seemed to multiply beneath my feet; but my resolution never faltered; and, at last, I reached a chamber, square, and immensely spacious, and paved with a marble that was of flesh color, and marked as with the veins and arteries of the human body. The walls of this place of terror were hidden by huge piles of carpets of a thousand kinds, and a thousand hues, and these moved slowly to and fro, as if painfully stirred by human creatures stifling beneath their weight. All around were ranged black chests, whose steel padlocks seemed encrusted with blood.* Muffled hissings appeared to issue from under the

---

*At this point Smith's conclusion begins.

lids of some of these chests; from others, groans and cries as of indistinct voices, and metallic clinkings. I thought that the voices were those of dives, or afrits, rather than men. I shuddered, and fled on, all the more precipitately because some of them had seemed to call me by name. The chamber was endless, and I saw that I had been mistaken as to its form. It enlarged itself before me, like the perspectives of a hall of ill dreams. Insensibly, and as if by the operation of some enchantment, it assumed a more frightful aspect. The marble pavement was now of that livid color seen in the flesh of bodies after death, its veinings were dark as if blood had coagulated within them, and were interspersed with mottlings such as would be made on human skin by the contusions of iron maces. Columns, higher than the monumental pillars of the old kings of Egypt, rose round me into gloom that the great taper was unable to pierce. A blue mist, such as might ascend from nether gulfs, wavered like a curtain before the removed walls, and the light flickered woefully in my arms, as it met the dank sighing exhaled by the subterranean reaches.

I had need of all my resolution, and was forced to summon up the loved image of Kalilah, with all possible clearness, before I could proceed any further. The vastness of the room, its dismal character and furnishings, terrified me more and more. A weakness seized upon my limbs and senses, the taper became an almost insupportable burden, and I could scarce uplift it to inspect the curious treasures piled about me. Notwithstanding this, I perceived that there were open caskets, overrunning with divers jewels, with goldwork wrought in the fashion of antiquity, and still untarnished; so that I felt sure, at first, that I had reached the treasury of Omoultakos, the Jinn to whom the cabalist kings had entrusted their wealth. But soon doubt came upon me, as I began to note the hideous confusion that prevailed everywhere, the human finger-bones, and other charnel relics, that were heaped without discrimination amid the precious stones, or stored in separate vessels of graven silver, as if they too had been of rare worth. I saw, also, that some of the larger caskets were really sarcophagi, such as were used by the Egyptians.

They had been brimmed with skulls, and the severed members of mummies, and gold coins. Serpents, milk-white, and wholly scaleless, crept to and fro, bringing in their mouths bright jewels, or fragments of bone, which they deposited in certain receptacles that were not yet filled to the rim.

A faintness, such as the dying must undergo, would have overcome me at the sight of these horrors, and the musty odors which they emitted; but I was revived by an extraordinary apparition, which, through the speed and brilliance of its descent from one of the topless pillars, I took for a moment to be the Palm-tree-climber. The apparition reached the floor in a flash; it rose up, and I saw my mistake. It was almost more than I could do to refrain from bursting into wild laughter, for the uncommon personage before me resembled, as much as anything else, a mangy baboon whose hair had fallen out in broad patches. His head and face, indeed, were altogether hairless, like those of the ancient priests, but the brows had been painted with kohl to relieve their blank appearance, and the same cosmetic had been applied in large mouches about the jowls. He carried at his side, from a girdle of human gut, a capacious and somewhat tattered pouch, in the form of a stomach sac, from whose rifts unmentionable objects protruded. More amazing than all this, however, was the long tail, seeming to be on fire perpetually, which the remarkable being flourished in my face like a torch.

Recalling the injunctions of the Climber, I succeeded in smothering my mirth, and maintained a strict silence. It was well, no doubt, that I did so. Omoultakos, for it was indeed the Jinn himself, addressed me in a hollow and lugubrious voice that accorded somewhat strangely with his aspect, saying: "Princess, you need carry no longer the immense taper whose weight has grown so burdensome to you. My tail, which burns with inexhaustible fire, will now serve as a flambeau for us both."

He indicated a half-empty sarcophagus, in which, with expressive signs, he told me to deposit the taper, leaving it upright, so that the grease would not gutter upon the rare contents of that reliquary. Then he said to me: "As a fitting reward for your perseverance in daring the shadows of the subterranean labyrinth, I shall show you the many treasures which have been amassed in this chamber, during the eras of my custodianship. To the wealth of the cabalist rulers, in itself quite prodigious, I have since added much that I prize peculiarly. Eblis, it is true, in his deep-lying halls, has been able to gather together a far more inclusive assortment of terrestrial riches; but I venture to assert that my collection, in some ways, is a little choicer than his. For example, in this casket, you behold, among other remnants of former delight and beauty, a thighbone that once belonged to Balkis."

He waved his tail, which flared brightly, above the relic in question, and then, with a ludicrous and proprietary air, passed on to others. At one time, during our tour, he paused before a small box of green bronze, filled with a dark brown powder, and lifting a pinch of the powder to his nostrils, gave vent to prolonged and violent sternutations. When these had ceased, he remarked with much satisfaction: "There is, to my knowledge, no sneezing-powder more efficacious than the one I have just employed, which was obtained through the atomizing of the mummies of antique embalmers."

My astonishment and disgust were mingled with a strange propensity to laughter, which I conquered again and yet again, with much difficulty. Omoultakos, in a most extensive circuit of inspection about the chamber, illumined for me with the unfailing light of his appendage, an infinite variety of objects that testified to mortal corruption. All the while, he discoursed upon their quondam ownership, and their history, in a fashion that was no less proud than funereal. He showed me, moreover, certain musical instruments, which he himself had designed during hours of leisure. Among them, I remember that there were lutes fashioned from the ribs and arm-bones of women, and stringed with male sinews, and also there were tabors of human skin, that had a deep sonority. On more than one of these instruments, he played a while for my diversion, and though I thought the airs he extorted from them were more than atrocious, I felt that it would be politic to commend, rather than criticize, his playing. In the meanwhile, I burned with desire to question him regarding the whereabouts of Kalilah, and the means through which we might again be united; but mindful of all that the Climber had told me, I restrained my eagerness.

At last, Omoultakos, who had led me on for a great distance between the columns, and the sarcophagi, and had laid aside his unusual instruments of music, turned on me, and said: "Think not, O princess, that all my treasures are things which have come down from antiquity. In the recesses of this unfathomable chamber, objects of more recent date are also conserved. One of them, at least, will interest you. Be patient, and follow the illumination of my tail."

With this adjuration, he conducted me to an open sarcophagus, gilded, and carved from end to end with hieroglyphics, that stood a little apart from the others. In it, with unutterable horror and anguish, I discerned the form of Kalilah, lying as if dead, with a mortal pallor on his cheeks, and lips, and eyelids. I noted that the bosom of his raiment was torn and bloody. I hurled myself upon him, and sought to revive him with kisses, but in vain.

Omoultakos, at this point, chose to interrupt my efforts by inserting the agile tip of his combustive tail between myself and the face of Kalilah. He observed, in a severe tone: "There is but one way in which the prince, your beloved brother, can be revived. The method, fortunately, lies at my immediate disposal. First, however, I will explain to you the presence of Kalilah in this place. The Emir Abou Taber Achmed, in attempting to continue the heroic education he designed for your brother, sent him forth with a small retinue the other day, to hunt the ferocious lions of the Nubian Desert. These lions, appearing in unwonted number, and with more than their usual rapacity, disposed of the followers of Kalilah, and would have served the prince in like manner, if some of my subordinate Jinns, who were watching over the expedition, had not intervened. Unluckily, they were too late to keep Kalilah from being wounded almost to death by the talons of the beasts.

They brought him here, only a few hours since, and I have permitted him to occupy the sarcophagus of an elder Pharaoh, though my wisdom has told me that the tenancy will be of brief duration, and that Kalilah can not be numbered among my permanent acquisitions. If you, Zulkaïs, will consent to a very simple matter, I will give into your hand, without delay, a supremely sovereign restorative."

"Anything! Anything!" I cried, wildly. "I consent to whatever you ask, if only Kalilah be brought back to life."

"You need promise only one thing," quoth Omoultakos. "Pledge your fealty to Eblis, the lord of the fiery globe, and the shadowy caverns."

"It is pledged," I replied, hastily. "Give me the restorative."

Omoultakos, with his apish fingers, began to fumble in the tattered pouch that hung at his girdle. I caught sight of certain highly nauseating oddments, from among which, presently, he produced a pale yellow fruit, having somewhat the form and size of a peach, and laid it in the palm of my hand.

"This fruit," he informed me, "was grown in a garden which, without ever having beheld the sun, is more fertile than the gardens of Irem. If you squeeze it very gently above the lips of Kalilah, a single drop of its juice, falling down upon them, will suffice to resuscitate him in all the bloom that you have loved so dearly. The fruit, after that, is yours to retain; but I trust that you will not be so careless as to devour it at any future time. If you were to do this, the results would be very surprising, since the action of the juice on those who languish at the gates of death, and those who exult in the fullness of life, is an altogether different thing."

Scarcely heeding any of his words, I hastened to squeeze the yellow fruit above Kalilah's lips, which were white as those of a cadaver. I was transported with joy when a living ruby returned into them beneath the dripping of the fluid, and the eyes of Kalilah opened, to give back my ardent gaze. He lifted his arms from the sarcophagus to embrace me, and I quite forgot the presence of Omoultakos. That personage, after a decorous interval, observed in a loud voice: "I am sorry to break in upon your reunion, since I cannot do otherwise than approve and admire the fervor which animates you, but it is more than probable that I shall have, before long, another use for the receptacle you are both occupying. For that reason, I shall conduct you to an alcove beyond my treasury. This alcove is fitted with comfortable couches that will serve your purpose fully as well."

Kalilah, rearing his head at the sound of Omoultakos' voice, perceived, for the first time, the remarkable baboon, who had hitherto been screened from his view by my bosom. He, in his turn, was no less amazed than I had been. However, heeding the injunction of our host, he got up from the sarcophagus. In low tones, I begged him to repress the injudicious laughter that quivered visibly upon his countenance. We both followed Omoultakos. As we went, I placed the yellow fruit in the bosom of my garment.

Kalilah, more impressed by the person of our guide than by the doleful surroundings, could not forbear commenting on the igneous properties of the tail, which emitted showers of sparks on the gloom, as the owner flourished it in his progress. He remarked to me, in great wonder, that the baboon seemed to experience no discomfort whatever from this unique process of combustion. Omoultakos, who had overheard him, turned and said: "Know, young prince, that it is the nature of my tail to burn in this manner, and the sensation it affords me is, in its degree, no more painful, or extraordinary, than that which women experience from the flushing of their cheeks, or men from an excitement of the blood."

After a journey that appeared brief indeed, and which I could not reconcile with my former impression of the vastness of the chamber, we came to an open portal. The flambeau of Omoultakos, reared aloft, illumined for us a much smaller room, with couches of golden cloth, and dark draperies. My father would have loved the draperies, since they were entirely covered with hieroglyphics; but the hieroglyphics, which appeared to change altogether from moment to moment, would have maddened the Sages whom he employed. Here the Jinn left us, after lighting with his torch the many lamps of brass, and copper censers, with which the room had been supplied. I thought that his departure was attended by an odd lack of ceremony, but recalled that he had come down from the pillar, on the occasion of his appearance before me, in a manner no less informal. Through the open doorway, Kalilah and I continued, for some time, to see the luminosity that he made in his movements about the treasury. He seemed to be very busy, and we caught glimpses of certain peculiar assistants, who were bringing in a new lot of treasures. But our joy in being together once more, preoccupied us so fully, that we paid little heed to these activities, and were enabled to disregard, for the time being, their somewhat sinister import.

Between our caresses, we asked each other a thousand questions, and told all that had happened to us severally, since the date of our separation. Kalilah was much dismayed when he learned the circumstances of my visit to the underground palace, and the promise I had made, on his behalf, to the Jinn. "Alas!" he said, "I fear that all this has been prearranged, and for no good purpose. The lions who attacked me were of supernatural size and fierceness. No doubt they were the very Jinns of whom Omoultakos told you, and after their talons had slain my followers, and had rendered me senseless, they brought me here. You, Zulkaïs, through your affection for me, have entered the trap. However, let us try to forget this. No matter how dark and precarious our situation, we have at least the consolation of each other's society."

"All that I have done was nothing," I replied. "Gladly would I pledge myself to Eblis a thousand times, for your sake."

In such converse, the hours went by, and we began to wonder at the long absence of Omoultakos, who had vanished after a while among the pillars of the treasury, and had not returned. He had left us without declaring his intentions as to our future destiny, and it seemed that he had forgotten us. Moreover, he had made no provision for us, beyond lighting the lamps and censers. By the illumination that these vessels yielded, we began to remark the moth-holes in the figured hangings, and the great age of the couches, whose coverings might have been exhumed from palaces long buried in the desert sand. We noted, also, that the lamps and censers were overspread with verdigris. The fumes of the latter vessels troubled us, being both musty and aromatic, like the balms that exhale from the cerements of the Pharaohs. We heard, at intervals, equivocal and disquieting sounds, in a direction of which we were not sure. Together with all this, I grew faint with hunger, but there were no viands in the room for my regalement. At last, I remembered the fruit which I had placed in my bosom, after using it to revive Kalilah. Forgetful of the warning of the Jinn, I drew it forth. I would have shared it with Kalilah, but he, noting my hunger, declined. I devoured it greedily, finding a strange and spicy savor in its pulp.

Almost immediately, I experienced a feeling of unbearable heat, an intense ardor of life rose within me, as if it would burst the confines of my heart. The chamber seemed to blaze with a light that was not that of the lamps. My senses burned with a confused delirium of desires, a madness possessed me, and Kalilah was lost to my perception, like the shadows of the apartment. Then I thought that a ball of fire, hued with a thousand colors that changed momently, swam up and floated before me in the air. An extravagant longing seized me, to possess the ball, and I sprang to my feet and tried to clasp it, but the globe eluded me, and fled swiftly, and I, without heeding the cries of Kalilah, pursued it. I ran through a small portal at the rear of the chamber, and down a labyrinth of cavernous corridors, which, save for the illumination of the globe, would have been altogether lightless. Intent only on overtaking the bright ball, I did not notice my surroundings, or the route I followed. At last, the light disappeared, leaving only a dim glimmer, like the afterglow of the sunken sun, and I came to the verge of a precipice. Far below, the ball receded, plunging into abysses from which the dismal and eternal roaring of lost waters came up to arrest me. However, in my delirium, I should still have followed the globe, if it had not seemed, after an interval, to return toward me from the depths. I waited, ready to seize it, but, as the light drew nearer, I perceived its true source. It was Omoultakos, climbing nimbly from the gulf, by means of the slight projections of the stone.

In an instant, he stood beside me, and said, with an air of reproof: "Princess, why this haste to fling yourself into the underground river that flows eternally toward the realms of Eblis? The destined hour of your departure thither, borne by that doleful tide, is not yet at hand. Fortunately, I met your brother, who was seeking you in the darkness of the caverns; and, learning what had happened, I came without delay, by another route than yours, to intercept you. Kalilah, in consideration of this act of succor, has plighted himself to the prince of the fiery globe, and the flaming hearts. Let us rejoin him, for I fear that he still wanders, lost and distracted, in the darkness. In a sense, I am to blame for what has occurred. Carried away by the duties of my custodianship of the treasury—duties that are often exigent—I forgot the obligations of a host, and failed to provide for your natural needs. If I had done as I should, hunger would never have prompted you to devour the fruit that gave rise to your delirium."

My madness had abated. I followed Omoultakos, perceiving, as I went, the horrors of the labyrinth of caverns, to which the orb with the thousand colors had blinded me. At every turn, there were scattered bones, and skeletons, which had belonged, mayhap, to wretches who had lost themselves in the maze, and had perished of famine. Some of the skeletons lay close together, but I could not tell whether the intimacy of their postures had been dictated by human love, or anthropophagism. Omoultakos did not enlighten me upon this point, nor did I care to question him. At last, we found Kalilah, whose joy was little less extravagant than the delirium which had led me to the floating ball.

"I must provide more adequately for your entertainment," said

Omoultakos. "Eblis permits me to keep you here a while, as my guests. My subterranean garden lies not far away, and in it is a pavilion, which you may occupy. Food and drink will be served regularly to you, and in plenteous quantities, and I trust that neither of you will be tempted, in view of what has occurred, to sample the fruit of my trees."

He conducted us along a short passage, from which we emerged into an immense cavern whose roof was purple like the vault of night, and was starred with effulgent ores that resembled the planets and the constellations. Here we beheld the garden of which he had spoken. It consisted of fantastic trees, heavily laden with divers fruits and blossoms, and cunningly illumed by lamps, which, very often, I could not distinguish from the fruits. In the midst was a small pavilion, built of a marble mottled with rose and black. It was furnished with luxurious divans, and a table on which delicious viands, and wines like molten ruby and topaz, had been spread for our refection. Omoultakos, after again assuring us of his hospitality, begged leave to excuse himself, and departed with the same celerity that had marked his former movements.

In the pavilion he had placed at our disposal, Kalilah and I dwelt for a period of time that neither of us could calculate. That period, however, in spite of certain forebodings, was the happiest we had known, since our childhood days when the Emir was still content to leave us together without interruption. In that place, there was no difference between day and night: for the lamps burned eternally amid the fruited foliage, and the star-like ores continued to sparkle ever in the vault above us. Often we wandered through the garden, which had a strange beauty, though we did not care, after certain indiscreet delvings, to examine too closely into its hidden particulars. The odors of the blossoms, richer than myrrh and santal, conduced to an agreeable languor; and since the Jinn supplied us with an infinity of savorous foods, and wines more delicate than those of Persia, we were well content to leave his fruits alone. In the happiness of being together, and in transports renewed perpetually, we almost forgot the rash pledges we had given. Nor were we troubled overmuch by the fact that the attendants who served us were invisible, and gave proof of their presence only by a sound that resembled the noise made by the flittering of great bats. Also, for the most part, we found ourselves able to ignore a sullen roaring that pervaded the garden continually, seeming to issue from subterranean waters, at a vague distance, and in a direction of which we were never sure. Indeed, we became so accustomed to the sound, mournful and menacing though it was, that it seemed to us little more than a quality of the silence in which we were sequestered.

Our host, who was no doubt busily engaged with the care of his acquisitions, and the treasure confided to him by the cabalist rulers, failed to visit us again. We remarked his negligence, but under the circumstances, we did not miss him.

Alas! though we knew it not, or strove to forget it, the malign forces of our destiny were always at work. Our sojourn in the garden of Omoultakos was to have a frightful denouement. By virtue of the allegiance we had both pledged to the Lord of Evil, we were to share, at the appointed time, the fate of all others who have thus damned themselves irretrievably. And yet—in order to live again those happy hours—I, and Kalilah, too, would repeat the same bond without hesitation. Dream not that we repent.

We were plighting other vows, as we had done a thousand times, and were seated upon a divan in the pavilion, when the date of perdition arrived. It came without announcement, save an insupportable thunder, that seemed to rive apart the foundations of the world. We were tossed as if by earthquake, the air darkened around us, and the ground gave way. Clasped in each other's arms, we had the sensation of falling, together with the pavilion, into a deep abyss. The thunder ceased, the vertigo of our descent grew less, and we heard on every side the woeful and furious noise of rushing waters. A melancholy glimmering dawned about us, and by it, we saw the pavilion had become a raft of serpents plaited together in the fashion of reeds, that was borne headlong on a dark tumultuous river. The serpents, large and rigid as beams of wood, had preserved on their skins the black and rosy mottling of the marble, and they had formed themselves into a cabin around us, like the super-structure of the pavilion. As we went, they added a loud and sinister hissing to the sound of the driven waters.

In this horrible manner, we were carried through unfathomable caves, ever deeper, toward the accursed realms of Eblis. Night surrounded us, we beheld no longer the least ray or glimmer, and, clasped tightly in each other's embrace, we sought by means of such contact to mitigate the noisome clamminess of the reptiles, and the terror of our situation. Thus we seemed to go on for a length of time that was equivalent to many days.

At last, a light broke upon us, lurid and doleful, and the clamor of the river deepened, with a thunder of mighty waterfalls before us. We thought surely that the torrent would precipitate us over some fatal verge, but at this point, the serpents of our raft began to exert themselves, and swimming vigorously, they landed us in the halls of Eblis, not far from that place where the Sultan Soliman listens eternally to the tumult of the cataract, and waits for the release that will come to him only with its cessation. After that, preserving no longer the form of a raft, they re-entered the stream, and swam back separately, in the direction of the garden of Omoultakos. Now, lord, we await, even as you, the moment when our hearts shall be kindled with the unconsuming fire, and shall burn brightly as the tail of the Baboon—but, alas! shall derive unutterable anguish, like the hearts of all other mortals, from that flame in which is the ecstasy of demons.

THE PRINCESS ALMEENA

From her balcony of pearl, the princess Almeena, clad in a gown of irisated silk, with her long and sable locks unbound, gazes toward the sunset-flooded sea beyond a terrace of green marble that peacocks guard. Below, in the tinted light, fantastic trees whose boles are serpentine, train fine and hair-like foliage, that mingling with the moon-shaped leaves of enormous lilies. Rainbow-coloured reeds cluster about the pools and fountains of black water that are rimmed with carven malachite. But these the princess does not heed, but gazes upon the far-off seas, where the golden ichors of the sun have gathered in a vast lake overflowing the horizon. Ere long, a wind from the west, from isles where palm trees blossom above the purple foam, brings in its breath the odour of unknown flowers to mingle with the balms of the garden, and the sweet suspiration of the princess—the princess who dreams, listening to the wind, that her lover, the captain of the emperor's most redoubtable trireme of war, sailing the sky-blue seas beyond the horizon and the sunset, has remembered her wild and royal loneliness, and has breathed in his heart a secret sigh.

THE KISS OF ZORAIDA

With one backward look at the bowery suburbs of Damascus, and the street that was peopled only by the long, faint shadows of a crescent moon, Selim dropped from the high wall among the leafing almonds and flowering lilacs of Abdur Ali's garden. The night was almost sultry; and the air was steeped with a distilled languor of voluptuous perfume. Even if he had been in some other garden, in another city, Selim could not have breathed that perfume without thinking of Zoraida, the young wife of Abdur Ali. Evening after evening, for the past fortnight, during her lord and master's absence, she had met him among the lilacs; till he had grown to associate the very odor of her hair and the savor of her lips with their fragrance.

The garden was silent, except for a silver-lisping fountain; and no leaf or petal stirred in the balmy stillness. Abdur Ali had gone to Aleppo on urgent business and was not expected back for several more days; so the slightly tepid thrill of anticipation which Selim felt was untinged by any thought of danger. The whole affair, even from the beginning, had been as safe as that sort of thing could possibly be: Zoraida was Abdur Ali's only wife, so there were no jealous women who might tattle to their common lord; and the servants and eunuchs of the household, like Zoraida herself, hated the severe and elderly jewel-merchant. It had been unnecessary even to bribe them into complaisance. Everything and everyone had helped to facilitate the amour. In fact, it was all too easy; and Selim was beginning to weary a little of this heavy-scented happiness and the over-sweet affection of Zoraida. Perhaps he would not come again after tonight, or tomorrow night. . . . There were other women, no less fair than the jeweler's wife, whom he had not kissed so often . . . or had not kissed at all.

He stepped forward among the flower-burdened bushes. Was there a figure standing in the shadow, near the fountain? The figure was dim, and darkly muffled, but it must be Zoraida. She had never failed to meet him there, she was ever the first at their rendezvous. Sometimes she had taken him into the luxurious harem; and sometimes, on warm evenings like this, they had spent their long hours of passion beneath the stars, amid the lilacs and almonds.

As Selim approached, he wondered why she did not rush to meet him, as was her wont. Perhaps she had not yet seen him. He called softly: "Zoraida!"

The waiting figure emerged from the shadow. It was not Zoraida, but Abdur Ali. The faint moon-rays glinted on the dull iron barrel and bright silver frettings of a heavy pistol which the old merchant held in his hand.

"You wish to see Zoraida?" The tone was harsh, metallically bitter.

Selim, to say the least, was taken aback. It was all too plain that his affair with Zoraida had been discovered, and that Abdur Ali had returned from Aleppo before the appointed time to catch him in a trap. The predicament was more than disagreeable, for a young man who had thought to spend the evening with a much-enamored mistress. And Abdur Ali's direct query was disconcerting. Selim was unable to think of an apt or judicious answer.

"Come, thou shalt see her." Selim felt the jealous fury, but not the savage irony, that underlay the words. He was full of unpleasant premonitions, most of which concerned himself rather than Zoraida. He knew that he could not look for mercy from this austere and terrible old man; and the probabilities before him were such as to preclude more than a passing thought of what might have befallen, or would befall, Zoraida. Selim was something of an egoist; and he would hardly have claimed (except for the ear of Zoraida) that he was deeply in love. His self-solicitude, under the circumstances, was perhaps to be expected, even if not wholly to be admired.

Abdur Ali had covered Selim with the pistol. The young man realized uncomfortably that he himself was unarmed, except for his yataghan. Even as he was remembering this, two more figures came forward from amid the lilac-shadows. They were the eunuchs, Cassim and Mustafa, who guarded Abdur Ali's harem, and whom the lovers had believed friendly to their intrigue. Each of the giant blacks was armed with a drawn scimitar. Mustafa stationed himself at Selim's right hand and Cassim at his left. He could see the whites of their eyes as they watched him with impassable vigilance.

"Now," said Abdur Ali, "you are about to enjoy the singular privilege of being admitted to my harem. This privilege, I believe, you have arrogated to yourself on certain former occasions, and without my knowledge. Tonight I shall grant it myself; though I doubt if there are many who would follow my example. Come: Zoraida is waiting for you, and you must not disappoint her, nor delay any longer. You are later than usual at the rendezvous, as I happen to know."

With the blacks beside him, with Abdur Ali and the levelled pistol in his rear, Selim traversed the dim garden and entered the courtyard of the jewel-merchant's house. It was like a journey in some evil dream; and nothing appeared wholly real to the young man. Even when he stood in the harem interior, by the soft light of Saracenic lamps of wrought brass, and saw the familiar divans with their deep-hued cushions and coverings, the rare Turkoman and Persian rugs, the taborets of Indian ebony freaked with precious metals and mother-of-pearl, he could not dispel his feeling of strange dubiety.

In his terror and bewilderment, amid the rich furnishings and somber splendor of the room, he did not see Zoraida for a moment. Abdur Ali perceived his confusion and pointed to one of the couches.

"Hast thou no greeting for Zoraida?" The low tone was indescribably sardonic and ferocious.

Zoraida, wearing the scanty harem costume of bright silks in which she was wont to receive her lover, was lying on the sullen crimson fabrics of the divan. She was very still, and seemed to be asleep. Her face was whiter than usual, though she had always been a little pale; and the soft, child-like features, with their hint of luxurious roundness, wore a vaguely troubled expression, with a touch of bitterness about the mouth. Selim approached her; but she did not stir.

"Speak to her," snarled the old man. His eyes burned like two spots of slowly eating fire in the brown and crumpled parchment of his face.

Selim was unable to utter a word. He had begun to surmise the truth; and the situation overwhelmed him with a horrible despair.

"What? Thou hast no greeting for one who loved thee so dearly and so unwisely?" The words were like the dripping of some corrosive acid.

"What hast thou done to her?" said Selim after awhile. He could not look at Zoraida any longer; nor could he lift his eyes to meet those of Abdur Ali.

"What have I done? I have dealt with her very gently, all things considered. As thou seest, I have not marred in any wise the perfection of her beauty—there is no wound, and not even the mark of a blow, on her white body. I did not play the butcher and slay her with the sword, as others would have done. Was I not more than generous ... to leave her thus ... for thee? Her lips and bosom are still warm—though doubtless you will not find them so responsive as usual."

Selim was not a coward, as men go; yet he gave an involuntary shudder.

"But . . . thou hast not told me."

"It was a rare and precious poison, which slays immediately and with little pain. A drop of it would have been enough—or even so much as still remains upon her lips. She drank it of her own choice. I was merciful to her . . . as I shall be to thee."

"I am at thy disposal," said Selim with all the hardihood he could muster. "Of course, it would be useless to deny anything."

The jewel-dealer's face became a mask of malignity, like that of some avenging fiend.

"You need not confess—I know everything—I knew it even from the first. My trip to Aleppo was only a blind so that I could make sure. I was here in Damascus, watching, when you thought me leagues and leagues away. It is not for you to affirm or deny your guilt—your place is only to obey and do my will. My eunuchs know their master, and they will slice thee limb from limb and member from member if I give the word."

Selim looked at the two Negroes. They returned his gaze with impassive eyes that were utterly devoid of all interest, either friendly or unfriendly. The light ran without a quiver along their gleaming muscles and upon their glittering swords.

"What is thy will?"

"Merely that you should prove yourself a good and faithful lover to Zoraida. In bringing you here tonight, I have performed an act of the most remarkable abnegation, as you must know. Other husbands would have slain you like a jackal when you entered the garden... However, I am capable of still further abnegation."

"But, I do not understand. What would you have me do?"

"I have already told you . . . Zoraida was untrue to me for your sake; but it is in my mind that you shall never be false to her, as one of your brood is certain to be sooner or later, if you are permitted to go hence alive."

"Dost thou mean to kill me?"

"I have no intention of slaying thee myself. Thy death will come from another source."

Selim looked again at the armed eunuchs.

"No, it will not be that—unless you prefer it."

"In Allah's name, what dost thou mean, then?" The tawny brown of Selim's face had turned ashen with the horror of suspense.

"Thy death will be one which any true lover would envy," said Abdur Ali.

Selim was powerless to ask another question. His nerves were be-ginning to crumble under the ordeal. The dead woman on the couch, the malevolent old man with his baleful half-hints and his obvious im-placability, the muscular Negroes who would hew a man into collops at their master's word—all were enough to break down the courage of har-dier men than he.

He became aware that Abdur Ali was speaking once more.

"I have brought thee to thy mistress. But it would seem that thou art not a very ardent lover. Have you nothing to say to her? Surely there is much to be said, under the circumstances?"

"In the name of the Prophet, cease thy mockery."

Abdur Ali did not seem to hear the tortured cry.

"It is true, of course, that she could not reply even if thou shouldst speak to her. But her lips are as fair as ever—even if they are growing a little cold with thy unlover-like delay. Hast thou no kiss to lay upon them, in memory of all the other kisses they have taken—and given?"

Selim was again speechless.

"Come—you are not very demonstrative, for one who was so amo-rous only yesternight."

"But ... you said there was a poison which—"

"Yes, and I told thee the truth. Even the touch of thy lips to hers, where a trace of the poison lingers, will be enough to cause thy death." There was an awful gloating in Abdur Ali's voice.

Selim shivered and looked again at Zoraida. Aside from her utter stillness and pallor, and the faintly bitter expression about the mouth, she differed in no apparent wise from the woman who had lain so often in his arms. Yet the very knowledge that she was dead was enough to make her seem unspeakably strange and even repulsive to Selim. It was hard to associate this still, marmoreal being with the affectionate mis-tress who had always welcomed him with eager smiles and caresses.

"Truly, you are a fortunate young man," said Abdur Ali. "She loved you to the end ... and you will die from her last kiss. Few men are so lucky."

"Is there no other way?" Selim's question was little louder than a whisper.

"There is none. And you delay too long." Abdur Ali made a sign to the Negroes, who stepped closer to Selim, lifting their swords in the lamplight.

"Unless thou dost my bidding, thy hands will be sliced off at the wrists, to begin with," the jeweler went on. "The next blows will sever a small portion of each forearm. Then a little temporary attention will be given to other parts of your body, before returning to the arms. And I leave the rest to your conjecture. I am sure thou wilt prefer the other death, which will be quick and almost painless, apart from its other advantages."

Selim stooped above the couch where Zoraida lay. Terror—the abject terror of death—was his one emotion. He had wholly forgotten his love for Zoraida, had forgotten her kisses and endearments. He feared the strange, pale woman before him as much as he had once desired her.

"Make haste." The voice of Abdur Ali was steely as the lifted scimitars.

Selim bent over and kissed Zoraida on the mouth. Her lips were not entirely cold, but there was a queer, bitter taste. Of course, it must the poison. The thought was hardly formulated when a searing agony seemed to run through all his veins. He could no longer see Zoraida, in the blinding flames that appeared before him and filled the room like ever-widening suns; and he did not know that he had fallen forward on the couch across her body. Then the flames began to shrink with an awful swiftness, and went out in a swirl of soft gloom. Selim felt that he was sinking into a great gulf, and that someone (whose name he could not remember) was sinking beside him. Then, all at once, he was alone . . . and was losing even the sense of solitude . . . till there was nothing anywhere but darkness and oblivion.

A Chinese Fable

The pine and the willow were once lovers, and they held affectionate converse together in the fashion of trees, and mingled their diverse foliage in secret.

But storm and flood and whirlwind came, and the willow was torn away from the pine, to take root again in the fashion of willows.

Now it is told that the willow has babbled to the winds, and has even murmured untrue things concerning the pine—who, all these years, has kept his own counsel and has retained in his dark boughs certain of her shed leaves.

It would seem that the willow has forgotten the worth of silence. But therein are many virtues—even as there are many meanings in this fable.

THE INVISIBLE CITY

"Confound you," said Langley, in a hoarse whisper that came with effort through swollen lips, blue-black with thirst. "You've gulped about twice your share of the last water in the Lob-nor Desert." He shook the canteen which Furnham had just returned to him, and listened with a savage frown to the ominously light gurgling of its contents.

The two surviving members of the Furnham Archaeological Expedition eyed each other with new-born but rapidly growing disfavor. Furnham, the leader, flushed with dark anger beneath his coat of deepening dust and sunburn. The accusation was unjust, for he had merely moistened his parched tongue from Langley's canteen. His own canteen, which he had shared equally with his companion, was now empty.

Up to that moment, the two men had been the best of friends. Their months of association in a hopeless search for the ruins of the semifabulous city of Kobar had given them abundant reason to respect each other. Their quarrel sprang from nothing else than the mental distortion and morbidity of sheer exhaustion, and the strain of a desperate predicament. Langley, at times, was even growing a trifle light-headed after their long ordeal of wandering on foot through a land without wells, beneath a sun whose flames poured down upon them like molten lead.

"We ought to reach the Tarim River pretty soon," said Furnham stiffly, ignoring the charge and repressing a desire to announce in mordant terms his unfavorable opinion of Langley.

"If we don't, I guess it will be your fault," the other snapped. "There's been a jinx on this expedition from the beginning; and I shouldn't wonder if the jinx were you. It was your idea to hunt for Kobar anyway. I've never believed there was any such place."

161

Furnham glowered at his companion, too near the breaking point himself to make due allowance for Langley's nerve-wrought condition, and then turned away, refusing to reply. The two plodded on, ignoring each other with sullen ostentatiousness.

The expedition, consisting of five Americans in the employ of a New York museum, had started from Khotan two months before to investigate the archaeological remains of Eastern Turkestan. Ill-luck had dogged them continually; and the ruins of Kobar, their main objective, said to have been built by the ancient Uighurs, had eluded them like a mirage. They had found other ruins, had exhumed a few Greek and Byzantine coins, and a few broken Buddhas; but nothing of much novelty or importance, from a museum viewpoint.

At the very outset, soon after leaving the oasis of Tchertchen, one member of the party had died from gangrene caused by the vicious bite of a Bactrian camel. Later on, a second, seized by a cramp while swimming in the shallow Tarim River, near the reedy marshes of Lob-nor, that strange remnant of a vast inland sea, had drowned before his companions could reach him. A third had died of some mysterious fever. Then in the desert south of the Tarim, where Furnham and Langley still persisted in a futile effort to locate the lost city, their Mongol guides had deserted them, taking all the camels and most of the provisions, and leaving to the two men only their rifles, their canteens, their other personal belongings, the various antique relics they had amassed, and a few tins of food.

The desertion was hard to explain, for the Mongols had heretofore shown themselves reliable enough. However, they had displayed a queer reluctance on the previous day, had seemed unwilling to venture further among the endless undulations of coiling sand and pebbly soil.

Furnham, who knew the language better than Langley, had gathered that they were afraid of something, were deterred by superstitious legends concerning this portion of the Lob-nor Desert. But they had been strangely vague and reticent as to the object of their fear; and Furnham had learned nothing of its actual nature.

Leaving everything but their food, water and rifles to the mercy of the drifting sands, the men had started northward toward the Tarim, which was sixty or seventy miles away. If they could reach it, they would find shelter in one of the sparse settlements of fishermen along its shores; and could eventually make their way back to civilization.

It was now afternoon of the second day of their wanderings. Langley had suffered most, and he staggered a little as they went on beneath the eternally cloudless heavens, across the glaring desolation of the dreary landscape. His heavy Winchester had become an insufferable burden, and he had thrown it away in spite of the remonstrance of Furnham, who still retained his own weapon.

The sun had lowered a little, but burned with grueling rays, tyrannically torrid, through the bright inferno of stagnant air. There was no wind, except for brief and furious puffs that whirled the light sand in the faces of the men, and then died as suddenly as they had risen. The ground gave back the heat and glare of the heavens in shimmering, blinding waves of refraction.

Langley and Furnham mounted a low, gradual ridge, and paused in sweltering exhaustion on its rocky spine. Before them was a broad, shallow valley, at which they stared in a sort of groggy wonderment, puzzled by the level and artificial-looking depression, perfectly square, and perhaps a third of a mile wide, which they descried in its center. The depression was bare and empty, with no sign of ruins, but was lined with numerous pits that suggested the ground-plan of a vanished city.

The men blinked, and both were prompted to rub their eyes as they peered through flickering heat-waves; for each had received a momentary impression of flashing light, broken into myriad spires and columns, that seemed to fill the shallow basin and fade like a mirage.

Still mindful of their quarrel, but animated by the same unspoken thought, they started down the long declivity, heading straight toward the depression. If the place were the site of some ancient city, they might possibly hope to find a well or water-spring.

They approached the basin's edge, and were puzzled more and more by its regularity. Certainly it was not the work of nature; and it might have been quarried yesterday, for seemingly there were no ravages of wind and weather in the sheer walls; and the floor was remarkably smooth, except for the multitude of square pits that ran in straight, intersecting lines, like the cellars of destroyed or unbuilt houses. A growing sense of strangeness and mystery troubled the two men; and they were blinded at intervals by the flash of evanescent light that seemed to overflow the basin with phantom towers and pillars.

They paused within a few feet of the edge, incredulous and bewildered. Each began to wonder if his brain had been affected by the sun. Their sensations were such as might mark the incipience of delirium. Amid the blasts of furnace-like heat, a sort of icy coolness appeared to come upon them from the broad basin. Clammy but refreshing, like the chill that might emanate from walls of sunless stone, it revived their fainting senses and quickened their awareness of unexplained mystery.

The coolness became even more noticeable when they reached the very verge of the precipice. Here, peering over, they saw that the sides fell unbroken at all points for a depth of twenty feet or more. In the smooth bottom, the cellar-like pits yawned darkly and unfathomably. The floor about the pits was free of sand, pebbles or detritus.

"Christ! What do you make of that?" muttered Furnham to himself rather than to Langley. He stooped over the edge, staring down with feverish and inconclusive speculations. The riddle was beyond his experience—he had met nothing like it in all his researches. His puzzlement, however, was partly submerged in the more pressing problem of how he and Langley were to descend the sheer walls. Thirst—and the hope of finding water in one of the pits—were more important at that moment than the origin and nature of the square basin.

Suddenly, in his stooping position, a kind of giddiness seized him, and the earth seemed to pitch deliriously beneath his feet. He staggered, he lost his balance, and fell forward from the verge.

Half-fainting, he closed his eyes against the hurtling descent and the crash twenty feet below. Instantly, it seemed, he struck bottom. Amazed and incomprehending, he found that he was lying at full length, prone on his stomach in mid-air, upborne by a hard, flat, invisible substance. His outflung hands encountered an obstruction, cool as ice and smooth as marble; and the chill of it smote through his clothing as he lay gazing down into the gulf. Wrenched from his grasp by the fall, his rifle hung beside him.

He heard the startled cry of Langley, and then realized that the latter had seized him by the ankles and was drawing him back to the precipice. He felt the unseen surface slide beneath him, level as a concrete pavement, glib as glass. Then Langley was helping him to his feet. Both, for the nonce, had forgotten their misunderstanding.

"Say, am I bughouse?" cried Langley. "I thought you were a goner when you fell. What have we stumbled on, anyhow?"

"Stumbled is good," said Furnham reflectively, as he tried to collect himself. "That basin is floored with something solid, but transparent as air—something unknown to geologists or chemists. God knows what it is, or where it came from or who put it there. We've found a mystery that puts Kobar in the shade. I move that we investigate."

He stepped forward, very cautiously, still half-fearful of falling, and stood suspended over the basin.

"If you can do it, I guess I can," said Langley, as he followed. With Furnham in the lead, the two began to cross the basin, moving slowly and gingerly along the invisible pavement. The sensation of peering down as if through empty air was indescribably weird.

They had started midway between two rows of the dark pits, which lay about fifty feet apart. Somehow, it was like following a street. After they had gone some little distance from the verge, Furnham deviated to the left, with the idea of looking directly down into one of these mysterious pits. Before he could reach a vertical vantage-point, he was arrested by a smooth, solid wall, like that of a building.

"I think we've discovered a city," he announced. Groping his way along the air-clear wall, which seemed free of angles or roughness, he came to an open doorway. It was about five feet wide and of indeterminable height. Fingering the wall like a blind man, he found that it was nearly six inches thick. He and Langley entered the door, still walking on a level pavement, and advanced without obstruction, as if in a large empty room.

For an instant, as they went forward, light seemed to flash above them in great arches and arcades, touched with evanescent colors like those in fountain-spray. Then it vanished, and the sun shone down as before from a void and desert heaven. The coolness emanating from the unknown substance was more pronounced than ever; and the men almost shivered. But they were vastly refreshed, and the torture of their thirst was somewhat mitigated.

Now they could look perpendicularly into the square pit below them in the stone floor of the excavation. They were unable to see its bottom, for it went down into shadow beyond the westering sun-rays. But both could see the bizarre and inexplicable object which appeared to float immobile in air just below the mouth of the pit. They felt a creeping chill that was more insidious, more penetrant than the iciness of the unseen walls.

"Now I'm seeing things," said Langley.

"Guess I'm seeing them too," added Furnham.

The object was a long, hairless, light-grey body, lying horizontally, as if in some invisible sarcophagus or tomb. Standing erect, it would have been fully nine feet in height. It was vaguely human in its outlines, and possessed two legs and two arms; but the head was quite unearthly. The thing seemed to have a double set of high, concave ears, lined with perforations; and in place of nose, mouth and chin, there was a long, tapering trunk which lay coiled on the bosom of the monstrosity like a serpent. The eyes—or what appeared to be such—were covered by leathery, lashless and hideously wrinkled lids.

The thing lay rigid; and its whole aspect was that of a well-preserved corpse or mummy. Half in light and half in shadow, it hung amid the funereal, fathomless pit; and beneath it, at some little distance, as their eyes became accustomed to the gloom, the men seemed to perceive another and similar body.

Neither could voice the mad, eerie thoughts that assailed them. The mystery was too macabre and overwhelming and impossible. It was Langley who spoke at last.

"Say, do you suppose they are *all* dead?"

Before Furnham could answer, he and Langley heard a thin, shrill, exiguous sound, like the piping off some unearthly flute whose notes were almost beyond human audition. They could not determine its direction; for it seemed to come from one side and then from another as it continued. Its degree of apparent nearness or distance was also variable. It went on ceaselessly and monotonously, thrilling them with an eeriness as of untrod worlds, a terror as of uncharted dimensions. It seemed to fade away in remote ultramundane gulfs; and then, louder and clearer than before, the piping came from the air beside them.

Inexpressibly startled, the two men stared from side to side in an effort to locate the source of the sound. They could find nothing. The air was clear and still about them; and their view of the rocky slopes that rimmed the basin was blurred only by the dancing haze of heat.

The piping ceased, and was followed by a dead, uncanny silence. But Furnham and Langley had the feeling that someone—or something—was near them—a stealthy presence that lurked and crouched and drew closer till they could have shrieked aloud with the terror of suspense. They seemed to wait amid the unrealities of delirium and mirage, haunted by some elusive, undeclared horror.

Tensely they peered and listened, but there was no sound or visual ostent. Then Langley cried out, and fell heavily to the unseen floor, borne backward by the onset of a cold and tangible thing, resistless as the launching coils of an anaconda. He lay helpless, unable to move, beneath the dead and fluid weight of the unknown incubus, which crushed down his limbs and body and almost benumbed him with an icy chill as of etheric space. Then something touched his throat, very lightly at first, and then with a pressure that deepened intolerably to a stabbing pain, as if he had been pierced by an icicle.

A black faintness swept upon him, and the pain seemed to recede as if the nerves that bore it to his brain were spun like lengthening gossamers across gulfs of anesthesia.

Furnham, in a momentary paralysis, heard the cry of his companion, and saw Langley fall and struggle feebly, to lie inert with closing eyes and whitening face. Mechanically, without realizing for some moments what had happened, he perceived that Langley's garments were oddly flattened and pressed down beneath an invisible weight. Then, from the hollow of Langley's neck, he saw the spurting of a thin rill of blood, which mounted straight in air for several inches, and vanished in a sort of red mist.

Bizarre, incoherent thoughts arose in Furnham's mind. It was all too incredible, too unreal. His brain must be wandering, it must have given way entirely … but something was attacking Langley—an invisible vampire of this invisible city.

He had retained his rifle. Now he stepped forward and stood beside the fallen man. His free hand, groping in the air, encountered a chill, clammy surface, rounded like the back of a stooping body. It numbed his finger-tips even as he touched it. Then something seemed to reach out like an arm and hurl him violently backward.

Reeling and staggering, he managed to retain his balance, and returned more cautiously. The blood still rose in a vanishing rill from Langley's throat. Estimating the position of the unseen attacker, Furnham raised his rifle and took careful aim, with the muzzle less than a yard away from its hidden mark.

The gun roared with deafening resonance, and its sound died away in slow echoes, as if repeated by a maze of walls. The blood ceased to rise from Langley's neck, and fell to a natural trickle. There was no sound, no manifestation of any kind from the thing that had assailed him. Furnham stood in doubt, wondering if his shot had taken effect. Perhaps the thing had been frightened away, perhaps it was still close at hand, and might leap upon him at any moment, or return to its prey.

He peered at Langley, who lay white and still. The blood was ceasing to flow from the tiny puncture. He stepped toward him, with the idea of trying to revive him, but was arrested by a strange circumstance. He saw that Langley's face and upper body were blurred by a grey mist that seemed to thicken and assume palpable outlines. It darkened apace, it took on solidity and form; and Furnham beheld the monstrous thing that lay prone between himself and his companion, with part of its fallen bulk still weighing upon Langley. From its inertness, and the bullet-wound in its side, whence oozed a viscid purple fluid, he felt sure that the thing was dead.

The monster was alien to all terrene biology—a huge, invertebrate body, formed like an elongated starfish, with the points ending in swollen tentacular limbs. It had a round, shapeless head with the curving, needle-tipped bill of some mammoth insect. It must have come from other planets or dimensions than ours. It was wholly unlike the mummified creature that floated in the pit below, and Furnham felt that it represented an inferior animal-like type. It was evidently composed of an unknown order of organic matter that became visible to human eyes only in death.

His brain was swamped by the mad enigma of it all. What was this place upon which he and Langley had stumbled? Was it an outpost of worlds beyond human knowledge or observation? What was the material of which these buildings had been wrought? Who were their builders? Whence had they come? And what had been their purpose? Was the city of recent date? Or was it, perhaps, a sort of ruin, whose builders lay dead in its vaults—a ruin haunted only by the vampire monster that had assailed Langley?

Shuddering with repulsion at the dead monster, he started to drag the still unconscious man from beneath the loathsome mass. He avoided touching the dark, semi-translucent body, which lapsed forward, quivering like a stiff jelly when he had pulled his companion away from it.

Like something very trivial and far away, he remembered the absurd quarrel which Langley had picked with him, and remembered his own resentment as part of a doubtful dream, now lost in the extra-human mystery of their surroundings. He bent over his comrade, anxiously, and saw that some of the natural tan was returning to the pale face and that the eyelids were beginning to flutter. The blood had clotted on the tiny wound. Taking Langley's canteen, he poured the last of its contents between the owner's teeth.

In a few moments, Langley was able to sit up. Furnham helped him to his feet, and the two began to grope their way from the crystal maze.

They found the doorway; and Furnham, still supporting the other, decided to retrace their course along the weird street by which they had started to cross the basin. They had gone but a few paces, when they heard a faint, almost inaudible rustling in the air before them, together with a mysterious grating noise. The rustling seemed to spread and multiply on every hand, as if an invisible crowd were gathering; but the grating soon ceased.

They went on, slowly and cautiously, with a sense of imminent, uncanny peril. Langley was now strong enough to walk without assistance; and Furnham held his cocked rifle ready for instant use. The vague rustling sounds receded, but still encircled them.

Midway between the underlying rows of pits, they moved on toward the desert precipice, keeping side by side. A dozen paces on the cold, solid pavement, and then they stepped into empty air and landed several feet below, with a terrific jar, on another hard surface. It must have been the top of a flight of giant stairs; for, losing their balance, they both lurched and fell, and rolled downward along a series of similar surfaces, and lay stunned at the bottom.

Langley had been rendered unconscious by the fall; but Furnham was vaguely aware of several strange, dream-like phenomena. He heard a faint, ghostly, sibilant rustling, he felt a light and clammy touch upon his face, and smelt an odor of suffocating sweetness, in which he seemed to sink as into an unfathomable sea. The rustling died to a vast and spatial silence; oblivion darkened above him; and he slid swiftly into nothingness.

It was night when Furnham awoke. His first impression was the white dazzle of a full moon, shining in his eyes. Then he became aware that the circle of the great orb was oddly distorted and broken, like a moon in some cubistic painting. All around and above him were bright, crystalline angles, crossing and intermingling—the outlines of a translucent architecture, dome on dome and wall on wall. As he moved his head, showers of ghostly iris—the lunar yellow and green and purple—fell in his eyes from the broken orb and vanished.

He saw that he was lying on a glass-like floor, which caught the light in moving sparkles. Langley, still unconscious, was beside him. Doubtless they were still in the mysterious oubliette down whose invisible stairs they had fallen. Far off to one side, through a mélange of the transparent partitions, he could see the vague rocks of the Gobi, twisted and refracted in the same manner as the moon.

Why, he wondered, was the city now visible? Was its substance rendered perceptible, in a partial sort of way, by some unknown ray which existed in moonlight but not in the direct beams of the sun? Such an explanation sounded altogether too unscientific; but he could not think of any other, at the moment.

Rising on his elbow, he saw the glassy outlines of the giant stairs down which he and Langley had plunged. A pale, diaphanous form, like a phantom of the mummified creature they had seen in the pit, was descending the stairs. It moved forward with fleet strides, longer than those of a man, and stooped above Furnham with its spectral trunk waving inquisitively and poising an inch or two from his face. Two round, phosphorescent eyes, emitting perceptible beams like lanterns, glowed solemnly in its head above the beginning of the proboscis.

The eyes seemed to transfix Furnham with their unearthly gaze. He felt that the light they emitted was flowing in a ceaseless stream into his own eyes—into his very brain. The light seemed to shape itself into images, formless and incomprehensible at first, but growing clearer and more coherent momently. Then, in some indescribable way, the images were associated with articulate words, as if a voice were speaking: words that he understood as one might understand the language of dreams.

"We mean you no harm," the voice seemed to say. "But you have stumbled upon our city; and we cannot afford to let you escape. We do not wish to have our presence known to men.

"We have dwelt here for many ages, The Lob-nor desert was a fertile realm when we first established our city. We came to your world as fugitives from a great planet that once formed part of the solar system— a planet composed entirely of ultra-violet substances, which was destroyed in a terrible cataclysm. Knowing the imminence of the catastrophe, some of us were able to build a huge space-flier, in which we fled to the Earth. From the materials of the flier, and other materials we had brought along for the express purpose, we built our city, whose name, as well as it can be conveyed in human phonetics, is Ciis.

"The things of your world have always been plainly visible to us; and, in fact, due to our immense scale of perceptions, we probably see much that is not manifest to you. Also, we have no need of artificial light at any time. We discovered, however, at an early date, that we ourselves and our buildings were invisible to men. Strangely enough, our bodies undergo in death a degradation of substance which brings them within the infra-violet range; and thus within the scope of your visual cognition."

The voice seemed to pause, and Furnham realized that it had spoken only in his thoughts by a sort of telepathy. In his own mind, he tried to shape a question:

"What do you intend to do with us?"

Again he heard the still, toneless voice:

"We plan to keep you with us permanently. After you fell through the trap-door we had opened, we overpowered you with an anesthetic; and during your period of unconsciousness, which lasted many hours, we injected into your bodies a drug which has already affected your vision, rendering visible, to a certain degree, the ultra-violet substances that surround you. Repeated injections, which must be given slowly, will make these substances no less plain and solid to you than the materials of your own world. Also, there are other processes to which we intend to subject you . . . processes that will serve to adjust and acclimate you in all ways to your new surroundings."

Behind Furnham's weird interlocutor, several more phantasmal figures had descended the half-visible steps. One of them was stooping over Langley, who had begun to stir and would recover full consciousness in a few instants. Furnham sought to frame other questions, and received an immediate reply.

"The creature that attacked your companion was a domestic animal. We were busy in our laboratories at the time, and did not know of your presence till we heard the rifle-shots.

"The flashes of light which you saw among our invisible walls on your arrival were due to some queer phenomenon of refraction. At certain angles the sunlight was broken or intensified by the molecular arrangement of the unseen substance."

At this juncture Langley sat up, looking about him in a bewildered fashion.

"What the hell is all this? And where the hell are we?" he inquired as he peered from Furnham to the people of the city.

Furnham proceeded to explain, repeating the telepathic information he had just received. By the time he had ceased speaking, Langley himself appeared to become the recipient of some sort of mental reassurance from the phantom-like creature who had been Furnham's interlocutor; for Langley stared at this being with a mixture of enlightenment and wonder in his expression.

Once more, there came the still, super-auditory voice, fraught now with imperious command.

"Come with us. Your initiation into our life is to begin immediately. My name is Aispha—if you wish to have a name for me in your thoughts. We ourselves, communicating with each other without language, have little need for names; and their use is a rare formality among us. Our generic name, as a people, is the Tiisins."

Furnham and Langley arose with an unquestioning alacrity, for which afterwards they could hardly account, and followed Aispha. It was as if a mesmeric compulsion had been laid upon them. Furnham noted, in an automatic sort of way, as they left the oubliette, that his rifle had vanished. No doubt it had been carefully removed during his period of insensibility.

He and Langley climbed the high steps with some difficulty. Queerly enough, considering their late fall, they found themselves quite free of stiffness and bruises; but, at the time they felt no surprise—only a drugged acquiescence in all the marvels and perplexities of their situation.

They emerged on the outer pavement, amid the bewildering outlines of the luminous buildings, which towered above them with intersections of multiform crystalline curves and angles. Aispha went on without pause, leading them toward the fantastic serpentine arch of an open doorway in one of the tallest of these edifices, whose pale domes and pinnacles were heaped in immaterial splendor athwart the zenith-nearing moon.

Four of the ultra-violet people—the companions of Aispha—brought up the rear. Aispha was apparently unarmed; but the others carried weapons like heavy-bladed and blunt-pointed sickles of glass or crystal. Many others of this incredible race, intent on their own enigmatic affairs, were passing to and fro in the open street and through the portals of the unearthly buildings. The city was a place of silent and phantasmal activity.

At the end of the street they were following, before they passed through the arched entrance, Furnham and Langley saw the rock-strewn slope of the Lob-nor, which seemed to have taken on a queer filminess and insubstantiality in the moon-light. It occurred to Furnham, with a sort of weird shock, that his visual perception of earthly objects, as well as of the ultra-violet city, was being affected by the injections of which Aispha told him.

The building they now entered was full of apparatuses made in the form of distorted spheres and irregular disks and cubes, some of which seemed to change their outlines from moment to moment in a confusing manner. Certain of them appeared to concentrate the moonlight like ultra-powerful lenses, turning it to a fiery, blinding brilliance. Neither Furnham nor Langley could imagine the purpose of these devices; and no telepathic explanation was vouchsafed by Aispha or any of his companions.

As they went on into the building, there was a queer sense of some importunate and subtle vibration in the air, which affected the men unpleasantly. They could not assign its source nor could they be sure whether their own perception of it was purely mental or came through the avenues of one or more of the physical senses. Somehow it was both disturbing and narcotic; and they sought instinctively to resist its influence.

The lower story of the edifice was seemingly one vast room. The strange apparatuses grew taller about them, rising as if in concentric tiers, as they went on. In the huge dome above them, living rays of mysterious light appeared to cross and re-cross at all angles of incidence, weaving a bright, ever-changing web that dazzled the eye.

They emerged in a clear, circular space at the center of the building. Here ten or twelve of the ultra-violet people were standing about a slim column, perhaps five feet high, that culminated in a shallow basin-like formation. There was a glowing oval-shaped object in the basin, large as the egg of some extinct bird. From this object, numerous spokes of light extended horizontally in all directions, seeming to transfix the heads and bodies of those who stood in a loose ring about the pillar. Furnham and Langley became aware of a high, thin, humming noise which emanated from the glowing egg and was somehow inseparable from the spokes of light, as if the radiance had become audible.

Aispha paused, facing the men; and a voice spoke in their minds.

"The glowing object is called the Dōir. An explanation of its real nature and origin would be beyond your present comprehension. It is allied, however, to that range of substances which you would classify as minerals; and is one of a number of similar objects which existed in our former world. It generates a mighty force which is intimately connected with our life-principle; and the rays emanating from it serve us in place of food. If the Dōir were lost or destroyed, the consequences would be serious; and our life-term, which, normally, is many thousand years, would be shortened for want of the nourishing and revivifying rays."

Fascinated, Furnham and Langley stared at the egg-shaped orb. The humming seemed to grow louder; and the spokes of light lengthened and increased in number. The men recognized it now as the source of the vibration that had troubled and oppressed them. The effect was insidious, heavy, hypnotic, as if there were a living brain in the object that sought to overcome their volition and subvert their senses and their minds in some unnatural thralldom.

They heard the mental command of Aispha:

"Go forward and join those who partake of the luminous emanations of the Dōir. We believe that by so doing you will, in course of time, become purged of your terrestrial grossness; that the very substance of your bodies may eventually be transformed into something not unlike that of our own; and your senses raised to a perceptional power such as we possess."

Half unwillingly, with an eerie consciousness of compulsion, the men started forward.

"I don't like this," said Furnham in a whisper to Langley. "I'm beginning to feel queer enough already." Summoning his utmost will-power, he stopped short of the emanating rays and put out his hand to arrest Langley.

With dazzled eyes, they stood peering at the Dōir. A cold, restless fire, alive with some nameless evil that was not akin to the evil of Earth, pulsated in its heart; and the long, sharp beams, quivering slightly, passed like javelins into the semi-crystalline bodies of the beings who stood immobile around the column.

"Hasten!" came the unvocal admonition of Aispha. "In a few moments the force in the Dōir, which has a regular rhythm of ebb and flow, will begin to draw back upon itself. The rays will be retracted; and you will have to wait for many minutes before the return of the emanation."

A quick, daring thought had occurred to Furnham. Eyeing the Dōir closely, he had been impressed by its seeming fragility. The thing was evidently not attached to the basin in which it reposed; and in all likelihood, it would shatter like glass if hurled or even dropped on the floor. He tried to suppress his thought, fearing that it would be read by Aispha or others of the ultra-violet people. At the same time, he sought to phrase, as innocently as possible, a mental question:

"What would happen if the Dōir were broken?"

Instantly, he received an impression of anger, turmoil and consternation in the mind of Aispha. His question, however, was apparently not answered; and it seemed that Aispha did not want to answer it— that he was concealing something too dangerous and dreadful to be revealed. Furnham felt, too, that Aispha was suspicious, had received an inkling of his own repressed thought.

It occurred to him that he must act quickly, if at all. Nerving himself, he leapt forward through the ring of bodies about the Dōir. The rays had already begun to shorten slightly; but he had the feeling of one who hurls himself upon an array of lance-points. There was an odd, indescribable sensation, as if he were being pierced by something that was both hot and cold; but neither the warmth nor the chill was beyond endurance. A moment, and he stood beside the column, lifting the glowing egg in his hands and poising it defiantly as he turned to face the ultra-violet people.

The thing was phenomenally light; and it seemed to burn his fingers and to freeze them at the same time. He felt a strange vertigo, an indescribable confusion; but he succeeded in mastering it. The contact of the Dōir might be deadlier to the human tissues than that of radium, for aught he knew. He would have to take his chances. At any rate, it would not kill him immediately; and if he played his cards with sufficient boldness and skill, he could make possible the escape of Langley—if not his own escape.

The ring of ultra-violet beings stood as if stupefied by his audacity. The retracting spokes of light were slowly drawing back into the egg; but Furnham himself was still impaled by them. His fingers seemed to be growing translucent where they clutched the weird ball.

He met the phosphoric gaze of Aispha, and heard the frantic thoughts that were pouring into his mind, not only from Aispha but from all the partakers of the Dōir's luminous beams. Dread, unhuman threats, desperate injunctions to return the Dōir to its pedestal, were being laid upon him. Rallying all his will, he defied them.

"Let us go free," he said mentally, addressing Aispha. "Give me back my weapon and permit my companion and me to leave your city. We wish you no harm; but we cannot allow you to detain us. Let us go— or I will shatter the Dōir—will smash it like an egg on the floor."

At the shaping of his destructive thought, a shudder passed among the semi-spectral beings; and he felt the dire fear that his threat had aroused in them. He had been right: the Dōir *was* fragile; and some awful catastrophe, whose nature he could not quite determine, would ensue instantly upon its shattering.

Step by step, glancing frequently about to see that no one approached him by stealth from behind, Furnham returned to Langley's

side. The Tiisins drew back from him in evident terror. All the while, he
continued to issue his demands and comminations:

"Bring the rifle quickly . . . the weapon you took from me . . . and
give it into my companion's hands. Let us go without hindrance or mo-
lestation—or I will drop the Dōir. When we are outside the city, one of
you—one only—shall be permitted to approach us, and I will deliver
the Dōir to him."

One of the Tiisins left the group, to return in less than a minute with
Furnham's Winchester. He handed it to Langley, who inspected the
weapon carefully and found that it had not been damaged or its loading
or mechanism tampered with in any way. Then, with the ultra-violet
creatures following them in manifest perturbation, Furnham and Langley made their way from the building and started along the open street
in the general direction (as Langley estimated from the compass he carried) of the Tarim River.

They went on amid the fantastic towering of the crystalline piles;
and the people of the city, called as if by some unworded summons,
poured from the doorways in an ever-swelling throng and gathered behind them. There was no active demonstration of any overt kind; but
both the men were increasingly aware of the rage and consternation that
had been aroused by Furnham's audacious theft of the Dōir—a theft
that seemed to be regarded in the light of actual blasphemy. The hatred
of the Tiisins, like a material radiation, dark, sullen, stupefying, stultify-
ing, beat upon them at every step. It seemed to clog their brains and
their feet like some viscid medium of nightmare; and their progression
toward the Gobi slope became painfully slow and tedious.

Before them, from one of the buildings, a tentacled, star-fish monster, like the thing that had assailed Langley, emerged and lay crouching
in the street as if to dispute their passage. Raising its evil beak, it glared
with filmy eyes, but slunk away from their approach, as if at the monition
of its owners.

Furnham and Langley, passing it with involuntary shivers of repugnance, went on. The air was oppressed with alien, unformulable menace. They felt an abnormal drowsiness creeping upon them at whiles. There was an unheard, narcotic music, which sought to overcome their vigilance, to beguile them into slumber.

Furnham's fingers grew numb with the unknown radiations of the Dōir; though the sharp beams of light, by accelerative degrees, had withdrawn into its center, leaving only a formless misty glow that filled the weird orb. The thing seemed latent with terrible life and power. The bones of his transparent hand were outlined against it like those of a skeleton.

Looking back, he saw that Aispha followed closely, walking in advance of the other Tiisins. He could not read the thoughts of Aispha as formerly. It was as if a blank, dark wall had been built up. Somehow, he had a premonition of evil—of danger and treachery in some form which he could not understand or imagine.

He and Langley came to the end of the street, where the ultra-violet pavement joined itself to the desert acclivity. As they began their ascent of the slope, both men realized that their visual powers had indeed been affected by the injective treatment of the Tiisins: for the soil seemed to glow beneath them, faintly translucent; and the boulders were like semi-crystalline masses, whose inner structure they could see dimly.

Aispha followed them on the slope; but the other people of Ciis, as had been stipulated by Furnham, paused at the juncture of their streets and buildings with the infra-violet substances of Earth.

After they had gone perhaps fifty yards on the gentle acclivity, Furnham came to a pause and waited for Aispha, holding out the Dōir at arm's length. Somehow, he had a feeling that it was unwise to return the mystic egg; but he would keep his promise, since the people of Ciis had kept their part of the bargain so far.

Aispha took the Dōir from Furnham's hands; but his thoughts, whatever they were, remained carefully shrouded. There was a sense of something ominous and sinister about him as he turned and went back down the slope with the fiery egg shining through his body like a great watchful eye. The beams of light were beginning to emanate from its center once more.

The two men, looking back ever and anon, resumed their journey. Ciis glimmered below them like the city of a mirage in the moonlit hollow. They saw the ultra-violet people crowding to await Aispha at the end of their streets.

Then, as Aispha neared his fellows, two rays of cold, writhing fire leaped forth from the base of a tower that glittered like glass at the city's verge. Clinging to the ground, the rays ran up the slope with the undulant motion of pythons, following Langley and Furnham at a speed that would soon overtake them.

"They're double-crossing us!" warned Furnham. He caught the Winchester from Langley, dropped to his knees and aimed carefully, drawing a bead on the luminous orb of the Dōir through the spectral form of Aispha, who had now reached the city and was about to enter the waiting throng.

"Run!" he called to Langley. "I'll make them pay for their treachery; and perhaps you can get away in the meanwhile."

He pulled the trigger, missing Aispha but dropping at least two of the Tiisins who stood near the Dōir. Again, steadily, he drew bead, while the rays from the tower serpentined onward, pale, chill and deadly-looking, till they were almost at his feet. Even as he aimed, Aispha took refuge in the foremost ranks of the crowd, through whose filmy bodies the Dōir still glowed.

This time, the high-powered bullet found its mark, though it must have passed through more than one of the ultra-violet beings before reaching Aispha and the mystic orb.

Furnham had hardly known what the result would be; but he had felt sure that some sort of catastrophe would ensue the destruction of the Dōir. What really happened was incalculable and almost beyond description.

Before the Dōir could fall from the hands of its stricken bearer, it seemed to expand in a rushing wheel of intense light, revolving as it grew and blotting out the forms of the ultra-violet people in the foreground. With awful velocity, the wheel struck the nearer buildings, which appeared to soar and vanish like towers of fading mirage. There was no audible explosion—no sound of any kind—only that silent, ever-spinning, ever-widening disk of light that threatened to involve by swift degrees the whole extent of Ciis.

Gazing spell-bound, Furnham had almost forgotten the serpentine rays. Too late, he saw that one of them was upon him. He leapt back, but the thing caught him, coiling about his limbs and body like an anaconda. There was a sensation of icy cold, of horrible constriction; and then, helpless, he found that the strange beam of force was dragging him back down the slope toward Ciis, while its fellow went on in pursuit of the fleeing Langley.

In the meanwhile, the spreading disk of fire had reached the tower from which the rays emanated. Suddenly Furnham was free—the serpentine beams had both vanished. He stood rooted to the spot in speechless awe; and Langley, returning to his aid, also paused, watching the mighty circle of light that seemed to fill the entire basin at their feet with a soundless vortex of destruction.

"My God!" cried Furnham, after a brief interval. "Look what's happening to the slope."

As if the force of the uncanny explosion were now extending beyond Ciis, boulders and masses of earth began to rise in air before the white, glowing maelstrom, and sailed in slow, silent levitation toward the men.

Furnham and Langley started to run, stumbling up the slope, and were overtaken by something that lifted them softly, buoyantly, irresistibly, with a strange feeling of utter weightlessness, and bore them like wind-wafted leaves or feathers through the air. They saw the bouldered

crest of the acclivity flowing far beneath them; and then they were floating, floating, ever higher in the moonlight, above leagues of dim desert.
A faintness came upon them both—a vague nausea—an illimitable vertigo—and slowly, somewhere in that incredible flight, they lapsed into
unconsciousness.

The moon had fallen low, and its rays were almost horizontal in
Furnham's eyes when he awoke. An utter confusion possessed him at
first; and his circumstances were more than bewildering. He was lying
on a sandy slope, among scattered shrubs, meager and stunted; and
Langley was lying not far away. Raising himself a little, he saw the white
and reed-fringed surface of a river—which could be none other than the
Tarim—at the slope's bottom. Half- incredulous, doubting his own
senses, he realized that the force of the weird explosion had carried
Langley and himself many miles and had deposited them, apparently
unhurt, beside the goal of their desert wanderings!

Furnham rose to his feet, feeling a queer lightness and unsteadiness.
He took a tentative step—and landed four or five feet away. It was as if
he had lost half his normal weight. Moving with great care he went over
to Langley, who had now started to sit up. He was reassured to find that
his eye-sight was becoming normal again; for he perceived merely a faint
glowing in the objects about him. The sand and boulders were comfort-
ably solid; and his own hands were no longer translucent.

"Gosh!" he said to Langley, "That was some explosion. The force
that was liberated by the shattering of the Dōir—must have done something to the gravity of all surrounding objects. I guess the city of Ciis
and its people have gone back into outer space; and even the infra-violet
substances about the city must have been more or less degravitated. But
I guess the effect is wearing off, as far as you and I are concerned—
otherwise we'd be travelling still."

Langley got up and tried to walk, with the same disconcerting result
that had characterized Furnham's attempt. He mastered his limbs and
his equilibrium after a few experiments.

"I still feel like a sort of dirigible," he commented. "Say, I think we'd better leave this out of our report to the museum. A city, a people, all invisible, in the heart of the Lob-nor—that would be too much for scientific credibility."

"I agree with you," said Furnham—"the whole business would be too fantastic, outside of a super-scientific story. In fact," he added a little maliciously, "it's even more incredible than the existence of the ruins of Kobar."

The Kingdom of the Worm

Foreword

This tale was suggested by the reading of *The Voyages and Travels of Sir John Maundeville*, in which the fantastic realm of Abchaz and the darkness-covered province of Hanyson are actually described! I recommend this colorful fourteenth-century book to lovers of fantasy. Sir John even tells, in one chapter, how diamonds propagate themselves! Truly, the world was a wonderful place in those times, when almost everyone believed in the verity of such marvels.

Now in his journeying Sir John Maundeville had passed well to one side of that remarkable province in the kingdom of Abchaz which was called Hanyson; and, unless he was greatly deceived by those of whom he had inquired the way, could deem himself within two days' travel of that neighboring realm of Georgia.

He had seen the river that flowed out from Hanyson, a land of hostile idolators on which there lay the curse of perpetual darkness; and wherein, it was told, the voices of people, the crowing of cocks and the neighing of horses had sometimes been heard by those who approached its confines. But he had not paused to investigate the verity of these marvels; since the direct route of his journey was through another region; and also Hanyson was a place into which no man, not even the most hardy, would care to enter without need.

However, as he pursued his wayfaring with the two Armenian Christians who formed his retinue, he began to hear from the inhabitants of that portion of Abchaz the rumor of an equally dread demesne, named

185

Antchar, lying before him on the road to Georgia. The tales they told were both vague and frightful, and were of varying import: some said that this country was a desolation peopled only by the liches of the dead and by loathly phantoms; others, that it was subject to the ghouls and afrits, who devoured the dead and would suffer no living mortal to trespass upon their dominions; and still others spoke of things all too hideous to be described, and of dire necromancies that prevailed even as the might of emperors doth prevail in more usually ordered lands. And the tales agreed only in this, that Antchar had been within mortal memory one of the fairest domains of Abchaz, but had been utterly laid waste by an unknown pestilence, so that its high cities and broad fields were long since abandoned to the desert and to such devils and other creatures as inhabit waste places. And the tellers of the tales agreed in warning Sir John to avoid this region and to take the road which ran deviously to the north of Antchar; for Antchar was a place into which no man had gone in latter times.

The good knight listened gravely to all these, as was his wont; but being a stout Christian, and valorous withal, he would not suffer them to deter him from his purpose. Even when the last inhabited village had been left behind, and he came to the division of the ways, and saw verily that the highway into Antchar had not been trodden by man or beast for generations, he refused to change his intention but rode forward stoutly while the Armenians followed with much protest and some trepidation.

Howbeit, he was not blind to the sundry disagreeable tokens that began to declare themselves along the way. There were neither trees, herbs nor lichens anywhere, such as would grow in any wholesome land; but low hills mottled with a leprosy of salt, and ridges bare as the bones of the dead.

Anon he came to a pass where the hills were strait and steep on each hand, with pinnacled cliffs of a dark stone crumbling slowly into dust and taking shapes of wild horror and strangeness, of demonry and Satanry as they crumbled. There were faces in the stone, having the semblance of ghouls or goblins, that appeared to move and twist as the travellers went by; and Sir John and his companions were troubled by the aspect of these faces and by the similitudes which they bore to one another. So much alike, indeed, were many of them, that it seemed as if their first exemplars were preceding the wayfarers, to mock them anew at each turn. And aside from those which were like ghouls or goblins, there were others having the features of heathen idols, uncouth and hideous to behold; and others still that were like the worm-gnawed visages of the dead; and these also appeared to repeat themselves on every hand in a doubtful and wildering fashion.

The Armenians would have turned back, for they swore that the rocks were alive and endowed with motion, in a land where naught else was living; and they sought to dissuade Sir John from his project. But he said merely, "Follow me, an ye will," and rode onward among the rocks and pinnacles.

Now, in the ancient dust of the unused road, they saw the tracks of a creature that was neither man nor any terrestrial beast; and the tracks were of such unwonted shape and number, and were so monstrous withal, that even Sir John was disquieted thereby; and perceiving them, the Armenians murmured more openly than before.

And now, as they pursued their way, the pinnacles of the pass grew tall as giants, and were riven into the likeness of mighty limbs and bodies, some of which were headless and others with heads of Typhoean enormity. And their shadows deepened between the travellers and the sun, to more than the umbrage of shadows cast by rocks. And in the darkest depth of the ravine, Sir John and his followers met a solitary jackal, which fled them not in the manner of its kind but passed them with articulate words, in a voice hollow and sepulchral as that of a demon, bidding them to turn back, since the land before them was an interdicted realm. All were much startled thereat, considering that this was indeed a thing of enchantment, for a jackal to speak thus, and being against nature, was foreominous of ill and peril. And the Armenians cried out, saying they would go no further; and when the jackal had passed from sight, they fled after it, spurring their horses like men who were themselves ridden by devils.

Seeing them thus abandon him, Sir John was somewhat wroth; and also he was perturbed by the warning of the jackal; and he liked not the thought of faring alone into Antchar. But, trusting in our Saviour to forfend him against all harmful enchantments and the necromancies of Satan, he rode on among the rocks till he came forth at length from their misshapen shadows; and emerging thus, he saw before him a grey plain that was like the ashes of some dead land under extinguished heavens.

At sight of this region, his heart misgave him sorely, and he misliked it even more than the twisted faces of the rocks and riven forms of the pinnacles. For here the bones of men, of horses and camels, had marked the way with their pitiable whiteness; and the topmost branches of long dead trees arose like supplicative arms from the sand that had sifted upon the older gardens. And here there were ruinous houses, with doors open to the high-drifting desert, and mausoleums sinking slowly in the dunes. And here, as Sir John rode forward, the sky darkened above him, though not with the passage of clouds or the coming of the simoon, but rather with the strange dusk of midmost eclipse, wherein the shadows of himself and his horse were blotted out, and the tombs and houses were wan as phantoms.

Sir John had not ridden much further, when he met a horned viper, or cerastes, crawling toilsomely away from Antchar in the deep dust of the road. And the viper spoke as it passed him, saying with a human voice, "Be warned, and go not onward to Antchar, for this is a realm forbidden to all mortal beings except the dead."

Now did Sir John address himself in prayer to God the Highest, and to Jesus Christ our Savior and all the blessed Saints, knowing surely that he had arrived in a place that was subject to Satanical dominion. And while he prayed the gloom continued to thicken, till the road before him was half nighted and was no longer easy to discern. And though he would have still ridden on, his charger halted in the gloom and would not respond to the spur, but stood and trembled like one who is smitten with palsy.

Then, from the twilight that was nigh to darkness, there came gigantic figures, muffled and silent and having, as he thought, neither mouths nor eyes beneath the brow-folds of their sable cerements. They uttered no word, nor could Sir John bespeak them in the fear that came upon him; and likewise he was powerless to draw his sword. And they plucked him from his saddle with fleshless hands, and led him away, half swooning at the horror of their touch, on paths that he perceived only with the dim senses of one who goes down into the shadow of death. And he knew not how far they led him nor in what direction; and he heard no sound as he went other than the screaming of his horse far off, like a soul in mortal dread and agony: for the footfalls of those who had taken him were soundless, and he could not tell if they were phantoms or haply were veritable demons. A coldness blew upon him, but without the whisper or soughing of wind; and the air he breathed was dense with corruption and such odors as may emanate from a broken charnel.

For a time, in the faintness that had come upon him, he saw not the things that were standing beside the way, nor the shrouded shapes that went by in funereal secrecy. Then, recovering his senses a little, he perceived that there were houses about him and the streets of a town, though these were but scantly to be discerned in the night that had fallen without bringing the stars. However, he saw, or deemed, that there were high mansions and broad thoroughfares and markets; and among them, as he went on, a building that bore the appearance of a great palace, with a facade that glimmered vaguely, and domes and turrets half swallowed up by the lowering darkness.

As he neared the facade, Sir John saw that the glimmering came from within and was cast obscurely through open doors and between broad-spaced pillars. Too feeble was the light for torch or cresset, too dim for any lamp; and Sir John marvelled amid his faintness and terror. But when he had drawn closer still, he saw that the strange gleaming was like the phosphor bred by the putrefaction of a charnel.

Beneath the guidance of those who held him helpless, he entered the building. They led him through a stately hall, in whose carven columns and ornate furniture the opulence of kings was manifest; and thence he came into the great audience-room, with a throne of gold and ebony set on a high dais, all of which was illumed by no other light than the glimmering of decay. And the throne was tenanted, not by any human lord or sultan, but a grey, prodigious creature, of height and bulk exceeding those of man, and having in all its over-swollen form the exact similitude of a charnel-worm. And the worm was alone, and except for the worm and Sir John and those beings who had brought him thither, the great chamber was empty as a mausoleum of old days, whose occupants were long since consumed by corruption.

Then, standing there with a horror upon him as no man had ever envisaged, Sir John became aware that the worm was scrutinizing him severely, with little eyes deep-folded in the obscene bloating of its face, and then, with a dreadful and solemn voice, it addressed him, saying:

"I am king of Antchar, by virtue of having conquered and devoured the mortal ruler thereof, as well as all those who were his subjects. Know then that this land is mine and that the intrusion of the living is unlawful and not readily to be condoned. The rashness and folly thou hast shown in thus coming here is verily most egregious; since thou wert warned by the peoples of Abchaz, and warned anew by the jackal and the viper which thou didst meet on the road into Antchar. Thy temerity hath earned a condign punishment. And before I suffer thee to go hence, I decree that thou shalt lie for a term among the dead, and dwell as they dwell, in a dark sepulcher, and learn the manner of their abiding and the things which none should behold with living eyes. Yea, still alive, it shall be thine to descend and remain in the very midst of death and putrefaction, for such length of time as seemeth meet to correct thy folly and punish thy presumption."

Sir John was one of the worthiest knights in Christendom, and his valor was beyond controversy. But when he heard the speech of the throned worm, and the judgement that it passed upon him, his fear became so excessive that once again he was nigh to swooning. And, still in this state, he was taken hence by those who had brought him to the audience-room. And somewhere in the outer darkness, in a place of tombs and graves and cenotaphs beyond the dim town, he was flung into a deep sepulcher of stone, and the brazen door of the sepulcher was closed upon him.

Lying there through the seasonless midnight, Sir John was companioned only by an unseen cadaver and by those ministrants of decay who were not yet wholly done with their appointed task. Himself as one half dead, in the sore extremity of his horror and loathing, he could not tell if it were day or night in Antchar; and in all the term of endless hours that he lay there, he heard no sound, other than the beating of his own heart, which soon became insufferably loud, and oppressed him like the noise and tumult of a great throng.

Appalled by the clamor of his heart, and affrighted by the thing which lay in perpetual silence beside him, and whelmed by the awesomeness and dire necromancy of all that had befallen him, Sir John was prone to despair, and scant was his hope of returning from that imprisonment amid the dead, or of standing once more under the sun as a living man. It was his to learn the voidness of death, to share the abomination of desolation, and to comprehend the unutterable mysteries of corruption; and to do all this not as one who is a mere insensible cadaver, but with soul and body still inseparate. His flesh crept, and his spirit cringed within him, as he felt the crawling of worms that went avidly to the dwindling corpse or came away in glutted slowness. And it seemed to Sir John at that time (and at all times thereafter) that the condition of his sojourn in the tomb was verily to be accounted a worse thing than death.

At last, when many hours or days had gone over him, leaving the tomb's darkness unchanged by the entrance of any beam or the departure of any shadow, Sir John was aware of a sullen clangor, and knew that the brazen door had been opened. And now, for the first time, by the dimness of twilight that had entered the tomb, he saw in all its piteousness and repulsion the thing with which he had abode so long. In the sickness that fell upon him at this sight, he was haled forth from the sepulcher by those who had thrust him therein; and, fainting once more with the terror of their touch, and shrinking from their gigantic shadowy stature and cerements whose black folds revealed no human visage or form, he was led through Antchar along the road whereby he had come into that dolorous realm.

His guides were silent as before; and the gloom which lay upon the land was even as when he had entered it, and was like the umbrage of some eternal occultation. But at length, in the very place where he had been taken captive, he was left to retrace his own way and to fare alone through the land of ruinous gardens toward the defile of the crumbling rocks.

Weak though he was from his confinement, and all bemazed with the things which had befallen him, he followed the road till the darkness lightened once more and he came forth from its penumbral shadow beneath a pale sun. And somewhere in the waste he met his charger, wandering through the sunken fields that were covered up by the sand; and he mounted the charger and rode hastily away from Antchar through the pass of the strange boulders with mocking forms and faces. And after a time he came once more to the northern road by which travellers commonly went to Georgia; and he was rejoined by the two Armenians, who had waited on the confines of Antchar, praying for his secure deliverance.

Long afterwards, when he had returned from his wayfaring in the East and among the peoples of remote isles, he told of the kingdom of Abchaz in the book that related his travels; and also he wrote therein concerning the province of Hanyson. But he made no mention of Antchar, that kingdom of darkness and decay ruled by the throned worm.

TOLD IN THE DESERT

Out of the fiery furnace of the desert sunset, he came to meet our caravan. He and his camel were a single silhouette of shadow-like thinness that emerged above the golden-crested dunes and disappeared by turns in their twilight-gathering hollows. When he descended the last dune and drew near, we had paused for the night, and we were pitching our black tents and lighting our little fires.

The man and his dromedary were like mummies that could find no repose in the subterranes of death, and that had wandered abroad beneath the goading of a cryptic spur, ever since the first division of the desert from the town. The face of the man was withered and blackened as by the torrefaction of a thousand flames; his beard was grey as ashes; and his eyes were expiring embers. His clothing was like tatters of the ancient dead, like the spoils of ghoulish rag-pickers. His camel was a mangy, moth-eaten skeleton such as might bear the souls of the damned on their dolorous ride to the realms of Iblis.

We greeted him in the name of Allah and bade him welcome. He shared our meal of dates and coffee and dried goat-flesh; and later, when we sat in a circle beneath the crowding stars, he told us his tale in a voice that had somehow taken on the loneliness, the eerie quavers and disconsolate overtones of the desert wind, as it seeks among infinitely parching horizons for the fertile, spicy valleys it has lost and cannot find.

Of my birth, my youth, and the appellation by which I was known and perhaps renowned among men, it would now be bootless to speak: for those days are one in remoteness with the reign of Al Raschid, they have gone by like the Afrit-builded halls of Suleiman. And in the bazaars or in the harems of my natal city, none would recall me; and if one spoke my name, it would be as a dying and never-repeated echo. And my own memories grow dim like the fires of hesternal wanderings, on which the sand are blown by an autumn gale.

But, though none will remember my songs, I was once a poet; and like other poets in their prime, I sang of vernal roses and autumnal rose-leaves, of the breasts of dead queens and the mouths of living cup-bearers, of stars that seek the fabled ocean-isles, and caravans that follow the eluding and illusory horizons. And because I was fevered with the strange disquietude of youth and poesy, for which there is neither name nor appeasement, I left the city of my boyhood, dreaming of other cities where wine and fame would be sweeter, and the lips of women more desirable.

It was a gallant and merry caravan with which I set forth in the month of the flowering of almonds. Wealthy and brave were the merchants with whom I travelled; and though they were lovers of gold and wrought ivory, of rugs and damascus blades and olibanum, they also loved my songs and could never weary of hearing them. And though our pilgrimage was long, it was evermore beguiled with recital of odes and telling of tales; and time was somehow cheated of its days, and distance of its miles, as only the divine necromancy of song can cheat them. And the merchants told me stories of the far-off, glamorous city which was our goal; and hearkening to their recountal of its splendors and delights, and pondering my own fancies, I was well content with the palm-less leagues as they faded behind our dromedaries.

Alas! For we were never to behold the bourn of our journey, with its auriphrygiate domes that were said to ascend above the greening of paradisal trees, and its minarets of nacre beyond waters of jade. We were waylaid by the fierce tribesmen of the desert in a deep valley between hills; and though we fought valiantly, they bore us down from our hamstrung camels with their over-numbering spears; and taking our corded bales of merchandise, and deeming us all securely dead, they left us to the gier-eagles of the sand.

All but myself, indeed, had perished; and sorely wounded in the side, I lay among the dead as one on whom there descends the pall-like shadow of Azrael. But when the robbers had departed, I somehow stanched my streaming wound with tatters of my torn raiment; and seeing that none stirred among my companions, I left them and tottered away on the route of our journey, sorrowing that so brave a caravan should have come to a death so inglorious. And beyond the defile in which we had been overtaken with such dastardy, I found a camel who had strayed away during the conflict. Even as myself, the animal was maimed, and it limped on three legs and left a trail of blood. But I made it kneel, and mounted it.

Of the hours that ensued I remember little. Blinded with pain and weakness, I heeded not the route that the camel followed, whether it were the track of caravans or a desert-ending path of Bedouins or jackals. But dimly I recalled how the merchants had told me at morn that there were two days of travelling in a desolation where the way was marked by serried bones, ere we should reach the next oasis. And I knew not how I should survive so arduous a journey, wounded and without water; but I clung dizzily to the camel.

The red demons of thirst assailed me; and fever came, and delirium, to people the waste with phantasmagoric shadows. And I fled through aeons from the frightful immemorial Things that held lordship of the desert, and would have proffered me the green, beguiling cups of an awful madness with Their bone-white hands. And though I fled, They dogged me always; and I heard Them gibbering all around me in the air that had turned to blood-red flame.

There were mirages on the waste; there were lucent meres and palms of fretted beryl that hovered always at an unattainable distance. I saw them in the interludes of my delirium; and one there was at length, which appeared greener and fairer than the rest; but I deemed it also an illusion. Yet it faded not nor receded like the others; and in each interval of my phantom-clouded fever it drew nearer still. And thinking it still a mirage,

I approached the palms and the water; and a great blackness fell upon me, like the web of oblivion from the hands of the final Weaver; and I was henceforth bereft of sight and knowledge.

Waking, I deemed perforce that I had died and was in a sequestered nook of Paradise. For surely the sward on which I lay, and the waving verdure about me, were lovelier than those of earth; and the face that leaned above me was that of the youngest and most compassionate houri. But when I saw my wounded camel grazing not far away, and felt the reviving pain of my own hurt, I knew that I still lived; and that the seeming mirage had been a veritable oasis.

Ah! Fair and kind as any houri was she who had found me lying on the desert's verge, when the riderless camel came to her hut amid the palms. Seeing that I had awakened from my swoon, she brought me water and fresh dates, and smiled like a mother as I ate and drank. And, uttering little cries of horror and pity, she bound my wound with the sootheness of healing balsams.

Her voice was gentle as her eyes; and her eyes were those of a dove that has dwelt aways in a vale of myrrh and cassia. When I had revived a little, she told me her name, which was Neria; and I deemed it lovelier and more melodious than the names of the sultanas who are most renowned in song, and remotest in time and fable. She said that she had lived from infancy with her parents amid the palms; and now her parents were dead, and there was none to companion her except the birds that nested and sang in the verdant frondage.

How shall I tell of the life that began for me now, while the spear-wound was mending? How shall I tell of the innocent grace, the child-like beauty, the maternal tenderness of Neria? It was a life remote from all the fevers of the world, and pure from every soilure; it was infinitely sweet and secure, as if in the whole of time and space there were no others than ourselves and naught that could ever trouble our happiness. My love for her, and hers for me, was inevitable as the flowering of the palms and their fruiting. Our hearts were drawn to each other with no shadow of doubt or reluctance; and the meeting of our mouths was simple as that of roses blown together by a summer wind.

We felt no needs, no hungers, other than those which were amply satisfied by the crystal well-water, by the purple fruit of the trees, and by each other. Ours were the dawns that poured through the feathering emerald of fronds; and the sunsets whose amber was flung on a blossom-purified sward more delicate than the rugs of Bokhara. Ours was the divine monotony of contentment, ours were the kisses and endearments ever the same in sweetness, yet illimitably various. Ours was a slumber enchanted by cloudless stars, and caresses without denial or regret. We spoke of naught but our love and the little things that filled our days; yet the words we uttered were more than the weighty discourse of the learned and the wise. I sang no more, I forgot my odes and ghazals; for life itself had become a sufficing music.

The annals of happiness are without event. I know not how long it was that I dwelt with Neria; for the days were molten together in a dulcet harmony of peace and rapture. I remember not if they were few or many; since time was touched by a supernal sorcery, and was no longer time.

Alas! For the tiny whisper of discontent that awakens sooner or later in the bosoms of the blest, that is heard through the central melodies of heaven! There came a day when the little oasis seemed no longer the infinite paradise I had dreamt, when the kisses of Neria were as honey too often tasted, when her bosom was a myrrh too often breathed. The sameness of the days was no longer divine, the remoteness was no longer security but a prison-house. Beyond the fringed horizon of the trees there hovered the opal and marble dream of the storied cities I had sought in former time; and the voices of fame, the tones of sultana-like women, besought me with far, seductive murmurs. I grew sad and silent and distraught; and, seeing the change that was on me, Neria saddened also and watched me with eyes that had darkened like nocturnal wells in which there lingers a single star. But she uttered no breath of reproach or remonstrance.

At last, with halting words, I told her of my longing to depart; and, hypocrite that I was, I spoke of urgent duties that called me and would not be denied. And I promised with many oaths to return as soon as these duties would permit. The pallor of Neria's face, and the darkening of her violet-shadowed eyes, were eloquent of mortal sorrow. But she said only, "Go not, I pray thee. For if thou goest, thou shalt not find me again."

I laughed at her words and kissed her; but her lips were cold as those of the dead, they were unresponsive as if the estranging miles had already intervened. And I, too, was sorrowful when I rode away on my dromedary.

Of that which followed there is much, and yet little, to tell. After many days among the veering boundaries of the sand, I came to a far city; and there I abode for awhile and found in a measure the glory and delight of which I had dreamed. But amid the loud and clamoring bazaars, and across the silken whisper of harems, there returned to me the parting words of Neria; and her eyes besought me through the flame of golden lamps and the luster of opulent attire; and a nostalgia fell upon me for the lost oasis and the lips of abandoned love. And because of it I knew no peace; and after a time I returned to the desert.

I retraced my way with exceeding care, by the dunes and remotely scattered wells that marked the route. But when I thought to have reached the oasis, and to see again the softly waving palms above Neria's abode, and the glimmering waters beside it, I saw no more than a stretch of featureless sand, where a lonely, futile wind was writing and erasing its aimless furrows. And I sought across the sand in every direction, till it seemed that I must overtake the very horizons as they fled; but I could not find a single palm, nor a blade of grass that was like the blossomy sward on which I had lain or wandered with Neria; and the wells to which I came were brackish with desolation and could never have held the crystalline sweetness of the well from which I had drunk with her....

Since then, I know not how many suns have crossed the brazen hell of the desert; nor how many moons have gone down on the waters of mirage and marah. But still I seek the oasis; and still I lament the hour of careless folly in which I forsook its perfect paradise. To no man, mayhap, it is given to attain twice the happiness and security, remote from all that can trouble or assail, which I knew with Neria in a bygone year. And woe to him who abandons such, who becomes a voluntary exile from an irretrievable Aidann. For him, henceforward, there are only the fading visions of memory, the tortures and despairs and illusions of the quested miles, the waste whereon there falls no lightest shadow of any leaf, and the wells whose taste is fire and madness...

We were all silent when the stranger ceased; and no one cared to speak. But among us all there was none who had not remembered the face of her to whom he would return when the caravan had ended its wayfaring.

After awhile, we slept; and we thought that the stranger also slumbered. But awakening before dawn, when a horned moon was low above the sands, we saw that the man and his dromedary had disappeared. And far-off in the ghostly light a doubtful shadow passed from dune to dune like a fever-driven phantom. And it seemed to us that the shadow was the single silhouette of a camel and its rider.

ENNUI

In the alcove whose curtains are cloth-of-gold, and whose pillars are fluted sapphire, reclines the emperor Chan, on his couch of ebony set with opals and rubies, and cushioned with the furs of unknown and gorgeous beasts. With implacable and weary gaze, from beneath unmoving lids that seem carven of purple-veined onyx, he stares at the crystal windows, giving upon the infinite fiery azures of a tropic sky and sea. Oppressive as nightmare, a formless, nameless fatigue, heavier than any burden the slaves of the mines must bear, lies forever at his heart: all deliriums of love and wine, the agonizing ecstasy of drugs, even the deepest and the faintest pulse of delight or pain—all are proven, all are futile, for the outworn but insatiate emperor. Even for a new grief, or a subtler pang than any felt before, he thinks, lying on his bed of ebony, that he would give the silver and vermilion of all his mines, with the crowded caskets, the carcanets and crowns that lie in his most immemorial treasure-vault. Vainly, with the verse of the more inventive poets, the fanciful purple-threaded fabrics of the subtlest looms, the unfamiliar gems and minerals from the uttermost land, the pallid leaves and blood-like petals of a rare and venomous blossom—vainly, with all these, and many stranger devices, wilder, more wonderful diversions, the slaves and sultanas have sought to alleviate the iron hours. One by one he has dismissed them with a weary gesture. And now, in the silence of the heavily curtained alcove, he lies alone, with the canker of ennui at his heart, like the undying mordant worm at the heart of the dead.

Anon, from between the curtains at the head of his couch, a dark and slender hand is slowly extended, clasping a dagger whose blade reflects the gold of the curtain in a thin and stealthily wavering gleam:

Slowly, in silence, the dagger is poised, then rises and falls like a splinter of lightning. The emperor cries out, as the blade, piercing his loosely-folded robe, wounds him slightly in the side. In a moment the alcove is filled with armed attendants, who seize and drag forth the would-be assassin—a slave-girl, the princess of a conquered people, who has often, but vainly, implored her freedom from the emperor. Pale, and panting with terror and rage, she faces Chan and the guardsmen, while stories of unimaginable monstrous tortures, of dooms unnamable, crowd upon her memory. But Chan, aroused and startled only for the instant, feels again the insuperable weariness, more strong than anger or fear, and delays to give the expected signal. And then, momentarily moved, perchance, by some ironical emotion, half-akin to gratitude—gratitude for the brief but diverting danger, which has served to alleviate his ennui for a little, he bids them free the princess; and, with a regal courtesy, places about her throat his own necklace of pearls and emeralds, each of which is the cost of an army.

Lemuria

In Lemuria

Rememberest thou? Enormous gongs of stone
Were stricken, and the storming trumpeteers
Acclaimed my deed to answering tides of spears,
And spoke the names of monsters overthrown—
Griffins whose angry gold, and fervid store
Of sapphires wrenched from mountain-plunged mines—
Carnelians, opals, agates, alamandines,
I brought to thee some scarlet eve of yore.

In the wide fane that shrined thee Venus-wise,
The fallen clamors died . . . I heard the tune
Of tiny bells of pearl and melanite,
Hung at thy knees, and arms of dreamt delight;
And placed my wealth before thy fabled eyes,
Pallid and pure as jaspers from the moon.

An Offering to the Moon

I

I believe," announced Morley, "that the roofless temples of Mu were not all devoted to solar worship, but that many of them were consecrated to the moon. And I am sure that the one we have now discovered proves my point. These hieroglyphics are lunar symbols beyond a doubt."

Thorway, his fellow-archaeologist, looked at Morley with a surprise not altogether due to the boldly authoritative pronouncement. He was struck anew by the singularity of Morley's tones and expression. The dreamy, beardless, olive features, that seemed to repeat some aboriginal Aryan type, were transfigured by a look of ecstatic absorption. Thorway himself was not incapable of enthusiasm when the occasion seemed to warrant it; but this well-nigh religious ardor was beyond his comprehension. He wondered (not for the only time) if his companion's mentality were not a trifle . . . eccentric.

However, he mumbled a rejoinder that was deferential even though non-committal. Morley had not only financed the expedition, but had been paying a liberal stipend to Thorway for more than two years. So Thorway could afford to be respectful, even though he was a little tired of his employer's odd and unauthorized notions, and the interminable series of sojourns they had made on Melanesian isles. From the monstrous and primordial stone images of Easter Island to the truncated pyramidal columns of the Ladrones, they had visited all the far-strewn remains which are held to prove the former existence of a great continent in the mid-Pacific. Now, on one of the lesser Marquesas, hitherto unexplored, they had located the massive walls of a large temple-like edifice. As usual, it had been difficult to find, for such places were universally feared and shunned by the natives, who believed them haunted by the immemorial dead, and could not be hired to visit them or even to reveal their whereabouts. It was Morley who had stumbled upon the place, almost as if he were led by a subconscious instinct.

Truly, they had made a significant discovery, as even Thorway was compelled to admit. Except for a few of the colossal topmost stones, which had fallen or splintered away, the walls were in well-nigh perfect preservation. The place was surrounded by a tangle of palms and jack-fruit and various tropical shrubs; but somehow none of them had taken root within the walls. Portions of a paved floor were still extant, amid centurial heaps of rubble. In the center was a huge, square block, rising four feet above the ground-level, which might well have served as an altar. It was carved with rude symbols which appeared to represent the moon in all its digits, and was curiously grooved across the top from the middle to one side with a trough that became deeper toward the edge. Like all other buildings of the sort, it was plain that the temple had never supported a roof.

"Yes, the symbols are undoubtedly lunar," admitted Thorway.

"Also," Morley went on, "I believe that rites of human sacrifice were performed in these temples. Oblations of blood were poured not only to the sun but to the moon."

"The idea is maintainable, of course," rejoined Thorway. "Human sacrifice was pretty widespread at a certain stage of evolution. It may well have been practiced by the people who built this edifice."

Morley did not perceive the dryness and formality of his confrere's assent. He was preoccupied with feelings and ideas, some of which could hardly have been the natural result of his investigations. Even as in visiting many others of the ancient remains, he had been troubled by a nervous agitation which was a compound of irresoluble awe and terror, of nameless, eager fascination and expectancy. Here, among these mighty walls, the feeling became stronger than it had been anywhere else; and it mounted to a pitch that was veritably distracting, and akin to the disturbed awareness that ushers in the illusions of delirium.

His idea, that the temple was a place of lunar worship, had seized him almost with the authority of an actual recollection, rather than a closely reasoned inference. Also, he was troubled by sensory impressions that bordered upon the hallucinative. Though the day was tropically warm, he was conscious of a strange chill that emanated from the walls—a chill as of bygone cycles; and it seemed to him that the narrow shadows wrought by a meridian sun were peopled with unseen faces. More than once, he was prompted to rub his eyes, for ghostly films of color, like flashes of yellow and purple garments, came and went in the most infinitesimal fraction of time. Though the air was utterly still, he had the sense of perpetual movement all around him, of the passing to and fro of intangible throngs. It was many thousand years, in all likelihood, since human feet had trodden these pavements; but Morley could have cried aloud with the imminence of the long-dead ages. It appeared to him, in a brief glimpse, that his whole life, as well as his journeyings and explorations in the South Seas, had been but a devious return to some earlier state of being; and that the resumption of this state was now at hand. All this, however, continued to perplex him mightily: it was as if he had suffered the intrusion of an alien entity.

He heard himself speaking to Thorway, and the words were unfamiliar and remote, as if they had issued from the lips of another.

"They were a joyous and a child-like race, those people of Mu," he was saying; "but not altogether joyous, not wholly child-like. There was a dark side . . . and a dark worship—the cult of death and night, personified by the moon, whose white, implacable, frozen lips were appeased only by the warm blood that flowed upon her altars. They caught the blood in goblets as it ran from the stone grooves . . . they raised it aloft . . . and the goblets were swiftly drained in mid-air by the remote goddess, if the sacrifice had proven acceptable."

"But how do you know all this?" Thorway was quite amazed, no less by his companion's air than by the actual words. Morley, he thought, was less like a modern, everyday American than ever. He remembered, inconsequently, how all the natives of the various island-groups had taken to Morley with an odd friendliness, without the reserve and suspicion often accorded to other white men. They had even warned Morley against the guardian spirits of the ruins—and they did not always trouble to warn others. It was almost as if they regarded him as being in some manner akin to themselves. Thorway wondered... though he was essentially unimaginative.

"I tell you, I *know*," Morley said, as he walked up and down beside the altar. "I have seen . . ." his voice trailed off in a frozen whisper, and he seemed to stiffen in every limb, and stood still as with some momentary catalepsy. His face grew deadly pale, his eyes were set and staring. Then, from between rigid lips; he uttered the strange words, *"Rhalu muvasa than,"* in a monotonous, hieratic tone, like a sort of invocation.

Morley could not have told what it was that he felt and saw in that moment. He was no longer his known and wonted self; and the man beside him was an unheeded stranger. But he could remember nothing afterward—not even the odd vocals he had uttered. Whatever his mental experience may have been, it was like a dream that fades instantly when one awakens. The moment passed, the extreme rigidity left his limbs and features, and he resumed his interrupted pacing.

His confrere was staring at him in astonishment, not unmingled with solicitude.

"Are you ill? The sun is pretty hot today. And one should be careful. Perhaps we had best return to the schooner."

Morley gave a mechanical assent and followed Thorway from the ruins toward the seashore, where the schooner they had used in their voyaging was anchored in a little harbor less than a mile distant. His mind was full of confusion and darkness. He no longer felt the queer emotions that had seized him beside the altar; nor could he recall them otherwise than dimly. All the while he was trying to recollect something which lay just below the rim of memory; something very momentous, which he had forgotten long, long ago.

II

Lying in a cane couch beneath an awning on the schooner's deck, Morley drifted back to his normal plane of consciousness. He was not unwilling to accept Thorway's suggestion, that he had suffered a touch of sun among the ruins. His ghostly sensations, the delirium-like approach to a state of awareness which had no relation to his daily life, were now unlikely and unreal. In an effort to dismiss them altogether, he went over in his mind the whole of the investigative tour he had undertaken, and the events of the years preceding it.

He remembered his youthful luctations against poverty, his desire for that wealth and leisure which alone makes possible the pursuit of every chimera; and his slow but accelerative progress when once he had acquired a modicum of capital and had gone into business for himself as an importer of Oriental rugs. Then he recalled the chance inception of his archaeological enthusiasm—the reading of an illustrated article which described the ancient remains on Easter Island. The insoluble strangeness of these little-known relics had thrilled him profoundly, though he knew not why; and he had resolved to visit them some day. The theory of a lost continent in the Pacific appealed to him with an almost intimate lure and imaginative charm; it became his own particular chimera, though he could not have traced to their psychal origin the feelings behind his interest. He read everything procurable on the subject; and as soon as his leisure permitted, he made a trip to Easter Island. A year later, he was able to leave his business indefinitely in the hands of an efficient manager. He hired Thorway, a professional archaeologist with much experience in Italy and Asia Minor, to accompany him; and purchasing an old schooner, manned by a Swedish crew and captain, he had set out on his long, devious voyage among the Islands.

Going over all this in his thoughts, Morley decided that it was now time to return home. He had learned all that was verifiable regarding the mysterious ruins. The study had fascinated him as nothing else in his life had ever done; but for some reason his health was beginning to suffer. Perhaps he had thrown himself too assiduously into his labors; the ruins had absorbed him too deeply. He must get away from them, must not risk a renewal of the queer, delusory sensations he had experienced. He recalled the superstitions of the natives, and wondered if there were something in them after all; if unwholesome influences were attached to those primeval stones. Did ghosts return or linger from a world that had been buried beneath the waves for unknown ages? Damn it, he had almost felt at times as if he were some sort of *revenant* himself.

He called to Thorway, who was standing beside the rail in conversation with one of the Norse sailors.

"I think we have done enough for one voyage, Thorway," he said. "We will lift anchor in the morning and return to San Francisco."

Thorway made little effort to conceal his relief. He did not consider the Polynesian isles a very fruitful field for research: the ruins were too old and fragmentary, the period to which they belonged was too conjectural, and did not deeply engage his interest.

"I agree," he rejoined. "Also, if you will pardon me for saying it, I don't think the South Sea climate is one of ideal salubriousness. I've noticed occasional indispositions on your part for some time past."

Morley nodded in a weary acquiescence. It would have been impossible to tell Thorway his actual thoughts and emotions. The man was abysmally unimaginative.

He only hoped that Thorway did not think him a little mad—though, after all, it was quite immaterial.

The day wore on; and the swift, purpureal darkness of eventide was curtailed by the rising of a full moon which inundated sea and land with warm, ethereous quicksilver. At dinner, Morley was lost in a taciturn abstraction; and Thorway was discreetly voluble, but made no reference to the late archaeological find. Svensen, the captain, who ate with them, maintained a monosyllabic reticence, even when he was told of the proposed return to San Francisco. After eating, Morley excused himself and went back to the cane couch. Somewhat to his relief, he was not joined by Thorway.

Moonlight had always aroused in Morley a vague but profound emotion. Even as the ruins had done, it stirred among the shadows of his mind a million ghostly intimations; and the thrill he felt was at times not unalloyed with a cryptic awe and trepidation, akin, perhaps, to the primal fear of darkness itself.

Now, as he gazed at the tropic plenilune, he conceived the sudden and obsessing idea that the orb was somehow larger, and its light more brilliant than usual; even as they might have been in ages when the moon and earth were much younger. Then he was possessed by a troublous doubt, by an inenarrable sense of dislocation, and a dream-like vagueness which attached itself to the world about him. A wave of terror surged upon him, and he felt that he was slipping irretrievably away from all familiar things. Then the terror ebbed; for that which he had lost was far-off and incredible; and a world of circumstances long-forgot was assuming, or resuming, the tinge of familiarity.

What, he wondered, was he doing on this queer ship? It was the night of sacrifice to Rhalu, the selenic goddess; and he, Matla, was to play an essential part in the ceremony. He must reach the temple ere the moon had mounted to her zenith above the altar-stone. And it now lacked only an hour of the appointed time.

He rose and peered about with questioning eyes. The deck was deserted, for it was unnecessary to keep watch in that tranquil harbor. Svensen and the mate were doubtless drinking themselves to sleep as usual; the sailors were playing their eternal whist and pedro; and Thorway was in his cabin, probably writing a no less eternal monograph on Etruscan tombs. It was only in the most remote and exiguous manner that Morley recollected their existence.

Somehow, he managed to recall that there was a boat which he and Thorway had used in their visits to the isle; and that this boat was moored to the schooner's side. With a tread as lithe and supple as that of a native, he was over the rail and was rowing silently shoreward. A hundred yards, or little more, and then he stood on the moon-washed sand.

Now he was climbing the palm-clustered hill above the shore, and was heading toward the temple. The air was suffused with a primal, brooding warmth, with the scent of colossal flowers and ferns not known to modern botanists. He could see them towering beside his way with their thick, archaic fronds and petals, though such things have not lifted to the moon for aeons. And mounting the crest of the hill, which had dominated the little isle and had looked down to the sea on two sides, he saw in the mellow light the far, unbounded reaches of a softly rolling plain, and sealess horizons everywhere, that glowed with the golden fires of cities. And he knew the names of these cities, and recalled the opulent life of Mu, whose prosperity had of late years been menaced by Atlantean earthquakes and volcanic upheavals. These, it was believed, were owing to the wrath of Rhalu, the goddess who controlled the planetary forces; and human blood was being poured in all her fanes to placate the mysterious deity.

Morley (or Matla) could have remembered a million things; he could have called to mind the simple but strange events of his entire pre-existence in Mu, and the lore and history of the far-flung continent. But there was little room in his consciousness for anything but the destined drama of the night. Long ago (how long he was not sure) he had been chosen among his people for an awful honor; but his heart had failed him ere the time ordained, and he had fled. Tonight, however, he would not flee. A solemn religious rapture, not untinged with fear, guided his steps toward the temple of the goddess.

As he went on, he noticed his raiment, and was puzzled. Why was he wearing these ugly and unseemly garments? He began to remove them and to cast them aside one by one. Nakedness was ordained by sacerdotal law for the role he was to play.

He heard the soft-vowelled murmur of voices about him, and saw the multi-colored robes or gleaming amber flesh of forms that flitted among the archaic plants. The priests and worshippers were also on their way to the temple.

His excitement rose, it became more mystical and more rhapsodic as he neared his destination. His being was flooded by the superstitious awe of ancient man, by the dreadful reverence due to the unknown powers of nature. He peered with a solemn trepidation at the moon as it rose higher in the heavens, and saw in its rounded orb the features of a divinity both benign and malevolent.

Now he beheld the temple, looming whitely above the tops of titan fronds. The walls were no longer ruinous, their fallen blocks were wholly restored. His visit to the place with Thorway was dim as a fever fantasy; but other visits during his life as Matla, and ceremonials of the priests of Rhalu which he had once beheld, were clear and immediate in his memory. He knew the faces he would see, and the ritual wherein he would participate. He thought mostly in pictures; but the words of a strange vocabulary were ready for his recollection; and phrases drifted through his mind with unconscious ease; phrases that would have seemed unintelligible gibberish an hour before.

Matla was aware of the concentrated gaze of several hundred eyes as he entered the great, roofless fane. The place was thronged with people, whose round features were of a pre-Aryan type; and many of the faces were familiar to him. But at that moment all of them were parcel of a mystic horror, and were awesome and obscure as the night. Nothing was clear before him, save an opening in the throng, which led to the altar-stone around which the priests of Rhalu were gathered, and wherein Rhalu herself looked down in relentless, icy splendor from an almost vertical elevation.

He went forward with firm steps. The priests, who were clad in lunar purple and yellow, received him in an impassive silence. Counting them, he found that there were only six instead of the usual seven. One there was among them who carried a large, shallow goblet of silver; but the seventh, whose hand would lift a long and curving knife of some copperish metal, had not yet arrived.

Thorway had found it curiously hard to apply himself to the half-written monograph on Etruscan tombs. An obscure and exasperating restlessness finally impelled him to abandon his wooing of the reluctant muse of archaeology. In a state of steadily mounting irritation, wishing that the bothersome and unprofitable voyage were over, he went on deck.

The moonlight dazzled him with its preternatural brilliance, and he did not perceive for a few moments that the cane couch was empty. When he saw that Morley was gone, he experienced a peculiar mixture of alarm and irritation. He felt sure that Morley had not returned to his cabin. Stepping to the schooner's shoreward side, he noted with little surprise the absence of the moored boat. Morley must have gone ashore for a moonlight visit to the ruined temple; and Thorway frowned heavily at this new presumptive evidence of his employer's eccentricity and aberration. An unwonted sense of responsibility, deep and solemn, stirred within him. He seemed to hear an inward injunction, a strange half-familiar voice, bidding him to take care of Morley. This unhealthy and exorbitant interest in a more than problematic past should be discouraged or at least supervised.

Very quickly, he made up his mind as to what he should do. Going below, he called two of the Swedish sailors from their game of pedro and had them row him ashore in the ship's dinghy. As they neared the beach the boat used by Morley was plainly visible in the plumy shadow of a clump of seaward-leaning palms.

Thorway, without offering any explanation of his purpose in going ashore, told the sailors to return to the ship. Then, following the well-worn trail toward the temple, he mounted the island-slope.

Step by step, as he went on, he became aware of a strange difference in the vegetation. What were these monstrous ferns and primordial-looking flowers about him? Surely it was some weird trick of the moonlight, distorting the familiar palms and shrubs. He had seen nothing of the sort in his daytime visits, and such forms were impossible, anyway. Then, by degrees, he was beset with terrible doubt and bewilderment. There came to him the ineffably horrifying sensation of passing beyond his proper self, beyond all that he knew as legitimate and verifiable. Fantastic, unspeakable thoughts, alien, abnormal impulses, thronged upon him from the sorcerous glare of the effulgent moon. He shuddered at repellent but insistent memories that were not his own, at the ghastly compulsion of an unbelievable command. What on earth was possessing him? Was he going mad like Morley? The moon-bright isle was like some bottomless abyss of nightmare fantasy, into which he sank with nightmare terror.

He sought to recover his hard, materialistic sanity, his belief in the safe literality of things. Then, suddenly and without surprise, he was no longer Thorway.

He knew the real purpose for which he had come ashore—the solemn rite in which he was to play an awful but necessary part. The ordained hour was near—the worshippers, the sacrifice and the six fellow-priests awaited his coming in the immemorial fane of Rhalu.

Unassisted by any of the priests, Matla had stretched himself on the cold altar. How long he lay there, waiting, he could not tell. But at last, by the rustling stir and murmur of the throng, he knew that the seventh priest had arrived.

All fear had left him, as if he were already beyond the pain and suffering of earth. But he knew with a precision well-nigh real as physical sight and sensation the use which would be made of the copperish knife and the silver goblet.

He lay gazing at the wan heavens, and saw dimly, with far-focused eyes, the leaning face of the seventh priest. The face was doubly familiar

. . . but he had forgotten something. He did not try to remember. Already it seemed to him that the white moon was drawing nearer, was stooping from her celestial station to quaff the awaited sacrifice. Her light blinded him with unearthly fulgor; but he saw dimly the flash of the falling knife ere it entered his heart. There was an instant of tearing pain that plunged on and on through his body, as if its tissues were a deep abyss. Then a sudden darkness took the heavens and blotted out the face of Rhalu; and all things, even pain, were erased for Matla by the black mist of an eternal nothing.

III

In the morning, Svensen and his sailors waited very patiently for the return of Morley and Thorway from the island. When afternoon came and the two were still absent, Svensen decided that it was time to investigate.

He had received orders to lift anchor for San Francisco that day; but he could not very well depart without Thorway and Morley.

With one of the crew, he rowed ashore and climbed the hill to the ruins. The roofless temple was empty, save for the plants that had taken root in the crevices of its pavement. Svensen and the sailor, looking about for the archaeologists, were horrified from their stolidity by the stains of newly dried blood that lined the great groove in the altar-block to its edge.

They summoned the remainder of the crew. A daylong search of the little island, however, was without result. The natives knew nothing of the whereabouts of Morley and Thorway, and were queerly reticent even in avowing their ignorance. There was no place where the two men could have hidden themselves, granting that they had any reason for a procedure so peculiar. Svensen and his men gave it up. If they had been imaginative, it might have seemed to them that the archaeologists had vanished bodily into the past.

THE UNCHARTED ISLE

I do not know how long I had been drifting in the boat. There are several days and nights that I remember only as alternate blanks of greyness and darkness; and, after these, there came a phantasmagoric eternity of delirium and an indeterminate lapse into pitch-black oblivion. The sea-water I had swallowed must have revived me; for when I came to myself, I was lying at the bottom of the boat with my head a little lifted in the stern, and six inches of brine lapping at my lips. I was gasping and strangling with the mouthfuls I had taken; the boat was tossing roughly, with more water coming over the sides at each toss; and I could hear the sound of breakers not far away.

I tried to sit up, and succeeded, after a prodigious effort. My thoughts and sensations were curiously confused, and I found it difficult to orient myself in any manner. The physical sensation of extreme thirst was dominant over all else—my mouth was lined with running, throbbing fire—and I felt light-headed, and the rest of my body was strangely limp and hollow. It was hard to remember just what had happened; and, for a moment, I was not even puzzled by the fact that I was alone in the boat. But, even to my dazed, uncertain senses, the roar of those breakers had conveyed a distinct warning of peril; and, sitting up, I reached for the oars.

The oars were gone, but, in my enfeebled state, it was not likely that I could have made much use of them anyway. I looked around, and saw that the boat was drifting rapidly in the wash of a shore-ward current, between two low-lying darkish reefs half-hidden by flying veils of foam. A steep and barren cliff loomed before me; but, as the boat neared it, the cliff seemed to divide miraculously, revealing a narrow chasm through which I floated into the mirror-like waters of a still lagoon. The passage from the rough sea without, to a realm of sheltered silence and seclusion, was no less abrupt than the transition of events and scenery which often occurs in a dream.

The lagoon was long and narrow, and ran sinuously away between level shores that were fringed with an ultra-tropical vegetation. There were many fern-palms, of a type I had never seen, and many stiff, gigantic cycads, and wide-leaved grasses taller than young trees. I wondered a little about them even then; though, as the boat drifted slowly toward the nearest beach, I was mainly preoccupied with the clarifying and assorting of my recollections. These gave me more trouble than one would think.

I must have been a trifle light-headed still; and the sea-water I had drunk couldn't have been very good for me, either, even though it had helped to revive me. I remembered, of course, that I was Mark Irwin, first mate of the freighter *Auckland,* plying between Callao and Wellington; and I recalled only too well the night when Captain Melville had wrenched me bodily from my bunk, from the dreamless under-sea of a dog-tired slumber, shouting that the ship was on fire. I recalled the roaring hell of flame and smoke through which we had fought our way to the deck, to find that the vessel was already past retrieving, since the fire had reached the oil that formed part of her cargo; and then the swift launching of boats in the lurid glare of the conflagration. Half the crew had been caught in the blazing fore-castle; and those of us who escaped were compelled to put off without water or provisions. We had rowed for days in a dead calm, without sighting any vessel, and were suffering the tortures of the damned, when a storm had arisen. In this storm, two of the boats were lost; and the third, which was manned by Captain Melville, the second mate, the boatswain and myself, had alone survived. But sometime during the storm, or during the days and nights of delirium that followed, my companions must have gone overboard. . . . This much I recalled; but all of it was somehow unreal and remote, and seemed to pertain only to another person than the one who was floating shore-ward on the waters of a still lagoon. I felt very dreamy and detached; and even my thirst didn't trouble me half as much now as it had on awakening.

The boat touched a beach of fine, pearly sand, before I began to wonder where I was and to speculate concerning the shores I had reached. I knew that we had been hundreds of miles south-west of Easter Island on the night of the fire, in a part of the Pacific where there is no other land; and certainly this couldn't be Easter Island. What, then, could it be? I realized with a sort of shock that I must have found something not on any charted course or geological map. Of course, it was an isle of some kind; but I could form no idea of its possible extent; and I had no way of deciding off-hand whether it was peopled or unpeopled. Except for the lush vegetation, and a few queer-looking birds and butterflies, and some equally queer-looking fish in the lagoon, there was no visible life anywhere.

I got out of the boat, feeling very weak and wobbly in the hot white sunshine that poured down upon everything like a motionless universal cataract. My first thought was to find fresh water; and I plunged at random among the mighty fern-trees, parting their enormous leaves with extreme effort, and sometimes reeling against their boles to save myself from falling. Twenty or thirty paces, however, and then I came to a tiny rill that sprang in shattered crystal from a low ledge, to collect in a placid pool where ten-inch mosses and broad, anemone-like blossoms mirrored themselves. The water was cool and sweet: I drank profoundly, and felt the benison of its freshness permeate all my parched tissues.

Now I began to look around for some sort of edible fruit. Close to the stream, I found a shrub that was trailing its burden of salmon-yellow drupes on the giant mosses. I couldn't identify the fruit; but its aspect was delicious, and I decided to take a chance. It was full of a sugary pulp; and strength returned to me even as I ate. My brain cleared, and I recovered many, if not all, of the faculties that had been in a state of partial abeyance.

I went back to the boat, and bailed out all the sea-water; then I tried to drag the boat as far up on the sand as I could, in case I might need it again at any future time. My strength was inadequate to the task; and still fearing that the tide might carry it away, I cut some of the high grasses with my clasp-knife and wove them into a long rope, with which I moored the boat to the nearest palm-tree.

Now, for the first time, I surveyed my situation with an analytic eye, and became aware of much that I had hitherto failed to observe or realize. A medley of queer impressions thronged upon me, some of which could not have arrived through the avenues of the known senses. To begin with, I saw more clearly the abnormal oddity of the plant-forms about me: they were not the palm-ferns, grasses and shrubs that are native to south sea islands: their leaves, their stems, their frondage, were mainly of uncouth archaic types, such as might have existed in former aeons, on the sea-lost littorals of Mu. They differed from anything I had seen in Australia or New Guinea, those asylums of a primeval flora; and, gazing upon them, I was overwhelmed with intimations of a dark and prehistoric antiquity. And the silence around me seemed to become the silence of dead ages and of things that have gone down beneath oblivion's tide. From that moment, I felt that there was something wrong about the island. But somehow I couldn't tell just what it was, or seize definitely upon everything that contributed to this impression.

Aside from the bizarre-looking vegetation, I noticed that there was a queerness about the very sun. It was too high in the heavens for any latitude to which I could conceivably have drifted; and it was too large anyway; and the sky was unnaturally bright, with a dazzling incandescence. There was a spell of perpetual quietude upon the air, and never the slightest rippling of leaves or water; and the whole landscape hung before me like a monstrous vision of unbelievable realms apart from time and space. According to all the maps, that island couldn't exist, anyhow. . . . More and more decisively, I knew that there was something wrong: I felt an eerie confusion, a weird bewilderment, like one who has been cast away on the shores of an alien planet; and it seemed to me that I was separated from my former life, and from everything I had ever known, by an interval of distance more irremeable than all the blue leagues of sea and sky; that, like the island itself, I was lost to all possible reorientation. For a few instants, this feeling became a nervous panic, a paralyzing horror.

In an effort to overcome my agitation, I set off along the shore of the lagoon, pacing with feverish rapidity. It occurred to me that I might as well explore the island; and perhaps, after all, I might find some clue to the mystery, might stumble on something of explanation or reassurance.

After several serpent-like turns of the winding water, I reached the end of the lagoon. Here the country began to slope upward toward a high ridge, heavily wooded with the same vegetation I had already met, to which a long-leaved araucaria was now added. This ridge was apparently the crest of the island; and, after a half-hour of groping among the ferns, the stiff archaic shrubs and araucarias, I managed to surmount it.

Here, through a rift in the foliage, I looked down upon a scene no less incredible than unexpected. The further shore of the island was visible below me; and, all along the curving beach of a land-locked harbor, were the stone roofs and towers of a town! Even at that distance, I could see that the architecture was of an unfamiliar type; and I was not sure at first glance whether the buildings were ancient ruins or the homes of a living people. Then, beyond the roofs, I saw that several strange-looking vessels were moored at a sort of mole, flaunting their orange sails in the sunlight.

My excitement was indescribable: at most (if the island were peopled at all) I had thought to find a few savage huts; and here below me were edifices that betokened a considerable degree of civilization! What they were, or who had builded them, were problems beyond surmise; but, as I hastened down the slope toward the harbor, a very human eagerness was mingled with the dumbfoundment and stupefaction I had been experiencing. At least, there were people on the island; and, at the realization of this, the horror that had been a part of my bewilderment was dissipated for the nonce.

When I drew nearer to the houses, I saw that they were indeed strange. But the strangeness was not wholly inherent in their architectural forms; nor was I able to trace its every source, or define it in any way, by word or image. The houses were built of a stone whose precise color I cannot recall, since it was neither brown nor red nor grey, but a hue that seemed to combine, yet differ from, all these; and I remember only that the general type of construction was low and square, with square towers. The strangeness lay in more than this—in the sense of a remote and stupefying antiquity that emanated from them like an odor: I knew at once that they were old as the uncouth primordial trees and grasses, and, like these, were parcel of a long-forgotten world.

Then I saw the people—those people before whom not only my ethnic knowledge, but my very reason, were to own themselves baffled. There were scores of them in sight among the buildings, and all of them appeared to be intensely preoccupied with something or other. At first I couldn't make out what they were doing, or trying to do; but plainly they were much in earnest about it. Some were looking at the sea or the sun, and then at long scrolls of a paper-like material which they held in their hands; and many were grouped on a stone platform around a large, intricate metal apparatus resembling an armillary. All of these people were dressed in tunic-like garments of unusual amber and azure and Tyrian shades, cut in a fashion that was unfamiliar to history; and when I came close, I saw that their faces were broad and flat, with a vague foreomening of the Mongolian in their oblique eyes. But, in an unspecifiable way, the character of their features was not that of any race that has seen the sun for a million years; and the low, liquid, many-vowelled words which they spoke to each other, were not denotive of any recorded language.

None of them appeared to notice me; and I went up to a group of three who were studying one of the long scrolls I have mentioned, and addressed them. For all answer, they bent closer above the scroll; and even when I plucked one of them by the sleeve, it was evident that he did not observe me. Much amazed, I peered into their faces, and was struck by the mingling of supreme perplexity and monomaniacal intentness which their expression displayed. There was much of the madman, and more of the scientist absorbed in some irresoluble problem. Their eyes were fixed and fiery, their lips moved and mumbled in a fever of perpetual disquiet; and, following their gaze, I saw that the thing they were studying was a sort of chart or map, whose yellowing paper and faded inks were manifestly of past ages. The continents and seas and isles on this map were not those of the world I knew; and their names were written in heteroclitic runes of a lost alphabet. There was one immense continent in particular, with a tiny isle close to its southern shore; and ever and anon, one of the beings who pored above the map would touch this isle with his finger-tip, and then would stare toward the empty horizon, as if he were seeking to recover a vanished shore-line. I received a distinct impression that these people were as irretrievably lost as I myself; that they too were disturbed and baffled by a situation not to be solved or redeemed.

I went on toward the stone platform, which stood in a broad open space among the foremost houses. It was perhaps ten feet high, and access to it was given by a flight of winding steps. I mounted the steps, and tried to accost the people who were crowding about the armillary-like instrument. But they too were utterly oblivious of me, and intent upon the observations they were making. Some of them were turning the great sphere; some were consulting various geographical and celestial maps; and, from my nautical knowledge, I could see that certain of their companions were taking the height of the sun with a kind of astrolabe. All of them wore the same look of perplexity and savant-like preoccupation which I had observed in the others.

Seeing that my efforts to attract their attention were fruitless, I left the platform and wandered along the streets toward the harbor. The strangeness and inexplicability of it all was too much for me: more and more, I felt that I was being alienated from the realms of all rational experience or conjecture; that I had fallen into some unearthly limbo of confoundment and unreason, into the *cul-de-sac* of an ultra-terrestrial dimension. These beings were so palpably astray and bewildered; it was so obvious that they knew as well as I that there was something wrong with the geography, and perhaps with the chronology, of their island.

I spent the rest of the day roaming around; but nowhere could I find anyone who was able to perceive my presence; and nowhere was there anything to reassure me, or resolve my ever-growing confusion of mind and spirit. Everywhere there were men, and also women; and though comparatively few of them were grey and wrinkled, they all conveyed to my apprehension a feeling of immemorial eld, of years and cycles beyond all record or computation. And all were troubled, all were feverously intent, and were perusing maps or reading ancient pells and volumes, or staring at the sea and sky, or studying the brazen tablets of astronomical parapegms along the streets, as if by so doing they could somehow find the flaw in their reckonings. There were men and women of mature years, and some with the fresh, unlined visages of youth; but in all the place I saw but one child; and the face of the child was no less perplexed and troubled than those of its elders. If anyone ate or drank or carried on the normal occupations of life, it was not done within my scope of vision; and I conceived the idea that they had lived in this manner, obsessed with the same problem, through a period of time which would have been practically eternal in any other world than theirs.

I came to a large building, whose open door was dark with the shadows of the interior. Peering in, I found that it was a temple; for across the deserted twilight, heavy with the stale fumes of burnt-out incense, the slant eyes of a baleful and monstrous image glared upon me. The thing was seemingly of stone or wood, with gorilla-like arms and the malignant features of a sub-human race. From what little I could see in the gloom, it was not pleasant to look upon; and I left the temple, and continued my perambulations.

Now I came to the water-front, where the vessels with orange sails were moored at a stone mole. There were five or six of them in all: they were small galleys, with single banks of oars and figure-heads of metal that were graven with the likeness of primordial gods. They were indescribably worn by the waves of untold years; their sails were rotting rags; and no less than all else on the island, they bore the impress of a dread antiquity. It was easy to believe that their grotesquely carven prows had touched the aeon-sunken wharves of Lemuria.

I returned to the town; and once again I sought to make my presence known to the inhabitants, but all in vain. And after awhile, as I trudged from street to street, the sun went down behind the island, and the stars came swiftly out in a heaven of purpureal velvet. The stars were large and lustrous and were innumerably thick: with the eye of a practiced mariner, I studied them eagerly; but I could not trace the wonted constellations, though here and there I thought that I perceived a distortion or elongation of some familiar grouping. All was hopelessly askew, and disorder crept into my very brain, as I tried once more to orient myself, and noticed that the inhabitants of the town were still busied with a similar endeavor. . . .

I have no way of computing the length of my sojourn on the island. Time didn't seem to have any proper meaning there; and, even if it had, my mental state was not one to admit of precise reckoning. It was all so impossible and unreal, so much like an absurd and troublesome hallucination; and half the time, I thought that it was merely a continuation of my delirium—that probably I was still drifting in the boat. After all, this was the most reasonable supposition; and I don't wonder that those who have heard my story refuse to entertain any other. I'd agree with them, if it weren't for one or two quite material details. . . .

The manner in which I lived is pretty vague to me, also. I remember sleeping under the stars, outside the town; I remember eating and drinking, and watching those people day after day, as they pursued their hopeless calculations. Sometimes I went into the houses and helped myself to food; and once or twice, if I remember rightly, I slept on a couch in one of them, without being disputed or heeded by the owners. There was nothing that could break the spell of their obsession or force them to notice me; and I soon gave up the attempt. And it seemed to me, as time went on, that I myself was no less unreal, no less doubtful and insubstantial, than their disregard would appear to indicate.

In the midst of my bewilderment, however, I found myself wondering if it would be possible to get away from the island. I remembered my boat, and remembered also that I had no oars. And forthwith I made tentative preparations for departure. In broad daylight, before the eyes of the townspeople, I took two oars from one of the galleys in the harbor, and carried them across the ridge to where my boat was hidden. The oars were very heavy, their blades were broad as fans, and their handles were fretted with hieroglyphs of silver. Also, I appropriated from one of the houses two earthen jars, painted with barbaric figures, and bore them away to the lagoon, intending to fill them with fresh water when I left. And also I collected a supply of food. But somehow the brain-muddling mystery of it all had paralyzed my initiative; and even when everything was ready, I delayed my departure. I felt, too, that the inhabitants must have tried innumerable times to get away in their galleys, and had always failed. And so I lingered on, like a man in the grip of some ridiculous nightmare.

One evening, when those distorted stars had all come out, I became aware that unusual things were going on. The people were no longer standing about in groups, with their customary porings and discussions, but were all hastening toward the temple-like edifice. I followed them, and peered in at the door.

The place was lit with flaring torches that flung demoniac shadows on the crowd and on the idol before whom they were bowing. Perfumes were burnt, and chants were sung in the myriad-vowelled language with which my ear had become familiarized. They were invoking that frightful image with gorilla-like arms and half-human, half-animal face; and it was not hard for me to surmise the purpose of the invocation. Then the voices died to a sorrowful whisper, the smoke of the censers thinned, and the little child I had once seen was thrust forward in a vacant space between the congregation and the idol.

I had thought, of course, that the god was of wood or stone; but now, in a flash of terror and consternation, I wondered if I had been mistaken. For the oblique eyes opened more widely, and glowered upon the child, and the long arms, ending in knife-taloned fingers, lifted slowly and reached forward. And arrow-sharp fangs were displayed in the bestial grin of the leaning face. The child was still as a bird beneath the hypnotic eyes of a serpent; and there was no movement, and no longer even a whisper, from the waiting throng....

I cannot recall what happened then: whenever I try to recall it, there is a cloud of horror and darkness in my brain. I must have left the temple and fled across the island by starlight; but of this, too, I remember nothing. My first recollection is of rowing sea-ward through the narrow chasm by which I had entered the lagoon, and of trying to steer a course by the wried and twisted constellations. After that, there were days and days on a bland, unrippling sea, beneath a heaven of dazzling incandescence; and more nights below the crazy stars; till the days and nights became an eternity of tortured weariness; and my food and water were all consumed; and hunger and thirst and a feverous calenture with tossing, seething hallucinations, were all that I knew.

One night, I came to myself for a little while, and lay staring up at the sky. And once more the stars were those of the rightful heavens; and I gave thanks to God for my sight of the Southern Cross, ere I slid back into coma and delirium. And when I recovered consciousness again, I was lying in a ship's cabin, and the ship's doctor was bending over me.

They were all very kind to me on that ship. But when I tried to tell them my tale, they smiled pityingly; and after a few attempts, I learned to keep my silence. They were very curious about the two oars with sil-ver-fretted handles, and the painted jars which they found with me in the boat; but they were all too frank in refusing to accept my explana-tion. No such island and no such people could possibly exist, they said: it was contrary to all the maps that had ever been made, and gave the direct lie to all the ethnologists and geographers.

Often I wonder about it, myself, for there are so many things I can't explain. Is there a part of the Pacific that extends beyond time and space—an oceanic limbo into which, by some unknowable cataclysm, that island passed in a bygone period, even as Lemuria sank beneath the wave? And if so, by what abrogation of dimensional laws was I enabled to reach the island and depart from it? These things are beyond specu-lation. But often in my dreams, I see again the incognizably distorted stars, and share the confusion and bafflement of a lost people, as they pore above their useless charts, and take the altitude of a deviated sun.

LEMURIENNE

From dawn to dawn your eyes of graven spar
For ever change, with chill, forgotten runes:
But all the while your spirit lies afar,
A sphinx that peers on prediluvian moons.

THE ABOMINATIONS OF YONDO

The sand of the desert of Yondo is not as the sand of other deserts; for Yondo lies nearest of all to the world's rim; and strange winds, blowing from a gulf no astronomer may hope to fathom, have sown its ruinous fields with the grey dust of corroding planets, the black ashes of extinguished suns. The dark, orb-like mountains which rise from its pitted and wrinkled plain are not all its own, for some are fallen asteroids half-buried in that abysmal sand. Things have crept in from nether space, whose incursion is forbid by the watchful gods of all proper and well-ordered lands; but there are no such gods in Yondo, where live the hoary genii of stars abolished, and decrepit demons left homeless by the destruction of antiquated hells.

It was noon of a vernal day when I came forth from that interminable cactus-forest in which the Inquisitors of Ong had left me, and saw at my feet the grey beginnings of Yondo. I repeat, it was noon of a vernal day; but in that fantastic wood, I had found no token or memory of spring; and the swollen, fulvous, dying and half-rotten growths through which I had pushed my way, were like no other cacti, but bore shapes of abomination scarcely to be described. The very air was heavy with stagnant odors of decay; and leprous lichens mottled the black soil and russet vegetation with increasing frequency. Pale-green vipers lifted their heads from prostrate cactus-boles, and watched me with eyes of bright ochre that had no lids or pupils. These things had disquieted me for hours past; and I did not like the monstrous fungi, with hueless stems and nodding heads of poisonous mauve, which grew from the sodden lips of fetid tarns; and the sinister ripples spreading and fading on the yellow water at my approach, were not reassuring to one whose nerves

231

were still taut from unmentionable tortures. Then, when even the blotched and sickly cacti became more sparse and stunted, and rills of ashen sand crept in among them, I began to suspect how great was the hatred my heresy had aroused in the priests of Ong; and to guess the ultimate malignancy of their vengeance.

I will not detail the indiscretions which had led me, a careless stranger from far-off lands, into the power of those dreadful magicians and mysteriarchs who serve the lion-headed Ong. These indiscretions, and the particulars of my arrest, are painful to remember; and least of all do I like to remember the racks of dragon-gut strewn with powdered adamant, on which men are stretched naked; or that unlit room with six-inch windows near the sill, where bloated corpse worms crawled in by hundreds from a neighboring catacomb. Sufficient to say that, after expending the resources of their frightful fantasy, my inquisitors had borne me blindfolded on camel-back for incomputable hours, to leave me at morning twilight in that sinister forest. I was free, they told me, to go whither I would; and in token of the clemency of Ong, they gave me a loaf of coarse bread and a leathern bottle of rank water by way of provision. It was at noon of the same day that I came to the desert of Yondo.

So far, I had not thought of turning back, for all the horror of those rotting cacti, or the evil things that dwelt among them. Now, I paused, knowing the abominable legend of the land to which I had come; for Yondo is a place where few have ventured wittingly, and of their own accord. Fewer still have returned—babbling of unknown horrors and strange treasure; and the life-long palsy which shakes their withered limbs, together with the mad gleam in their starting eyes beneath whitened brows and lashes, is not an incentive for others to follow in their footsteps. So it was that I hesitated on the verge of those ashen sands, and felt the tremor of a new fear in my wrenched vitals. It was dreadful to go on, and dreadful to go back, for I felt sure that the priests had made provision against the latter contingency. So, after a little, I went forward, sinking at each step in a loathly softness, and followed by certain long-legged insects that I had met among the cacti. These insects were the color of a week-old corpse, and were as large as tarantulas; but when I turned and trod upon the foremost, a mephitic stench arose that was more nauseous even than their color. So, for the nonce, I ignored them as much as possible.

Indeed, such things were minor horrors in my predicament. Before me, under a huge sun of sickly scarlet, Yondo reached interminable as the land of a hashish-dream against the black heavens. Far-off, on the utmost rim, were those orb-like mountains of which I have told; but in between were awful blanks of grey desolation, and low, treeless hills like the backs of half-buried monsters. Struggling on, I saw great pits where meteors had sunk from sight; and divers-colored jewels that I could not name glared or glistened from the dust. There were fallen cypresses that rotted by crumbling mausoleums, on whose lichen blotted marble fat chameleons crept with royal pearls in their mouths. Hidden by the low ridges, were cities of which no stela remained unbroken—immense and immemorial cities lapsing shard by shard, atom by atom, to feed infinities of desolation. I dragged my torture-weakened limbs over vast rubbish-heaps that had once been mighty temples; and fallen gods frowned in rotting psammite, or leered in riven porphyry at my feet. Over all was an evil silence, broken only by the satanic laughter of hyenas, and the rustling of adders in thickets of dead thorn, or antique gardens given to the perishing nettle and fumitory.

Topping one of the many mound-like ridges, I saw the waters of a weird lake, unfathomably dark and green as malachite, and set with bars of profulgent salt. These waters lay far beneath me in a cup-like basin; but almost at my feet on the wave-worn slopes were heaps of that ancient salt; and I knew that the lake was only the bitter and ebbing dregs of some former sea. Climbing down, I came to the dark waters, and began to lave my hands; but there was a sharp and corrosive sting in that immemorial brine, and I desisted quickly, preferring the desert dust that had wrapped about me like a slow shroud.

Here I decided to rest for a little; and hunger forced me to consume part of the meager and mocking fare with which I had been provided by the priests. It was my intention to push on, if my strength would allow, and reach the lands that lie to the north of Yondo. These lands are desolate, indeed, but their desolation is of a more usual order than that of Yondo; and certain tribes of nomads have been known to visit them occasionally. If fortune favored me, I might fall in with one of these tribes.

The scant fare revived me, and, for the first time in weeks of which I had lost all reckoning, I heard the whisper of a faint hope. The corpse-colored insects had long since ceased to follow me; and so far, despite the eeriness of the sepulchral silence and the mounded dust of timeless ruin, I had met nothing half so horrible as those insects. I began to think that the terrors of Yondo were somewhat exaggerated.

It was then that I heard a diabolic chuckle on the hillside above me. The sound began with a sharp abruptness that startled me beyond all reason, and continued endlessly, never varying its single note, like the mirth of some idiotic demon. I looked up, and saw the mouth of a dark cave, fanged with green stalactites, which I had not perceived before. The sound appeared to come from within this cave.

With a fearful intentness, I stared at the black opening. The chuckle grew louder, but for a while I could see nothing. At last I caught a whitish glimmer in the darkness; then, with all the rapidity of nightmare, a monstrous Thing emerged. It had a pale, hairless, egg-shaped body, large as that of a gravid she-goat; and this body was mounted on nine long, wavering legs with many flanges, like the legs of some enormous spider. The creature ran past me to the water's edge; and I saw that there were no eyes in its oddly sloping face; but two knife-like ears rose high above its head, and a thin, wrinkled snout hung down across its mouth, whose flabby lips, parted in that eternal chuckle, revealed rows of bats' teeth.

It drank avidly of the bitter lake; then, with thirst satisfied, it turned and seemed to sense my presence, for the wrinkled snout rose and pointed toward me, sniffing audibly. Whether the creature would have fled, or whether it meant to assail me, I do not know; for I could bear the sight no longer, but ran with trembling limbs amid the massive boulders and great bars of salt along the lake-shore.

Utterly breathless, I stopped at last, and saw that I was not pursued. I sat down, still trembling, in the shadow of a boulder, but I was to find little respite, for now began the second of those bizarre adventures which forced me to believe all the mad legends I had heard.

More startling even than that diabolic chuckle, was the scream that rose at my very elbow, from the salt-compounded sand—the scream of a woman possessed by some atrocious agony, or helpless in the grip of devils. Turning, I beheld a veritable Venus, naked in a white perfection that could fear no scrutiny, but immersed to her navel in the sand. Her terror-widened eyes implored me, and her lotus hands reached out with beseeching gesture. I sprang to her side—and touched a marble statue, whose carven lids were drooped in some enigmatic dream of dead cycles, and whose hands were buried with the lost loveliness of hips and thighs. Again I fled, shaken with a new fear; and again I heard the scream of a woman's agony. But I did not turn once more to see the imploring eyes and hands.

Up the long slope to the north of that accursed lake, stumbling over boulders of basanite, and ledges that were sharp with verdigris-covered metals; floundering in pits of salt or innominable ashes, on terraces wrought by the receding tide in ancient aeons, I fled as a man flees from dream to baleful dream of some cacodemoniacal night. At whiles there was a cold whisper in my ear, which did not come from the wind of my flight; and looking back as I reached one of the upper terraces, I perceived a singular shadow that ran pace by pace with my own. This shadow was not the shadow of man, nor ape, nor any known beast: the head was too grotesquely elongated, the squat body too gibbous; and I was unable to determine whether the shadow possessed five legs, or whether what appeared to be the fifth was merely a tail.

Terror lent me new strength, and I had reached the hill-top when I dared to look back again. But still the fantastic shadow kept pace by pace with mine; and now I caught a curious and utterly sickening odor, foul as the odor of bats who have hung in a charnel-house amid the mould of corruption. I ran for leagues, while the red sun slanted above the asteroidal mountains to the west; and the weird shadow lengthened with mine but kept always at the same distance behind me.

An hour before sunset, I came to a circle of small pillars that rose miraculously unbroken amid ruins that were like a vast pile of potsherds. As I passed among these pillars, I heard a whimper, like the whimper of some fierce animal, between rage and fear, and saw that the shadow had not followed me within the circle. I stopped and waited, conjecturing at once that I had found a sanctuary my unwelcome familiar would not dare to enter; and in this the action of the shadow confirmed me, the Thing hesitated, then ran about the circle of columns, pausing often between them; and, whimpering all the while, at last went away and disappeared in the desert toward the setting sun.

For a full half hour, I did not dare to move; then, the imminence of night, with all its probabilities of fresh terror, urged me to push on as far as I could to the north. For I was now in the very heart of Yondo where demons or phantoms might dwell who would not respect the sanctuary of the unbroken columns.

Now, as I toiled on, the sunlight altered strangely; for the red orb, nearing the mounded horizon, sank and smouldered in a belt of miasmal haze, where floating dust from all the shattered fanes and necropoli of Yondo was mixed with evil vapors coiling skyward from black enormous gulfs lying beyond the utmost rim of the world. In that light, the entire waste, the rounded mountains, the serpentine hills, the lost cities, were drenched with phantasmal and darkening scarlet.

Then, out of the north, where shadows mustered, there came a curious figure—a tall man, fully caparisoned in chain-mail—or, rather, what I assumed to be a man. As the figure approached me, clanking dismally at each step on the sharded ground, I saw that its armor was of brass mottled with verdigris; and a casque of the same metal, furnished with coiling horns and a serrate comb, rose high above its head. I say its head, for the sunset was darkening, and I could not see clearly at any distance; but when the apparition came abreast, I perceived that there was no face beneath the brows of that bizarre helmet, whose empty edges were outlined for a moment against the smouldering light. Then the figure passed on, still clanking dismally, and vanished.

But on its heels, ere the sunset faded, there came a second apparition, striding with incredible strides, and halting when it loomed almost upon me in the red twilight—the monstrous mummy of some ancient king, still crowned with untarnished gold, but turning to my gaze a visage that more than time or the worm had wasted. Broken swathings flapped about the skeleton legs, and above the crown that was set with sapphires and balas-rubies, a black Something swayed and nodded horribly; but, for an instant, I did not dream what it was. Then, in its middle, two oblique and scarlet eyes opened and glowed like hellish coals, and two ophidian fangs glittered in an ape-like mouth. A squat, furless, shapeless head on a neck of disproportionate extent leaned unspeakably down and whispered in the mummy's ear. Then, with one stride, the titanic lich took half the distance between us, and from out the folds of the tattered sere-cloth a gaunt arm arose, and fleshless, taloned fingers laden with glowering gems, reached out and fumbled for my throat. . . .

Back, back through aeons of madness and dread, in a prone, precipitate flight I ran from those fumbling fingers that hung always on the dusk behind me, back, back forever, unthinking, unhesitating, to all the abominations I had left; back in the thickening twilight toward the nameless and sharded ruins, the haunted lake, the forest of evil cacti, and the cruel and cynical inquisitors of Ong who waited my return.

THE ABOMINATION OF DESOLATION

The desert of Soom is said to lie at the world's unchartable extreme, between the lands that are little known and those that are scarcely even conjectured. It is dreaded by travellers, for its bare and ever-moving sands are without oases, and a strange horror is rumored to dwell among them. Of this horror many tales are told, and nearly all of the tales are different. Some say that the thing has neither visible form nor audible voice, and others that it is a dire chimera with multitudinous heads, horns and tails, and a tongue whose sound is like the tolling of bells in deep funereal vaults. Of the caravans and solitary wanderers who have ventured into Soom, none has returned without a story to tell; and some have never returned at all, or have come back with brains devoured to madness by the terror and vertigo and delirium of infinite empty space . . . Yes, there are many tales, of a thing that follows furtively or with the pandemonium of a thousand devils; of a thing that lurks and lies in wait behind the shifting dunes; of a thing that roars or whispers balefully from the sand or from the wind, or stirs unseen in the coiling silence, or falls from the air like a crushing incubus, or yawns like a sudden pit before the feet of the traveller.

But once on a time there were two lovers who came to the desert of Soom, and who had occasion to cross the sterile sands. They knew not the evil rumor of the place; and, since they had found an abiding Eden in each other's eyes, it is perhaps doubtful if they even knew that they were passing through a desert. And they alone, of all who have dared this fearsome desolation, have had no tale to relate of any troublous thing, of any horror that followed or lurked before them, either seen or unseen, inaudible or heard; and for them there was no multi-headed chimera, no yawning pit or incubus. And never, never could they comprehend the stories that were told by less fortunate wayfarers.

THE VENUS OF AZOMBEII

The statuette was not more than twelve inches in height, and represented a female figure that somehow reminded me of the Medicean Venus, despite many differences of feature and proportion. It was wrought of a black wood, almost as heavy as marble; and the unknown artist had certainly made the most of his material to suggest the admixture of a negroid strain with a type of beauty well-nigh classic in its perfection of line. It stood on a pedestal formed in imitation of a half-moon, with the cloven side of the hemisphere constituting the base. On studying it more closely, I found that the resemblance to the Venus de Medici was largely in the pose and in the curves of the hips and shoulders; but the right hand was more elevated than hers in its position, and seemed to caress the polished abdomen; and the face was fuller, with a smile of enigmatic voluptuousness about the heavy lips, and a sensuous droop to the deep eyelids, which were like the petals of some exotic flower when they fold beneath a sultry velvet evening. The workmanship was quite amazing, and would not have been unworthy of the more archaic and primitive periods of Roman art.

My friend Marsden had brought the figurine with him on his return from Africa; and it stood always on his library table. It had fascinated me and had stirred my curiosity from the first; but Marsden was singularly reticent concerning it; and beyond telling me that it was of negro workmanship and represented the goddess of a little-known tribe on the upper Benuwe, in Adamawa, he had so far declined to gratify my inquisitiveness. But his very reserve, and something of significant import, even of emotional perturbation in his tone whenever we spoke of the statuette, had made me believe that a story hung thereon; and, knowing

Marsden as I did, remembering his habitual reticence recurrently varied by outbursts of a well-nigh garrulous confidentiality, I felt sure that he would tell me the story in due time.

I had known Marsden ever since our school-days, for we had both been in the same year at Berkeley. He possessed few friends, and none, perhaps, who had been intimate with him as long as I. So no one was better fitted than I to perceive the inexplicable change that had come over him since his two years of traveling in Africa. This change was both physical and spiritual, and some of its features were of so subtle a character that one could hardly give them a name or seize upon them with any degree of clearness. Others, though, were all too plainly marked: the increase of Marsden's natural melancholia, turning now into fits of ferocious depression; and the woeful deterioration in his health, never too robust even in its prime, would have been noticeable to the merest acquaintance. I remembered him as being very tall and wiry, with a sallow complexion, black hair, and eyes of a clear azure blue; but since his return, he was far thinner than of old, and he stooped so much that he gave the impression of having actually lost in height; his features were shrunken and wrinkled, his skin had become corpse-like in its pallor, his hair was heavily sprinkled with grey, and his eyes had darkened in an unaccountable manner, as if they had somehow absorbed the mysteriously profound and sinister blue of tropic nights. In them, there burned a fire that they had never before possessed—a macabre fire such as one would find in the eyes of a man consumed by some equatorial fever. Indeed, it often occurred to me that the readiest explanation of the change in Marsden was that he had been seized by some lethal sickness of the jungle, from which he had not yet fully recovered. But this he had always denied when I questioned him.

The more elusive alterations at which I have hinted were mainly mental, and I shall not try to define all of them. But one, in particular, was quite signal: Marsden had always been a man of undoubted courage and hardihood, with nerves that were unshakable in spite of his melancholic disposition; but now I perceived in him at times a queer furtiveness, an undefinable apprehensiveness quite at variance with his former character. Even in the midst of some trivial or commonplace conversation, a look of manifest fear would suddenly pass over his face, he would scrutinize the shadows of the room with an apprehensive stare, and would stop half-way in a sentence, apparently forgetting what he had started to say. Then, in a few moments, he would recover himself and go on with the interrupted speech. He had developed some odd mannerisms, too: one of them was that he could never enter or leave a room without looking behind him, with the air of a man who fears that he is being followed or that some imminent doom is dogging his every footstep. But all this, of course, could have been explained as nervousness attendant upon, or resulting from, the illness that I suspected. Marsden himself would never discuss the matter; so after a few discreet suggestions that might have led him to unbosom himself, if he so wished, I had tacitly ignored the visible changes in his manner and personality. But I sensed a real and perhaps tragic mystery, and felt also that the black figurine on Marsden's table was in some way connected with it. He had told me much concerning his trip to Africa, which had been undertaken because of a life-long fascination which that continent had held for him; but I knew intuitively that much more was being kept back.

One morning, about six weeks after Marsden's return, I called to see him, following several days of absence during which I had been extremely busy. He was living alone, with one servant, in the large house on Russian Hill, San Francisco, which he had inherited together with a considerable fortune from his parents, who were long dead. He did not come to answer my knock, as was his wont; and if my hearing were not exceptionally keen, I do not think I should have heard the feeble voice in which he called out, telling me to enter. Pushing open the door, I went through the hall into the library, from which his voice had issued, and found him lying on a sofa, near the table on which stood the black statuette. It was obvious to me at a glance that he was very ill; his thinness and pallor had increased to a shocking degree in the few days since I had seen him last, and I was immediately impressed by the singular fact that he had even shrunken more in stature than could be explained by the crouch of his shoulders. Everything about him had shriveled, and had actually withered as if a flame were consuming him, and the form on the couch was that of a smaller man than my friend. He had aged, also, and his hair had taken on a new hoariness, as if white ashes had fallen upon it. His eyes were pitifully sunken, and they burned as embers burn in deep caverns. I could scarcely repress a cry of astonishment and consternation when I saw him.

"Well, Holly," he greeted me, "I guess my days are numbered. I knew the thing would get me in time—I knew it when I left the shores of the Benuwe with that image of the goddess Wanaôs for a keepsake. . . . There are dreadful things in Africa, Holly . . . malignant lust, and corruption, and poison, and sorcery . . . things that are deadlier than death itself—at least, deadlier than death in any form that we know. Don't ever go there . . . if you have any care for the safety of body and soul."

I tried to reassure him, without paying ostensible heed to the more cryptic references, the more oracular hints in his utterance.

"There is some low African fever in your system," I said. "You should see a doctor—should, in fact, have seen one weeks or months ago. There's no reason why you shouldn't get rid of the trouble, whatever it is, now that you are back in America. But of course you need expert medical attention: you can't afford to neglect anything so insidious and obscure."

Marsden smiled—if the ghastly contortion of his lips could be called a smile. "It's no use, old man. I know my malady better than any doctor could know it. Of course, it may be that I have a little fever—that wouldn't be surprising; but the fever isn't one that has ever been classified in medical lore. And there's no cure for it in any pharmacopoeia."

With the last word, his countenance assumed a horrible grimace of pain, and seemed to shrivel before me like a sheet of paper that turns ashen with fire. He no longer appeared to notice my presence, and began to mutter brokenly, in tones of a peculiar huskiness, in a harsh, grating whisper, as if the very cords of his throat were involved in the same shrinking that affected his face. I caught most, if not all, of the words:

"She is dying, too... as I am... even though she is a living goddess. ... Mybaloë, why did you drink the palm-wine? ... You, too, will shrivel up, and suffer these gnawing, clawing tortures ... Your beautiful body ... how perfect, how magnificent it was! ... You will shrivel up in a few weeks, like a little old woman ... you will suffer the torments of hell-fire ... Mybaloë! Mybaloë!" ... His speech became an indistinct moaning, in which portions of words were now and then audible. He had all the aspect of a dying man: his whole body seemed to contract, as if all the muscles, all the nerves, even the very bones, were dwindling in size, were tightening to a locked rigidity; and his lips were drawn in a horrible rictus, showing a thin white line of teeth.

I ran to Marsden's dining-room, where I knew that a decanter full of old Scotch usually stood on the sideboard, and filled a sherry-glass with the liquor. Hastening back, I succeeded, though with extreme difficulty, in forcing some of the strong spirit between his teeth. The effect was almost immediate: he revived into full consciousness, his facial muscles relaxed, and he no longer wore the look of tetanic agony that had possessed his whole body.

"I'm sorry to have been such a bother," he said. "But the crisis is past for today ... Tomorrow, though ... that'll be another matter." He shuddered, and his eyes were dark with the haunting of some incombatable horror.

I made him drink the remainder of the whisky, and going to the telephone, took the liberty of summoning a doctor whose abilities were personally known to both of us. My friend smiled a little, in grateful recognition of my solicitude, but shook his head.

"The end won't be so very far off now," he said. "I know the symptoms; it's a matter of a fortnight, or little more, when matters reach the point that they have reached today."

"But what is it?" I cried. The query was prompted by horror and solicitude, more than curiosity.

"You will learn soon enough," he replied, pointing to the library table with a forefinger of skeleton thinness. "Do you see that manuscript?"

Following his direction, I perceived on the table, close to the wooden statuette, a pile of written sheets, which, in my natural concern regarding Marsden's illness, I had not before noticed.

"You are my oldest friend," he went on, "and I have been aware for quite a while past that I owe you an explanation of certain things that have puzzled you. But the matters involved are so strange, and so peculiarly intimate, that I have been unable to bring myself to a frank confession face to face. So I have written for you a full narration of the final two months of my stay in Africa, concerning which I have spoken so little heretofore. You are to take it home with you when you leave; but I must beg you not to read the manuscript till after my death. I am sure I can trust you to respect my wishes in this regard. When you read it, you will learn the cause of my illness, and the story of the black figurine which has tantalized your curiosity so much."

A few minutes later, there came a knock on the door, and I went to answer it. As I expected, it was Dr. Pelton, who lived only a few blocks away, and who had left home immediately in reply to my summons. He was a brisk and confident type of person, with the air of habitual reassurance, of professional good cheer, that goes so far in building up a doctor's reputation for proficiency. But I could see beneath his manner an undertone of doubt, of real bafflement, as he examined Marsden.

"I'm not altogether sure what is wrong," he admitted, "but I think the trouble is mainly digestive and nervous. Doubtless the African climate, and the food, must have upset you quite radically. You will need a nurse, if there is any recurrence of the attack you have had today." He wrote a prescription, and left shortly after. Since I had a pressing engagement, I was obliged to follow him in about half an hour, taking with me the manuscript that Marsden had indicated. But before going I called a nurse by telephone, with Marsden's authority, and left her in charge, promising to return as soon as possible.

Of the fortnight that followed, with the frightful protracted agonies, the brief and illusory shifts for the better, the ghastly relapses that characterized my friend's condition, I cannot bear to write a full account. I spent with him all the time I could spare, for my presence seemed to comfort him a little, except during the awful daily crises, when he was beyond all consciousness of his surroundings. Toward the last, there were lengthening intervals of delirium, when he muttered wildly, or screamed aloud in terror of things or persons visible only to himself. To be with him, to watch him, was an ordeal without parallel; and to me, the most dreadful thing about it all was the progressive shriveling, the perpetual diminution of Marsden's head and body, and the lessening of his very stature, which went on hour by hour and day by day with paroxysmal accompaniments of a suffering not to be borne by human flesh without lapsing into madness or oblivion… But I cannot enter into details, or describe the final stages; and I hardly dare even hint the condition in which he died and in which his body went to the undertaker. I can only say that in their extreme, their more than infantile dwarfage and devolution of form, the remains bore no likeness to anything that it would be permissible to name; also, that the task of the undertaker and the pall-bearers was phenomenally light . . . When the end came, I gave thanks to God for the belated mercy of my friend's death. I was completely worn out, and it was not until after the funeral that I summoned enough energy and resolution for a perusal of Marsden's manuscript.

The account was clearly written, in a fine, feline script, though the handwriting bore evidence of stress and agitation toward the end. I tran-

scribe the narrative hereunder, with no liberties of abridgment or ampli-
fication:

I, Julius Marsden, have experienced all my life the ineffable nostalgia
of the far-off and the unknown. I have loved the very names of remote
places, of antipodean seas and continents and isles. But I have never
found in any other word even a tithe of the untellable charm that has
lain inherent for me ever since childhood in the three syllables of the
word *Africa*. They have conjured up for me, as by some necromantic
spell, the very quintessence of all mystery, of all romance, and no
woman's name could have been dearer to me, or more eloquent of delight and allure, than the name of this obscure continent. By a happy
dispensation, which, alas! does not invariably attend the fulfillment of
our dreams, my twenty-two months of sojourning in Morocco, Tunis,
Egypt, Zanzibar, Senegal, Dahomey and Nigeria had in no way disappointed me, for the reality was astoundingly like my vision. In the hot
and heavy azure of the skies, the great levels of desert sand or of ram-
pant jungles, the long and mighty rivers winding through landscapes of
unbelievable diversity, I found something that was deeply congenial to
my spirit. It was a realm in which my rarest dreams could dwell and
expand with a sense of freedom never achievable elsewhere.

At the end of the twenty-second month of my sojourn, I was travelling on the upper reaches of the river Benuwe, that great eastern tributary of the Niger. My immediate objective was Lake Tchad, with whose
confluent rivers the Benuwe is connected by means of an upland
swamp. I had left Yollah, with several boatmen of the Foulah tribe, a
race of negroid Mohammedans, and we had now rounded the eastern
slope of Mount Alantika, that enormous granite bulk that looms for nine
thousand feet from the fertile plains of Adamawa.

It was a picturesque and beautiful country through which we were
passing. There were occasional villages surrounded by fields of durrah,
of cotton and yams, and great stretches of wild, luxuriant forest, of baobabs, bananas, deleb-palms, and pandanus, beyond which arose the

castellated tops of ridgy hills and fantastically-carven cliffs.

Toward sunset, Alantika had become a bluish blur in the distance, above the green sea of the jungle. As we went onward in our two small barges, one of which was mainly laden with my personal effects, I perceived that my boatmen were conversing among themselves in low voices, and caught a frequent repetition of the word "Azombeii," always with a note of fear and warning.

I had already picked up a little of the Foulah language; and one of the boatmen, a tall, well-featured fellow, bronze rather than black, was master of a sort of broken German variegated with a few words of English. I questioned him as to the subject and import of the conversation, and learned that Azombeii was the name of the district we were now approaching, which, he declared, was peopled by a pagan tribe of unusual ferocity, who were still suspected of cannibalism and human sacrifice. They had never been properly subdued, either by the Mohammedan conquerors of the country or by the present

German administration, and lived very much to themselves in their own primeval way, worshipping a goddess named Wanaôs—a goddess unfamiliar even to the other pagan tribes of Adamawa, who were all fetishists. They were especially inimical toward the Mohammedan negroes, and it was perilous to intrude upon their territory, particularly during the annual religious festival now being celebrated. He and his fellows, he confessed, were loath to proceed much further.

On all this, at the time, I made no express comment. To me, the story seemed none too credible, and savored of the ignorant prejudices of insular peoples, who are ever suspicious and fearful of those beyond their own borders. But I was a little disturbed, for I did not want the course of my journey to be suspended by any difficulty with my boatmen or the natives.

The sun had now gone down with a tropical abruptness, and in the brief twilight I saw that the forest on the river-banks had become more dense and exuberant than any through which we had before passed.

There were ancient baobabs, enormous in the gloom; and the pendant leaves of mammoth plants fell down to the river like cataracts of emerald. Over all, a primordial silence reigned—a silence fraught with the burden of things unutterable by human speech—with the furtive pulse of an esoteric and exotic life, the secret breathing of unformulable passion, of unapprehended peril, the spirit of a vast and insuppressible fecundity.

We landed on a grassy margin, and proceeded to make our camp for the night. After a meal of yams and ground-nuts and tinned meat, to which I added a little palm-wine, I brought up the matter of continuing our journey on the morrow; but not until I had pledged myself to triple the boatmen's wages, would they promise to take me through the Azombeii country. I was more than ever inclined to make light of their fears, and, in fact, had begun to suspect that the whole business was mere play-acting, with no other purpose than the extortion of an increase of pay. But this, of course, I could not prove; and the boatmen were full of an apparent reluctance, vowing by Allah and his prophet Mohammed that the danger they would incur was incomparably dire— that they, and even myself, might furnish soup-meat for the revels of Azombeii, or smoke on a pagan altar, before the setting of tomorrow's sun. They also told me some curious details concerning the customs and beliefs of the people of Azombeii. These people, they said, were ruled by a woman who was looked upon as the living representative of the goddess Wanaôs, and who shared the divine honors accorded to her. Wanaôs, as far as I could gather, appeared to be a goddess of love and procreation, resembling somewhat in her character both the Roman Venus and the Carthaginian Tanit. I was struck even then by a certain etymological similarity of her name to that of Venus—a similarity regarding which I was soon to learn more. She was worshipped, they told me, with rites and ceremonies of an orgiastic license beyond all parallel—a license which shocked even the neighboring pagans, who were themselves given to vile practices not to be tolerated by any virtuous Moslem. They went on to say that the Azombeiians were also addicted to sorcery, and that their witch-doctors were feared throughout Adamawa.

My curiosity was aroused, though I told myself that in all probability the rumors related by the boatmen were fables or gross exaggerations. But I had seen something of negro religious rites, and was able to credit the tales of orgiastic excess, at any rate. Pondering the strange stories I had heard, my imagination became excited, and I did not fall asleep till after an unwonted interval.

My slumber was heavy, and full of troubled dreams that appeared to prolong intolerably the duration of the night. I awoke a little before dawn, when the red horn of a waning moon had begun to set behind the serrate edges of palm-trees in the west. Looking about in the half-light, with eyes that were still bemused with sleep, I found myself entirely alone: The boatmen and their barges were gone, though all of my personal property and some of the provisions had been left behind with an honesty quite scrupulous, considering the circumstances. Evidently the fears expressed by the Foulahs had been genuine, and discretion had overpowered their desire for gain.

Somewhat dismayed by the prospect of having to continue my journey alone—if it were to be continued at all—and without means of navigation or conveyance, I stood irresolute on the river-bank, as the dawn began to brighten. I did not like the idea of turning back; and, since I did not consider it at all probable that I could be in any bodily danger at the hands of the natives, in a region under German rule, I finally resolved to go on and try to engage bearers or boatmen in the Azombeii district. It would be necessary for me to leave most of my effects by the river for the present, and return for them later, trusting to find them undisturbed.

I had no sooner made up my mind to this course of procedure, when I heard a soft rustling in the long grasses behind me. Turning, I perceived that I was no longer alone, though my companions were not the missing Foulahs, as I had hoped for a brief instant. Two negro women, attired in little more than the lightening amber air of morn, stood close beside me. Both were fairly tall, and well-proportioned, but it was the foremost of the two who caught my attention with a veritable shock of surprise not altogether due to the suddenness of her approach.

Her appearance would have surprised me anywhere, at any time. Her skin was a lustrous velvet black, with subtle gleams of rapid-running bronze; but all her features and proportions, by some astounding anomaly, were those of an antique Venus. Indeed, I have seldom seen in Caucasian women a more consummate regularity of profile and facial contour. As she stood before me without moving, she might have been a woman of Rome or Pompeii, sculptured in black marble by a statuary of the Latin decadence. She wore a look that was both demure and sensual, an expression full of cryptic poise allied with great sweetness. Her hair was done in a rich coil on the nape of a comely neck. Between her breasts, on a chain of beaten silver, hung several ruddy garnets, carven with rough intaglios whose precise nature I did not notice at the time. Her eyes met mine with perfect frankness, and she smiled with an air of naive delight and mischief at my all-too-obvious dumbfoundment. That smile made me her voluntary captive henceforward.

The second woman was of a more negroid type, though personable enough in her way. By her bearing and demeanor, she gave the impression of being somehow subordinate to the first, and I assumed that she was a slave or servant. The one semblance of a garment worn by both was a little square of cloth depending in front from a girdle of palm-fibre; but the fabric of the square worn by the first was finer than that of the other, and differed from it in having a fringe of silky tassels.

The leader turned and spoke a few words to her companion in mellifluous liquid tones, and the servant replied in a voice almost equally soft and musical. The word *"Aroumani"* was repeated several times, with accompanying glances at me, and I readily surmised that I was the theme of their conversation. I could not understand their speech, which bore no likeness to the Foulah language, and, indeed, was different from that of any pagan tribe I had so far encountered in Adamawa. But some of the vocables teased me with a vague sense of familiarity, though I could not define or align this familiarity at the moment.

I addressed the two women in the scant Foulah that I knew, asking if they were of the Azombeii tribe. They smiled, and nodded their heads in recognition of the word, and made signs to me that I was to follow them.

The sun had now leapt above the horizon, and the forest was filled with a green and golden radiance as the women led me away from the river-shore and along a meandering path among gigantic baobabs. They walked before me with a grave and effortless grace, and the leader looked back every now and then over her shapely shoulder, smiling with a complaisant curve of the full lips and a delicious droop of the carven lids that had in them a trace of simple coquetry. I followed, half overcome by emotions that were new to me—by the first pulsations of a mounting fever of the senses and the mind, the stirring of unfamiliar curiosities, the subtle languor, the poppy-drowsy delight of a Circean enchantment. I felt as if the immemorial attraction of Africa had suddenly become embodied for me in a human shape.

The forest began to thin, and we came to cultivated fields, and then to a large village of clay huts. My sable guides pointed to the village, saying the one word: "Azombeii," which, as I learned later, was the name of the principal town as well as of the district in general.

The place was astir with negroes, many of whom, both male and female, were possessed of a clear-cut type of feature unaccountably reminiscent of the classical, and similar to that of the two women. Their skins varied from darkest ebony to a sultry, tarnished copper. Many of them crowded around us immediately, regarding me with a sort of friendly inquisitiveness, and making signs of obeisance and reverence before my Venus-like companion. It was clear that she occupied a place of high importance among them, and I wondered, not for the first time, if she were the woman of whom the Foulahs had spoken—the ruler of the Azombeii and the living viceregent of the goddess Wanaôs.

I tried to converse with the natives, but could not make myself understood till an old man with a bald head and a straggling fringe of grey beard came forward and hailed me in broken English. He, it seemed, had traveled as far afield as Nigeria during his youth, which accounted for his linguistic accomplishments. None of the others had ever been more than a few miles beyond the confines of his own territory; and apparently the tribe had little intercourse with outsiders, either negro or Caucasian.

The old man was most affable and loquacious, evidently delighting in an opportunity to air his command of a foreign tongue. It was hardly necessary to question him, for he began at once to volunteer the information which I desired. His people, he announced, were very glad to see me, for they were friendly toward the whites, though they had no manner of use for the Moslem negroes of Adamawa. Also, he went on, it was manifest that I had won the favor and protection of the goddess Wanaôs, since I appeared among them under the guidance of Mybaloë, their beloved ruler, in whom the spirit of the goddess resided. At this, he made an humble obeisance toward my lovely guide, who smiled, and addressed a few sentences to him, which he forthwith interpreted, saying that Mybaloë had proffered me an invitation to remain in Azombeii as her guest.

I had intended to broach immediately the matter of hiring bearers, or engaging boatmen for the continuance of my journey on the Benuwe; but at this invitation, and the sweet, wistful, almost supplicating look which Mybaloë directed upon me as her words were being translated, I forgot all about my plans, and told the interpreter to thank Mybaloë and say that I accepted the invitation. A few hours earlier, I should not have dreamt of the possibility of feeling any specific interest in a black woman, since that aspect of the charm of Africa was one which had never really touched me heretofore. But now, the first weavings of an unforeseen magic were upon me: my senses had become preternaturally active, and my normal processes of thought were benumbed as by the working of some insidious opiate. I had been eager to reach Lake Tchad, and the idea of tarrying by the way had never before occurred to me: now, it seemed the most natural thing in the world to remain in Azombeii, and Lake Tchad became a dimly receding mirage, far off on the borders of oblivion.

Mybaloë's face grew radiant as a summer morn, when my acceptance was interpreted. She spoke to some of the people about her, obviously giving them instructions. Then she disappeared among the crowd, and the old interpreter, with several others, led me to a hut which they put at my disposal. The hut was quite clean, and the floors were strewn with strips of palm-leaf, which exhaled an agreeable odor. Food and wine were set before me and the old man and two girls remained in attendance, saying that they had been appointed as my servants. I had barely finished my meal, when some more natives entered, bearing the belongings I had left by the river-side.

Now, in reply to my queries, the interpreter, whose name was Nygaza, told me as much as his rudimentary English would convey regarding the history, habits and religion of the people of Azombeii. According to their traditions, the worship of Wanaôs among them was almost as old as the world itself, and had been introduced ages and ages ago by some white strangers from the north, who called themselves *Aroumani*. These strangers had settled and married among the natives, and their blood had gradually become disseminated throughout the whole tribe, who had always remained apart from the other pagans of Adamawa. All white people were called *Aroumani* by them, and were looked upon with peculiar respect, on account of these traditions. Wanaôs, as the Foulahs had said, was a deity of love and fecundation, the mother of all life, the mistress of the world, and her image had been accurately graven in wood by the pale strangers, so that the Azombeiians might have an exemplar for their idol. It had always been customary to associate a living woman with her worship, as a sort of avatar or embodiment of the goddess, and the most beautiful maiden of the district was chosen by the priests and priestesses for this role, and filled also the office of queen, with the privilege of taking to herself a male consort. Mybaloë, a girl of eighteen, had recently been elected; and the annual festival of Wanaôs, which consisted of liberal drinking and feasting, together with nightly ceremonies of worship, was now in progress.

While I listened to the old man, I indulged in certain speculations of a surprising order. I deemed it not impossible that the pale strangers of whom he spoke had been a party of Roman explorers, who had crossed the Sahara from Carthage and penetrated the Soudan. This would account for the classic features of Mybaloë and others of the Azombeiians, and for the name and character of the local goddess. Also, the vague familiarity of some of the words spoken by Mybaloë was now explicable, since I realized that these words had borne a partial resemblance to Latin vocables. Much amazed by what I had learned and by all that I had succeeded in piecing together, I lost myself in odd reveries, while Nygaza continued his babbling.

The day wore on, and I did not see Mybaloë, as I had fully expected, nor did I receive word from her. I began to wonder a little. Nygaza said that her absence was attributable only to urgent duties; he leered discreetly, as he assured me that I would soon see her again.

I went for a walk through the village, accompanied by the interpreter and the girls, who refused to leave me for a moment. The town, as I have said, was large for an African village, and must have comprised two or three thousand people. All was neat and orderly, and the general degree of cleanliness was quite remarkable. The Azombeiians, I could see, were thrifty and industrious, and gave evidence of many civilized qualities.

Toward the hour of sunset, a messenger came, bearing an invitation from Mybaloë, which Nygaza translated. I was to dine with her in her palace, and then attend the evening rites in the local temple.

The palace stood on the very outskirts of the town, among palms and pandanus, and was merely an overgrown hut, as African palaces are wont to be. But the interior proved to be quite comfortable, even luxurious, and a certain barbaric taste had been displayed in its furnishing. There were low couches along the walls, covered with draperies of native weaving, or the skins of the *ayu*, a sort of fresh-water seal found in the Benuwe. In the center was a long table, not more than a foot in height from the floor, around which the guests were squatted. In one corner, as in a niche, I noticed a small wooden image of a female figure, which I rightly took to be a representation of Wanaôs. The figure bore a strange resemblance to the Roman Venus; but I need not describe it further, since you have often seen it on my library table.

Mybaloë greeted me with many compliments, which were duly translated by Nygaza; and I, not to be outdone, replied with speeches of a flowery fervor by no means insincere. My hostess had me seated at her right hand, and the feast began. The guests, I learned, were mostly priests and priestesses of Wanaôs. All of them regarded me with friendly smiles, with the exception of one man, who wore a murderous frown. This man, Nygaza told me in a whisper almost inaudible, was the high-priest Mergawe, a mighty sorcerer or witch-doctor, much feared rather than revered, who had long been in love with Mybaloë and had hoped to be chosen for her consort.

As unobtrusively as I could, I surveyed Mergawe with more attention. He was a muscular brute, over six feet in height, and broad without being stout. His face was regular in outline, and would have been handsome, were it not for the distortion due to a most malignant expression. Whenever Mybaloë smiled upon me or addressed some remark to me through Nygaza, his look became a demoniacal glare. I readily perceived that the first day of my visit in Azombeii had brought me a powerful enemy, as well as a possible sweetheart.

The table was laden with equatorial delicacies, with the meat of young rhinoceros, several kinds of wild fowl, bananas, papayas, and a sweet, highly-intoxicating palm-wine. Most of the guests were prone to gorge themselves in true African fashion, but Mybaloë's manner of eating was as dainty as that of any European girl, and she endeared herself to me all the more by her restraint. Mergawe also ate little, but drank immoderately, in a seeming attempt to achieve inebriation as rapidly as possible. The eating and drinking went on for hours, but I paid less and less attention to it and to my fellow-guests, in the ever-growing enchantment of Mybaloë's presence. Her sinuous youthful grace of figure, her lovely tender eyes and lips, were far more potent than the wine, and soon I forgot to notice even the baleful glaring of Mergawe. On her part, Mybaloë displayed toward me a frank favor, swiftly conceived and avowed, which she did not even dream of disguising. She and I had begun to speak a language which did not require the interpretation of old Nygaza. With the one exception of Mergawe, no one seemed to regard our mutual infatuation with anything but approval.

Presently the time of the evening rites approached, and Mybaloë excused herself, telling me that she would meet me later in the temple. The gathering broke up, and Nygaza led me through the nocturnal village, where groups of people were feasting and revelling about their fires in the open air. We entered the jungle, which was full of voices and flitting shadowy forms, all on their way to the fane of Wanaôs. I had no idea what the temple would be like, though somehow I did not expect the usual African fetish-house. To my surprise, it proved to be an enormous cave in a hill back of the village. It was illumined by many torches, and had already become crowded with the worshippers. At the farther end of the huge chamber, whose lofty vault was dark with impenetrable shadow, there stood on a sort of natural dais an image of Wanaôs, carved in the customary black wood of a tree that is native to Azombeii. The image was somewhat more than life-size. Beside it, on a wooden seat that could easily have accommodated another person, sat Mybaloë, statuesque and immobile as the goddess herself. Fragrant leaves and grasses were burning on a low altar, and tom-toms were throbbing with delirious insistence, regular as the beating of turgid pulses, in the gloom behind the goddess and her mortal viceregent. The priests, priestesses and devotees were all naked, except for little squares of cloth similar to that worn by Mybaloë, and their bodies gleamed like polished metal in the wildly flickering light of the torches. All were chanting a solemn monotonous litany, and they swayed in the slow movements of a hieratic dance, lifting their arms toward Wanaôs, as if to invoke her favor.

There was an undeniable impressiveness about it all; and as if by contagion, a bizarre excitement began to invade me, and something of the sacred fervor felt by the devotees found its way into my own blood. With eyes intent upon Mybaloë, who seemed to be in a veritable trance, unconscious or unheedful of all about her, I felt the resurgence of atavistic impulses, of barbaric passions and superstitions latent in the subterranean depths of being. I knew the promptings of a savage hysteria, of a lust both animal and religious.

The old interpreter, who had disappeared in the throng, returned to my side anon, saying that Mybaloë had requested that I come forward to her seat. How the request had been communicated I can not imagine, for surely her lips had never opened or moved beneath my intent and passionate watching. The worshippers made way for me, and I stood before her, thrilling almost with a kind of awe, as well as a frenetic desire, when I met her eyes that were filled by the solemn possession of the amorous deity. She motioned me to seat myself beside her. By this act, as I learned later, she selected me before all the world as her consort, and I, by accepting the invitation, became her official lover.

Now, as if my enthronement with Mybaloë were a signal, the ceremonies took on a new excitation, with an orgiastic trend at which I can only hint. Things were done at which Tiberius would have blushed: Elephantis itself could have learned more than one secret from these savages. The cavern became a scene of indiscriminate revel, and the goddess and her representative were alike forgotten in the practice of rites that were doubtless appropriate enough, considering the nature of Wanaôs, even though they were highly improper from a civilized viewpoint. Through it all, Mybaloë maintained a perfect immobility, with open eyes whose lids were still as those of the statue. At last she arose and looked around the cavern upon her oblivious devotees with a gaze that was wholly inscrutable. Then she turned to me, with a demure smile and a slight movement of the hand, and beckoned me to follow her. Unnoticed by any one, we left the orgies and came forth upon the open jungle, where warm gusts of perfume wandered beneath the tropical stars....

From that night there began for me a new life—a life which I will not try to defend, but will only describe, as far as any description is possible. I had never before conceived of anything of the sort; I should never have believed myself capable of the sensuous fervor I felt for Mybaloë, and the almost inenarrable experiences into which her love initiated me. The dark electric vitality of the very earth upon which I trod, the humid warmth of the atmosphere, the life of the swiftly-grown luxuriant plants, all became an intimate part of my own entity, were mingled with the ebb and flow of my blood, and I drew nearer than ever before to the secret of the charm that had lured me across the world to that esoteric continent. A powerful fever exalted all my senses, a deep indolence bedrugged my brain. I lived, as never before, and never again, to the full capacity of my physical being. I knew, as an aborigine knows, the mystic impact of perfume and color and savor and tactual sensation. Through the flesh of Mybaloë, I touched the primal reality of the physical world. I had no longer any thoughts, or even dreams, in the abstract meaning of such terms, but existed wholly in relation to my surroundings, to the diurnal flux of light and darkness, of sleep and passion, and all sensory impressions.

Mybaloë, I am sure, was indeed lovable, and her charm, though highly voluptuous, was not altogether of the body. She had a fresh and naive nature, laughter loving and kindly, with less of actual or latent cruelty than is common to the African. And always I found in her, even apart from her form and features, a delightful suggestion of the elder pagan world, a hint of the classic woman and the goddess of old myths. Her sorcery, perhaps, was not really complex; but its power was complete, and lay as far beyond analysis as beyond denial. I became the ecstatic slave of a loving and indulgent queen.

The flowers of an equatorial spring were now in bloom, and our nights were opiate or aphrodisiac with their fragrance. The nocturnal heavens were full of fervid stars, the moons were balmy and propitious, and the people of Azombeii looked with favor upon our love, since the will of Mybaloë was to them the will of the goddess.

One cloud alone—a cloud which we scarcely regarded at first—was visible in our firmament. This cloud was the jealousy and ill-will of Mergawe, the high-priest of Wanaôs. He glowered with a lethal malignity, sullen as a negro Satan, whenever I happened to meet him; but his ill-will was not otherwise demonstrated, either by word or act; and Nygaza and Mybaloë both assured me that overt hostility on his part would be most improbable at any time, since because of Mybaloë's divine office and my position as her lover, anything of the sort would savor of actual blasphemy.

As for me, I felt an intuitive distrust of the sorcerer, though I was far too happy to expend much thought on the problem of his potential maleficence. However, the man was an interesting type, and his reputation was literally something with which to conjure. People believed that he knew the language of animals, and could even hold converse with trees and stones, which accorded him whatever information he might require. He was reputed to be a master of what is known as "bad fetish"—that is to say, he could lay an evil spell on the person or possessions of whosoever had incurred his enmity. He was a practitioner of invultuation, and was also said to know the secret of a terrible slow poison, which caused its victims to wither up and shrivel to the stature of a new-born child, with prolonged and hellish agonies—a poison which did not begin to operate for weeks or even months after the time of its consumption.

The days went by, and I lost all proper count of their passage, reckoning time only by the hours I spent with Mybaloë. The world and its fullness were ours—ours were the deep-blue heavens and the flowering forest and the grassy meadows by the river-side. As lovers are prone to do, we found for ourselves more than one favorite haunt, to which we liked to repair at recurrent intervals. One of these haunts was a grotto behind the cave-temple of Wanaôs, in whose center was a great pool fed by the river Benuwe through subterranean channels. At some remote time, the roof of the grotto had broken in, leaving a palm-fringed aperture in the hill-top, through which the sunlight or moonlight fell with precipitate rays upon the somber waters. Around the sides there were many broad ledges and fantastic alcoves of columnar stone. It was a place of weird beauty, and Mybaloë and I had spent more than one moon-lit hour on the couch-like shelves above the pool. The waters were inhabited by several crocodiles, but of these we took little heed, absorbed in each other and in the bizarre loveliness of the grotto, that always changed with the changing light.

One day, Mybaloë had been summoned away from the village on some errand whose nature I can not now remember. Doubtless it concerned some problem of justice or native politics. At any rate, she was not expected back till the following noon. Therefore, I was quite surprised when a messenger came to me at evening, with word that Mybaloë would return sooner than she had planned, and that she requested me to meet her in the grotto behind the cave of Wanaôs at the hour when the rays of the moon, now slightly gibbous, would first fall through the opening above. The native who brought the message was a man I had never seen before, but of this I thought nothing, since he purported to come from the outlying village to which Mybaloë had been called.

I reached the cavern at the hour appointed, and paused on the verge of one of the ledges, looking about in the uncertain light for Mybaloë. The moon had begun to pour a faëry radiance over the rough edge of the pit in the cavern-dome. I saw a stealthy movement in the waters beneath me, where a crocodile slid through the silver-gleaming ebony of the surface; but of Mybaloë herself I could find no visible sign anywhere. I wondered if she were not hiding from me in some prankish mood, and resolved to make a search of the alcoves and shelves on tip-toe, in order to surprise her.

I was about to leave the ledge on which I stood, when I received a violent push from behind, which precipitated me with a headlong suddenness into the black pool seven or eight feet below. The waters were deep, and I sank almost to the bottom before I recovered myself or even realized what had happened. Then I rose and struck out blindly for the shore, remembering with a thrill of terror the crocodile I had seen a moment before my fall. I reached the edge, where it shelved down with accessible gradations, but the water was still deep, and my fingers slipped on the smooth stone. Behind me, I heard a furtive rippling, and knew its causation all too well. Turning my head, I saw two of the great saurians, whose eyes burned with unholy phosphorescence in the moonlight as they glided toward me.

I think that I must have cried aloud; for, as if in answer, I heard a woman's voice cry out on the ledge above, and then the rippled waters were cleft by a falling form that shone for an instant with a flash as of black marble. A breathless interval, while the waters foamed, and then a well-known head arose beside me, and an arm that held aloft a glittering knife. It was Mybaloë herself. With miraculous adroitness, she drove the knife to its hilt in the side of the foremost crocodile, as the monster opened his formidable jaws to seize me. Her stroke had found the heart, and the crocodile slipped back beneath the surface, thrashing about in a brief agony. But its companion came on without pausing, and met the same unerring thrust of Mybaloë's knife. There were stirrings in the pool, and the dark bodies of others began to appear. With a superhuman agility, in what was seemingly no more than a single movement, Mybaloë drew herself out on the rocks of the margent, and caught my hands in hers. An instant more, and I stood beside her, hardly knowing how I had come there, so light and swift had been my ascent. The crocodiles were nosing the shore beneath us when I turned to look back.

Breathless and dripping, we sat on a moon-bright shelf of the cavern and began to question each other, with tender interludes of silence and caresses. In a few weeks, I had learned much of the Azombeiian tongue, and we no longer required an interpreter at any time.

To my astonishment, Mybaloë denied having sent me a messenger that evening. She had returned because of an overwhelming premonition of some imminent evil that menaced me, and had felt herself drawn irresistibly to the grotto, arriving just in time to find me floundering in the pool. While passing through the cave of Wanaôs, from which a low tunnel led to the open grotto, she had met a man in the darkness, and thought that it might have been Mergawe. He had passed without speaking, in as much haste as Mybaloë herself. I told her of the push I had received from behind as I stood on the ledge. It was all too evident that I had been lured to the cavern by some one who desired to make away with me; and, as far as we knew, Mergawe was the one person in Azombeii capable of conceiving or nurturing such a motive. Mybaloë became very grave, and little more was said between us regarding the matter.

After our return to the village, Mybaloë sent several men to search for Mergawe and bring him before her. But the sorcerer had disappeared, and no one could tell his whereabouts, though more than one person had seen him earlier in the evening. He did not return to his dwelling on the morrow; and though a sedulous and thorough quest was instituted throughout the whole of Azombeii, no trace of him could be found during the days following. His very disappearance, of course, was taken for an implicit confession of guilt. Supreme indignation was rife among the people when the episode in the grotto became publicly known; and in spite of the fear his reputation had evoked, Mergawe would have fared disastrously at their hands, and the sentence of death pronounced against him by Mybaloë would have been needless, if he had dared to show himself among his fellow-tribesmen.

The unexpected peril I had faced, and the marvellous rescue effected by Mybaloë, served to draw us even closer together, and our passion found a new depth and gravity henceforward. But as time went on, and nothing was heard of Mergawe, who seemed to have been literally swallowed up by the wide and sultry silence of the equatorial spaces, the episode began to recede, and gradually dwindled to our view in a lengthening perspective of blissful days. We ceased to apprehend any further attempt at harm on the part of the witch-doctor, and were lulled to an indolent security, in which our happiness took on the hues of its maturing summer.

One night, the priests of Wanaôs were giving a dinner in my honor. Forty or fifty people were already gathered in a banqueting-hall not far from the temple, but Mybaloë had not yet arrived. As we sat awaiting her, a man entered, bearing a large calabash full of palm-wine. The man was a stranger to me, though he was evidently known to some of the people present, who hailed him by name, calling him Marvasi.

Addressing me, Marvasi explained that he had been sent by the people of an outland community with a gift of palm-wine, which they hoped that I, as the consort of Mybaloë, would deign to accept. I thanked him, and bade him convey my acknowledgement to the donors of the wine.

"Will you not taste the wine now?" he said, "I must return immediately; but before leaving, I should like to learn if the gift meets with your approval, so that I can tell my people."

I poured out some of the wine into a cup and drank it very slowly, as one does in testing the savor and quality of a beverage. It was quite sweet and heavy, with a peculiar after-flavor of puckerish bitterness which I did not find altogether agreeable. However, I praised the wine, not wishing to hurt Marvasi's feelings. He grinned with apparent pleasure at my words, and was about to depart, when Mybaloë entered. She was panting with haste, her expression was both wild and stern, and her eyes blazed with unnatural fire. Rushing up to me, she snatched the empty wine-cup from my fingers.

"You have drunk it?" she cried, in a tone of statement more than of query.

"Yes," I replied, in great wonder and perplexity.

The look that she turned upon me was indescribable, and full of conflicting elements. Horror, agony, devotion, love and fury were mingled in it, but I knew somehow that the fury was not directed toward me. For one intense moment her eyes held mine; then, averting her face, she pointed to Marvasi and bade the priests of Wanaôs to seize and bind him. The command was instantly obeyed. But before offering any explanation, and without saying a word to me or to anyone, Mybaloë poured out a cupful of the palm-wine and drank it at a single draught. Beginning to suspect the truth, I would have seized it from her hand, but she was too quick for me.

"Now we will both die," she said, when she had emptied the cup. For a moment, her face assumed a tranquil smile, then it became the countenance of an avenging goddess as she turned her attention to the wretched Marvasi. Every one present had now surmised the truth, and mutterings of rage and horror were heard on all sides. Marvasi would have been torn limb from limb, joint from joint, muscle from muscle, by the bare hands of the priests if it had not been for Mybaloë, who intervened and told them to wait. Stricken with abject terror, the man cowered among his captors, knowing too well the manner of doom that would be meted out to him in spite of any momentary reprieve.

Mybaloë began to interrogate him in brief, stern sentences, and Marvasi, whose awe of her was even more patent than his fear of the priests, made answer with many stammerings as he cringed and fawned. He confessed that the wine was poisoned; also, that he had been hired by the sorcerer and high-priest Mergawe to proffer it to me and see that I drank some of it at once, if possible. Mergawe, he said, had been hiding in the forest on the borders of Azombeii for weeks, living in a secret cavern known only to himself and a few adherents, who had brought him food and such news as he desired to learn. Marvasi, who was under certain intimate obligations to Mergawe, and had been used by him as a tool on other occasions, was one of these adherents.

"Where is Mergawe now?" questioned Mybaloë. Marvasi would have hesitated, but the eyes of the queen, ablaze with anger and with superhuman mesmerism, dragged the very truth from his reluctant lips. He said that Mergawe was now lurking in the jungle, on the outskirts of the town of Azombeii, waiting for assurance that the poison had been drunk by its intended victim.

A number of the priests were at once dispatched to find Mergawe. While they were absent, Mybaloë told me how warning of the plan to poison me had been brought to her by another of Mergawe's friends, who had recoiled at the final hour from the atrociousness and audacity of such a design.

The priests returned in a little while, bringing the captive sorcerer. They had succeeded in coming upon him unaware, and though he struggled with demoniacal strength and fury, they bore him down and bound him with thongs of rhinoceros hide. They brought him into the banqueting-hall amid a horror-frozen silence.

In spite of his desperate predicament, the face of the sorcerer was full of a malevolent triumph, as he stood before us. Proud, and superbly erect, he gave no evidence of fear, but his mien proclaimed the Satanic possession of an evil exultation. Before Mybaloë could question or address him, he began to pour forth a torrent of dreadful mouthings, intermingled with maledictions and vituperations. He told us how he had prepared the poison, he enumerated the fearsome ingredients, the slowly chanted and lethiferous runes, the manifold and mighty power of the baleful fetishes that had gone into or had helped in its making. Then he described the action of the poison, the preliminary months during which Mybaloë and I would suffer innumerable pangs, would die uncounted deaths in our anticipation of the deferred agonies to come; and then the interminable tortures themselves, the slow and hideous contraction of all our fibers, all our organs, the drying-up of the very sources of life, and the shrinkage to infantile, or even pre-infantile, stature and dimensions before the relief of death. Forgetful of all but his mad hatred, his insensate jealousy, he lingered over these details, he repeated them again and again with so vile a gloating, so horrible and rapturous a relish, that a sort of paralyzing spell was laid upon the assembly, and no one stepped forward to silence him with a knife or a spear.

At last, while his mouthings continued, Mybaloë filled another cup with the poisoned wine; and while the priests held Mergawe and forced his teeth apart with their spear-blades, she poured the wine down his throat. Oblivious or contemptuous of his doom, he betrayed no slightest quiver or shrinking of fear, but glared with that awful look of exultation all the while, like a black fiend who rejoices over the damned, even though he himself is numbered among them. Marvasi was also compelled to drink the wine, and he cringed and cried with terror, frothing at the mouth when the lethal liquor touched his tongue. Then the two men, by Mybaloë's order, were led away and imprisoned, and were left under a strong guard to await the working of the poison. But later in the night, when their deed became known to the populace, a multitude of men and women, maddened beyond all measure or control, broke in and overpowered the guards and carried Marvasi and Mergawe to the grotto behind the cave of Wanaôs, where they were flung like offal to the crocodiles in the black pool.

Now, for Mybaloë and me, there began a life of indepictable horror. Dead was all our former joy and happiness, for the blackness of the doom to come lay on us like the charnel shadow cast by the gathering of a myriad vultures. Love, it is true, was still ours, but love that already seemed to have entered the hideous gloom and nothingness of the grave . . . But of these things I can not tell you, though I have told you so much . . . They were too sacred and too terrible. . . .

After the leaden lapse of funereal days, beneath heavens from which for us the very azure had now departed, it was agreed between Mybaloë and me that I should leave Azombeii and return to my native land. Neither of us could bear the thought of having to witness day by day the eventual torments and progressive physical disintegration of the other when Mergawe's poison should begin to operate. Of our farewell meeting, I can say only that it was infinitely sorrowful, and that I shall remember the love and grief in Mybaloë's eyes amid the culminative pangs and disordered illusions of my last delirium. Before I left, she gave me for a keepsake the little image of Wanaôs, concerning which you have asked me so often.

It is needless to detail my return to America. Now, after months of a delay that has had in it nothing of mercy or mitigation, I feel the first workings of the poison; I have recognized all its preliminary symptoms, and the sickening expectations of haunted days and sleep-forbidden nights are being realized. And knowing all that is yet to come, and seeing with a clarity of imaginative vision that sears my soul the coincidental agonies of Mybaloë, I have begun to envy the death of Marvasi and Mergawe in the pool of crocodiles.

THE PASSING OF APHRODITE

In all the lands of Illarion, from mountain-valleys rimmed with unmelting snow, to the great cliffs of sard whose reflex darkens a sleepy, tepid sea, were lit as of old the green and amethystine fires of summer. Spices were on the wind that mountaineers had met in the high glaciers; and the eldest wood of cypress, frowning on a sky-clear bay, was illumined by scarlet orchids. . . . But the heart of the poet Phaniol was an urn of black jade overfraught by love with sodden ashes. And because he wished to forget for a time the mockery of myrtles, Phaniol walked alone in the waste bordering upon Illarion; in a place that great fires had blackened long ago, and which knew not the pine or the violet, the cypress or the myrtle. There, as the day grew old, he came to an unsailed ocean, whose waters were dark and still under the falling sun, and bore not the memorial voices of other seas. And Phaniol paused, and lingered upon the ashen shore; and dreamt awhile of that sea whose name is Oblivion.

Then, from beneath the westering sun, whose bleak light was prone on his forehead, a barge appeared and swiftly drew to the land: albeit there was no wind, and the oars hung idly on the foamless wave. And Phaniol saw that the barge was wrought of ebony fretted with curious anaglyphs, and carved with luxurious forms of gods and beasts, of satyrs and goddesses and women; and the figurehead was a black Eros with full unsmiling mouth and implacable sapphire eyes averted, as if intent upon things not lightly to be named or revealed. Upon the deck of the barge were two women, one pale as the northern moon, and the other swart as equatorial midnight. But both were clad imperially, and bore the mien of goddesses or of those who dwell near to the goddesses.

Gravely, without word or gesture, they regarded Phaniol; and, marvelling, he inquired, "What seek ye?"

Then, with one voice that was like the voice of Hesperian airs among palms at evening twilight in the Fortunate Isles, they answered, saying:

"We wait the goddess Aphrodite, who departs in weariness and sorrow from Illarion, and from all the lands of this world of petty loves and pettier mortalities. Thou, because thou art a poet, and hast known the great sovereignty of love, shall behold her departure. But they, the men of the court, the market-place and the temple, shall receive no message nor sign of her going-forth, and will scarcely dream that she is gone…. Now, O Phaniol, the time, the goddess and the going-forth are at hand."

Lo, even as they ceased, One came across the desert; and her coming was a light on the far hills; and where she trod the lengthening shadows shrunk, and the grey waste put on the purple asphodels and the deep verdure it had worn when those queens were young, that now are a darkening legend and a dust of mummia. Even to the shore she came and stood before Phaniol, while the sunset greatened, filling sky and sea with a flush as of new-blown blossoms, or the inmost rose of that coiling shell which was consecrate to her in old time. Without robe or circlet or garland, crowned and clad only with the sunset, fair with the dreams of man but fairer yet than all dreams: thus she waited, smiling tranquilly, who is life or death, despair or rapture, vision or flesh, to gods and poets and galaxies unknowable. But, filled with a wonder that was also love, or much more than love, the poet could find no greeting.

"Farewell, O Phaniol," she said, and her voice was the sighing of remote waters, the murmur of water moon-withdrawn, forsaking not without sorrow a proud island tall with palms. "Thou hast known me and worshipped all thy days till now, but the hour of my departure is come: I go, and when I am gone, thou shalt worship still and shalt not know me. For the destinies are thus, and not forever to any man, to any world or to any god, is it given to possess me wholly. Autumn and spring will return when I am past, the one with yellow leaves, the other with yellow violets; birds will haunt the renewing myrtles; and many little loves will be thine. Not again to thee or to any man will return the perfect vision and the perfect flesh of the goddess."

Ending thus, she stepped from that ashen strand to the dark prow of the barge; and even as it had come, without wafture of wind or movement of oar, the barge put out on a sea covered with the fallen, fading petals of sunset. Quickly it vanished from view, while the desert lost those ancient asphodels and the deep verdure it had worn again for a little. Darkness, having conquered Illarion, came slow and furtive on the path of Aphrodite; shadows mustered innumerably to the grey hills, and the heart of the poet Phaniol was an urn of black jade overfraught by love with sodden ashes.

THE PRIMAL CITY

In these after-days, when all things are touched with insoluble doubt and dereliction, I am not sure of the purpose that had taken us into that little-visited land. I recall, however, that we had found explicit mention, in a volume of which we possessed the one existing copy, of certain vast prehuman ruins lying amid the bare plateaus and stark pinnacles of the region. How we had acquired the volume I do not remember: but Sebastian Polder and I had given our youth and much of our manhood to the quest of hidden knowledge; and this book was a compendium of all things that men have forgotten or ignored in their desire to repudiate the inexplicable.

We, being enamored of mystery, and seeking ever for the clues that material science has disregarded, pondered much upon those pages written in an antique alphabet. The location of the ruins was clearly stated, though in terms of an obsolete geography; and I remember our excitement when we had marked the position on a terrestrial globe. We were consumed by a wild eagerness to behold the alien city, and certain of our ability to find it. Perhaps we wished to verify a strange and fearful theory which we had formed regarding the nature of the earth's primal inhabitants; perhaps we sought to recover the buried records of a lost science . . . or perhaps there was some other and darker objective....

I recall nothing of the first stages of our journey, which must have been long and arduous. But I recall distinctly that we traveled for many days amid the bleak, treeless uplands that rose rapidly like a many-tiered embankment toward the range of high pyramidal summits guarding our destination. Our guide was a native of the country, sodden and taciturn, with intelligence little above that of the llamas who carried our supplies.

He had never visited the ruins, but we had been assured that he knew the way, which was a secret remembered by few of his fellow countrymen. Rare and scant was the local legendry concerning the place and its builders; and, after many queries, we could add nothing to the knowledge gained from the immemorial volume. The city, it seemed, was nameless; and the region about it was untrodden by man.

Desire and curiosity raged within us like a calenture; and we gave no heed to the hazards and travails of exploration. Over us stood the eternal azure of vacant heavens, matching in their desolation the empty landscape. The route steepened; and above us now was a wilderness of cragged and chasmed rock, where nothing dwelt but the sinister wide-winged condors.

Often we lost sight of certain eminent peaks that had served us for landmarks. But it seemed that our guide knew the way, as if led by an instinct more subtle than memory or intelligence; and at no time did he hesitate. At intervals we came to the broken fragments of a paved road that had formerly traversed the whole of this rugged region: broad, cyclopean flags of gneiss, channeled as if by the storms of cycles older than human history. And in some of the deeper chasms we saw the eroded piers of great bridges that had spanned them in other time. These ruins reassured us; for in the primordial volume there was mention of a highway and of mighty bridges, leading to the fabulous city.

Polder and I were exultant; and yet I think that we both shivered with a curious terror when we tried to read certain inscriptions that were still deeply engraved on the worn stones. No living man, though erudite in all the tongues of Earth, could have deciphered those characters; and perhaps it was their very alienage that frightened us. We had sought diligently during many laborious years for all that transcends the dead level of mortality through age or remoteness or strangeness; we had longed ardently for the esoteric and bizarre: but such longing was not incompatible with fear and repulsion. Better than those who had walked always in the common paths, we knew the perils that might attend our exorbitant and solitary researches.

Often we had debated, with variously fantastic conjectures, the enigma of the mountain-builded city. But, toward our journey's end, when the vestiges of that pristine people multiplied around us, we fell into long periods of silence, sharing the taciturnity of our stolid guide. Thoughts came to us that were overly strange for utterance; the chill of elder aeons entered our hearts from the ruins—and did not depart.

We toiled on between the desolate rocks and the sterile heavens, breathing an air that became thin and painful to the lungs, as if with some admixture of cosmic ether. At high noon we reached an open pass, and saw before and above us, at the end of a long and vertiginous perspective, the city that had been described as an unnamed ruin in a volume antedating all other known books.

The place was built on an inner peak of the range, surrounded by snowless summits little sterner and loftier than itself. On one side the peak fell in a thousand-foot precipice from the overhanging ramparts; on another, it was terraced with wild cliffs; but the third side, facing toward us, was a steep acclivity with broken-down scarps and chimneys that would offer small difficulty to expert mountaineers. The rock of the whole mountain was strangely ruinous and black; but the city walls, though gapped and worn to a like dilapidation, were conspicuous above it at a distance of leagues.

Polder and I beheld the bourn of our world-wide search with thoughts and emotions which we did not voice. The Indian made no comment, pointing impassively toward the far summit with its crown of ruins. We hurried on, wishing to complete our journey by daylight; and, after plunging into an abysmal valley, we began at mid-afternoon the ascent of the slope toward the city.

We were impressed anew by the abnormal blackness and manifold cleavages of the rock. It was like climbing amid the overthrown and fire-blasted blocks of a Titan citadel. Everywhere the slope was rent into huge, obliquely angled masses, often partly vitrified, which made the ascent a more arduous problem than we had expected. Plainly, at some former time, it had been subjected to the action of intense heat; and yet there were no volcanic craters amid the nearby mountains. Puzzling greatly, I recalled a passage in that old volume, hinting ambiguously at the dark fate that long ago destroyed the city's inhabitants: "For the people of that city had reared its walls and towers too high amid the region of the clouds; and the clouds came down in their anger and smote the city with dreadful fires; and thereafter the place was peopled no more by those primal giants who had built it, but had only the clouds for inhabitants and custodians." But from this passage I could still draw no definite conclusion: for the ideation was too fantastic to be understood as anything more than a dubious figure of speech.

We had left our three llamas at the slope's bottom, merely taking with us provisions for a night. Thus unhampered, we made fair progress in spite of the ever-varying obstacles offered by the shattered scarps. After a while we came to the hewn steps of a stairway mounting toward the summit; but the steps had been wrought for the feet of colossi, and, in many places, they were part of the heaved and tilted ruin; so they did not greatly facilitate our climbing.

The sun was still high above the western pass behind us; and for this reason, as we went on, I was much surprised by a sudden deepening of the char-like blackness on the rocks. Turning, I saw that several greyish vapory masses, which might have been either clouds or smoke, were drifting idly about the summits that overlooked the pass; and one of these masses, rearing like a limbless figure, upright and colossal, had interposed itself between us and the sun.

Sebastian and the guide had also noted this phenomenon. Clouds were almost unheard-of amid those arid mountains in summer; and the presence of smoke would have been equally hard to explain. Moreover, the grey masses were wholly detached from each other and showed a peculiar opacity and sharpness of outline. At second glance they did not really resemble any cloud-forms we had ever seen; for about them there was a baffling suggestion of weight and solidity. Moving sluggishly into the heavens above the pass, they preserved their original contours and their separateness. They seemed to swell and tower, coming toward us on the blue air from which, as yet, no lightest stirring of wind had reached us. Floating thus, they maintained the rectitude of massive columns or of giants marching on a broad plain.

I think we all felt an alarm that was none the less urgent for its vagueness. Somehow, from that instant, it seemed that we were penned up by unknown powers and were cut off from all possibility of retreat. All at once, the dim legends of the ancient volume had assumed a menacing reality. We had ventured into a place of hidden peril—and the peril was upon us. In the movement of the clouds there was something alert, deliberate and implacable. Polder spoke with a sort of horror in his voice, uttering the thought which had already occurred to me:

"They are the sentinels who guard this region—and they have espied us!"

We heard a harsh cry from the Indian. Following his gaze, we saw that several of the unnatural cloud-shapes had appeared on the summit toward which we were climbing, above the megalithic ruins. Some arose half hidden by the walls, as if from behind a breastwork; others stood, as it were, on the topmost towers and battlements, bulking in portentous menace, like the cumuli of a thunder-storm.

Then, with terrifying swiftness, many more of the cloud-presences towered simultaneously from the four quarters, emerging from behind the gaunt peaks or assuming sudden visibility in mid-air. With equal and effortless speed, as if convoked by an unheard command, they gathered in converging lines upon the eyrie-like ruins. We the climbers, and the whole slope about us and the valley below, were plunged in a twilight weird and awesome as that of central eclipse.

The air was still windless, but it weighed upon us as if burdened with the wings of a thousand cacodemons. I remembered that I was conscious of our exposed position, for we had paused on a wide landing of the mountain-hewn steps. We could have concealed ourselves amid the huge fragments on the surrounding slope; but, for the nonce, we were incapable of the simplest movement. The rarity of the air had left us weak and gasping. And the chill of altitude crept into us.

In a close-ranged army, the Clouds mustered above and around us. They rose into the very zenith, swelling to insuperable vastness, and darkening like Tartarean gods. The sun had disappeared, leaving no faintest beam to prove that it still hung unfallen and undestroyed in the heavens.

I felt that I was crushed into the very stone by the eyeless regard of that awful assemblage, judging and condemning. We had trespassed upon a region conquered long ago by strange elemental entities; we had approached their very citadel—and now we must meet the doom our rashness had invited. Such thoughts, like a black lightning, flared in my brain.

Now, for the first time, I became aware of sound—if the word can be applied to a sensation so anomalous. It was as if the oppression that weighed upon me had become audible; as if palpable thunders poured over and past me. I felt, I *heard* them in every nerve, and they roared through my brain like torrents from the opened floodgates of some tremendous weir in a world of genii.

Downward upon us, with limbless Atlantean stridings, there swept the cloudy cohorts. Their swiftness was that of mountain-sweeping winds. The air was riven as if by the tumult of a thousand tempests, was rife with an unmeasured elemental malignity. I recall but partially the events that ensued; but the impression of insufferable darkness, of demonic clamor and trampling, and the pressure of thunderous burdenous onset, remains forever indelible. Also, there were voices that called out with the stridor of clarions in a war of gods, uttering ominous syllables that the ears of man could never seize.

Before those vengeful Shapes, we could not stand for an instant. We hurled ourselves madly down the darkly shadowed steps of the giant stairs. Polder and the guide were a little ahead of me, to the left hand,

and I saw them in that baleful twilight through sheets of sudden rain, on the verge of a deep chasm, which, in our ascent, had compelled us to much circumambulation. I saw them leap together—and yet I swear that they did not fall into the chasm: for one of the Shapes was upon them, whirling and stooping over them, even as they sprang. There was a blasphemous, unthinkable fusion as of forms beheld in delirium: for an instant the two men were like vapors that swelled and swirled, towering high as the thing that had covered them; and the thing itself was a misty Janus, with two heads and bodies melting, no longer human, into its unearthly column. . . .

After that, I remember nothing more, except the sense of vertiginous falling. By some miracle I must have reached the edge of the chasm and flung myself into its depths without being overtaken as the others had been. How I escaped the pursuit of those cloudy Guardians is forevermore an enigma. Perhaps, for some inscrutable reason of their own, they permitted me to go.

When I returned to awareness, stars were peering down upon me like chill incurious eyes between black and jagged lips of rock. The air had turned sharp with the coldness of nightfall in a mountain land. My body ached with a hundred bruises and my right forearm was limp and useless when I tried to raise myself. A dark mist of horror stifled my thoughts. Struggling to my feet with pain-racked effort, I called aloud, though I knew that none would answer me. Then, striking match after match, I searched the chasm and found myself, as I had expected, alone. Nowhere was there any trace of my companions: they had vanished utterly—as clouds vanish....

Somehow, by night, with a broken arm, I must have climbed from the steep fissure, I must have made my way down the frightful mountainside and out of that namelessly haunted and guarded land. I remember that the sky was clear, that the stars were undimmed by any semblance of cloud; and that somewhere in the valley I found one of our llamas, still laden with its stock of provisions. . . .

Plainly I was not pursued by the Guardians. Perhaps They were concerned only with the warding of that mysterious primal city from human intrusion. Never shall I learn the secret of those ruinous walls and crumbling keeps, nor the fate of my companions. But still, through my nightly dreams and diurnal visions, the dark Shapes move with the tumult and thunder of a thousand storms; and my soul is crushed into the earth with the burden of Their imminence; and They pass over me with the speed and vastness of vengeful gods; and I hear Their voices calling like clarions in the sky, with ominous, world-shaking syllables that the ear can never seize.

THE SEED FROM THE SEPULCHER

"Yes, I found the place," said Falmer. "It's a queer sort of place, pretty much as the legends describe it." He spat quickly into the fire, as if the act of speech had been physically distasteful to him, and, half averting his face from the scrutiny of Thone, stared with morose and somber eyes into the jungle-matted Venezuelan darkness.

Thone, still weak and dizzy from the fever that had incapacitated him for continuing their journey to its end, was curiously puzzled. Falmer, it seemed to him, had undergone an inexplicable change during the three days of his absence—a change so elusive and shadowy in some of its phases that Thone was unable to delimit it fully in his thoughts.

Other phases, however, were all too obvious. Falmer, even during extreme hardship or jungle illness, had been heretofore unquenchably loquacious and cheerful. Now he seemed sullen, uncommunicative, as if his mind were preoccupied with far-off things of disagreeable import. His bluff face had grown hollow—even pointed—and his eyes had narrowed to secretive slits. Thone was troubled by these changes, though he tried to dismiss his impressions as mere distempered fancies due to the influence of the ebbing fever.

"But can't you tell me what the place was like?" he persisted.

"There isn't much to tell," said Falmer, in a queer grumbling tone. "Just a few crumbling walls overgrown and half-displaced by the forest trees, and a few falling pillars netted with lianas."

"But didn't you find the burial-pit of the Indian legend, where the gold was supposed to be?"

"Oh, yes, I found it. The place has started to cave in from above, so there wasn't much difficulty about that—but there was no treasure."

279

Falmer's voice had taken on a forbidding surliness; and Thone decided to refrain from further questioning.

"I guess," he commented lightly, "that we had better stick to orchid-hunting. Treasure trove doesn't seem to be in our line. By the way, did you find any unusual flowers or plants during the trip?"

"Hell, no," Falmer snapped. His face had gone suddenly ashen in the firelight, and his eyes had assumed a set glare that might have meant either fear or anger. "Shut up, can't you? I don't want to talk. I've had a headache all day—some damned Venezuelan fever coming on, I suppose. We'd better head for the Orinoco tomorrow, even if we are both sick. I've had all I want of this trip."

James Falmer and Roderick Thone, professional orchid-hunters, with two Indian guides, had been following an obscure tributary of the upper Orinoco. The country was rich in rare flowers; and, beyond its floral wealth, they had been drawn by vague but persistent rumors among the local tribes concerning the existence of a ruined city somewhere on this tributary: a city that contained a burial-pit in which vast treasures of gold, silver and jewels had been interred together with the dead of some nameless people. These rumors were never first hand, but the two men had thought it worthwhile to investigate them. Thone had fallen sick while they were still a full day's journey from the supposed site of the ruins, and Falmer had gone on in a canoe with one of the Indians, leaving the other to attend to Thone. He had returned at nightfall of the third day following his departure.

Thone decided after a while, as he lay staring at his companion, that the latter's taciturnity and moroseness were perhaps due to disappointment over his failure to find the treasure. It must have been that—together with some tropical infection working in his blood. However, he admitted doubtfully to himself, it was not like Falmer to be disappointed or downcast under such circumstances. Greediness for mere wealth, as far as he had occasion to observe, was not in the man's nature.

Falmer did not speak again, but sat glaring before him as if he saw something invisible to others beyond the labyrinth of fire-touched boughs and lianas in which the whispering, stealthy darkness crouched. Somehow, there was a shadowy fear in his aspect. Thone continued to watch him, and saw that the Indians, impassive and cryptic, were also watching him, as if with some obscure expectancy. The riddle was too much for Thone, and he gave it up after a while, lapsing into restless, fever-turbulent slumber, from which he awakened at intervals to see the set face of Falmer, dimmer and more distorted each time with the slowly dying fire. At last it became a half-human thing, devoured by inhuman shadows and twisted by the ever-changing horror of those febrile dreams.

Thone felt stronger in the morning: his brain was clear, his pulse tranquil once more; and he saw with mounting concern the mysterious indisposition of Falmer, who seemed to rouse and exert himself with great difficulty, speaking hardly a word and moving with singular stiffness and sluggishness. He appeared to have forgotten his announced project of returning toward the Orinoco, and Thone took entire charge of the preparations for departure. His companion's condition puzzled him more and more: the signs were not born of any malady with which he was familiar. There was no fever and the symptoms were wholly obscure and ambiguous. However, on general principles, he administered a stiff dose of quinine to Falmer before they started.

The paling saffron of a sultry dawn sifted upon them through the jungle-tops as they loaded their belongings into the dugouts and pushed off down the slow current. Thone sat near the bow of one of the boats, with Falmer in the rear, and a large bundle of orchid roots and part of their equipment filling the middle. The two Indians, taciturn and stolid, occupied the other boat, together with the rest of the supplies.

It was a monotonous journey. The river wound like a sluggish olive snake between dark, interminable walls of forest, from which, at intervals, the goblin faces of orchids leaned and leered. There were no sounds other than the splash of paddles, the furious chattering of monkeys and petulant cries of strange, fiery-colored birds. The sun rose above the jungle and poured down a waveless tide of torrid brilliance.

Thone rowed steadily, looking back over his shoulder at times to address Falmer with some casual remark or friendly question. The latter, with dazed eyes and features that were queerly pale and pinched in the sunlight, sat dully erect and made no effort to use his paddle, seeming to lack both the strength and the inclination. He offered no reply to the solicitous queries of Thone, but shook his head at intervals with a sort of shuddering motion that was plainly automatic and involuntary, rather than the expression of common negation. After a while he began to moan thickly, as if in pain or delirium.

They went on in this manner for several hours; the heat grew more oppressive between the stifling, airless walls of jungle. Thone became aware of a shriller cadence in the moans of his sick companion. Looking back, he saw that Falmer had removed his sun-helmet, seemingly oblivious of the murderous heat, and was clawing at the crown of his head with frantic fingers. Convulsions shook his entire body, and the dugout began to rock dangerously as he tossed to and fro in a long paroxysm of manifest agony. His voice mounted to a ceaseless, high, unhuman shrieking.

Thone made a quick decision. There was a break in the lining palisade of somber forest, and he headed the boat for shore immediately. The Indians followed, whispering between themselves and eyeing the sick man with glances of apprehensive awe and terror that puzzled Thone tremendously. He felt that there was some devilish mystery about the whole affair; and he could not imagine what was wrong with Falmer. All the known manifestations of malignant tropical diseases rose before him like a rout of hideous phantasms; but among them, he could not recognize the thing that had assailed his companion.

Having gotten Falmer ashore on a semi-circle of liana-latticed beach without the aid of the reluctant guides, who seemed unwilling to touch or approach the sick man, Thone administered a heavy hypodermic injection of morphine from his medicine chest. This appeared to ease Falmer's suffering, and the convulsions ceased. Thone, taking advantage of their remission, proceeded to examine the crown of Falmer's head.

He was startled to find amid the thick disheveled hair a hard and pointed lump which resembled strangely the tip of a beginning horn, rising under the still unbroken skin. As if endowed with erectile and resistless life, it seemed to grow beneath his fingers.

At the same time, abruptly and mysteriously, Falmer opened his eyes and appeared to regain full consciousness, as if he had overcome not only the effects of the hypodermic but the stupor of the unknown malady. For a few minutes, he was more his normal self than at any time since his return from the ruins. He began to talk, as if he were anxious to relieve his mind of some oppressing burden. His voice was peculiarly thick and toneless, but Thone, listening in half-comprehending horror, was able to follow his mutterings and piece them together.

"The pit! The pit!" said Falmer. "The infernal thing that was in the pit, in the deep sepulcher! . . . I wouldn't go back there for the treasure of a dozen El Dorados . . . I didn't tell you much about those ruins, Thone. Somehow it was hard—impossibly hard—to talk.

"I guess the Indian knew there was something wrong with those ruins. He led me to the place all right . . . but he wouldn't tell me anything about it; and he waited by the river-side while I searched for the treasure.

"Great grey walls there were, older than the jungle—old as death and time—not like anything I have ever seen. They must have been quarried and reared by people from some forgotten continent or lost planet. They loomed and leaned at mad, unnatural angles, threatening to crush the trees about them. And there were columns, too: thick, swollen columns of unholy form, whose abominable carvings the jungle had not wholly screened from view.

"My God! that accursed burial-pit! There was no trouble finding it.

The pavement above had broken through quite recently, I think. A big tree had pried with its boa-like roots between the yard-deep flagstones that were buried beneath centuries of mould. One of the flags had been tilted back on the pavement, and another had fallen through into the pit. There was a large hole, whose bottom I could see dimly in the forest-strangled light. Something glimmered palely at the bottom; but I could not be sure what it was.

"I had taken along a coil of rope, as you remember. I tied one end to a main root of the tree, dropped the other through the opening, and went down like a monkey. When I got to the bottom I could see little at first in the gloom, except for the whitish glimmering all around me, at my feet. Something broke and crunched beneath me when I began to move—something that was unspeakably brittle and friable. I turned on my flash-light, and saw that the place was fairly littered with bones—human skeletons lay tumbled everywhere. They must have been very old, for they dissolved into powder at a touch.

"The place was a huge sepulchral chamber. After awhile, as I wandered about with the flash-light, I found the steps that led to the blocked-up entrance. But if any treasure had been buried with the bodies, it must have been removed long ago. I groped around amid the bones and dust, feeling pretty much like a ghoul, but couldn't find anything of value, not even a bracelet or a finger-ring on any of the skeletons.

"It wasn't until I thought of climbing out that I noticed the real horror. I didn't mind those skeletons so much: they were lying in attitudes of repose, even if they were a little crowded and it seemed that their owners must have died natural deaths—natural, that is, as we reckon such things.

"Then, in one of the corners—the corner nearest to the opening in the roof—I looked up and saw it in the webby shadows. Ten feet above my head it hung, and I had almost touched it, unknowingly, when I descended the rope.

"It looked like a sort of weird lattice-work at first. Then I saw that the lattice was partly formed of human bones—a complete skeleton, very tall and stalwart, like that of a warrior. I wouldn't have cared if it had been hanging there in any normal fashion—if it had been suspended by metal chains, for instance, or had merely been nailed to the walls. The horror lay in the thing that grew out of the skull—the white, withered thing like a set of fantastic antlers ending in myriads of long and stringy tendrils that had spread themselves on the wall, climbing upward till they reached the roof. They must have lifted the skeleton, or body, along with them as they climbed.

"I examined the thing with my flash-light, and found new horrors. It must have been a plant of some sort, and apparently it had started to grow in the cranium. Some of the branches had issued from the cloven crown, others through the eye-holes and the nose-holes, to flare upward. And the roots of the blasphemous thing had gone downward, trellising themselves on every bone. The very toes and fingers were ringed with them, and they drooped in writhing coils. Worst of all, the ones that had issued from the toe-ends *were rooted in a second skull,* which dangled just below, with fragments of the broken-off root system. There was a litter of fallen bones on the floor in the corner, but I didn't care to inspect it.

"The sight made me feel a little weak, somehow—and more than a little nauseated—that abhorrent, inexplicable mingling of the human and the plant. I started to climb the rope, in a feverish hurry to get out, but the thing fascinated me, in its abominable fashion, and I couldn't help pausing to study it a little more when I had climbed half-way. I leaned toward it too fast, I guess, and the rope began to sway, bringing my face lightly against the leprous, antler-shaped boughs above the skull.

"Something broke—I don't know what—possibly a sort of pod on one of the branches. Anyway, I found my head enveloped in a cloud of pearl-grey powder, very light, fine, and scentless. The stuff settled on my hair, it got into my nose and eyes, nearly choking and blinding me. I tried to shake it off as well as I could. Then I climbed on and pulled myself through the opening. . . ."

As if the effort of coherent narration had been too heavy a strain, Falmer lapsed into disconnected mumblings, some of which were inaudible. The mysterious malady, whatever it was, returned upon him, and his delirious ramblings were mixed with groans of torture. But at moments he regained a flash of coherence.

"My head! My head!" he muttered. "There must be something in my brain, something that grows and spreads; I tell you, I can feel it there. I haven't felt right at any time since I left the burial-pit. . . . My mind has been queer ever since. . . . It must have been the spores of the ancient devil-plant. . . . The spores have taken root . . . the thing is splitting my skull, going down into my brain—a plant that springs out of a human cranium, as if from a flower-pot!"

The dreadful convulsions began once more, and Falmer writhed uncontrollably in his companion's arms, shrieking with agony. Thone, sick at heart, and horribly shocked by his sufferings, abandoned all effort at restraint and took up the hypodermic. With much difficulty, he managed to inject a triple dose into one of the wildly tossing arms, and Falmer grew quiet by degrees and lay with open glassy eyes, breathing stertorously. Thone, for the first time, perceived an odd protrusion of his eyeballs, which seemed about to start from their sockets, making it impossible for the lids to close, and lending the drawn, contorted features an expression of mad horror and extravagant ghastliness. It was as if something were pushing Falmer's eyes from his head.

Thone, trembling with sudden weakness and terror, felt that he was involved in some unnatural web of nightmare. He could not, dared not, believe the story Falmer had told him, and its implications. The thing was too monstrous, too fantastic; and, assuring himself that his companion had imagined it all, had been ill throughout with the incubation of some strange fever, he stooped over and found that the horn-shaped lump on Falmer's head had now broken through the skin.

Increasingly, with a sense of unreality, he stared at the object that his prying fingers had touched and revealed amid the matted hair. It was unmistakably a plant-bud of some sort, with involuted folds of pale green and bloody pink that seemed about to expand. The thing issued from above the central suture of the skull; and the thought occurred to the horror-sick observer that it had somehow taken root in the very bone; had gone downward, as Falmer had feared, into the brain.

A nausea swept upon Thone, and he recoiled from the lolling head and its baleful outgrowth, averting his gaze. His fever, he felt, was returning; there was a woeful debility in all his limbs; and he heard the muttering voices of incipient delirium through the quinine-induced ringing in his ears. His eyes blurred with a deathly mist, as if the miasma of some equatorial fen had arisen visibly before him.

He fought to subdue his illness and impotence. He must not give way to it wholly; he must go on with Falmer and the Indians, and reach the nearest trading station, many days away on the Orinoco, where Falmer could receive aid.

As if through sheer volition, the clinging vapor cleared from his eyes, and he felt a resurgence of strength. He looked around for the two guides, and saw, with a start of uncomprehending surprise, that they had vanished. Then, peering further, he observed that one of the boats—the dugout used by the Indians—had also disappeared. It was all too evident that he and Falmer had been deserted. Perhaps the Indians had known what was wrong with the sick man, and had been afraid. Their apprehensive glances, their covert whisperings, their patent unwillingness to approach Falmer, all seemed to confirm this. At any rate, they were gone, and they had taken much of the camp equipment and most of the provisions with them.

Thone turned once more to the supine body of Falmer, conquering his fear and repugnance with effort. Something must be done, and they must go on while Falmer still lived. One of the boats remained; and even if Thone became too ill to ply the paddle, the current would still carry them downstream.

Resolutely, he drew out his clasp-knife and, stooping over the stricken man, he excised the protruding bud, cutting as close to the scalp itself as he could with safety. The thing was unnaturally tough and rubbery; it exuded a thin, sanious fluid; and he shuddered when he saw its internal structure, full of nerve-like filaments, with a core that suggested cartilage. He flung it aside quickly on the river sand. Then, lifting Falmer in his arms, he lurched and staggered toward the remaining boat. He fell more than once, and lay half-swooning across the inert body. Alternately carrying and dragging his burden, he reached the boat at last. With the remainder of his failing strength, he contrived to prop Falmer in the stern against the pile of equipment.

His fever was mounting apace. Dimly, with a swimming brain, and legs that bent beneath him like river reeds, he went back for the medicine-kit. After much delay, with tedious, half-delirious exertions, he pushed off from the shore, and got the boat into mid-stream. He paddled with nerveless, mechanical strokes, hardly knowing what he did, till the fever mastered him wholly and the oar slipped from oblivious fingers. . . .

After that, he seemed to be drifting through a hell of strange dreams illumed by an intolerable, glaring sun. He went on in this way for cycles, and then floated into a phantom-peopled darkness, and slumber haunted by innominable voices and faces, all of which became at last the voice and face of Falmer, detailing over and over again a hideous story which Thone still seemed to hear in the utmost abyss of sleep.

He awoke in the yellow glare of dawn, with his brain and his senses comparatively clear. His illness had left a great languor, but his first thought was of Falmer. He twisted about, nearly falling overboard in his debility, and sat facing his companion.

Falmer still reclined, half-sitting, half-lying, against the pile of blankets and other impedimenta. His knees were drawn up, his hands clasping them as if in tetanic rigor. His features had grown as wan and stark and ghastly as those of a dead man, and his whole aspect was one of mortal rigidity. It was this, however, that caused Thone to gasp with unbelieving horror—a horror in which he found himself hoping that Falmer really *was* dead.

During the interim of Thone's delirium and his lapse into slumber, which must have been a whole afternoon and night, the monstrous plant-bud, merely stimulated, it would seem, by the act of excision, had grown again with preternatural and abhorrent rapidity, from Falmer's head. A loathsome pale-green stem was mounting thickly and had started to branch like antlers after attaining a height of six or seven inches.

More dreadful than this, if possible, similar growths had issued from the eyes; and their heavy stems, climbing vertically across the forehead, had entirely displaced the eye-balls. Already they were branching like the thing that mounted from the crown. The antlers were all tipped with pale vermilion. Each of them appeared to quiver with repulsive animation, nodding rhythmically in the warm, windless air. . . . From the mouth another stem protruded, curling upward like a long and whitish tongue. It had not yet begun to bifurcate.

Thone closed his eyes to shut away the shocking vision. Behind his lids, in a yellow dazzle of light, he still saw the cadaverous, deathly features, the climbing stems that quivered against the dawn like ghastly hydras of tomb-etiolated green. They seemed to be waving toward him, growing and lengthening visibly as they waved. He opened his eyes again, and fancied, with a start of new terror, that the antlers *were* actually taller than they had been a few moments previous.

After that, he sat watching them in a sort of baleful paralysis, with horror curdled at his heart. The illusion of the plant's visible growth and freer movement—if it was illusion—increased upon him by accelerative degrees. Falmer, however, did not stir, and his white, parchment face seemed to shrivel and fall in, as if the roots of the growth were draining him of blood, were devouring his very flesh in their insatiable and ghoulish hunger.

Shuddering, Thone wrenched his eyes away and stared at the river shore. The stream had widened, and the current had grown more slug-gish. He sought to recognize their location, looking in vain for some familiar landmark in the monotonous dull-green cliffs of jungle that lined the margin. All was strange to him, and he felt hopelessly lost and alienated. He seemed to be drifting on an unknown tide of nightmare and madness, companioned by something more frightful than corrup-tion itself.

His mind began to wander with an odd inconsequence, coming back always, in a sort of closed circle, to the growth that was devouring Falmer. With a flash of scientific curiosity, he found himself wondering to what genus it belonged. It was neither fungus nor pitcher-plant, nor anything that he had ever encountered or heard of in his explorations. It must have come, as Falmer had suggested, from an alien world; it was nothing that the earth could conceivably have nourished.

He felt, with a comforting assurance, that Falmer was dead, for the roots of the thing must have long since penetrated the brain. That at least, was a mercy. But even as he shaped the thought, he heard a low, guttural moaning, and, peering at Falmer in horrible startlement, saw that his limbs and body were twitching slightly. The twitching increased, and took on a rhythmic regularity, though at no time did it resemble the agonized and violent convulsions of the previous day. It was plainly au-tomatic, like a sort of galvanism; and Thone saw that it was timed with the languorous and loathsome swaying of the plant. The effect on the watcher was insidiously mesmeric and somnolent; and once he caught himself beating the detestable rhythm with his foot.

He tried to pull himself together, groping desperately for something to which his sanity could cling. Ineluctably, he felt the return of his sick-ness: fever, nausea, and revulsion worse than the loathliness of death. But before he yielded to it utterly, he drew his loaded revolver from the holster and fired six times into Falmer's quivering body. He knew that he had not missed, but, after the final bullet, Falmer still moaned and twitched in unison with the evil swaying of the plant, and Thone, sliding into delirium, heard still the ceaseless, automatic moaning.

There was no time in the world of seething unreality and shoreless oblivion through which he drifted. When he came to himself again, he could not know if hours or weeks had elapsed. But he knew at once that the boat was no longer moving; and lifting himself dizzily, he saw that it had floated into shallow water and mud and was nosing the beach of a tiny, jungle-tufted isle in mid-river. The putrid odor of slime was about him like a stagnant pool, and he heard a strident humming of insects.

It was either late morning or early afternoon, for the sun was high in the still heavens. Lianas were drooping above him from the island trees like uncoiled serpents, and epiphytic orchids, marked with ophidian mottlings, leaned toward him grotesquely from lowering boughs. Immense butterflies went past on sumptuously spotted wings.

He sat up, feeling very giddy and light-headed, and faced again the horror that companioned him. The thing had grown incredibly, enormously: the three-antlered stems, mounting above Falmer's head, had become gigantic and had put out masses of ropy feelers that tossed uneasily in the air, as if searching for support—or new provender. In the topmost antler, issuing from the crown and towering above the others, a prodigious blossom had opened—a sort of fleshy disk, broad as a man's face and pale as leprosy.

Falmer's features had shrunken till the outlines of every bone were visible as if beneath tightened paper. He was a mere death's head in a mask of human skin, and his body seemed to have collapsed and fallen, leaving little more than a skeleton beneath his clothing. He was quite still now, except for the communicated quivering of the stems. The atrocious plant had sucked him dry, had eaten his vitals and his flesh.

Thone wanted to hurl himself forward in a mad impulse to grapple with the loathly growth. But a strange paralysis held him back. The plant was like a living and sentient thing—a thing that watched him, that dominated him with its unclean but superior will. And the huge blossom, as he stared, took on the dim, unnatural semblance of a face. It was some-how like the face of Falmer, but the lineaments were twisted all awry, and were mingled with those of something wholly devilish and non-human. Thone could not move—and he could not take his eyes from the blasphemous, unthinkable abnormality.

By some miracle, his fever had left him; and it did not return. Instead, there came an eternity of frozen fright and madness, in which he sat facing the mesmeric plant. It towered before him from the dry, dead shell that had been Falmer, its swollen, glutted stems and branches swaying in a gentle rhythm, its huge flower leering perpetually upon him with its impious travesty of a human face. He thought that he heard a low singing sound, ineffably, demoniacally sweet, but whether it emanated from the plant or was a mere hallucination of his overwrought senses, he could not know.

The sluggish hours went by, and a gruelling sun poured down upon him like molten lead from some titanic vessel of torture. His head swam with weakness and the fetor-laden heat; but he could not relax the rigor of his posture. There was no change in the nodding monstrosity, which seemed to have attained its full growth above the head of its victim. But after a long interim, Thone's eyes were drawn to the rigid, shrunken hands of Falmer, which still clasped the drawn-up knees in a spasmodic clutch. From the back of each hand, from the ends of the skeleton fingers, tiny white rootlets had broken and were writhing slowly in the air, groping, it seemed, for a new source of nourishment. Then, from the neck and chin, other tips were breaking, and over the whole body the clothing stirred in a curious manner, as if with the crawling and lifting of hidden lizards.

At the same time the singing grew louder, sweeter, more imperious in Thone's ears, and the swaying of the great plant assumed an indescribably seductive tempo. It was like the allurement of voluptuous sirens, the deadly languor of dancing cobras. Thone felt an irresistible compulsion: a summons was being laid upon him, and his drugged mind and body must obey it. The very fingers of Falmer, twisting viperishly, seemed beckoning to him. Then, suddenly he was on his hands and knees in the bottom of the boat.

Inch by inch, with baleful terror and equally baleful fascination contending in his brain, he crept forward, dragging himself over the disregarded bundle of orchid-plants—inch by inch, foot by foot, till his head was against the withered hands of Falmer, from which hung and floated the questing roots.

Some cataleptic spell had made him helpless. He felt the rootlets as they moved like delving fingers through his hair and over his face and neck, and started to strike in with agonizing, needle-sharp tips. He could not stir, he could not even close his lids. In a frozen stare, he saw the gold and carmine flash of a hovering butterfly as the roots began to pierce his pupils.

Deeper and deeper went the greedy roots, while new filaments grew out to enmesh him like a witch's net. . . . For a while, it seemed that the dead and the living writhed together in leashed convulsions. . . . At last Thone hung supine amid the lethal, ever-growing web; bloated and colossal, the plant lived on; and in its upper branches, through the still, stifling afternoon, a second flower began to unfold.

THE LETTER FROM MOHAUN LOS

Introduction

Some who read this narrative will no doubt remember the disappearance of the eccentric millionaire Domitian Malgraff and his Chinese servant Li Wong, which provided the newspapers of 1940 with flamboyant headlines and many columns of rumor and speculation.

Reams were written concerning the case; but, stripped of all reportorial embellishments and luridities of surmise, it can hardly have been said to constitute a story. There were no verifiable motives nor explanatory circumstances, no clues nor traces of any kind. The two men had passed from all mundane knowledge, between one hour and the next, as if they had evaporated like some of the queer volatile chemicals with which Malgraff had been experimenting in his private laboratory. No one knew the use of these chemicals; and no one knew what had happened to Malgraff and Li Wong.

Few, perhaps, will consider that any reliable solution of these problems is now afforded through the publication of the manuscript received by Sylvia Talbot a year ago in the fall of 1941.

Miss Talbot had formerly been affianced to Malgraff, but had broken off the engagement three years prior to his disappearance. She had been fond of him; but his dreamy disposition and impractical leanings had formed a decided barrier from her view-point. The youth had seemed to take his dismissal lightly and had afterwards plunged into scientific researches whose nature and object he had confided to no one. But neither then nor at any other time had he shown the least inclination to supplement by his own efforts the huge fortune inherited from his father.

Regarding his vanishment, Miss Talbot was as much in the dark as everyone else. After the breaking-off of the engagement she had continued to hear from him at intervals; but his letters had grown more and more infrequent through his absorption in unnamed studies and labors. She was both surprised and shocked by the news of his disappearance.

A world-wide search was made by his lawyers and relations; but without result. Then, in the late summer of 1941, the strange vessel containing the aforesaid manuscript was found floating in the Banda Sea, between Celebes and the Spice Islands, by a Dutch pearler.

The vessel was a sphere of some unknown crystalline substance, with flattened ends. It was eighteen inches in diameter and possessed an interior mechanism of miniature dynamos and induction coils, all of the same clear material, together with an apparatus resembling an hourglass, which was half-filled with a grey powder. The outer surface was studded with several tiny knobs. In the very center, in a small cylindrical compartment, was a thick roll of greenish-yellow paper on which the name and address of Miss Sylvia Talbot were plainly legible through the various layers of the sphere. The writing had been done with some sort of brush or an extremely heavy pen, in pigment of a rare shade of purple.

Two months later, the thing reached Miss Talbot, who was startled and amazed when she recognized the writing as that of Domitian Malgraff.

After many vain experiments, by manipulating certain of the exterior knobs, the vessel was opened; and it came apart in two hemispheric sections. Miss Talbot found that the roll of paper contained a voluminous letter from Malgraff, written on yard-long sheets. This letter, with the omission of a few intimate paragraphs and sentences, is now offered to the public in obedience to the writer's wish.

Malgraff's incredible tale, of course, is easily enough to be explained on the ground of imaginative fabrication. Such, in the opinion of those who knew him, would be far from incompatible with his character. In his own whimsical and fantastic way, he is said to have been something of a joker. A new search has now been instituted, on the supposition that he may be living somewhere in the Orient; and all the isles adjacent to the Banda Sea will be carefully examined.

However, certain collateral details are somewhat mysterious and baffling. The material and mechanism of the sphere are unfamiliar to scientists, and are still unexplained; and the fabric on which the letter was written, as well as the pigment used, have so far defied analysis. The paper, in its chemical composition, seems to present affinities with both vellum and papyrus; and the pigment has no terrestrial analogue.

The Letter

Dear Sylvia:

You have always considered me a hopeless dreamer; and I am the last person who would endeavor or even wish to dispute your summary. It might be added that I am one of those dreamers who have not been able to content themselves with dreams. Such persons, as a rule, are unfortunate and unhappy, since few of them are capable of realizing, or even approximating, their visionary conceptions.

In my case, the attempted realization has led to a singular result: I am writing this letter from a world that lies far-off in the twofold labyrinth of time and space; a world removed by many million years from the one wherein you live, the one whereto I am native.

As you know, I have never cared greatly for the material things of earth. I have always been irked by the present age, have always been devoured by a sort of nostalgia for other times and places. It has seemed so oddly and capriciously arbitrary that I should be *here* and not *otherwhere*, in the infinite, eternal ranges of being; and I have long wondered if it would not be possible to gain control of the laws that determine our temporal or cosmic situation, and pass at will from world to world or from cycle to cycle.

It was after you dismissed me that my speculations along such lines began to take a practical turn. You had told me that my dreamings were no less impossible than useless. Perhaps, among other things, I desired to prove that they were not impossible. Their utility or inutility was not a problem that concerned me, nor one which any man could decide.

I shall not weary you with a full recountal of my labors and researches. I sought above all else to invent a machine by which I could travel in time, could penetrate the past or the future. I started from the theory that movement in the time-dimension could be controlled, accelerated, or reversed by the action of some special force. By virtue of such regulation, one would be able to remove forward or backward along the aeons.

I shall say only that I succeeded in isolating the theoretic time-force, though without learning its ultimate nature and origin. It is an all-pervading energy, with a shorter wave-length than that of the cosmic rays. Then I invented a compound metal, perfectly transparent and of great toughness, which was peculiarly fitted for use in conducting and concentrating the force.

From this metal I constructed my machine, with dynamos in which I could develop an almost illimitable power. The reversal of the force, compelling a retrograde movement in time, could be secured by passing the current through certain rare volatile chemicals imprisoned in a special device resembling a large hour-glass.

After many months of arduous effort, the mechanism stood completed on the floor of my Chicago laboratory. Its outward form was more or less spherical, with flattened ends like those of a Chinese orange. It was capable of being hermetically sealed, and the machinery included an oxygen-apparatus. Within, there was ample room for three people amid the great tubular dynamos, the array of chronometric dials, and the board of regulative levers and switches. All the parts, being made of the same material, were transparent as glass.

Though I have never loved machinery, I surveyed it with a certain pride. There was a delightful irony in the thought that by using this super-mechanical device I could escape from the machine-ridden era in which I had been born.

My first intention was to explore the future. By travelling far enough in forward time, I expected to find one of two things: men would either have learned to discard their cumbrous and complicated engines, or would have been destroyed by them, giving place to some other and more sensible species in the course of mundane evolution. However, if the human future failed to inveigle me in any of its phases, I could reverse the working of the time-force and go back into the aeons that were posterior to my own epoch. In these, unless history and fable had lied, the conditions of life would be more congenial to my own tastes. But my most urgent curiosity was concerning the unknown and problematic years of ages to come.

All my labors had been carried on in private, with no other aid than that of Li Wong, my Chinese cook, valet, and housekeeper. And at first I did not confide the purpose of the mechanism even to Li Wong, though I knew him to be the most discreet and intelligent of mortals. People in general would have laughed if they had known what I was trying to do. Also there were cousins and other relations, all enviously watchful of my inherited wealth . . . and a country full of lawyers, alienists, and lunatic asylums. I have always had a reputation for eccentricity; and I did not choose to give my dear relatives an opportunity which might have been considered legally sufficient for the well-known process of "rail-roading."

I had fully intended to take the time-voyage alone. But when I had finished building the machine, and all was in readiness for departure, I realized that it would be impossible to go without my factotum, Li Wong. Apart from his usefulness and trustworthiness, the little Chinaman was good company. He was something of a scholar in his own tongue, and did not belong to the coolie class. Though his mastery of English was still imperfect, and my knowledge of Chinese altogether rudimentary, we had often discussed the poetry and philosophy of his own land, as well as certain less erudite topics.

Li Wong received the announcement of our projected journey with the same blandness and aplomb which he would have shown if I had told him we were going into the next state.

"Me go pack," he said. "You want plentee shirt?"

Our preparations were soon made. Apart from the changes of raiment suggested by Li Wong, we took with us a ten days' supply of provisions, a medicine kit, and a bottle of brandy, all of which were stored in lockers I had built for the purpose. Not knowing what we might find, or what might happen by the way, it was well to be prepared for emergencies.

All was now ready. I locked Li Wong and myself within the time-sphere, and then sat down before the instrument-board on which the controlling levers were ranged. I felt the thrill of a new Columbus or a Magellan, about to sail for undiscovered continents. Compared with this, all former human explorations would be as the crawling of emmets and pismires.

Even in the exultation of that moment, though everything had been calculated with mathematical precision, had been worked out to an algebraic degree, I recognized the element of uncertainty and danger. The effect of time-travelling on the human constitution was an unknown quantity. Neither of us might survive the process of acceleration in which lustrums and decades and centuries would be reduced to mere seconds.

I pointed this out to Li Wong. "Maybe you had better stay behind after all," I suggested.

He shook his head vigorously. "You go, I go," he said with an imperturbable smile.

Making a mental note of the hour, day, and minute of our departure. I pulled a lever and turned on the accelerative force.

I had hardly known what to anticipate in the way of physical reactions and sensations. Among other contingencies, it had even occurred to me that I might become partially or wholly unconscious; and I had clamped myself to the seat to avoid falling in case of this.

However, the real effect was very strange and unforeseen. My first feeling was that of sudden bodily lightness and immateriality. At the same time, the machine seemed to have expanded, its walls, dynamos, and other portions were a dim and shining blur, and appeared to repeat themselves in an endless succession of momentary images. My own person, and that of Li Wong, were multiplied in the same manner. I was incredibly conscious of myself as a mere flickering shadow, from which was projected a series of other shadows. I tried to speak, and the words became an indefinitely repeated echo.

For a brief interval, the sphere seemed to be hanging in a sea of light. Then, incomprehensibly, it began to darken. A great blackness pressed upon it from without; but the outlines of everything within the sphere were still visible through a sort of luminosity that clung to them like a feeble phosphorescence.

I was puzzled by these phenomena, and, in particular, by the outside darkness, for which I could not account. Theoretically, the days and nights through which we were passing at such supreme velocity would merge in a sort of greyness.

Centuries, aeons, *kalpas* of time, were going by in the strange night. Then, mysterious as the darkness, there came a sudden, blinding glare of light, intenser than anything I have yet known, which pervaded the sphere, and died away like a lightning-flash. It was followed shortly by two lesser flashes, very close together; and then the outer gloom returned once more.

I reached out, with a hand that became a hundred hands, and succeeded somehow in turning on the light that hung above my instrument board and chronometric dials. One of these dials was designed to register my forward motion in time. It was hard to distinguish the real hands and figures in the ghostly blur by which they were surrounded; but somehow, after much poring, I found that I had gone onward into the future for no less than twenty thousand years!

Surely this would be enough, at least for the initial stage of my flight.

I groped for the levers, and turned off the accelerative power.

Instantly, my visual sensations became those of a normal three-dimensional being in normal time and space. But the feeling of lightness and immateriality still persisted. It seemed to me that I should have floated in mid-air like a feather, if it had not been for the metal clamps that held me to the seat.

I heard the voice of Li Wong, whom I had practically forgotten for the moment. The voice came from above! Startled, I saw that the Chinese, with his wide sleeves flapping ludicrously, had floated upward and was bobbing about in the air, trying vainly to recover his equilibrium and re-establish his feet on the floor!

"Me fly all same sea-gull," he tittered, seeming to be amused rather than frightened by his novel predicament.

What on earth had happened? Was the force of gravity non-existent in this future world? I peered out through the glassy walls, trying to determine the geographical features of the terrain in which we had landed.

It must be night, I thought, for all was darkness, shot with a million cold and piercing stars. But why were the stars all around us, as well as above? Even if we were on a mountain-top, we should be surrounded by the vague masses of remote nocturnal horizons. But there were no horizons anywhere—only the swarming lights of irrecognizable constellations. With growing bewilderment, I looked down at the crystalline floor, and beneath me, as in some awful gulf, there swam the icy fires of unknown galaxies! I saw, with a terrific mental shock, that we were suspended in mid-space.

My first thought was, that the earth and the solar system had been annihilated. Somewhile during the past twenty thousand years, there had been a cosmic cataclysm; and Li Wong and myself, moving at inconceivable speed in the abstract time-dimension, had somehow managed to escape it.

Then, like a thunder-clap, there came the realization of the truth. *The sphere had moved only in time;* but, in the interim, the earth and the sun

had been travelling away from us in space, even as all stellar and planetary bodies are said to travel. I had never dreamt of such a contingency
in all my calculations, thinking that the laws of gravitation would keep
us automatically in the same position relative to the earth itself at which
we had started. But evidently these laws were non-effective in the ultra-
spatial dimension known as time. We had stood still in regard to ordinary space, and were now separated from the earth by twenty thousand
years of cosmic drift! Considered as a time-machine, my invention was
a pretty fair vehicle for interstellar transit.

To say that I was dumbfounded would only prove the inadequacy
of human words. The feeling that surged upon me was the most utter
and abominable panic that I have ever experienced. The sensations of
an explorer lost without a compass amid the eternal, unhorizoned ice of
some Arctic desert would have been mild and infantile in comparison.
Never before had I understood the true awfulness of intersidereal depth
and distance, of the gulf wherein there is neither limitation nor direction.
I seemed to whirl like a lost mote on the winds of immeasurable chaos,
in a vertigo of the spirit as well as of the body.

I reached out for the lever that would reverse the time-energy and
send the sphere backward to its starting-point. Then, in the midst of all
my panic, of all my violent fear and reeling, topsy-turvy confusion, I felt
a reluctance to return. Even in the bleak abyss that yawns unbridgeable
between the stars, I was not allured by the thought of the stale commonplace world I had left.

Miraculously, I began to recover something of stability, of mental
equipoise. I remembered the bright flashes that had puzzled me. These,
I now realized, had marked the passage of an alien sun and planetary
system, coinciding in its orbit with the former position of the earth in
space. If I went on in abstract time, other bodies would doubtless occupy the same position, in the everlasting drift of the universe. By slow-
ing the movement of the sphere, it might be feasible to land on one of
them.

To you, no doubt, the sheer folly and madness of such a project will be more than obvious. Indeed, I must have been a little mad, from the physical and psychic strain of my unparalleled experience. Otherwise, the difficulties of the landing which I so coolly proposed to myself—not to mention the dangers—would have been glaringly manifest.

I resumed the time-flight, at a speed reduced by half. This, I calculated, would enable me to sight the next approaching orb in time to prepare for landing.

The darkness about us was unbroken for an interval of many ages. It seemed to me that eternity itself had gone by in the rayless void ere a brilliant glare of light betokened a nearing sun. It passed us very close, filling half the heavens for an instant. Apparently there were no planets—or, at least none that came within sight.

Steadily we went on in time; till I ceased to watch the dial with its blurred and multiplied ciphers. I lived only in a dream of unreal and spectral duration. But somehow, after awhile, I knew that more than a million years had been travelled by the sphere.

Then, suddenly, another solar orb swam up before us. We must have passed through it, for the sphere was briefly surrounded by an incandescent flame, that seemed as if it would annihilate us with its intolerable flare. Then we were out of it, were suspended in black space, and a smaller, gleaming body was hurtling toward us.

This, I knew, would be a planet. I slowed the sphere to a rate of speed that would permit me to examine it. The thing loomed upon us, it whirled beneath us in a riot of massed images. I thought that I could distinguish seas and continents, isles and mountains. It rose still nearer, and appeared to surround us with swirling forms that were suggestive of enormous vegetable growths.

My hand was poised in readiness on the lever that would terminate our flight. As we swung dizzily amid the swirling forest, I brought the machine to a full stop, no doubt risking an instantaneous destruction. I heard a violent crash, and the vessel rocked and reeled deliriously. Then it seemed to right itself, and stood still. It was lurching half to one side, and I had nearly been wrenched from my seat, while Li Wong was sprawling in an undignified position on the floor. But nevertheless, we had landed!

Still giddy, and trying to regain my equilibrium, I peered through the crystalline walls on a weird and exuberant tangle of bewildering plant-forms. The time-machine was lodged between the swollen, liver-colored boles of certain of these plants and was hanging four or five feet in air above a pink and marshy soil from which protruded like sinister horns the brownish-purple tips of unknown growths. Overhead, there were huge, pale, flabby leaves with violet veinings in which I seemed to detect the arterial throb of sluggish pulses. The leaves depended from the bulbous top of each plant like a circle of flattened arms from a headless torso.

There were other vegetable forms, all crowding and looming grotesquely in the green, vaporous air whose density was such as to give almost the appearance of a submarine garden to the odd scene. From every side, I received a confused impression of python-like rattans, of poddy, fulsome, coral-tinted fronds and white or vermilion fungoid blossoms that were large as firkins. Above the jungle-tops, an olive-golden glimmering in the thick atmosphere betokened the meridian rays of a muffled sun.

My first feelings were those of astonishment—the scene before me was a source of giddiness to eye and brain. Then, as I began to distinguish new details in the medley of towering, outlandish shapes, I conceived a super-added emotion of horror, of veritable disgust. At intervals there were certain immense, bowl-like flowers, supported on strong, hispid stems of a curious tripodal sort, and hued with the ghastly greens and purples of putrefying flesh. In these bowls the squat bulks of mammoth insects—or, rather, of what I took to be such at the moment—were crouching in an evil immobility with strange antennae and other organs or members hanging down over the rims of the bowls.

These monsters appeared to mock the cadaverous coloring of the flowers. They were inexpressibly loathsome, and I shall not endeavor to describe their anatomy with any degree of minuteness. I shall, however, mention the three snail-like horns, ending in ruby-red eyes, that rose above their bodies and watched the forest around them with a baleful vigilance.

About the base of each of the tripodal stems, I perceived the carcasses of quaint animals, lying in a circle, in varying stages of decomposition. From many of these carrion, new plants of the same type as the bowl-flowers were issuing, with dark, ghoulish buds that had not yet unfolded.

As I studied these plants and their guardians with growing repulsion, a six-legged creature, something between a wart-hog and an iguana, emerged from the jungle and trotted past within a dozen feet of the time-sphere. It approached one of the bowl-shaped blossoms, and sniffed at the hairy triple stem with a thin ant-eater snout. Then, to my horror, the squatting form in the huge bowl sprang forth with lightning rapidity and landed on the spine of the hapless animal. I saw the flash of a knife-like sting that was buried in the grotesque body. The victim struggled feebly, and then lay supine, while its assailant proceeded to make use of an organ that resembled the ovipositor of the ichnemon-fly.

All this was highly revolting; and even more repulsive was my discovery that the insect-form was actually a part of the flower in which it had been reposing! It hung by a long, pallid, snaky rope, like a sort of umbilical cord, from the center of the tilted bowl; and after the hideous thing had finished with its victim, the cord began to shorten, drawing the monster back to its lurking-place. There it squatted as before, watching for fresh prey with its ruby eyes. It was damnably obvious that the plant belonged to a semi-faunal genus and was wont to deposit its seeds (or eggs) in animal bodies.

I turned to Li Wong, who was surveying the scene with manifest disapprobation in his almond eyes.

"Me no likee this." He shook his head gravely as he spoke.

"Can't say that I care much for it, either," I returned. "Considered as a landing-place, this particular planet leaves a good deal to be desired. I fear we'll have to go on for a few more million or trillion years, and try our luck elsewhere."

I peered out once more, wondering if the other plant-types around us were all possessed of some disagreeable and aggressive character or ability, like the bowl-flowers. I was not reassured when I noticed that some of the serpentine rattans were swaying sluggishly toward the time-sphere, and that one of them had already reached it and was creeping along the wall with tiny tendrils that ended in suction-cups.

Then, from amid the curling vapors and crowding growths, a bizarre being appeared and ran toward the time-machine, barely avoiding one of the cord-suspended monsters as it launched itself from a tall blossom. The thing fell short of its intended prey by a mere inch or two, and swung horribly in mid-air like a goblin pendulum before it was retracted by the long, elastic cord.

The aforesaid being was about the height of an average man. He was bipedal, but exhibited four arms, two of which issued from either side of his elongated, pillar-like neck and the other two from positions half way down on his wasp-waisted thorax. His facial features were of elfin delicacy, and a high, fluted comb of ivory rose from his broad and hairless crown. His nose, or what appeared to be such, was equipped with mobile feelers that hung down beside his tiny puckered mouth like Oriental mustaches; and his round, discoid ears were furnished with fluttering, streamer-like diaphanous membranes, thin as strips of parchment, on which were curious hieroglyphic markings. His small, sapphire-brilliant eyes were set far apart beneath ebon semi-circles that seemed to have been drawn with pigment on his pearly skin. A short cape of some flossy vermilion fabric served to cover his upper body; but, apart from this, there was nothing that one could distinguish as artificial raiment.

Avoiding several more of the plant-monsters, who lunged viciously, he neared the time-machine. Plainly he had seen us; and it seemed to me that his sapphire eyes implored us for succor and refuge.

I pressed a button which served to unlock and open the door of the sphere. As the door swung outward, Li Wong and I were assailed by numerous unearthly smells, many of which were far from pleasant. We breathed the surge of an air that was heavy with oxygen and was also laden with the vapors of unfamiliar chemical elements.

With a long, flying leap, the strange entity sprang in air and gained the crystal sill of the open machine. I caught the flexible three-fingered hands of his lower arms and drew him to safety. Then I closed the door, just as one of the cord-hung monsters hurtled against it, breaking its keen, steely-looking sting and staining the clear metal with a rill of amber-yellow venom.

"Welcome, stranger," I said.

Our guest was breathing heavily; and his facial feelers trembled and swayed with the palpitation of his fine, membranous nostrils. Apparently he was too breathless for speech; but he made a series of profound inclinations with his crested head, and moved his tenuous fingers with fluttering gestures that were somehow expressive of regard and gratitude.

When he had recovered his breath, and had composed himself a little, he began to talk in a voice of unearthly pitch, with sharp cadences and slowly rising intonations which I can compare only to the notes of certain tropic birds. Of course, Li Wong and I could only guess at his meaning, since the words, whenever distinguishable as such, were totally different from those of any human tongue or dialect.

We surmised, however, that he was thanking us and was also offering us an explanation of the perils from which we had rescued him. He seemed to be telling us a lengthy tale, accompanied with many dramatic gestures of an odd but eloquent sort, and from certain of these, we gathered that his presence in that evil jungle was involuntary; that he had been abandoned there by enemies, in the hope that he would never escape from the wilderness of monstrous plants. By signs, he told us that the jungle was of enormous extent, and was filled with growths that were even more dreadful than the bowl-flowers.

Afterwards, when we had learned to understand the language of this quaint being, we found that our surmises had been correct; but the narrative, in its entirety, was even stranger and more fantastical than we had imagined.

As I listened to our guest, and watched the swiftly weaving movements of his four hands, I became aware that a shadow had fallen upon us, intercepting the green, watery light of the blurred heavens. Looking up, I saw that a small air-vessel, of discoid form, surrounded with turning wheels and pointed wings that whirred like the sails of a wind-mill, was descending toward us and was hovering just above the time-machine.

Our guest perceived it also, and broke off abruptly in his story-telling. I could see that he was greatly alarmed and agitated. I inferred that the air-vessel belonged, perhaps, to his enemies, to the very beings who had left him to a cruel doom in that fearsome terrain. No doubt they had returned to make sure of his fate; or else their attention had in some manner been attracted by the appearance of the time-sphere.

The alien air-ship was now hanging near the tops of the giant plants between whose boles the sphere had become lodged in landing. Through the silvery whirl of its rotating wings and wheels, I saw the faces of several entities who bore a general likeness to our guest, and were plainly of the same racial type. One of these beings was holding a many-mouthed instrument with a far-off resemblance to the Gatling gun, or mitrailleuse, and was aiming it at the time-machine.

Our passenger gave a piercing cry, and clutched my arm with two of his hands while he pointed upward with the others. I required no interpreter, and no lengthy process of reasoning, to understand that we were in grave danger from the foreign vessel and its occupants. I sprang immediately to the instrument board, and released the lever that would send us onward in time at the utmost speed of which the machine was capable.

Even as I pulled the lever, there came from the air-ship a flash of cold and violescent light that seemed to envelop the time-sphere. Then all things in the world without were resolved to a flying riot of formless, evanescent images, and around us once more, after a brief interval, was the ebon darkness of interstellar space. Again the machine was filled with momentary, repeated phantoms, to which were added those of our curious guest. Again the dials, the levers and the dynamos multiplied themselves infinitely in a dim, phosphorescent glow.

Later, I learned that our flight into forward aeons had saved us from utter annihilation only by the fraction of a second. The force emitted by the many-mouthed weapon on the air-vessel would have turned the sphere into vanishing vapor if we had sustained it for more than a moment.

Somehow, I managed to clamp myself into the seat once more, and sat watching the weirdly manifolded hands and ciphers that registered our progress in universal time. Fifty thousand years—a hundred thousand—a million—and still we floated alone in the awesome gulf of the everlasting cosmic midnight. If any suns or planets had passed us during the interim, they had gone by at a distance which rendered them invisible.

Li Wong and the new passenger had clutched at the handles of the lockers in which our provisions were stored, to keep themselves from drifting aimlessly about in mid-air. I heard the babble of their voices, whose every tone and syllable was subdivided into a million echoes.

A peculiar faintness came upon me, and a dream-like sense of the unreal and irrational attached itself to all my impressions and ideas. I seemed to have gone beyond all that was conceivable or comprehensible, to have overpassed the very boundaries of creation. The black chaos in which I wandered was infinitely lost from all direction and orientation, was beyond life itself or the memory of life; and my consciousness seemed to flicker and drown in the dark nullitude of an incommensurable void.

Still we went on along the ages. On the far-off, receding earth, as well as on other planets, whole civilizations had evolved and elapsed and been forgotten, and many historical epochs and geological eras had gone by. Moons and worlds and even great suns had been destroyed. Travelling down their eternal orbits, the very constellations had all shifted their stances amid the infinite. These were inconceivable thoughts; and my brain was overwhelmed by the mere effort to visualize and comprehend their awfulness. Strangest of all was the thought that the world I had known was lost not only in sidereal immensity, but in the rayless night of a remote antiquity!

With more than the longing of a derelict sailor, adrift on chartless seas, I desired to feel underfoot once more the stable soil of Terra Firma—no matter where, or what. We had already made one landing in the dizzy labyrinth of time and space; and somewhere, somehow, among the aeons through which we were passing, another cosmic body might offer itself, intersecting in its spatial path our own position in abstract time.

Again, as before our initial landing, I slowed our progress to a rate that would allow inspection of any sun or world we might happen to approach.

There was a long, dreary interval of waiting, in which it seemed that the whole universe, with all its systems and galaxies, must have gone by us and left us hanging alone in the void that lies beyond organized matter. Then I became aware of a growing light; and, retarding the time-machine still further, I saw that a planet was nearing us; and beyond the planet were two larger and fierier bodies that I took for a binary system of suns.

Now was our opportunity, and I determined to seize it. The new planet whirled beneath us, it rolled upon us again, as we still moved in time at a rate whereby whole days were reduced to minutes. A moment more, and it rose from the gulf like some gigantically swelling bubble to surround us with a maze of half-cognizable imageries. There were atlantean mountain-tops through which we seemed to pass, and seas or level deserts above which we appeared to hover in the midst of broken cloud-strata. Now, for an instant, we were among buildings, or what I assumed to be such; then we were hurled onward to a broad, open space. I caught a confused glittering of many-pointed lights and unidentifiable, thronging forms, as I reached out and brought the sphere to a sudden halt.

As I have said before, it was a perilous thing to stop thus in accelerated time above a moving planet. There might well have been a collision that would have destroyed the machine; or we might have found ourselves embedded beneath fathoms of soil or stone. Indeed, there were any number of undesirable possibilities; and the only wonder is that we escaped annihilation.

As it was, we must have come to a halt in mid-air, perhaps fifteen or twenty feet above the ground. Of course, we were seized immediately by the gravitational influence of the new world. Even as my sense-impressions cleared with the cessation of the time-flight, we fell with a terrible, ear-splitting crash, and the sphere almost seemed to rebound and then rolled over, careening on its side. I was torn from my seat by the shock of impact, and Li Wong and our passenger were hurled to the floor beside me. The stranger and myself, though sorely bruised and shaken, contrived to retain consciousness; but I saw that Li Wong had been stunned by the fall.

Giddily, with swaying limbs and reeling senses, I tried to stand up, and somehow succeeded. My first thought was for Li Wong, who was lying inert against the tilted dynamos. A hasty examination showed me that he was uninjured. My second thought was for the time-machine, whose tough metal revealed no visible damage. Then, inevitably, the world into which we had fallen in a manner so precipitate, was forced upon my attention.

We had come down in the very center of what appeared to be an active battle-field! All around us was a formidable array of chariot-like vehicles, high-wheeled and high-bodied, drawn by quaint monsters that recalled the dragons of heraldry, and driven by beings of an unearthly kind who were little more than pygmies. There were many foot-soldiers, too, and all were armed with weapons such as have never been used in human history. There were spears that ended in curving, saw-toothed blades, and swords whose hilts were in the middle, and spiked balls at the end of long, leathern thongs, which were hurled at the enemy and then drawn back by their owners. Also, each of the chariots was fitted with a catapult, from which similar balls were flung.

The users of these weapons had paused in the midst of what was plainly a ferocious battle, and were all staring at the time-machine. Some, I saw, had been crushed beneath the heavy sphere as it plunged among them. Others had drawn back, and were eyeing us doubtfully.

Even as I surveyed this singular scene, with bewilderment that permitted no more than a partial cognizance of its baffling details, I saw that the interrupted combat was being resumed. The monster-drawn chariots swayed back and forth, and the air was thick with flying missiles, some of which hurtled against the walls of the sphere. It seemed, perhaps, that our presence was having an effect on the morale of these fantastic warriors. Many of those who were nearest to the sphere began to retreat, while others pressed forward; and I was able for the first time to distinguish the members of the two factions, who obviously belonged to different races.

Those of one faction, who were all foot-soldiers armed with spears and swords, were seemingly a rude barbaric type. They outnumbered the others greatly. Their fearsome, uncouth features were like graven masks of fury and malignity; and they fought with a savage desperation.

Their opponents, who comprised all the chariot-drivers, as well as a smaller body of foot-soldiers, were more delicate and civilized in appearance, with slighter limbs and anatomies. They made a skillful use of their catapults; and the tide of the battle seemed to be turning in their favor. When I perceived that all those who had been struck down by the time-machine belonged to the more barbarous type, I inferred that possibly our apparition had been construed as favorable to one faction and inimical to the other. The catapult-users were gaining courage; and the spear and sword bearers were becoming visibly demoralized.

The combat turned to an ever-growing rout. The corps of chariots gathered in a crushing mass about the time-sphere and drove the enemy swiftly back, while, in the heat of conflict, a barrage of singular weapons continued to assail our hyaline walls.

Ferocious-looking as they were, the dragons seemed to take no active part in the struggle, and were plainly mere beasts of draught or burden. But the slaughter was terrific; and crushed or trodden bodies were lying everywhere. The role of *deus ex machina* which I appeared to be playing in this outlandish battle was not one that I should have chosen of my own accord; and I soon decided that it would be better to fare even further afield in universal time.

I pulled the starting-lever; but, to my confoundment and consternation, there was no result. The mechanism in some manner had been jarred or disconnected by the violence of our fall, though I could not locate the precise difficulty at that moment. Afterwards, I found that the connection between the instrument-board and the dynamos had been broken, thus rendering the force inoperative.

Li Wong had now recovered consciousness. Rubbing his head, he sat up and appeared to be pondering our remarkable milieu with all the gravity of an Oriental philosopher. Our passenger was peering out with his brilliant sapphire eyes on this world to which he was no less alien than Li Wong and myself. He seemed to be eyeing the odd warriors and their dragon-teams with a cool scientific interest.

The more civilized of the two factions was now driving its enemies from the field in a tide of carnage. Our sound-proof walls prevented us from hearing the clash and rumble of chariot-wheels, the clangor of clashing weapons, and the cries that were doubtless being emitted by the warriors.

Since nothing could be done at the moment to repair our machinery, I resigned myself, not without misgivings, to an indefinite sojourn in the world whereon we had landed so fortuitously.

In perhaps ten minutes, the raging battle was over, the unslain remnant of the barbarians was in full flight, and the conquerors, who had poured past us in an irresistible torrent, were returning and massing about the sphere at a little distance.

Several, whom I took for commanding officers, descended from their cars and approached us. They prostrated themselves before the machine in the universal posture of reverence.

For the first time, I was able to form an exact impression of the appearance of these beings. The tallest of them was barely four feet in height, and their limbs, which were normal in number according to human ideas, were slender as those of elves or leprechauns. Their movements were very swift and graceful, and were seemingly aided by a pair of small wings or erigible membranes attached to their sloping shoulders.

Their faces were marked by a most elaborate development of the nostrils and eyes; and the ears and mouths were little more than vestigial by contrast. The nasal apparatus was convoluted like those of certain bats, with mobile valves arranged in rosettes, and a nether appendage that recalled the petals of a butterfly orchid. The eyes were proportionately enormous and were set obliquely. They were furnished with vertical lids and possessed a power of semi-circular rotation and also of protrusion and retraction in their deep orbits. This power, we learned later, enabled them to magnify or reduce any visual image at will, and also to alter or invert the perspective in which it was seen.

These peculiar beings were equipped with body-armor of red metal marked off in ovoid scales. Their light-brown arms and legs were bare. Somehow their whole aspect was very gentle and un-warlike. I marvelled at the prowess and bravery which they had shown in the late battle.

They continued their obeisances before the time-machine, rising and prostrating themselves anew, in an alternation like a set ritual with gestures and genuflections of hieratic significance. I conceived the idea that they regarded the machine itself as a conscious, intelligent and perhaps supernal entity; and that we the occupants, if perceived at all, were considered as internal and integral parts of the mechanism.

Li Wong and I began to debate the advisability of opening the doors and revealing ourselves to these fantastic devotees. Unluckily, I had neglected to provide the sphere with any device for determining the chemical composition of otherworld atmospheres; and I was not sure that the outside air would prove wholly suitable for human respiration. It was this consideration, rather than any actual fear of the mild, quaint warriors, that caused me to hesitate.

I decided to defer our epiphany; and I was about to resume my examination of the deranged machinery, when I noticed an ebullition in the massed ranks of soldiers that were drawn up around us at some little distance. The ranks parted with a swift, flowing motion, leaving a wide lane through which, presently, a remarkable vehicle advanced.

The vehicle was a sort of open platform mounted on numerous low, squat wheels, and drawn by a dozen of the dragon-creatures, arranged in teams of four. The platform was rectangular, and the small, castor-like wheels served to elevate it little more than a foot above the ground. I could not determine its material, which was copperish in color and suggested a heavy metallic stone rather than a pure, smelted metal. It was without furnishings or superstructure, aside from a low breast-work at the front, behind which three drivers stood, each holding the separate reins of a tandem of monsters; and at the rear, a strange outward-curving arm or crane of some black, lustrous material ending in a thick disk, which rose high in the air. One of the elfin people stood beside this crane.

With exquisite and admirable skill, the drivers brought their unwieldy conveyance forward in a sweeping arc through the empty space between the time-vessel and the surrounding army. The devotees of the sphere, who must have been commanding officers, retired to one side;

and the monster-hauled vehicle, passing us closely, was adroitly maneu-
vered and drawn about till it came to a halt with its rear end opposite
the sphere and the black arm inclining above our very heads with its
heavy horizontal disk.

The being who stood beside the curving arm began to manipulate
an oddly shaped and movable projection (which must have been a sort
of lever or control) in its dark surface. Watching him curiously, I became
aware of a sudden and increasing glare of light overhead; and looking
up, I saw that a lid-like cover was sliding back from the disk at the arm's
end, revealing a fire-bright substance that dazzled the eye.

Simultaneously, I felt a sensation of corporeal lightness, of growing
weightlessness. I reeled with vertigo, and reaching toward the wall in an
effort to steady myself, I floated buoyantly from the floor and drifted in
mid-air. Li Wong and the stranger, I perceived, were floundering eerily
and helplessly about amid the machinery.

Perplexed by this phenomenon of degravitation, I did not realize at
first that there had been a similar levitation of the time-sphere itself.
Then, as I turned in my aerial tumbling, I saw that the sphere had risen
from the ground and was now on a level with the floor of the strange
conveyance. It occurred to me that an unknown magnetic force was being emitted by the bright disk above our heads; and no sooner had I
conceived this idea, when the outward-curving arm began to rotate,
swinging back upon the vehicle of which it formed a part; and the time-
machine, as if suspended by invisible chains, swung with it, maintaining
a vertical position beneath the moving disk. In a trice, it was gently deposited on the platform. Then, like the switching-off of a light, the glaring disk was covered again by its dark lid, and the properties of normal
weight returned to my companions and to me.

The whole process of loading the sphere upon the platform had
been accomplished with remarkable celerity and efficiency. As soon as
it was completed the three drivers, with perfect concertion, reined their
tandems of dragons about in a long semi-circle, and started off on the

route by which they had come. Moving at considerable speed, we rolled easily along the wide lane that had been opened through the quaint army. The chariots and foot-soldiers closed behind us as we went; and looking back, I saw them wheel about and reform, with the chariots in the van. Passing through the outermost ranks, we took the lead, and the whole army followed us in martial order across a low plain.

I was struck by the seeming discrepancy between the preter-human control of gravitation possessed by this curious people, and their somewhat primitive modes of warfare and conveyance. Judging them, as I did, by terrestrial standards, I could not reconcile these things; and the true explanation was too bizarre and fantastic for me to have imagined it beforehand.

We proceeded toward our unknown destination, with the dragons trotting at a leisurely pace that covered more ground than one would have expected. I began to observe the surrounding milieu and to take note of much that had escaped me heretofore.

The plain, I saw, was treeless, with low hummocks and intervals of winding mounds, and was wholly covered with a short, lichenous growth that formed a kind of yellow-green turf. One of the two suns was hanging at meridian; and the other was either just rising or setting, for it hovered close to a far-off horizon of glaucous hills. The sky was tinted with deep green, and I saw that this color was due to the combined light of the suns, one of which was azure blue and the other verging upon amber.

After we had gone on for several miles and had passed a row of intervening hummocks, I beheld a strange city in the near distance, with low mushroom domes and peristyles of massive pillars that gleamed like rosy marble in the sunlight amid plots of orange and indigo and violet vegetation.

This city proved to be our objective. It was thronged with people among whom we passed on the dragon-drawn platform, borne like the trophies of a triumph. The buildings were roomy and well-spaced and were characterized by deep porticoes with swelling, bulbous columns. We learned subsequently that the material used in their construction was a sort of petrified wood, belonging to a genus of giant prehistoric trees, that had been quarried in enormous blocks.

After passing through many streets, we neared, in what was apparently the center of the town, a huge circular edifice. It consisted of a single dome upborne on rows of open, colossal pillars, with an entrance broad and high enough to admit with ease the vehicle on which the time-sphere was being carried. We rolled smoothly through the portals and along a level pavement beneath the vast dome.

The place was illumed by the horizontal rays of the sinking yellow sun, which fell on the ruddy floor in broad shafts between the massy pillars. I received an impression of immense empty space, of rosy-golden air and light. Then, in the center, as we went forward, I saw a sort of dais on which stood an extraordinary machine or contrivance of parti-colored metals, towering alone like an idol in some pagan fane. The dais, like the building, was circular, and rose four or five feet above the main pavement. It was perhaps sixty feet in diameter, and there were several stairs, graduated to the steps of the pygmy people, that gave access to it. Around the dais, in semi-circles on the pavement, with ample space between, there stood many low tables, supported on carven cubes and with benches about them, all of the same material as the edifice itself. The tables were set with numerous black pots, deep and shallow and multi-form, in which grew flowers of opulent orange and cassava colors, together with others of delicate white, of frail pink and silvery green.

These details I perceived hastily and confusedly as our conveyance moved on toward the central dais without endangering any of the tables. A sprinkling of people, who gave the impression of menials, were hurrying about the place, bringing new flower-pots or re-arranging certain of the ones that had already been disposed. Many of the elfin warriors, dismounting from their chariots, had followed us through the great portals.

Now the vehicle had drawn up beside the dais. By the operation of the black arm with its magnetic disk, the time-machine was lifted from the platform and deposited on the dais not far from the tall contrivance of multi-colored metals. Then, circling the dais, the vehicle withdrew with its dragon-team and vanished through the open entrance.

Whether the place was a temple or merely a public hall, I could not decide. It was like the phantasmagoria of some bewildering dream, and the mystery of it all was not solved when I noticed that hundreds of the faërypeople were seating themselves at the flower-laden tables and were bending toward the blossoms with a regular contraction and expansion of their voluted nostrils, as if they were inhaling delicious perfumes. To complicate my bewilderment still further, I could distinguish nothing on any of the tables in the form of food, nourishment or even drink, such as these heroic warriors might well be expected to require after an arduous battle.

Dismissing temporarily the baffling enigma, I turned my attention to the peculiar mechanism which occupied the dais together with the time-sphere. Here, too, I found myself at a loss, for I could not even surmise its nature and purpose. I had never seen anything like it among the most ingenious, pernicious and grotesque inventions of terrene mechanics.

The thing was quite gigantic, with a bristling, serried and fearsome array of highly polished rods and pistons, of long, spiral bands and abrupt, angular flanges, behind which I made out the half-hidden outlines of a squat cylindrical body, mounted on at least seven or eight ponderous legs that terminated in huge pads like the feet of hippopotami.

Above the complicated mass, there towered a sort of triple head, or superstructure of three globes, one above the other on a long metal neck. The heads were fitted with rows of eye-like facets, cold and bright as diamonds, and possessed numerous antennae and queer, unnamable appendages, some of great length. The whole apparatus had the air of some mysterious living entity—a super-machine endowed with sentience and with intellect; and the three-tiered head with its chill eyes appeared to watch us malignly and inscrutably like a metal Argus.

The thing was a miracle of machinery; and it gleamed with hues of gold and steel, of copper and malachite, of silver and azurite and cinnabar. But more and more I was impressed by an evil and brooding intentness, an aura of the sinister and the inimical. The monstrosity was motionless—but intelligent. Then, as I continued my inspection, I saw a movement of the foremost legs, and became aware that the machine was advancing stiffly on its massive pads toward the time-vessel.

It paused at an interval of five or six feet, and put out a long, thin, supple, many-jointed tentacle from the mass of appendages that adorned its topmost head. With this tentacle, like a raised whip, it struck smartly several times at the curving wall of the sphere.

I could not help feeling somewhat alarmed as well as puzzled; for the action was unmistakably hostile. The blows of the tentacle were somehow like a challenge—the equivalent, so to speak, of an actual slap in the face. And the wary movement with which the machine stepped back and stood facing us, after delivering the whip-sharp blows, was curiously like the manœuvre of a fighter, squaring himself for combat. The thing seemed almost to crouch on its elephantine metal legs and pads; and there was an air of covert menace in its poised array of mysterious, deadly-looking parts and appendages.

At this moment there occurred a singular interruption which, in all likelihood, was the means of averting our death and the destruction of the time-globe. A group of the elfin people, four in number, ascended the stairs of the dais and approached us, bearing among them a large vessel, like an open shallow urn or deep basin, which was filled to the brim with a sluggish, hueless liquid, suggesting immediately some sort of mineral oil. Behind this group there came a second, carrying another vessel full of the same oleaginous fluid.

The two delegations, moving forward in perfect unison, deposited their burdens at the same instant, with the same peculiar genuflections, setting one of the basins before the time-sphere and the other at the feet of the belligerent alien mechanism. Afterwards they retired discreetly as they had come. The whole performance had the air of a religious rite— a sacrificial offering, intended to appease doubtful or angry deities.

Not without inward amusement, I wondered what use the time-sphere was supposed to make of the oily liquid. It seemed probable that we and our conveyance were regarded as a single mechanism, active and intelligent, and perhaps similar in kind to the curious Robot we had found occupying the dais.

The latter machine, however, was manifestly familiar with such offerings; for, without acknowledgement or ceremony, it proceeded to stoop over and dip certain of its metal proboscides in the oil. These organs, I perceived, were hollow at the ends, like the trunks of elephants; and I saw that the liquid in the basin was diminishing rapidly, as if it were being sucked up. When the vessel was half empty, the monster withdrew its proboscides; and then, by the simultaneous use of these members, turning and coiling with great suppleness in different directions, it began to oil the innumerable joints and flanges of its intricate machinery. Several times it suspended this remarkable process, eyeing the time-sphere balefully as if watching for a hostile movement. The whole performance was inconceivably grotesque and ludicrous—and sinister.

The main floor of the huge pillared hall, I now saw, had filled with the pygmy warriors, who were seated about the flower-burdened tables. All of them seemed to be inhaling the odors of these flowers in a manner that resembled actual ingestion; and I conceived the idea that they were regaling themselves with a feast of perfumes and perhaps required no other nutrient.

Turning from this quaint spectacle, to which I had given only a cursory glance, I perceived that the metal monster had apparently finished the anointing of its complex machinery and was again posting itself in an attitude preparatory for battle. There was a stealthy turning of half-hidden wheels and cogs, a covert throbbing of well-oiled pistons, as the mechanism faced us; and certain of its tentacles were poised in air like lifted weapons.

What would have happened next, in the normal course of events, I am not altogether sure; but the probabilities are that we would have been blotted out of existence very promptly, efficiently and summarily. Again, by a singular intervention, the time-vessel was saved from the anger of its strange antagonist.

Without warning, there came a flash of brilliant blinding flame, as if a thunder-bolt had issued from mid-air between the dais and the dome. There was a crashing, shivering noise that shook and penetrated our virtually sound-proof walls; and everything about us seemed to rock with the convulsions of a violent earthquake. The concussion hurled us back upon our dynamos; and I thought for an instant that the sphere would be flung from the dais. Recovering myself, I saw that a third machine had materialized on the dais, opposite the time-sphere and its opponent!

This machine differed as much from the hostile Robot as the latter, in its turn, differed from the time-globe. It was a sort of immense polyhedron, with an arrangement of numberless facets alternately opaque and transparent. Through some of the facets, clearer than glass, I was horrified and astonished to behold the thronging faces of entities similar to, or perhaps identical with, the beings who had threatened us from the air-vessel in that far-off world where we had picked up our unusual passenger.

There could be only one explanation: we had been pursued through the cosmic continuum by these vengeful and pertinacious creatures, who had evidently employed a time-space vehicle of their own; and who must have possessed unique instruments of incredible range and delicacy by which to detect and follow our course in the labyrinth of stellar gulfs and ages! Turning to our passenger, I saw by his troubled air and frantic gestures that he too had recognized the pursuers. Since I had not yet been able to repair our machinery, the position in which we now stood was a serious dilemma. We were without weapons of any kind, for it had not even occurred to me to bring along a revolver. I began to wish that I had fitted the time-machine with the arsenal of an American racketeer.

However, there was little time for either regret or apprehension. The course of events was now taking an unforeseen and incalculable turn. The formidable Robot, diverted from its war-like designs upon us by the appearance of the newcomer, had immediately squared itself around to face the polyhedron, with its metal members raised in a flailing gesture of menace. The occupants of the polyhedron, on their part, seemed to disregard the Robot. Several of the opaque facets began to slide back in the manner of ports, and revealed the yawning mouths of tubular weapons, all of which were levelled at the time-sphere. It appeared that these people were intent only on destroying us, after having followed us with fantastical vindictiveness through many aeons.

The Robot, it would seem, construed the opening of the ports as an act inimical to itself. Or perhaps it did not wish to yield its legitimate prey, the time-sphere, to another and foreign mechanism. At any rate, it bristled forward, winnowing the air with all its tentacles and proboscides, and tramping heavily on the dais with its myriad pads, till it stood within grappling-distance of the polyhedron. Coils of greyish vapor were beginning to issue from valves in its cylindrical body and pipe-like throat; and raising one of its hollow proboscides, it snorted forth a sudden jet of crimson flame—a briefly flaring tongue that struck an upper facet of the polyhedron, causing it to melt and collapse inward like so much solder.

The occupants of the alien time-machine were now slewing their tube-weapons around to face the Robot. A violescent fire leapt from one of the tubes, spreading like a fan, and severing cleanly an upraised tentacle of the monster. At this the angry mechanism seemed to go mad, and hurled itself at the polyhedron like some enormous octopus of metal. Jets of scarlet fire were issuing from several of its trunk-shaped organs, and great ruinous rents appeared in the facets of the polyhedron beneath their incessant playing. Undismayed by this, the wielders of the tube-weapons concentrated their violet beams on the Robot, inflicting terrific damage. The uppermost of the three globular heads was partly shot away, and metal filaments trailed from its broken rim like a shredded brain. The serried array of tossing members was torn and lopped like a flame-swept forest. Rods, cogs, pistons, and other parts dripped on the dais in a molten rain. Two of the foremost legs crumpled in shapeless ruin—but still the monster fought on; and the polyhedron became a twisted wreck beneath the focussing of the red fires.

Soon several of the violet beams were extinguished, and their wielders had dissolved into vapor and ashes. But other beams were still in action; and one of them struck the central cylinder of the Robot, after demolishing the outer machinery, and bored into it steadily like an acetylene torch. The beam must have penetrated a vital part, for suddenly there was a tremendous, all-engulfing flare, a cataclysmic explosion. The immense dome appeared to totter on its trembling columns, and the dais shook like a stormy sea. Then, an instant later, there fell from a dark cloud of swelling steam, a rain of metal fragments, glancing along our crystalline sides and strewing the dais and the main floor for some distance around. The monster, in its explosion, had involved the alien time-vessel, which was wholly riven asunder; and nothing remained of our pursuers but a few blackened cinders. Apart from this mutual and highly providential destruction of the inimical mechanisms, no serious damage had been done; for the main building, I now perceived for the first time, was deserted—the pygmies had abandoned their feast of odors and had retired discreetly, perhaps at the very onset of the battle. The time-sphere, though it had taken no part in the combat, was left by a singular and ironic fortuity in sole possession of the field.

I decided that fortune, being so favorably disposed toward us, might be tempted even further with impunity. So I opened the vessel's door, and found that the atmosphere of the world outside was perfectly breathable, though laden with an odd mixture of metallic fumes that lingered from the late explosion, and fruity and luscious fragrances from the potted blossoms.

Li Wong and the passenger and I emerged on the dais. The yellow sun had gone down, and the place swam with the blue, religious light of its ascendant binary. We were examining the littered ruins of the strange machines when a large delegation of elfin warriors re-entered and approached us. We could not divine their thoughts and emotions; but it seemed to me that their genuflections were even more expressive of profound reverence and gratitude than those with which the time-sphere had been hailed after the routing of the barbarian army. I received an almost telepathic impression that they were thanking us for a supposed act of deliverance at which we had been merely the onlookers.

In time, this impression was to be fully confirmed. The metal monster, it seemed, had come originally, like ourselves, from the outside universe, and had settled itself among this perfume-eating people. They had treated it with all due respect, had housed it in their public hall of assembly and had supplied it liberally with certain mineral lubricants which it required. The machine, in exchange, had deigned to instruct them regarding a few scientific and mechanical secrets such as that of degravitation by means of a reverse magnetic force; but the people, being somewhat non-inventive and non-mechanical by nature, had made little use of this Robot-imparted knowledge.

The metal monster, in time, had become disagreeably exacting and tyrannical; and moreover, it had flatly refused to help the pygmies in their war with another people when need arose. Therefore they were glad to be rid of it; and they seemed to take it for granted that we had made away with the monster as well as with the invading time-machine. So far, I have not thought it worth while to disillusion them in this regard.

No less than seven terrestrial months have now gone by since the landing of the sphere. My companions and I are still sojourning among the perfume-eaters; and we have no reason to complain of our lot, and no cause to lament the worlds we have left so far behind us in time and space.

In the interim, we have learned many things, and are now able to hold converse with our hosts, having familiarized ourselves by slow degrees with the peculiar phonetics of their speech.

The name of the world, as well as I can render it in human spelling, is Mohaun Los. Being subject to the gravitational pull of two solar bodies, it follows a somewhat eccentric and prolonged annual orbit. Nevertheless, the climate is equable and salubrious; though marked by meteoric phenomena of an unearthly sort.

The people among whom we are dwelling call themselves the Psounas. They are a fine and estimable race, though bizarre from a human standpoint as any of the mythic tribes whose anatomy and customs were described by Herodotus. They are the ruling race of the planet, and are inconceivably more advanced in many ways than their rude weapons and methods of warfare would lead one to imagine. Astronomy and mathematics, in particular, have been developed by them to a degree that is far beyond the achievement of human savants.

Their food consists of nothing grosser than perfumes; and at first, it was not easy to convince them that we required a more material nourishment. However, once they had grasped the idea, they supplied us abundantly with the meaty fruits in which Mohaun Los abounds; and they did not seem to be shocked or scandalized by our base appetites— even though fruits and other non-atomizable matters are eaten only by animals and the more aboriginal races of this world. The Psounas, indeed, have shown toward us at all times a spirit of urbane tolerance and *laissez faire*.

They are a peaceful race, and during their whole former history have had little need to acquire the martial arts. But the recent evolutionary development of a half-bestial tribe, the Gholpos, who have now learned to organize themselves and to make weapons, and have become quite aggressive as a consequence, has compelled the Psounas to take the field in self-defense.

The descent of the time-machine, falling upon their enemies during a crucial battle, was a most fortunate happening; for these ignorant savages, the Gholpos, regarded it as a manifestation of some divine or demoniac power in league with the Psounas, and were henceforward altogether broken and cowed.

The Psounas, it seems, were prone even from the first to a more naturalistic supposition regarding the character and origin of the time-sphere. Their long familiarity with the strange ultra-stellar Robot may have helped to disabuse them of any belief in the supernaturalism of mere machinery. I have had no difficulty in explaining to them the mechanism of our vessel and the voyage we have made along the aeons. My efforts, however, to tell them something of my own world, of its peoples and customs, have so far met with polite incredulity or sheer incomprehension. Such a world, they say, is quite unheard-of; and if they were not so courteous, probably they would tell me that it could not even be imagined by any rational being.

Li Wong and I, as well as the Psounas, have learned to talk with the singular entity whom I rescued from the diabolic living flowers on a world midway between the earth and Mohaun Los. This person calls himself Tuoquan, and he is a most erudite savant. His ideas and discoveries, being somewhat at variance with the notions that prevail in his own world, had caused him to be regarded with suspicion and hatred by his fellows; and, as I surmised, he had been abandoned by them, after due process of law, to a cruel doom in the jungle. The time-machine in which they had followed us to Mohaun Los was, he believed, the only vessel of the kind that had so far been invented by this people. Their zealous and fanatic devotion to legality and law-enforcement would have led them to pursue us beyond the boundaries of the universal continuum. Fortunately, there was small likelihood that they would ever dispatch another time-machine on our trail: for the lingering etheric vibrations that had enabled them to follow us, as dogs follow the scent of their quarry, would die out long before they could construct a duplicate of the unreturning polyhedron.

With the aid of the Psounas, who have supplied me with the necessary metallic elements, I have repaired the broken connection in the time-sphere. I have also made a miniature duplicate of the mechanism, in which I am planning to enclose this letter and send it backward through time, in the seemingly far-fetched and fantastic hope that it may somehow reach the earth and be received by you.

The astronomers of the Psounas have helped me to make the needful computations and adjustments which, indeed, would be utterly beyond my own skill or the mathematical knowledge of any human being. By combining in these calculations the chronometric records of the dials in the time-sphere with the ephemerides of Mohaun Los during the past seven months, and allowing for the pauses and changes of speed which we made during our journey, it has been possible to chart the incredibly complicated course which the mechanism must follow in time and space. If the calculations are correct to the most infinitesimal degree, and the movement of the device is perfectly synchronized, the thing will stop at the very moment and in the very same place from which I left the earth in retrograde time. But of course it will be a miracle if it reaches the earth at all. The Psounas have pointed out to me a ninth-magnitude star which they think is the solar orb of the system in which I was born.

If the letter should ever reach you, I have no reason to think that you will believe my tale. Nevertheless, I am going to ask you to publish it, even though the world in general will regard it as the fantasy of a madman or a practical joker. It pleases an obscure sense of irony in my mental make-up, to know that the truth will be heard by those among whom it must pass for a fantastic lie. Such an eventuation, perhaps, will be far from novel or unprecedented.

As I have said before, I am well enough contented with life in Mohaun Los. Even death, I am told, is a pleasant thing in this world, for when the Psounas wax old and weary, they repair to a hidden valley in which they are overcome by the lethal and voluptuous perfumes of narcotic flowers.

However, it may be that the nostalgia of new ages and new planets will seize me anon, and I shall feel impelled to continue my journey among future cycles. Li Wong, it goes without saying, will accompany me in any such venture: though he is quite happily engaged at present in translating the Odes of Confucius and other Chinese classics for the benefit of the people of Mohaun Los. (This poetry, I might add, is meeting with a better reception than my tales regarding Occidental civilization.)

Tuoquan, who is teaching the Psounas to make the fearfully destructive weapons of his own world, may decide to go with us; for he is full of intellectual curiosities. Perhaps we shall follow the great circle of time, till the years and aeons without number have returned upon themselves once more, and the past is made a sequel to the future!

Yours ever,
DOMITIAN

Editor's Note: Granting the truth of Domitian Malgraff's narrative, and admitting that his letter was launched from a world in future time, there are still certain problems that baffle explanation. No one knows how long the mechanism containing the letter had been floating in the Banda Sea before it was picked up: but in order to reach the earth at all, in the unimaginably complicated maze of temporal and spatial movement, it must have fallen there not long after the departure of the time-machine from Malgraff's laboratory. As Malgraff himself indicates in his letter, if the timing had been absolutely perfect it would have landed in his laboratory at the very moment when he and Li Wong began their journey!

FROM THE CRYPTS OF MEMORY

Aeons of aeons ago, in an epoch whose marvellous worlds have crumbled, and whose mighty suns are less than shadow, I dwelt in a star whose course, decadent from the high, irremeable heavens of the past, was even then verging upon the abyss in which, said astronomers, its immemorial cycle should find a dark and disastrous close.

Ah, strange was that gulf-forgotten star—how stranger than any dream of dreamers in the present, or than any vision that hath risen upon visionaries in their retrospection of the universal Past: There, thru inestimable cycles of a history whose records were beyond the computation of savants, the dead had come to infinitely outnumber the living; And, reared of a stone not destructible save in the enormous furnace of suns, their cities rose beside those of the living like Titan metropoli whose mighty precincts have begun to overgloom the vicinal villages. And over all was the black, funereal vault of the cryptic heavens—a dome of infinite shadows wherein the dismal sun, suspended like a sole, enormous lamp, failed to illumine, and, drawing back its fires from the face of the irresolvable ether, threw a baffled and despairing beam on the vague, remote horizons, and shrouded vistas interminate of the visionary land.

We were a sombre, melancholy people, who dwelt beneath the palls of twilight and silence thrown about the towering tombs and monuments of the Past: In our veins was the chill of the ancient night of Time, with a premonition of the lentor of Lethe; over us, like invisible vampires, brooded the innumerous hours on their sable and unremoving pinions; the very skies were fraught with oppression, and we breathed beneath them as in a sepulcher, forever sealed with all its stagnancies of corruption and of darkness.

Vaguely we lived, and loved as in dreams—the dim and mystic dreams that hover upon the verge of unfathomable sleep. We felt for our women, with their pale and spectral beauty, the same desire that the dead may feel for the phantom lilies of Hadean meads. Our days were spent in roaming through the ruins of lone and immemorial cities, or in the vast and shadowy fanes from whose awful and everlasting glooms of elder mystery, the simulachres of century-forgotten gods looked forth with unalterable eyes on the hopeless heavens, and saw but night and oblivion. Or, wandering through ashen fields of perennial autumn, we found the flowers of wan funebrial immortelles, that wept with a melancholy dew by the flowing silence of Acherontic waters.

And one by one we died, and were lost in the dust of accumulated time. We knew the years as a passing of shadows, and death itself as the yielding of twilight unto night.

Acknowledgments

"The Abomination of Desolation." *Phantasmagoria* 1, No. 4 (November 1938): 11. Text taken from *Poems in Prose* (Arkham House, 1964).

"The Abominations of Yondo." *Overland Monthly* 84, No. 4 (April 1926): 100–101, 114, 126. In *The Abominations of Yondo* (Arkham House, 1960). Text taken from *The End of the Story* (Night Shade, 2006).

"Atlantis." In *The Star-Treader and Other Poems* (A. M. Robertson, 1912). In *Selected Poems* (Arkham House, 1971). Text taken from *The Complete Poetry and Translations* (Hippocampus Press, 2008).

"A Chinese Fable." Text taken from *Lost Worlds* No. 2 (2004): 2.

"Chinoiserie." *Philippine Magazine* 27, No. 12 (November 1931): 728, 752, 756. Text taken from *Poems in Prose* (Arkham House, 1964).

"The Death of Malygris." *Weird Tales* 23, No. 4 (April 1934): 488–96. In *Lost Worlds* (Arkham House, 1944). Text taken from *The Last Hieroglyph* (Night Shade, 2010).

"The Double Shadow." In *The Double Shadow and Other Fantasies* ([Auburn Journal Print], 1933). *Weird Tales* 33, No. 2 (February 1939): 47–55. In *Out of Space and Time* (Arkham House, 1942). Text taken from *A Vintage from Atlantis* (Night Shade, 2007).

"Ennui." *Smart Set* 56, No. 1 (September 1918): 32. In *Ebony and Crystal* (The Auburn Journal, 1922). Text taken from *Poems in Prose* (Arkham House, 1964).

"From a Letter." In *Ebony and Crystal* (The Auburn Journal, 1922). Text taken from *Poems in Prose* (Arkham House, 1964).

"From the Crypts of Memory." *Bohemia* 2, No. 3 (April 1917): 27. In *Ebony and Crystal* (The Auburn Journal, 1922). In *Out of Space and Time* (Arkham House, 1942). Text taken from *Poems in Prose* (Arkham House, 1964).

"The Ghoul." *Fantasy Fan* 1, No. 5 (January 1934): 69–72. In *Other Dimensions* (Arkham House, 1970). Text taken from *The Door to Saturn* (Night Shade, 2007).

"In Lemuria." *Lyric West* 1, No. 4 (July–August 1921): 6. In *Ebony and Crystal* (The Auburn Journal, 1922). In *Selected Poems* (Arkham House, 1971). Text taken from *The Complete Poetry and Translations* (Hippocampus Press, 2008).

"The Invisible City." *Wonder Stories* 4, No. 1 (June 1932): 6–13. In *Other Dimensions* (Arkham House, 1970). Text taken from *A Vintage from Atlantis* (Night Shade, 2007).

"The Justice of the Elephant." *Oriental Stories* 1, No. 6 (Autumn 1931): 856, 858, 863–64. In *Other Dimensions* (Arkham House, 1970). Text taken from *The Door to Saturn* (Night Shade, 2007).

"The Kingdom of the Worm." *Fantasy Fan* 1, No. 2 (October 1933): 17–22. In *Other Dimensions* (Arkham House, 1970). Text taken from *The Door to Saturn* (Night Shade, 2007).

"The Kiss of Zoraida." *Magic Carpet Magazine* 3, No. 3 (July 1933): 373–76. In *Other Dimensions* (Arkham House, 1970). Text taken from *The Door to Saturn* (Night Shade, 2007).

"The Last Incantation." *Weird Tales* 15, No. 6 (June 1930): 783–86. In *Lost Worlds* (Arkham House, 1944). Text taken from *The End of the Story* (Night Shade, 2006).

"The Letter from Mohaun Los." *Wonder Stories* 4, No. 3 (August 1932): 218–29 (as "Flight into Super-Time"). In *Lost Worlds* (Arkham House, 1944). Text taken from *The Door to Saturn* (Night Shade, 2007).

"An Offering to the Moon." *Weird Tales* 45, No. 4 (September 1953): 54–61. In *Other Dimensions* (Arkham House, 1970). Text taken from *The Door to Saturn* (Night Shade, 2007).

"The Passing of Aphrodite." *Fantasy Fan* 2, No. 4 (December 1934): 59–60. In *The Abominations of Yondo* (Arkham House, 1960). Text taken from *Poems in Prose* (Arkham House, 1964).

"The Primal City." *Fantasy Fan* 2, No. 3 (November 1934): 41–45. In *Genius Loci* (Arkham House, 1948). Text taken from *The Last Hieroglyph* (Night Shade, 2010).

"The Princess Almeena." *Smart Set* 61, No. 2 (February 1920): 1. In *Ebony and Crystal* (The Auburn Journal, 1922). Text taken from *Poems in Prose* (Arkham House, 1964).

"The Seed from the Sepulcher." *Weird Tales* 22, No. 4 (October 1933): 497–505. In *Tales of Science and Sorcery* (Arkham House, 1964). Text taken from *A Vintage from Atlantis* (Night Shade, 2007).

"The Third Episode of Vathek" (with William Beckford). *Leaves* No. 1 (Summer 1937): 1–24. In *The Abominations of Yondo* (Arkham House, 1960). Text taken from *The Maze of the Enchanter* (Night Shade, 2009).

"Told in the Desert." In August Derleth, ed. *Over the Edge: New Stories of the Macabre* (Arkham House, 1964). In *Other Dimensions* (Arkham House, 1970). Text taken from *The Door to Saturn* (Night Shade, 2007).

"Tolometh." In *Spells and Philtres* (Arkham House, 1958). In *Selected Poems* (Arkham House, 1971). Text taken from *The Complete Poetry and Translations* (Hippocampus Press, 2008).

"The Uncharted Isle." *Weird Tales* 16, No. 5 (November 1930): 605–8, 710–14. In *Out of Space and Time* (Arkham House, 1942). Text taken from *The End of the Story* (Night Shade, 2006).

"The Venus of Azombeii." *Weird Tales* 17, No. 4 (June–July 1931): 496–514. In *Other Dimensions* (Arkham House, 1970). Text taken from *The End of the Story* (Night Shade, 2006).

"A Vintage from Atlantis." *Weird Tales* 22, No. 3 (September 1933): 394–99. In *The Abominations of Yondo* (Arkham House, 1960). Text taken from *A Vintage from Atlantis* (Night Shade, 2007).

"A Voyage to Sfanomoë." *Weird Tales* 18, No. 1 (August 1931): 111–15. In *Lost Worlds* (Arkham House, 1944). Text taken from *The End of the Story* (Night Shade, 2006).

"The Willow Landscape." *Philippine Magazine* 27, No. 12 (May 1931): 728, 752, 756. In *Genius Loci* (Arkham House, 1948). Text taken from *The Door to Saturn* (Night Shade, 2007).